# KINGS

# &

# PRIESTS

by
Evelyn M. Exley

ISBN-13: (trade paperback) 978-1-954448-17-9
ISBN-13: (ebook) 978-1-954448-22-3

Library of Congress Control Number: 2026902127



First Printing Edition 2026

exleybooks.com

# EXLEY BOOKS

## EXLEY FANTASY

*Kings and Priests*

TALES OF KING JUSTICE

*King Justice, The Legend Begins*

*The Scarlet Lady*

*First Knight*

*The Silver Knight*

*Captain of Dragons*

FATIMA'S STORY (YOUNG ADULT)

*Book 1: The Forgotten Palace*

*Book 2: The Forgotten Prince*

COMPANION NOVELS:

*Guardian of the City* (A NOVELLA)

NOVELS OF ALAMETH

*Red*

*Legend of the Hunt*

*Creation*

EVANSWOOD SERIES

*Part I*

*Part II*

CHRONICLES OF IKE:

*A Prophet Named Ike*

NOVELLAS:

*Elue*

CAVALCADE SERIES:

*Book 1: The Nepa Republic*

## EXLEY LEGACY

*The Warm Planet*

*Blood Moon*

*For the Whisper,*
*Who sets the race*
*and chooses the runners*

# *Part 1: Priests*

# 1.

*I have always loved to run.*

Malachi, my grandfather, said running was my destiny... but he had other reasons for saying it.

I never outgrew it. Even at the age of thirty, as I am now, I find that feeling comes over me, especially when I'm in the Lush Meadows outside of our tribal community, with the warm sun beating down on my shoulders and the tall wheat grass licking at my fingertips. I'm rarely out there anymore with all the pressing duties that sit on my shoulders, but if I am, the urge comes over me nearly every time.

*Run.*

That afternoon I was in the Meadows because I needed a moment away from the Temple. Those are hardly words I thought I'd ever hear myself say, no less actually feel. The Temple was the very place where its Priests were expected to find refuge and strength, where the people of the Rivermouth Tribes could seek out that same refuge and constancy in their lives for those moments when they needed it. But the work of rebuilding the Temple and setting to order all the little things in the tribe I belonged to, the Halevi, had been especially unyielding in the past five years. This year the work of it had reached a grueling level of demand, until I had begun to wonder if this was all my future held. I kept telling myself that living out my destiny and fulfilling a prophecy didn't always have to be exciting or filled with thrilling satisfaction; but these words rarely comforted or encouraged me anymore. They might have worked before, in the first two or three years after I returned from the Exile, but not now.

Not even the urge to run was enough to take hold today. I was by simple truth too bone-tired, too weary, too weary of mind to roust myself into action. Around me the gentle music of spring was in the air — the hum of insects rushing to accomplish their tasks, the call of song-birds in the distant trees on all sides of the fields where I stood. Any sounds of our large tribal community were kept at bay by the distant trees, further swallowed by the small range of granite mountains to the west named the Silent Heights. A refreshing wind swept through the open glade, gently kissing my face as it brushed past and returned. The afternoon sunshine was a coaxing warmth as it lay like a heavy blanket on my tense shoulders and seeped through my plain, well-worn clothing. It was enough just to stand there and take it all in.

Almost at once I could feel my soul beginning to reach out in the silence, reaching for the heavens, stretching for that Unseen Presence I knew was always here, always with me. When I was very young, this had been a discipline Malachi taught me, but now came naturally. I knew I could reach out… and my Creator would reach back. In a manner of speaking, He would grasp the hand I offered and hold firm. *I was not alone...* How grateful I was for even that brief connection, His constancy, His faithfulness to me. After all that I had faced, after the heart-wrenching troubles, and even now the trials that came with peace, He never failed to reach back. He knew — in spite of the fact I was surrounded by many who looked to me for answers and guidance — that I walked through life alone. I had a great need to be assured that He was not going anywhere.

But alas, my moment of peace was not destined to last long. I had given instructions not to be disturbed for the span of a prayer watch, but I heard a call and opened my eyes, the connection with the Whisper broken at once. This would be Ishtob. He was a young priest in the tribe, eager to please, thrilled as I had been at thirteen to be part of the work we did. One couldn't help but love him even when he was irksome. His youthfulness was most heard in the breaks and shrill cracks in his voice when he tried to speak, which lately had grown so hard to bear that the priests around him would burst into a small communal moan when he opened his mouth.

As he came today, he repeated my name several times, rushing through the tall grass of the Meadows, nearly stumbling in his eagerness. His shrill voice desecrated the tranquil silence about him. Ishtob was always wearing our priestly robes even when unnecessary and he was never seen without them. He had irreverently hiked these up today with both hands and looked as though he had run here from the Temple at a neck-break speed.

Whatever the news was, it had caused a great flush in his pale cheeks that was not caused by his recent run, and his blue eyes were overly bright. His blonde hair dripped in his eyes as he slid to a stop in front of me and an eager smile broke out on his handsome boyish face. *Nothing urgent,* I determined from his expression.

I restrained a heavy sigh and smoothed my face, purposing not to hurt him with my desperate need for rest. "Ish, what is it? I gave word that I was not to be disturbed —"

"Eren!" He nearly caught at me in his excitement, then seemed to recall who I was and stumbled back. "We have visitors." He recovered himself. "*You* — I mean, *you* have visitors!"

My mind went blank. I could see he did not mean the Rivermouth Tribes had a sudden visitor — this wouldn't have been so uncommon, seeing as our four tribes remained a central trading community for all of eastern Avan and had been so for the last two generations. There were often outsiders roaming our marketplaces and strolling through our dirt streets. *He no doubt meant that the Halevi have a visitor,* I thought. This would be more rare. Very few except the members of the tribes themselves ever passed through the gates of the Halevi compound and paid court to any of the priests. We purposefully lived an isolated life. This was something that might excite a thirteen-year-old priest whose life was always on the cusp of some great possibility.

"You mean the Halevi have a visitor from outside the community," I confirmed.

Ish remained as wide-eyed as ever, shaking his head with vigor."No. *You. You have a visitor.* Cohen said I was to come get you at once."

This announcement carried a much greater weight. Cohen was our Chief Priest; unless the matter was urgent, he would most surely have held back from disturbing me. He was a great lover of ceremony and held my position as High Priestess in the highest regard — probably with more regard than I held it at the moment. But more than that, it was the sheer unlikelihood of anyone seeking me out at all that caused me hesitation. I hadn't had a visitor in the five years since my return.

A great sinking feeling washed my mouth dry. "How many? How many are there?"

Ish hadn't noticed the sudden change in my tone. He was far too preoccupied. "Six!" he burst out. "Five arms men and a nobleman. They're escorting him, I think, an armed guard. Cohen said the nobleman is asking for you. Their horses are beautiful, more beautiful than I've seen." His thoughts changed suddenly. "When you were at King Cyric's city, did every nobleman stand so guarded, Eren? With dangerous weapons such as these?"

My mind reeled. His boyish description and enthusiastic questions sparked me into action. Suddenly that great burden of mental weariness I had walked out here with vanished. And there it was... *the urge to run...*

Without word, I drew an unsteady breath, hiked up my own drab skirts a modest distance, and burst into forward motion. I fairly flew over the Meadows, pushing through the tall grass towards the southern trees, legs pumping, heart pounding in my ears at the suddenness of it. I was no longer aware of Ish, nor did I care what his reaction might be at the sight of his dignified High Priestess running headlong away from him. My thoughts were racing with my own possibilities... *Surely this wasn't who I thought it was... Not after all of this time... If so, why had he come? What did he want? Nothing good could come of it, surely. Surely not...*

I never rightly knew why my heart always loved to run. It was hard work. By the time I reached the edges of the trees that would lead to the Halevi compound, sweat was running in my eyes and my heartbeat was thunderous.

Malachi always said I ran because I was born for it. When I was a child of ten, only months after I came to live with him permanently among the Halevi, we attended the Tribal Fair, a yearly event where each of the tribes brought out their display of goods and animals after a long hard winter. There were amusements, games, and competitions. I had never before been allowed to attend, but this year Grandfather had decided we would take a pause from my life of seclusion with him and from my training. He was aware I missed my mother and my brother and his soft heart was unable to watch me languish. The two of them were in attendance that day, and we came as a family — it is the only memory I hold of the four of us ever being together in all my years. Ordinarily my mother and Devland kept to their tribe and Malachi to his.

During the competitions that day, we stood together and watched a foot race. This was represented by three members specially chosen from the three other tribes — the Builders, the Planters, and the Governors.

In my innocence, I turned to Malachi and said with a frown, "The Halevi have no runner, Grandfather."

Malachi always had a twinkle in his eye. As a child, I often thought he carried a secret and hoped one day he would share it with me if I was diligent enough at the various assignments he gave me. "We don't participate in these games, Meeshka," he said.

*Meeshka* meant *gift of love.*

"These are for the community."

I stood and considered this briefly, trying not to feel disappointed. At that age I was still grasping why the Halevi had to be so different in so many things. Around us, the happy crowd cheered the runners, encouraging them, watching with great excitement as the contestants raced down the dusty track that had been marked with yellow flags through the streets of the community.

Malachi knew well that I loved to run; he had often teased that I ran more than I walked. He looked sidelong down at me that afternoon and added, "We do have a runner, though."

"We do?"

"Yes." His wise eyes warmly took me in above his heavy silver beard. "*You*. You run for us, Meeshka. It is you who runs for the Halevi."

The People of the Rivermouth had established their community around the land arc that connected the River Trowich to The Great Expanse, a great ocean at the southern end of the known world. We were also at the eastern tip of the nation known as Avan. We shared our small continent with only one other country, our western neighbor, Waldony. Everywhere in the community all one had to do was look to the east in order to catch sight of the sea-green body of water that we were settled by; the foaming surf broiled and churned far out to sea, driving choppy waves into the shore. None of our people were fishermen, but we still lived our lives by the constant tides and the summer storms that often came off the ocean. Almost all of our recreation was spent along its sandy shores in some activity or other.

The Halevi were located in the very center of the land arc, farthest from the river that ran west to east, and were the only tribe surrounded by four stone walls which separated us from the other tribes. There was a time when this physical separation was deeply resented by the community and bore some part in the Exile, but since the King's edict five years ago when I returned home, the Halevi had been accepted again — with little heart for it at first, but with more kindness in recent days after much work on my part and that of the other priests.

A dusty road ran past the front of the compound and I followed this from the trees until I reached the wooden gates that opened to my home, thoughts still running. The road was full as it nearly always was during the spring season; Rivermouth was a thriving community and drew a great many visitors. Wagons laden with supplies rumbled past; horsemen ambled by; women in linen dresses and wool kirtles moved to and from the market, woven baskets resting at their hips. No one gave me much heed. The community had grown familiar with seeing me beyond the Temple, even without my ceremonial robes, which I found ill-suited for the press of my daily labors. I spent more time training young priests, maintaining the compound, and laboring for peace with the other tribes than I did in prayer and worship... *which Malachi would have hated...*

"Everything worships," he told me, when I was five. "Have you noticed it, Meeshka?"

I had just begun to visit him at the Temple during my week days and it is nearly the first memory I have of him. This question he posed was a great revelation to me. I was only beginning to take notice of the world outside the safe nest my mother had created for my brother and me.

"Like the birds?" I asked.

"Everything," he confirmed warmly. "We were created to worship. But some choose to worship their pain. Some worship love. Some worship power. They pay homage to what they worship. They nurture and nurse it. They find their identity in it. These are all words you will eventually understand. But all things were created to worship."

He always asked me questions as a way to teach me. *"What is it you worship, Meeshka?"*

That day he did not look for an answer — and I had none ready to give.

For months after this I attended services in the Temple when Malachi attended. I followed him everywhere on the grounds of the compound and imitated his every action. He dressed me in a simple linen robe he had commissioned the community seamstress to create for me and I followed him as his little priestess shadow, dogging his every step. As the High Priest, much of his time was spent in worship and intercession, both in the Outer Courts with the other priests, and the Inner Court within the sanctuary of the Temple with just Cohen and Joel, the Chief Priests.

What began for me as simple imitation and fond admiration of my loving grandfather was quick to grow into something true and living of my own, even at so tender and delicate an age. I discovered a Presence Who loved me, Who filled my heart and soul with a warm fullness I could not explain. This surpassed any love I felt from my mother or Malachi, who were the closest people in my life. This moved within me and through me as a great flowing river that never ran dry.

This Unseen Presence held power and authority, yet extended itself with the greatest kindness and most delicate touch.

There came a day while in singing and prayer that I reached such a point of fullness and satisfaction that I whispered to the Presence, my Creator, *"I am yours. Every part of me is yours to claim."*

Something changed for me then. Something awakened within me that would never go to sleep. I remember racing to Malachi afterwards, who was never far away. I tugged on his decorated robes until I had his attention and declared, "I know the answer, Grandfather. I know the answer to the question."

Somehow Malachi always knew the difference between a childish discovery that did not bear much of his attention and when I had a revelation which very much deserved his complete acknowledgement. "What is the answer, Meeshka?" he asked kindly.

"I worship the Whisper, the Creator, the One True God."

His eyes were sparkling with light more brilliantly than ever as he knelt there beside me. "And where does He live?" he asked.

"My heart," I told him.

"And where does He reign?"

"My heart, if I will let Him," I answered.

"And will you let Him?"

I felt very alive in that moment, more alive than I had either the strength to express or the words of an adult to describe. This was a life that streamed through me and over me, like wind blowing through my being.

"I will let Him," I vowed. "I will let Him reign in my heart. I will worship Him forever."

"Very good," he said, unable to resist resting his large palm on my shoulder in pleased affection. His eyes were sparkling with more than light now. "You're a good girl, Meeshka. *More than good."*

The tall wooden gates of the Halevi compound were open during the days, an invitation to all in the community that they could enter at any time for prayer or spiritual counsel. We never assigned any watchmen at the walls, though there was a time when the priests were tempted. For this reason I was able to easily pass through that afternoon. I had by now slowed my steps, as well as my breathing, and smoothed my features even more so as I crossed the threshold, trying to appear calm and unmoved. This appearance was not wholly true, but there was no sense in laying myself bare.

The primary courtyard of the compound was sectioned off by a stone wall to the left and to the right. Beyond the wall to my right was the housing area for the unmarried priests. Those few who were married lived in the community with their families. Though Malachi could have lived with my mother, he had never chosen to and had instead made his life here within the compound, where I came to live with him at ten. This had been my home until I was nearly twenty.

Beyond the wall to my left was the Outer Court, which was just now filled with priests making incense offerings and prayers. Even as I made my initial steps, I could hear them in song, a rough chorus of male voices raising their voices as they performed their rituals. I had always loved the sound of their deep tonal voices lifted as one to the heavenlies while they worshipped and worked. The Halevi loved to sing and there were many psalmists among us. We sang songs that contained Old Prophecies; great ballads that told stories of our history and our interaction with God; odes that repeated The Sacred Text, for teaching and remembering; hymns that taught spiritual lessons; intimate songs speaking of love and adoration for the Whisper; and happy melodies, woven of all these things together, shaped chiefly to encourage the heart. Today the priests had chosen a melody; and they sounded much more at rest within themselves than I was at the moment.

Just ahead was the primary courtyard where visitors arrived, a beautiful section of the compound thriving just now with well-tended trees and thoughtfully planted flowers and foliage. Lining the courtyard were stone benches where visitors could wait or meditate. A round stone well and a trough sat in its center, but these were rarely used. We had worked very hard in the past five years to restore it to the beauty that it was today.

At the end of this courtyard was the Temple, easily the most stately building in the Rivermouth Community. The impressive edifice rose high above the walls of the compound, able to be seen all the way from the western mountains in the backdrop behind it. Even in King Cyric's city, Periburn, the Temple would be considered an impressive sight, as I had good cause to know. The single square building was constructed with a mix of manilla-colored marble and stone, with five small stone steps at its opening leading to four massive columns boldly upholding the A-frame stone roof. There were a total of twelve columns in all — four on each side and two in the center, upholding the portico. Beyond the portico, buried in shadow at all times, was an understated entrance to the Temple itself. Services were held there weekly in its general sanctuary, considered the Inner Court; living quarters were maintained in its back corner for the High Priest;

and there was, of course, the most important room in the compound, the Holy Place. Only the High Priest was ever allowed in this private room.

"Some places are Holy," Malachi told me the first time he ever took me there. "We must keep them that way. It is the High Priest's job to ensure this room is kept holy for God."

"Why does God need a Holy Place, Malachi?" I asked him. "He's God. He owns everything."

He was ever patient with me. "He has given the earth to us, Meeshka. It is ours to do with as we please. Yet He still desires to commune with us, and to reign here as an act of our own free will. He will not force us. He wants us to see Him for who He is, instead of commanding us. He once came in the form of a cloud, Meeshka, and would rest on the Holy Room itself. Now He rests upon His people. He has made you His Holy Place. In truth, we don't need this room."

It would be years before the impact of these truths settled into my soul, but I grasped their importance even at that tender age.

He continued, "The Sacred Text tells us, *I have set you apart from the people to be my own.* Not everyone is asked to live the life of a priest. We need Builders, and Planters, and Governors. God needs them also. We are not greater than they; they serve Him too. But for the Halevi, holiness is bound to two things — rest, and being held separate. We give this room to God — indeed, our entire way of life — as a way to show Him we ourselves are willing to be separated and will be His Holy Place. It is an outward physical act of an inward spiritual choice. The Sacred Text tells us, *The Whisper your God has chosen you out of all the people on the face of the earth to be His treasured possession.* You are His treasured possession, Meeshka. You live to bring Him pleasure."

*I lived to bring Him pleasure.* Little did I know how those very words would come to define my self-worth and shape the whole of who I would become.

Having lived here for so many years within the very confines of the Halevi compound, I had grown familiar with the sight of the Temple, but since my return from the Exile, I never could take it for granted. I was grateful every time I laid eyes on it, as I did today. Malachi would have been deeply proud that the Priesthood had been restored to its rightful place again. But more than all of that, I knew I was doing God's own work — making certain that, at least among the people of Rivermouth, He knew He was remembered, honored, and we desired to commune with Him.

My eyes fell from the pinnacle of the Temple, which held a stone cross, to the courtyard before it, where a tight cluster of dark horsemen were dismounted and waiting. No one else stood in the bailey except Cohen, who had skipped our evening rituals to host them until I arrived. Beyond doubt these were men of importance for him not to assign the matter to another priest, particularly at this hour of the day. My heart began thundering again.

I came upon them slowly, hoping my cheeks weren't too flushed nor my hair too rumpled, yet knowing these hopes were pointless. Some part of me had to confirm for myself who this was, and yet I dreaded the knowing of it.

A few of the men looked up and noticed me at once, though they did not take any more than a precursory glance to ensure that I was harmless. Today I looked like a village woman instead of the leader of this establishment and they weren't waiting for a villager.

Ishtob was right — they were impressively armed. Each man carried a pair of crossed swords in leather harnesses at their backs; arbalests, steel shields and full quivers hung from their ornate saddles; gilded, sheathed knives were tucked in their belts, and the hilt of gleaming silver daggers were noticeable at their boot tops. Their stern faces alone said they were deadly men, sober and intent, and their horses said the rest for them. These were beautiful black steeds, taller than the average stock horse currently seen on the streets of Rivermouth, standing with a disciplined stillness while they waited.

This company of men was the Royal Guard. I identified them at once. They were a specialized group who protected the Royal family when they left the castle. Most of the members of the Guard had a dark history, but they were loyal and had never given me trouble the few times I had crossed paths with them. Thankfully, the Halevi had nothing to fear from them, though what they were doing here was another matter altogether…

One of the earliest prophecies Malachi gave me was when I was at the tender age of six. He had been in prayer in the Holy Room and came to wake me from my afternoon lie-down so we could have supper together. Before I lived at the compound, this was our routine every day; then, after supper, my mother came and collected me, where I spent my nights with her and Devland.

Malachi was nearly unable to contain himself that day. In his small quarters at the back of the Temple, lit by the light of colorful stained glass windows on this side of the building, he rushed through preparations for the meal. He never ate elaborately, but even the simple assortment of cheeses, milk, ripe fruit and fresh slices of bread were almost too much distraction for him to be bothered with. Over the years I suspected that, had I not been in his life, he might well not have eaten at all.

"Such a curious visitation from God I've had, Meeshka," he told me, as I munched on the food he served me.

We were seated at his bare stone table, which I could scarcely reach from my place on the bench across from him. My young appetite was too demanding to pay him much heed, but he carried on, regardless.

"God has told me you will know kings, little Meeshka," he told me. "You will know the Kings and Princes of the earth. This is truly remarkable."

I was still old enough — and my hunger was not so great — that I fully comprehended what he had just told me. I stared at him openmouthed. It had been well explained to me from birth that my life and my future would be spent here in the Rivermouth Community; more specifically, within the walls of the Halevi compound, where I would one day stand in my grandfather's place as High Priestess. There was no other future for me outside of this.

But Malachi had gone on, heedless. His gray eyes sparkled with a dazzling light as he considered it. "*Imagine that* – one of our humble Halevi in the company and presence of kings and princes. *Our little Meeshka.*"

"Why would they wish to know me?" I asked him through a mouthful, shocked.

Malachi leaned forward across the table, still picturing it, laughing softly at the idea.

His appearance never changed in all the years I knew him, until the final month of his life when death began to settle upon him. Even amongst the other priests who looked so like him and worshipped with as much fervency, there was something strikingly set apart about Malachi. His smooth skin was the dark olive of our people, deeply sun-kissed by the many hours he spent outdoors in the Outer Court beside the other priests. Few lines carved his face save at the brow, revealing a lifetime spent with his expression drawn tight in prayer and thought. Hair of bright silver hung to his shoulders in full, wavy curls, the only color I ever knew it to be, while he always wore a full silver beard in which traces of black still lingered. Yet it was his gray eyes that held the greatest wonder — young with life, and deep enough to pierce the soul with their endless beauty. He nearly always had a quick smile and a soft word, especially for me. When he was not clad in his rich ceremonial garments, he wore dark gray linen robes with a long prayer shawl about his neck for those swift moments when he must give himself quickly to prayer. I always thought he was a beautiful man, both warm and mysterious… like God Himself.

"You will interpret their dreams," he told me, in delight. "You will interpret their dreams, Meeshka."

He grew more sober then, looking over at me. "I will have to teach you about kings," he added. "Their ways, their calling. How to speak to them with dignity and good words. The common language of our Rivermouth community and the priestly way we speak in the compound is well enough while you are here, but a king requires different words. We will start soon."

I always found it interesting that he never volunteered to train me in interpreting dreams. This was, he presumed, something that would come naturally, from God Himself.

Today I walked up to the men in the Royal Guard and they parted ways for me, presuming that I was headed for Cohen. As I did so, I gained a few more glances, this time with a touch more curiosity. They were still men of the world, after all, and I was scanned over for any distinguishing characteristics which would appeal to their senses. One dark-faced man arched a brow and gave me a half-smile, as if he wasn't too displeased. Perhaps if I had dressed anything but plain he would have kept his thoughts to himself. These men were strictly forbidden to keep company with women outside of their station, and a priestess was especially considered the most forbidden manner of woman in Periburn.

None of them recognized me, though I identified a few of them. They had been deeply engaged with the prospect of warfare the last time I'd seen any of them, then the battle itself that came afterward. I was not foremost on their minds at the time, except as someone under their protection. But I would never forget those events, nor the battle they fought that day. It still visited my dreams at times when I least expected it and usually when I least wanted it. *No, I was not surprised at all that I remembered a few of their faces.*

Then, finally, here was the elderly Cohen in his long gray robes, leaning on his old crook as he spoke in quiet tones to the nobleman.

The two of them turned at the sound of the men making way for me. My eyes quickly rushed past the familiar Cohen… and my breath caught and held.

Axel never considered himself to look like a prince. He was the second son of King Cyric and a statesman, which he was fond of saying about himself, seeing as everyone in his household prided themselves in being warriors. He never carried weapons, as if this proved his point, though I knew from shocking experience he was well able to use them. To the humble people of Rivermouth, and particularly to me the first time I ever spoke with him, he exuded a princeliness. Just now I could see Cohen's somewhat awed expression as he stood next to him, and understood well why Ishtob had reacted the way he did.

Axel had a habit of wearing finely woven doublets, usually in black or dark green, decorated and overlaid with gold or silver brocade, and kept his dark hair well-coiffed and his thin beard well-groomed. It came as little surprise to me that he was dressed much the same today. He had always claimed his place within his father's house, as an ambassador of good will, required him to dress with grace and exactness, but I never believed him. He loved finery, plain and simple. Yet his princely air did not spring from any special choice of finery, or his natural good looks — something I never dared to tell him when I knew him. It was somewhere in the strong shoulder line, in the set purposeful way he carried himself, in the keen blue-gray gaze that caught and held those who came within his line of sight. He took in the world with a sharp intelligent eye and very little passed him by. *That* was what made him a prince…

Today those sharp intelligent eyes were observing me for the first time in five years, somehow able to gather everything he needed without scanning me over as his men had done. He read me instantly.

When we parted ways, I had never expected to see him again, and was shocked and disturbed to see him now.

"Eren," he acknowledged.

Even his voice was suddenly very familiar. Neither loud nor soft, neither churlish nor bold, neither low nor high. Steady and even, like he was. He was indeed very different from any other member of his loud, brazen, warrior-class household. He would be about thirty-five now, I reasoned.

I couldn't help it. Memories came crashing back, like waves tearing into the shore of Rivermouth on a stormy day. My time at Periburn had developed me and for that I was grateful; I had fulfilled my God-given purpose there and was glad that I could; but in all other regards I had hoped to leave it behind forever. I honestly never wished to see him or any one of them again…

Something fell over him as he said my name aloud. To my shock, he crossed the three feet between us in one, heedless of the group of men around, ignoring the five years of distance that stood between us. His hands gripped my elbows with a manly grasp and he bent and brushed my cheek with a light kiss. This was the way his household greeted a familiar friend, though he had never once given me this greeting in our history together. For just a moment the smell of him — rich and musky — drifted over me. I was stunned speechless. *What was he doing here?*

When he drew back, his strong eyes were soft. He briefly took in my expression; recognized it even after all of this time.

"I need to speak with you," he said, low. "Are you comfortable with that?"

He was also a deeply intimate man, especially for a Prince; and I had met plenty by now. He never demanded, never commanded, never assumed. He was as humble with me as if we were equals, which we were not. He responded to those he knew with a soft closeness I had never seen in anyone but Malachi. Axel liked to say his softness, his ability to humbly request instead of proudly demand, also made him a good ambassador for his father. His name, I knew, meant *father of peace* and he lived up to this fully.

He had once asked me if I knew the meaning of my name and I told him, "Saint, or holy person."

He smiled at me. "I expected as much."

Today, he was expecting me to refuse his request. I sensed this at once. The truth of the matter was, however, he had the power to command me to do anything he wanted if he so desired or I would risk immediate death. Everyone in the Halevi community was subject to his authority. He could turn us out on the street in the next five turnings of breath if he wished to, and welcome us back in the next ten.

Somehow, I was able to find my voice and school it to a reasonably level tone. "We can talk. Of course."

But then my thoughts failed me and my mind went wholly blank. I had no idea where or how. Most of all, I couldn't move past the *why. Why was he here? What did he want?* The agony of living those days in Periburn was behind me and I wished to keep them that way, especially the final few. There were some events that had happened which had marked me forever.

Axel's eyes scanned my face. "We could walk," he suggested gently. "Somewhere nearby, perhaps, where we might have some privacy?"

This was helpful to my slow, stuttering thoughts. I turned quickly to Cohen, but he was already nodding with an easy, pleasant air. I could see from his expression he already knew or had guessed who this person of importance was.

"Perhaps the Lush Meadows would suit," he offered, smiling a little too generously. "There, no one will disturb you."

So we walked to the Meadows, with Axel's dark-faced men trailing at a distance behind and before on foot, their sharp eagle eyes scanning the area, clearing the way as we went. Fortunately, we gathered little enough attention along the way, though Ishtob passed us by with an open mouth and scurried on to the compound to discuss what he had seen with any priest who was willing to listen.

Soon enough, we reached the tree line, then the Meadows shortly after. The sun was already settling on the western horizon and the colors were changing. Somehow even the sight and feel of this did not give me any comfort just now. Axel was saying nothing, simply taking his long easy steps in the tall grass, looking around him with a quiet, sharp-eyed interest. I wondered which one of us would be the one to break the uneasy stillness.

"I always hoped one day to see the Rivermouth Community," he said eventually. "Especially the Temple. You spoke so much about it."

I glanced over at him. There were a thousand unspoken things between us, the least of which was the Rivermouth Community, but I followed his lead. "And now that you've seen it?"

He caught my eye with a light smile. He didn't answer. "You look well, Eren."

He had seen me at my worst and would know this was true more than most. Yet, like him, I did not feel inclined to answer every thought. "I'm High Priestess here," I said.

"Your Chief Priest told me, but I supposed. I pictured you here," he added suddenly, in a friendly manner. "Like *this.*"

A thought must have crossed my face, because he said, keenly, "What did you picture for me?"

*Still the same Axel,* I thought. Always attempting to draw me out when I didn't speak. I knew it was a practice he used often in his profession. He was very useful to his father, much more so than his bawdy and brash older brother or his thorny younger sister. King Cyric would never admit to this, of course. Agnar had been his pride and joy, his Crown Prince, the beloved heir to his prized throne, while Princess Onyx was the blameless delight of his heart. I came to know them all well before my time there was brought to a crashing halt after the terrible Uprising.

I wanted to tell Axel I hadn't pictured him at all. All the gruesome events that occurred were better left behind. I'd had no choice but to do so if I wanted to find a happy future. "Married with children, of course."

Axel laughed. He had a low, brief laugh that came easy for him, though he didn't always make use of it. "Did you? When did I ever plant that idea? Of marriage and children?"

I was still taking steps in the grass a few feet parallel to him. There was once a time when we were never direct about certain matters. "It's what is expected of you, isn't it? Things haven't changed for you." Then, suddenly, my questions surfaced. "What are doing here, milord? What's happened? Something must have or you wouldn't be here, like this, *now.*"

I was being very formal with him. He stopped and faced me.

We were the same height, something that had once made interacting with him a challenge seeing as we caught each other's eye evenly. Just now the falling sun from the west illuminated his princely features with a golden light and sparked the gray in his eyes in a way that was difficult to take in.

"Yes, something has happened," he said, with simple authority. "Something of importance, in fact. But now that I'm here, I don't feel inclined to come directly to the reason for my visit. I sense you want me gone as soon as possible." A little gleam entered his eye. "So I think I'll stay, at least for a day or two. As I said, I always hoped to visit the Rivermouth Community. I believe I'll take in the sights, perhaps even worship in your great Temple."

*Stubborn, too,* I thought. He'd always been stubborn, though never with me. With his father. Our last interaction with each other had made it very clear we would never see each other again. This visit today probably had to do with a need for me to interpret dreams or advise the King on spiritual matters, which was nearly the only purpose I had ever served in their household; but even this surprised me. Cyric had never asked for me again after I returned home and I knew he never would. Not after the Uprising. Not after what happened.

Quickly, I reached for the appropriate words, drawing myself up. "Well, if it's our community you've come to see, we are most honored to have you, of course, milord. I will be happy to alert the tribal leaders so that they can pay your visit proper homage. I can arrange for one of them to give you a viewing —"

I was already turning back now, ready to be done with this troubling conversation, thoroughly ready to pass the responsibility of his presence off to someone else. He was correct in that I wished to be gone from him as quickly as possible.

*"No."* His voice stopped me.

He waited until I turned back before adding, "I desire you to do it, Eren. You show me the sights. You know this place better than anyone. It's not such an odd request to ask you, as High Priestess, to provide yourself as an escort. Aside from that, I'd rather keep my visit as discreet as possible. If anyone should see us together, let them think you are simply escorting a nobleman from Periburn around the community upon request of the King. While I'm here, I would like the chance to see you worshipping in your beloved Temple," he added softly.

This was a rather intimate statement, but not shocking for the Axel I once knew. He spoke this way to many of his people. Today, however, his sentiment made me uncomfortable.

I held his blue-gray gaze. "Are you ordering me to escort you during your stay, milord?"

A brief silence fell after the stiff question. Somewhere in the past twenty or so steps through the Meadows he had plucked a strand of wheat grass and now looked down on it, fingering the fragile blade, turning my words over. He knew why it was I had asked. My question brought up the unspoken things between us in a coded way, the reasons why we had both understood, in one harsh instant, that there was no future for us even as friends and never could be. The Uprising had changed things forever.

When he glanced up again, his tone was soft and quiet, and he held my gaze evenly as he spoke. “Do you really need the answer to that question, Eren?”

No, I didn’t. Axel had never commanded anyone in his life and certainly never me.

My gaze fell before his, undone. “You would never insist.”

He allowed a heartbeat or two to pass, acknowledging the answer. Then he said with a quiet firmness, “I’ve missed you, Eren. I only want a little of your company, I promise. Then I will tell you everything and be on my way."

There were some people and some words, phrased so excellently, that could reduce you from a High Priestess of authority to a gentle song-bird singing softly in the trees. I had missed him, too, more than I cared to admit.

"So will you do it?" he asked. "Will you show me the sights?”

Somehow the fact that he was a prince made his humility strike all the deeper. I nodded in silence, weakened.

“Good.” He sounded somewhat relieved, as if he thought I might refuse him. “We can begin tomorrow then as soon as you have availability. I know you have morning prayer first.”

How well he knew my life. How uncomfortable it was to realize he had not forgotten a whipstitch of it in five years. Right now I was wishing, very contrarily, that he could have come here and found my ways so utterly changed he could not presume so much. That would feel much more satisfying in this moment. Marriage would have been one such change, but this had never been an option for me.

A priest's life was not a royal one, where position and responsibilities were volatile, altered at a king's pleasure and caught in the shifting course of events. When I knew him, Axel carried a constant awareness of the fickleness of his career, his responsibilities, his favor with his father, even his position in the King's household if his brother should perish through some unforeseen event… at least until Agnar produced several of his own heirs to secure the throne. Royal power only lasted if the Royal family could hold onto it, while a priest's life was steady, like time itself. His power and favor came from God and was eternal. Axel knew — or could safely guess — everything about my life if I was living in the Temple.

*What is happening?* I asked the Whisper, in a near panic. *Why is he here? Can you not encourage him on? You could bring a messenger who sends him away in a gallop.*

My frantic prayers continued. *I am not asking that you arrange a crisis, only something of importance that he alone must attend to. You have ample means. He is a prince of Avan, a man in great demand… Let the King send for him…*

"Allow me to escort you back to the Temple," Axel said in a courtly fashion, and began making his way back to the compound.

Sadly, it appeared that the Whisper did not intend to heed my cry. I had no choice but to follow.

# 2.

As I look back now and watch the events that led to the Uprising, I see so many things I was blind to as I was living them. I suppose this is true for everyone when they reflect on their yesteryears, but now I feel I was especially blind. *Perhaps everyone feels that way, too.* The careful construction of events began long before I became aware of the troubles around me, long before I realized the great significance of all that Malachi taught and told me. I'm thankful now I listened to all that he said, that I was a good student and he was such a skilled teacher. I can see the great Hand of Destiny upon me from the very moment I was brought into the world.

After Malachi received the prophecy concerning my destiny with kings and princes, I think he taught me near as much on the ways of a king as he did on the Priesthood, in preparation for the day when I would need this knowledge.

"The King has a calling just as we the Priests do," he told me. "His kingdom has been entrusted to him by the Whisper to rule and reign over the people. Only God raises up kings and takes them down. Promotion and demotion comes from Him alone. He uses the will of man for His purposes very artfully. Kings do not always know it, but their power is not given to them by their bloodline, or by their dissensions and rebellions. It is given to them by the Whisper. A king is established by God. If he places his trust in the Whisper, God will help him hold his place. If he does not, he is in constant danger of losing his kingdom if his people are not satisfied with his authority and leadership."

This intrigued me. Until I was ten, I had access to nightly conversation with my mother and Devland. They often talked of King Cyric and other men of power in the known world. My mother had decided opinions on the leaders of the world and did not wish for Devland in particular to be ignorant. She had strong hopes that when he came of age he would join the Governor Tribe of our people and help lead the Rivermouth Community into the future.

"Do kings believe in the Whisper?" I asked Malachi, though I already knew the answer.

Even with this difficult question his eyes were twinkling, as if he held a secret in spite of the troubles of the world. "Sometimes. Sometimes — alas — they believe in many gods. But it is on us to do two things: live as peaceably as we can with the King and his laws, and if the opportunity should arise, we show him the true God we serve. The reading of a dream is one such door, Meeshka, though in times past God has used many wonders and many ways besides."

My mother and Malachi did not agree on much, even their beliefs about the Whisper, and especially their ideas about authority in the lands. They never once set their differing beliefs into spoken words for me, yet I carried the knowing of it even at a tender age. The two kept to their own tribes and rarely claimed any association with each other. Miri believed in taking action, in carrying out your own authority. She was an insurgent at heart and found fault with every decision of King Cyric that came to her ears, even when it had no bearing on our community. She plainly did not hold that God had set the Sovereign in his place. It seemed to her that he shouldn't be King at all and should be dethroned altogether. She never offered an alternative to his rule, but it was always clear she didn't wish for him — or what she described as his *shoddy* bloodline — to rule Avan.

All through my childhood, she was deeply involved in our community and I knew she often regretted that she did not join the Governor Tribe when she had the chance at eighteen, instead of marrying my father and becoming a part of the Planters Tribe where she remained all of her life. When she could be spared from the fields, there were nights she dropped me off at the Temple and took Devland to community meetings so she could express her voice on local matters. She was a strong woman, which I admired her for, but she was much stronger than I would ever be. My very calling kept me softer than most any soul I knew beyond the Halevi. My mother and I were on very different paths, and she was aware of this early on and accepted it.

"You have your own destiny," she told me once, just before I went to dwell at the Temple for good. "I am proud of you, Eren. Walk in what has been set before you. You have your own place in the world, even if it is not mine or Devland's. Follow Malachi — that is the way appointed to you. And if, in time, your heart should choose a way beyond his, then let it be so. That is right as well."

My mother was the one, after all, who committed my life to the work of the Priesthood in the first place. She had gone childless for a long stretch of years, near ten into her marriage — then, when she was finally able to conceive, she lost two in pregnancy and another in childbirth. Our Healers told her to make her heart ready for the truth that she would never bear a child, and even warned her to set aside all hope of trying again.

While she carried me — her fourth attempt in fifteen years — she grew so desperate that she was often at the Temple in prayer, seeking solace while she waited hopefully. I was told she nearly lived there, making offerings, joining the singing and the prayers with the other priests. In those days she made a vow to the Whisper that, should He grant her a child, she would dedicate the child's life to Him and to the Priesthood.

This was a shocking vow considering that she and Malachi, her father-in-law, had never been of one mind on many things. She knew even as she prayed it that she would be turning me over to his close care and leadership. She would scarcely be able to experience many of the joys of motherhood as others did. Custom also held that I would one day stand as High Priestess after him. Yet her longing to bring a child into the world — which she saw as both a calling and a fulfillment of her womanhood — was so great that she laid aside her own desires, if only God would grant her this wonder.

After I was born without struggle or complication, Miri chose to keep her word. I think Malachi was as astonished as I was by her actions when I was finally old enough to understand the story and knew my mother as I did. He was deeply honored and often told me so over the years. Being a father to only one son who did not pursue the Priesthood, he would have had no heir at all if she had not consecrated me to the Temple. The position of High Priest would have been left to Cohen's sons.

"Which I don't mind so much," Malachi told me wryly, softly laughing; "They're good boys. *More than good.* But I like you better, Meeshka. I'm glad God saw to it to give me you. Thanks be to Him, the Priesthood is not cut off in our family line, which we have held for three generations."

To the wonder of all in my mother's close community — herself included — she bore Devland safely only a year after my own birth. She tearfully thanked God for this and embraced my brother in a way that she could not embrace me. While I was proof that God had heard her cry and accepted her terms, Devland was her child of blessing.

The ways of our household were never much account to me, not even when my father died without warning a year after Devland's birth. While my mother ranted about King Cyric and snuggled Devland in a way she never did with me, I always had Malachi, the one constant in my life. And like most children, I was content within the small world that had been set before me.

"You will be High Priestess," Miri told me once, and there was a bright pride in her dark eyes. "And Devland will be a Governor of the Rivermouth Community. You will both be great — in all the ways I could not be."

I knew this was enough for her.

As I grew into my womanhood, I carried a quiet knowing that I bore no likeness to Miri at all. She was dark of hair, short, and had a fiery spirit that showed through her black eyes. Devland was the one who took after her. He had the same stocky build and shared the hearty laugh that she did. I was the one who did not belong, somehow, not even among the tribes. There was no one in all the community who had auburn hair and blue eyes. From a very early age I had searched and determined this for myself. My eyes in particular carried no fire or strength as my mother and Devland's did; instead they glowed with light, especially after I worshipped. Malachi took me to a looking glass in his quarters in the Temple and showed me himself.

"You are clothed in the glory of God," he told me with warmth. "Look how His light still rests upon you after you have stood in His Presence. This, Meeshka — this is true beauty."

Everyone around me had dark olive skin, even Malachi, while my complexion remained coolly pale. Neither were any of the girls as tall as I was; I stood eye to eye with most men in our village by the time I was fifteen. Malachi explained this was not so unusual.

"Every so often," he said, "a child is born among our people who bears the look you carry — with fiery red hair and shining blue eyes. I will teach you a song of Elric the Red, a true tale of a priest whom the Whisper used to save our forefathers from a great storm that near destroyed the entire eastern coast of Avan. He looked as you do — tall and straight. A great intercessor he was for the people. Do not be tempted to fret over your appearance, Meeshka. God will make good use of it yet, when the hour is ready."

Tempted or no, these traits did mark me apart through the years, both in body and in heart. They separated me out from my own family and the tribal community. My consecrated life in the Temple only served to sharpen our differences even further.

Daily, Malachi taught me about priests and kings, while I wisely kept these teachings to myself when I did return home to Miri. I knew by an inward knowing — as if I was protecting a precious seedling promise within me as it grew into a strong tree of belief — that I should not let her know that I would one day walk with kings and princes. The very idea would have incensed her; I somehow knew this was the one thing that might cause her to end my time at the Temple.

"Kings have weaknesses," Malachi would say to me, "do not doubt it — all the more if they have not first submitted themselves to the Whisper. Power, it creeps into the heart and makes a man forget himself. It bends them, it spoils them, and they begin to abuse what was given for guarding. And the people, Meeshka — always the people — they are the ones who pay the price. So what is our work as Priests? To stand before God with the authority He gives us and to contend for the people through intercession."

At home, my mother told Devland, "It is for us to rein in men of power. They are near always bent toward corruption. They do not see that the only authority they possess is what we have allowed them to take — and we may take it back as swiftly. There are times when they must be made to learn this."

She gave him history lessons citing men who had done so in the past, just as Malachi gave me instruction on priests and Holy Men who had gone before us, giving counsel to the powerful and using their sacred gifts to better the world for the people.

There was a time when I told Devland about Malachi's prophecy. I remember it well. When he turned seven, he took a sudden interest in the Temple and began visiting me daily after his schooling in the community. I was thrilled every time he came. Miri was pleased that we were spending time together and permitted it for this reason, but I do not think she ever reckoned that Devland would take to his time with us so deeply.

He was such a dear little soul to me, and I delighted in showing him everything I knew. We explored every corner of the Temple, took part in all the prayers and offerings, laughed together in private at the older priests who fell asleep during services, and solemnly stood beside Malachi as he conducted the ceremonies. Those are some of my fondest memories of my childhood, aside from Malachi.

Before more than a few sennights had passed, Devland began spending time worshipping for himself, drawing away as I did for short periods to interact with the Whisper. How I delighted in seeing him in the sanctuary some rows away from me, knelt in reverent worship, speaking quietly in prayer. I felt some missing part of my heart was complete witnessing his communion with the Whisper, the sincerity of his tears, the earnestness on his expression.

"I have found something," he told me with eager brightness after a few months of visiting us. "I understand now why you love to come here, Eren. This is truly a wondrous place. A place where God visits."

He grew very attached to Malachi, who often rumpled his hair fondly as the little boy stood nearby, or gave him extra cheese when we ate supper because this was Devland's favorite.

"The cheese at the Temple is *far* better than Mother's cheese," he explained, in his bright happy way.

Malachi's love for his grandson was as deep as his affection for me, and I was glad to share him with Devland. I knew I had a singular purpose at the Temple, and it was Malachi's duty — and his delight — to pass that calling on to me; but my brother brought a tender warmth into both our lives for a special reason. While Devland gave me the gift of sharing my small world with him, of passing on the little I knew, Malachi and I were both granted the quiet joy of watching as Dev took up the Way of the Whisper by his own choosing.

During this time Devland arrived one day at the Temple and seemed troubled. This was unusual for him. When we were given a small time from Malachi to roam the compound, we wandered outside to the receiving courtyard, where the two of us sat on one of the stone benches. It was here, at last, I asked him the matter.

"You've been sorrowful today, Dev," I told him. "What has touched you so?"

He was much shorter than I was. With only a year between us, his feet could not yet touch the stone of the courtyard, while mine were already well-anchored. He looked over at me with dark anxious eyes. "I had a dream," he told me. "It kept me wakeful the whole night through. I did not tell Mother — I felt she would scold me for foolishness."

Somehow Dev always seemed much younger than I was. He was less certain, more easily troubled. Even with the great amount of attention and affection I knew he received from Miri, he was never very strong. I quickly put an arm around him in comfort, hugging his warm little body to my side. "Something grave must have met you there in the dream. What was it, love? Will you share it with me?"

As he nodded, his memory of the events returned and his dark eyes misted over in fright. "A black bear came into the house in the middle of the night and set upon Mother and me. Again and again he came at us. But then a beautiful lion appeared and devoured the bear. It is not the first time I have dreamt it," he added. "I am starting to fear it, Eren."

Unlike Devland, I wasn't afraid. Just that quick, I knew what the message meant. "The dream speaks about something that will happen, Dev," I told him. "The bear and the lion are images of the event. But I think you already know that much."

His black eyes — so like our mother's — widened with even greater fear. "What does it mean, Eren? There's a fear in my heart."

I squeezed him to me again, smiling. "Do not be afraid. It is a dream of preparation, and of promise. The Whisper is setting your heart at ease. A sickness will come into the house — that is the bear — and it will return more than once. But the lion — that is the Whisper — will come in time and drive the bear away, and you and Mother will be made well again."

He considered this with a very serious gravity. "That rings true —" One of his stubby hands covered his heart over his tunic. "In my heart."

"Malachi would say that the truth bears witness with you," I told him. "You can sense the truth. It is good to the taste. And I'm glad for it. I don't want for you to be afraid anymore; and I take comfort in knowing that the two of you will be safe in the end as well."

He cast me a quick upward glance, this time with a little awe. "You carry so much knowing, Eren. I wish I knew all that you know. How did you read the meaning of the dream?"

"The Whisper told me," I said. "I have never done it before, but Malachi said I could. He says I have a gift in me for the reading of dreams."

It was then, in this simple moment of closeness and affection, that I told him what God had said to Malachi. My gift would make room for me one day and bring me before kings and princes as a way to speak to them about the Whisper.

"Malachi says I will walk among them," I explained.

To my delight, Devland accepted this as solemnly as he accepted the interpretation of the dream. "You have been richly blessed by God, Eren."

He was also wise beyond his young years. "I will not speak of it to Mother," he promised me solemnly. "It is God's promise to you and she need never know."

We never discussed why she should not know, but both of our young instincts understood that this news would only stir her anger. Somehow, too, I knew Devland would keep his vow to me. I was grateful to him. He was my first friend, and my best friend.

"We should go and make a prayer offering," I told him, "asking the Whisper to keep you and Mother safe."

This quickly removed whatever remained of his fear and we moved on with the day before us, the frightening dream and its reassuring interpretation left behind.

After I turned ten, when I lived at the Temple, Malachi still permitted me to go home every six days and spend an entire day with Miri and Devland. At first I kept these faithfully. I missed my nights with them, especially Devland, and for a time the Temple felt like a dark mysterious place at night. Malachi had fashioned for me a small room next to his, separated by a heavy curtain, but even with the comfort of his presence nearby, the space felt foreign to me in the dark after so many years of sleeping in a single room with Devland across from me.

When I did come home again at the end of a sennight, I happily joined whatever activities Devland engaged in and took part in his life. Through this I came to know many of his friends and schoolmates, played at many games with children my age, and still remained connected to him and to Miri. Malachi encouraged this, seeing as he knew one day I would need a good understanding of the Rivermouth Community. When I should one day stand as High Priestess, he said, I would also serve as a go-between for our tribe, and so it was all the more needful that I be seen and come to know those outside my own tribe.

This is where I met Connor and Garwin, two of Devland's constant companions after the age of twelve. They were both from the Planters Tribe and were often with him when I visited. Of the two, Garwin was most like Devland, and I always held a fondness for him. He was warm of heart and gentle in manner, even though I was always the odd one out — in my looks, and in that I did not attend the common school of the Tribes. He never spoke of our differences, only made room for them without a word.

But never did I meet a soul who vexed me as much as Connor Shannasee.

At near thirteen, Connor was auburn-haired, with dark, probing eyes and freckled skin that stayed with him into manhood. His hair and lighter coloring marked him out among the tribes as surely as mine marked me, though in build he was like his own people — short of stature and strong of frame. Yet the tireless well of energy he carried was wholly his own. His most striking trait was his quick mouth — there was nearly always a witty remark or laughing comment on his lips, most often aimed at me if I was near. He tossed jests at my clothing, the color of my hair, my height — any and all differences he could find between us. I was two years his senior and that fact seemed to delight him from the first moment he laid eyes on me. He made constant sport of my looming height and of what he claimed was my grim, over-serious nature, taking especial pleasure in declaring that I would reach old age and frailty long before he ever did. And oh, the fun he had knowing I lived at the Temple and would be the next High Priestess.

"There's the towering Holy Woman," he'd say to Devland and Garwin. "She's come today to show us how to live, my brothers."

When I would leave for the day, his parting shot was often, "Make sure you say a prayer for us, Air. We will die in our guilt and sin if you don't."

I could never guess where he learned such wit or such notions. I did not see him or his mother at the Temple as I did the other children our age. I met his father years later, a quiet, slow-spoken man with little to say. It seemed unlikely Connor had learned his ways from either of them. He appeared simply to have been born with a sharp tongue and a clever mind. To my further dismay, Devland found his friend amusing even before he grasped half of what was said. Connor never failed to set the other two boys laughing and eager for fresh mischief. They were more daring because of him, more restless and eager. To my thinking, Connor was a man bent on stirring adversity and trouble from the start of his life.

At first I was only wounded and would draw back in quiet when the boy was about. I had never been spoken to so brashly before and did not know how to answer his clever, cutting remarks. In my childish thinking, I kept Connor's behavior from Malachi for fear he would protectively bar my visits to Devland. Then, eventually, I learned to ignore Connor altogether, though this was only a slight improvement.

"You must answer him in return," Devland told me at one point. "The girls at the school snap back sharp as flame to wick. It wins a measure of his regard."

I gave him a dry look. "Somehow I'm very much in doubt that anyone wins a measure of Connor's regard, especially not the girls in your school. I've seen them. There's not a boy they don't giggle at. And I have no wish for Connor's respect, Dev. Even aside from that, I've never been one for a sharp tongue."

"Perhaps you should be," he argued.

We were sitting in his room at Miri's house on the one day I had come to call, waiting for the boys to arrive for a planned outing to the shore. Though I made no complaint, Devland could see that I took little pleasure in his wish to include Connor that day. This feeling had only deepened with the months, and for some time now I had been coming to visit less and less. I chose instead to run errands for Malachi, or would visit the beach by myself with a Holy Textbook borrowed from the Temple. Devland, too, had visited the Temple less and less in his free time as his schooling made greater demands of him and Mother began to ask for his help in the fields to bring in more income. The rest of his time was occupied with his friends.

"You ought to stand your ground, Air," he said flatly. "You ought to, whether it suits you or not."

I frowned over at him, unable to understand the source of his persistence. "Do not use that name. Connor uses that word. That, and *Priestess.* My name is Eren."

Devland was sitting before the lone glass window in his humble room, casting his gaze now and again toward the lane beyond the cottage for any sign of the boys. In his hands, he was restlessly turning a wooden ball from palm to palm. He was very skilled with his hands and often wondered aloud — when safely beyond Miri's sharp hearing — whether he ought not join the Planters Tribe when he came of age, so he could work beside his friends. He did not think he was shaped to make a very good governor of the people, as she hoped. Among close ears, he thought her future for him sounded dull.

At the edge in my voice, he looked over and met me with a frown. "He means no ill by it. Connor calls you Air because it is the shortened version of your name. I like it. You take things too much to heart."

"Perhaps you should show honor for my wishes instead," I told him. "You know as well as I that he calls me Air for his own amusement, as though I were full of air and short on sense. Besides that, Connor's tongue has something to say about all things, but that neither makes his sayings true or right. And my *name* is Eren."

"He only speaks his mind," Devland said, his tone touched now with sullenness. My counsel as an elder sister had begun to chafe on him, all the more since he had taken such a liking to Connor. "Maybe it is you who should learn to face a man's opinions instead of flinching from them, or hating him for them. Strong opinions are the mark of a man. That's what Miri says."

I gave a short, unguarded snort — something I would have shown to no one else, but Devland was my only true friend besides Garwin, and he knew me best. "I could never hate anyone… and Connor is a mere boy. His thoughts are small and stuffed with himself. He's no man."

The ball stopped. Devland was glowering across the room. He shook his head at me in disgust. "You really are a prig. So lofty from your high perch of holiness. All voices are to be reckoned with, even Connor's. He may be twelve, but his thoughts have weight, and they will only gain strength. If you wish for respect, you must raise your voice and take it — not ask sweetly and pull back like a babe. And if I choose to call you Air, or even Priestess, I will do so."

I sprang to my feet, surprised by the stubborn cruelty of his words. Devland and I had never quarreled before. "I am *leaving,*" I declared. "There is no reason for me to stay here another breath."

With these final words, I left the house without a goodbye. Miri had gone to the market, so there was no one to slow me down or prevent me. Once outside, I took to the road with strong steps and my head held high, still upset, mostly disturbed by the strife between the two of us. It was true, Devland had never stood up for me to his friends, though I had truthfully never really expected it; but he had also never defended their actions to me like he had today. It seemed to me he had taken a side against me. He knew how precious he was to me, and I would surely never make the same choice about him. His acts were driving a quiet wedge between us.

Before long, I came upon the two boys as they made the last stretch toward the cottage. The road was a quiet one along the shore, leading to one of the scattered settlements on the edge of the fields where the Planters labored each day. Hard-packed sand lay beneath my feet; dry weeds and tall grass lined either side of the narrow, empty lane. In the distance I could hear the uneven pulse of the ocean waves beating at the shore beneath the late-summer sun that just now burned bright in the cloudless sky above.

I had no course but to pass the boys in the road unless I chose to leave it altogether. They were both clad in linen shirts and trousers, their worn clothing indication that today was dedicated to play. From the short space between us, Garwin met my eye at once and offered a friendly smile, but it was Connor whose look shifted to a quick, impish delight — like a fisherman who has felt the sure tug of a fine catch and knows a good supper lies ahead.

"Hi, Priestess!" he crowed.

I ignored this witless remark, in no mood to acknowledge him.

"Hello, Garwin," I greeted politely.

Garwin was a naturally affectionate boy. He reached out one hand and squeezed mine as he passed. "Eren? Are you not coming with us today?"

Connor paused to take me in with his bold eyes, searching my face. "She's troubled," he declared.

I found it unsettling, how keen his eye could be. "I have to go back to Malachi," I lied. "I came only to give a quick hello today."

Connor was never offended when I made a plain show of ignoring him; instead, he seemed to take pleasure in knowing how he nettled me. It was Garwin who appeared disheartened by my words. He had dark, expressive eyes and little skill in hiding what he felt. "Perhaps we'll see you in a sennight's time, when you come again?"

I had begun by now to wonder if he might have a special kind of attachment for me. I smiled at him, still taking steps away, backwards now. "Perhaps. See you."

It was not until I had turned my back on the two and was safely on my way that I heard Connor call after me, his voice edged with taunt, "Priestesses ought not to lie. *What would the Whisper say?"*

His loud voice carried out across the shore, catching in the wind. Anyone within a stone's throw could have heard it. I set my teeth and moved on without answering, trying hard not to stomp ahead.

For the next two months, I did not return to Miri's house and avoided Devland in the street if I saw him as I ran errands for Malachi. I was not willfully avoiding him; I simply could not decide how I felt about the conflict that lay between us, nor see any clear way through it. He had made plain that he did not favor the choices I had made and wished that I were a different person. I could not help but think this sprang from Connor's influence upon his life — yet there was nothing I could do to turn that tide either.

Oddly, I chose not to confide in Malachi, though I told him everything else of my thoughts and feelings. Some part of me hoped the situation would work itself out without having to involve Grandfather. I was always aware that he carried many pressing responsibilities, as well as his great passion for prayer and worship. I assumed minor differences between a brother and sister were very common and I did not wish for my little troubles to turn into a needless weight for him.

That fall Malachi hurried into his quarters at the back of the Temple one evening after a meeting outside the compound with leaders of the other tribes.

"Meeshka, I have news," he said at once. "Come, join me at the table here."

This was unusual. Even his tone was different, concerned somehow. I moved away from my place at the little wood stove range nearby where I was finishing his supper and sat down across from him. Only then did I truly look at him. In his haste, he hadn't bothered to remove his outer coat and hat, and these bore evidence of snowfall outside. Powder had settled in the dark fringe of his lashes as well, which he did not trouble to brush away. The soft gray of his eyes neither caught nor gave back the kitchen lamplight, yet the quiet radiance within them remained. Tonight, however, he was unusually solemn. My concern rose immediately.

"There is a strange illness moving through the community," he said. "Thanks be to the Whisper I did not send you on errands these past few days. The sickness is passing from house to house with great haste. As of this night, the tribal leaders have called for a shut-in of the whole community. Only the strongest in each household may go out to fetch what is needful until the sickness passes. All others must stay within, save the Healers."

He saw my reaction and added quickly, "I have been to your mother's house already, to see how she and Devland fare. They are both ill, but not gravely so, thank God. Meeshka, I know your heart will wish to be with them, but I must ask you to remain here within the Temple. You are not to leave it until the sickness has passed over the community."

This very idea caused my stomach to sink. How I wished to be there with them, especially Devland, even with the knowledge that Mother would sacrifice herself and her own health to see that he was well taken care of. I knew he wouldn't struggle. But I didn't like the thought of their suffering.

"Are you sure, Malachi?" I asked him softly; "That I could not remain with them until this passes?"

He reached out for my hand with compassion, his sober eyes filled with warmth. "My heart feels for you, Meeshka, but the sickness seems most violent among the youth of our tribes. Here in these walls you will be safest. You should also know, every available man or woman with healing skills has been asked to tend to the sick. I have volunteered the Halevi. Our people have long been called upon in times past to aid with plagues and illnesses. God keeps us safe as we do His work. So you must ready yourself — this may be a long empty winter for you. You will need to fill your time with prayers and offerings for the community from within the shelter of the Temple. I will mostly be taken up with the charge laid upon the Halevi, and you should not be out in the compound, even among the other priests."

"I could be taught to help you, Malachi —" I protested softly. "Could I not?"

His expression grew even more sober. "When you are older — not now, my child. You are my only heir, and my heart is fierce for you. When you are older, Meeshka," he repeated, gently, at the look in my eyes.

It was only after Malachi had already risen hastily and scurried away to report all of this to Cohen and the others that I remembered Devland's dream from long ago. I had all but forgotten it entirely. This brought some measure of calm, though I still did not like the idea of Mother and Devland alone during this struggle. They had only had each other since I had left home... and my uneasy conscience was whispering too that Devland and I were at odds. I hadn't seen him in several sennights.

That winter was indeed a long, slow terrible one. A life of quiet had always somehow suited me, yet this silence asked something wholly new of me. Not only was I deeply mindful of the great affliction upon our people, with no power in my hands to ease it, but the solitude bore down on me more heavily than anything I had ever known. I lived for the moments when Malachi returned home after days outside the compound and gave me the news. He was often tired and cold, and I thrilled at being able to care for him as much as he would let me.

Only once did I complain after a particularly long sennight of boredom. My life had become endless watches of silent prayer and incense offerings; I'd cleaned the Temple so many times even the stone benches gleamed with the polishing.

"I think the Whisper has abandoned the Temple right now," I said aloud. "He must be in the community with the priests where the truer work is being done. He isn't making Himself known here at all."

It was then Malachi looked at me in his wise gentle way across the little stone table in our living quarters. He could have used the moment for a rebuke, to remind me of the terrible calamity pressing upon Rivermouth and how small my own was beside it, yet instead he said, "Doing nothing is still doing something for the Halevi, Meeshka. Even our manner of living apart shows our faithfulness to the Whisper — this separation itself is a work of holiness. If you seem to do nothing, yet you live set apart unto the Whisper — for His will, at His calling, for His honor — then you are a royal priesthood still, and you are leaving a legacy behind you. Never forget how dear your place is to Him."

My eyes stung with tears at his gentle sermon. His words were ones I would never forget, even if I struggled to hold onto them in the days ahead. How like Malachi to make me feel important, and my life beautiful even in a moment like this one.

"The Priest has favor with God," Malachi told me once in that hard winter, "and the King has favor with men. You must use the favor given you — your standing with God — to plead for our people, Meeshka. Truly, they are in great suffering."

Indeed, they were suffering. When at last I was allowed to step out again, many months later, creeping forth at winter's end as the plague at last loosened its hold, I found that many of our young had either died or were wasted so thin they were scarcely recognizable. Sadly, the Planters Tribe had suffered the worst. Garwin alone had lost three of his five siblings. Malachi had kept much of this from me through the months of isolation, wishing to spare me any more anxiety than I already felt.

With this tragedy came great pain among the people. A sadness rested over the community like a heavy blanket, much heavier than the persistent presence of snow which seemed to take forever before finally giving way to spring. There was also a sharp concern that the harvest would be poor this year seeing as the work force had taken such a blow. In addition, news of the plague in Rivermouth had spread far and wide, to the wounding of the community's good name.

"This may be the opening of hard days for us, and for more reasons than one," Malachi said to me with quiet gravity. "It is likely to be several seasons yet before all of Avan will feel easy in returning here to trade."

He had also kept from me how much Miri had suffered through the winter. Few adults who were stricken with the disease were as laid low as she was. I soon discovered that it was Devland who had nursed her faithfully even in spite of his own illness, rather than the other way around as I had thought it would be. Malachi had brought them food and fresh water and tended to Miri some himself.

When I was allowed to see her, Devland was not home, but I was shocked at the change in her. It seemed that the prolonged illness had stripped her of any extra weight she carried, as well as her strength. She was as tiny as a child and weak as a butterfly. The bitter light in her eye had strengthened, however, and she cursed many times at life — and King Cyrus — when I visited her. She never directed this anger at me, but strangely, I did not feel my presence was welcomed by her. Mostly she ignored me. I looked fat and happy compared to her... compared to most of the community, who staggered like transparent spirits through the streets, feebly bent over from emotional pain or physical suffering.

When I returned to the Temple that day, Malachi found me crying in a darkened corner of the sanctuary. The plague had managed to isolate me twice over, first with separation, and now with the plain-faced fact I had been untouched by it. I wondered if my relationship with my mother would ever be the same again.

This question would never be answered, sadly. Only a few days after my visit to see her, Malachi brought the terrible news that Miri had passed away.

I leapt up at the news, startled in surprise. "Malachi, no! Devland has need of her — *I prayed for her* —"

He merely shook his head at me, placing a strong hand on my shoulder. "Draw strength from the Whisper, Meeshka," he told me sadly. "During such hours we must lean ourselves into Him. He is the One who can bring true comfort to our souls, when all other comforts fail."

After this there were restless nights until the burial service a few days later. I sought out Devland as soon as word reached me, but Miri's house was already brimming with the company of mourners, and he greeted me with little time and fewer words than I had hoped. He and Miri had been part of another world in life, and were now part of that world in death, joined by those who understood the illness and were suffering together at its end. Just as I had found in my final visit with Miri, there was no place for me here.

"What will become of Devland?" I asked Malachi through my tears afterward. "Will he come live here with us at the Temple? He is still but a boy."

Malachi must have known how much I wanted this. He bore the answer with the same soft care he had shown when he brought me word of Miri, and his eyes sought mine with a doleful kindness through his heavy beard. "It has already been weighed and settled. His heart is set on living with Garwin's people. They made their offer the very hour your mother passed. And in this, Meeshka, I believe it is a kindness. It would be a heavy loneliness for him to always dwell here. He is shaped more for the life of the community. Garwin's house has lost three children, as you know — and after such grief and want, they will take him in with open hands."

I knew the choice was true and right, though it wounded me all the same. Devland had not so much as considered a life with me or with Malachi; most of all, he had not discussed it with me beforehand. I was worried for him… and for our relationship.

I looked at Malachi with quiet fear. "Everything is changing."

His warm eyes were filled with compassion as he took me gently in his arms and held me close to him for a moment. "Change comes always, just as the seasons turn — this we cannot stop. But it grieves me that it has come so harshly upon you, little Meeshka. This is not what I would have chosen for you… nor for Devland. And in my heart I foresee this is only the first stirring. You must try to ready yourself."

Malachi's words proved prophetic in many ways. At the burial service, a full crowd gathered for the brief ceremony led by Cohen, who offered the prayers and a few quiet words over Miri's life. The young men had labored all day to thaw the frozen earth so that the grave might be cut, and though heavy patches of snow still lay across the ground, the air was warmed by the first bursts of spring sunshine. At the close of the small proceeding, we stood in quiet watch as the young men of the village lowered Miri's wooden casket into the earth with heavy ropes. Strangely, Devland did not stand beside Malachi and me, but remained instead with Garwin and Connor and their families, set apart from us.

Instead of crying as I thought I would, or thinking on any favorable memories of Miri, I found memories of Devland's dream crowding my mind. *The lion was meant to* eat *the bear.* That was the way it was meant to come to pass.

Not for the first time in the last little while, I glanced at Devland across the casket between us. He was clean and handsome, dressed in a dark wool tunic beneath a weathered cloak, his boots freshly brushed. He looked almost startlingly healthy — far more so than most of the villagers, whose frames had been stripped thin and whose skin had turned yellow and sallow. He had always been short and stocky, and he stood so now with squared shoulders and solid bearing. For all that Miri had suffered, he seemingly had not. Just now his eyes were downcast and his dark features were unreadable, though I thought he clutched the pale flower in his hand with a crushing grip.

In interpreting the dream, I had assured him of a peaceful end to the struggle. And while it was true he had survived and looked well, neither of us had been prepared for *this.* Not Mother. *Not Miri.* I wondered how his heart stood in all of it.

I longed to reach across the casket and hug him. Of the two of us, he had always been the more fragile one when it came to emotional matters. At the very least, I wanted to stand with him, *be with him.* He was my brother, and was now nearly the only family I had. I belonged with him, and he belonged with me. With Miri gone, we had no one else but Malachi.

Cohen gave some signal now, which prompted everyone in attendance to throw flowers they had been given beforehand onto the casket before the grave diggers covered it with soil. As one by one the attendees stopped and ceremoniously tossed their flowers, a few gripped Devland's shoulder affectionally or gave Malachi a solemn nod from across the grave, paying their respects before slowly drifting away. This was a quiet, sober few moments. There had been many burials in the past many sennights, and every face appeared especially devastated, still tender with the memory of its own loss.

As Garwin threw his flower in, he caught my eye and nodded kindly. He looked gaunt and terribly pale after the long winter. In that brief heartbeat alone, he gave me more notice than Devland had through the whole of the ceremony. I nodded back, teary-eyed at the other boy's sacrifice. After all, he had already endured three burials of his own family in the short span of these bitter months. It was good of him to spare me a little kindness.

As the people continued streaming by, the priests who stood behind Malachi and myself began singing a quiet hymn that carried the moment. Their harmonious voices rose over the burial grounds at the village's edge, filling the spring air with beautiful reminders of hope and courage. I felt the Presence of the Whisper move over me and was grateful to them — and to Him. Malachi's hand came down to settle on my shoulder, a securing comfort as he always was in my darkest moments.

When finally everyone had drifted away but the priests and the gravediggers, Devland and I cast our flowers in… and then he was moving away with Garwin's family, as if he was with them. Once again I was taken aback. His grief had swallowed him whole, leaving no room to see me, or to see that this loss had fallen on us both.

Standing there, left behind, I tried telling myself that he was just a boy, so very young to have lost our mother. He was in shock… and the two had been very close, much closer than I had ever been to Miri.

As these thoughts settled uneasily in me, the priests began filtering away from our side of the grave, headed back through the grave yard in a close cluster of dark robes and colorful prayer cloths. I went after Malachi with a numbness in my steps, uncertain whether my grief lay more with the loss of Miri or with the disturbing fear of what was unfolding in my brother's heart just then.

I was just hurrying forward to reach for Malachi's hand when I heard my name and paused in my steps on the snow-trodden ground, looking up. To my surprise, it was Connor who appeared at my side. I had hardly paid any attention to him during the ceremony, though I knew he was there. Out of long mental habit, I always kept some watch on where he was so I could avoid his tongue and bold stares. Not even Miri's burial service could change that. But here he was, taking me in with a freckled face and solemn dark eyes, surprising me with his unexpected appearance. I thought he had drifted away with his family some time ago.

He looked well after the long winter, as if he had not been afflicted with the plague as everyone else had. Like Devland, he too had polished himself up, having scavenged a dark fustian waistcoat from somewhere for the occasion that made him look older than his mere thirteen years, especially with the unusually sober light in his eye. I had to wonder if he had stolen it.

I waited for him to speak, my heart too unsettled to find words, even if I had wanted to reach for them. There was no telling what he had to say; I half-expected some mocking statement after the winter I had spent in hiding. He had never been one for much respect. It would be in Connor's manner to draw notice to my differences from those about me in a moment of weakness, and just now I was sharply aware of it. Even Miri had made me notice them in my last visit with her.

In his hands he held a flower. Without warning, he held this out to me.

"For you, Priestess," he said. "Seems wasted on Miri's grave. You should have it."

This left me at a loss altogether. I had to wonder if he had lingered back just to give it to me. I reached out to take the small blossom very slowly, aware Malachi was watching our interaction nearby. He would desire for me to show kindness in return for such a small gesture of consideration. How I wished even in that low moment of life that I didn't have to take it at all.

And then, all at once, without another word or waiting for my answer, Connor turned and departed.

# 3.

The troubles for Rivermouth continued for the next two years. As a result of the plague, the harvest was poor and patrons were few. Many families came near to starving, and there was a common unrest among the community. The Halevi gave what little food we had to those who came to our door begging for a penny or two, and the priests themselves worked even longer turns of labor than those in the fields — answering calls day and night for prayer and encouragement, tending to small illnesses in homes, and conducting burial rites. There were few happy times for anyone. Our annual Tribal Fair was set aside, and with it most other feasts and days of celebration. If any were wed or a child newly born to them, they did not presume to celebrate it in public, out of regard for those who suffered.

For my own part, I was touched by it very little, being kept within the shelter of the Temple as I was, where food never failed us even through the lean seasons that weighed upon the people. Our income came from a yearly tithe from Rivermouth which was required of every citizen and had been in place for generations. This was the way they showed the priests honor and recognized the value of the Halevi, who gave to the community in other ways beside economic contribution. Aside from that, the priests already lived a life of little, and celebrations were of no matter to us. Our lives kept a steady course, untouched by favorable or harsh conditions… at least so long as we had the Temple, one another, and the shelter of the compound. We drew our strength from the Whisper and took comfort in our quiet, constant traditions.

I did miss Devland, however. Miri and I had not been especially close since I was ten, but Devland held a piece of my heart which he would claim for all of his days. Whether he knew this or understood it, I didn't know, but I was aware of it. He never once came to find me, and when our paths met in the street, his words were few and thin. There was no returning to our last troubling conversation the autumn before Miri died; when I did mention it, he shrugged it off, as though our petty disagreement mattered little in light of the tragic winter that followed. I went to see him at Garwin's family home more than once, but in time I ceased my visits when I always found him either gone or withdrawn at the sight of me. He seemed far more taken in play with Garwin and the rest of his new kin, and spent the remainder of his time in finding ways to keep far from me. Malachi assured me that he kept watch with Garwin's parents from time to time, and that their word was Devland was content and well-settled in his new home. So I could do nothing but smile through the change and let it be as it was.

Malachi was always challenging me in small ways. That was a difficult thing, *allowing it to be as it was…* I desired nothing more than to be restored to my brother again. Life was emptier without him and Miri… but especially without him.

"Our choices — this is where our true strength is born," Malachi would say. "And our agreement. Agreement is no small matter, Meeshka. It has the power to bend the whole course of a life, even to reshape the fortunes of a nation. Yet there are hours when the only choice left to you is to let a thing be as it is. In such hours you must not move — not until a new door is given to you. Even the choosing to let it be is still a choice, you see. And that choice, whether it feels so or not, carries freedom within it. If you can receive that moment of seeming powerlessness, and even learn to rest in it with the Whisper's help, then you have gained a very great mastery indeed."

How different his teachings were from Miri's, who would have encouraged persistence and possibly aggression to bring about change. She would have bade me confront Devland outright, even to come to blows with him, until the matter was settled between us. Malachi believed in careful strategy, quiet trust, and self-control; she believed in reckless demand and public outcries.

"But how will I ever know when I am meant to act?" I asked Malachi.

He chuckled a little at my bewilderment. "Do not be anxious, Meeshka — you will know. The Whisper has His own way of making Himself known. We wait upon His wisdom to learn what is right, and we watch for His turning to learn when to move. And the moments for change, even the smallest ones, they come all at once. *You will know.*"

When I was eighteen, I stumbled upon a rumor that marked those days for me and seemed to begin a string of troubling events, each worse than the last. I had gone to the market to fetch some food staples for Malachi, armed with a little basket for carrying my purchases. I had promised him I would serve him fish, which had become a frequent dish in our diet, seeing as cheese, milk, and grains were in less abundance. More and more men in the community had taken to the Great Expanse to add to our dwindling stores, and for the first time that I could recall, small fishing boats could be seen riding at anchor just off the shore. The busy marketplace was located in the center of the community on the eastern bank of the river, full of chattering women, less full of buyers. The booths and tables were not as full as they once were, nor the awnings that shaded them as bright and colorful. Everything about the community had a look of tattered wear about it these days, including its buildings and streets. Even the skies, ordinarily populous with billowing clouds and dazzling color at this time of the year, were overcast and dull, as if reflecting the poor people below.

Today I was wearing plainclothes, but this did nothing to help me blend in. I still stood awkwardly tall and pale among all the short dark women with flashing eyes. By then I had more or less grown used to my differences among the folk of the community, and so had they — yet that afternoon, strangely, I felt it keenly again, for many of the women cast glances after me as I wandered from booth to booth, looking over the food and other wares. When I caught their eyes, most slid away, avoiding; but there was an amused glitter in their expressions, and they often sought out another woman after I passed to exchange a hidden smile with them. I had to wonder what was happening. Never before had I attracted any especial attention.

Fortunately, I didn't have to guess for long. Malachi had taught me that if I was patient long enough, someone would surely speak.

Even living somewhat apart from these people, he had been among them his entire life and understood there were always a few who could not resist passing on news — especially to the one whom it most concerned.

"I've come to depend on that fact," he sighed once. "Sadly. There's an advantage and a disadvantage to it." He gave me a knowing wink, eyes suddenly glimmering. "Cohen probably has a wise saying about it. He always has a wise saying when life is predictable."

A woman by the name of Flora was the one who caught me just before I left the marketplace and said, with a low chuckle, *"Girl —* everyone's talking about you… Your little adventure in the forest…"

She did not even know my name, though I knew hers. I paused in my steps and stared at her in simple surprise. *What could she mean?*

"You heard I was in the forest?" I rarely left the compound, and even less so now with Miri gone and Devland uninterested in my company.

She gave me a sly glance, as if I was playing the innocent. "You and that boy…"

To my irritation, a slow, betraying flush rose in my cheeks. "I don't know any boys. You must have the wrong girl."

I was going to turn away as quickly as that, but she insisted, "You're the Temple girl, aren't you? There's no mistaking who you are."

*The Temple girl.* I almost sighed. "I live with the priests in the Temple, yes. So you can see how I wouldn't know any boys at all. You must be mistaken —"

"Well, it seems this one knows you well enough," she cut in with a knowing laugh. *"Very well."*

That flush quickly kindled into a burning sensation in my face at her insinuation. I was surely confirming for her with my reaction that I was guilty of whatever they were saying about me. For a moment I wanted to turn and run, but I felt certain that the entire marketplace was watching now, eager for my response. It seemed to me even the air was tingling with anticipation. *How different these women were from the calm, orderly priests I was so accustomed to…*

"I'm afraid I don't know any boys," I repeated, faintly.

At my continued bewilderment, she at last gave voice to it. "I mean the Shannesee boy. You were seen with him. *Well* — " She broke off with a coarse little laugh, casting a glance toward another woman nearby. "— you were seen in closer company than *that*. There was heavy kissing, they say. He doesn't deny it. Folk have questioned him."

*Connor Shannesee.* I was utterly horrified. Never before had I been the talk of any local whispering, at least so far as I was aware, and the thought of it left me both sickened and ashamed. I was certain the color drained out of my face altogether. *What would Malachi say?*

"The women are all abuzz over you, seeing as you are the High Priest's granddaughter," she laughed. "You've always seemed like such a good, quiet soul. So virtuous." She flicked me a sudden wink, full of a meaning far from Malachi's loving one. "I've been telling them — you'll not be a *dull* High Priestess."

How amused she was. How pleased at the thought of my supposed wantonness. How she seemed to relish the notion of a sinful High Priestess. I couldn't respond. I turned sharply and hurried away, so miserable I no longer cared what they thought, her coarse words burning in my ears.

I didn't wait to tell Malachi or seek his counsel; I didn't even wait to drop the basket off at the Temple. I was too humiliated and infuriated. Images flashed through my mind of the news being spread from mouth to mouth, passed like an illness between the households of the community. *Connor has done this,* I thought angrily. *Connor has done this and enjoyed it.* He probably delighted in creating the story as much as the telling of it, spreading the tale that I had agreed to sneak into the forest with him for a secret tryst. That would have stirred little interest for a village girl foolishly taken with him — no one would have marveled at that — but what gave the tale intrigue was that it was *me,* the High Priest's novice. *How could I ever live down such foul, wretched lies?*

With grim determination, I marched all the way to the oat and barley fields on the edge of town where I knew the Planters would be working at this time of day. We were finishing the harvest season and every able-bodied man and woman in the tribe would be on hand, working to bring in the last of the season's crop. Just now the survival of the community through the upcoming winter months depended largely on a successful crop from the Planters.

It didn't take but a few inquiries and I located Conner in a large stretch of barley farthest away from the ocean's shore. He and a group of men and women had set themselves to the hard task of gathering, binding, and tying the cut stalks into sheaves, while in other parts of the fields rows of muscle-bound men were busy harvesting the barley with heavy sickles and scythes. The smell of grain, earthy dirt, and the faint, sweet scent of oats hung in the air; gnats and flies, stirred from their nests by the activity, hovered in swarms over the fields.

Connor wasn't difficult to spot. His auburn hair was less fiery and more jewel-toned in gray lighting, but it stood out among the other dark-haired workers; and the young man was forever talking. His laughing voice reached me even as I threaded my way through the shorn field. He was too busy at work and distracted with his story-telling to notice me until I was almost upon him, and then he looked up with surprise.

His entire face came alive as he recognized me. "Eren!" His nose scrunched as impishly as a ten-year-old boy, his eyes instantly sparking with mischievous scrutiny. "What brings *you* here?"

I couldn't remember when last I had seen him — perhaps only in a fleeting crossing of paths, when every part of me had worked to avoid him. He so rarely ever called me by name. Today, in light of what I had just heard in the marketplace, the sound of it on his lips irritated me as much as all the other names he had invented for me over the years.

"I need to speak with you," I demanded. *"At once."*

This stirred his curiosity, I could see that. Laughter was already pulling at his mouth just at the tone in my voice. The men and women who were scattered around us released a low moan, as if entertained by the prospect of trouble for him.

Unmoved, Connor acknowledged this with a brief laugh and a wry glance at me. "She's the High Priest's granddaughter. She couldn't hurt a butterfly."

"It could be," someone countered. "But it looks as though she'd like to fillet you alive with her tongue."

Tying up the sheaves was hot work for these men and women, and Connor looked it. Sweat ran down his face in dirty streaks, mixing and mingling with the sweat-stained shirt and filthy breeches he wore.

Though he was only seventeen, all of the young men in the Planters and Builders Tribes were required to work as hard as any full-grown man as soon as they left school at fifteen. He paused a moment to make vain effort at wiping the grime and sweat away from his forehead with a dark rag that hung at his leather belt, giving little heed to the snickering that moved among the others.

"I need water," he told them. "Be back shortly." His dark eyes fell to me, nodding towards the edge of the field beyond us where a wagon and team stood in the shade of a belt of trees. "This way, Priestess. You can tell me all about it."

This wry statement made the field workers laugh again.

Just being in this position, subject to the humor of these men and women, made me burn with new irritation. But I was determined to confront him for what he had done; he had gone too far with his disrespect. I moved after him stiffly, walking behind by a few feet, not willing to stride alongside him. I didn't wait until we reached the edge of the trees; I told him straight out.

"I know you are at the root of it, Connor Shannesee," I declared to his back. "You should be ashamed."

At this, he stopped in his tracks and turned fully around. Though we had moved beyond those at work, we hadn't yet made it to the water wagon. He laughed in my face. "It pains me to disappoint you, Priestess, but I never said any of those things."

I didn't believe him for an instant. "They can mar my reputation terribly! It's just plain wrong." There was heat in my voice now as I said the words through clinched teeth. *"And you know better."*

His laughter swelled and brimmed over, bubbling up like some mocking well of gladness meant to plague me. "What a glare you have, Priestess! I didn't know you had it in you."

*"Are you listening to me?"*

"Of course I am. And I'm telling you, I didn't spread that story —" Now he was choking out the words, hardly able to contain his mirth.

"It's on every tongue in the marketplace that you did it. Who else would utter such abominable lies?"

"Those women were *wishing* you did those things is more likely," he chortled. "They relish a juicy story, like a good cut of meat."

This was true, I couldn't deny it. The women in the marketplace were by far the worst gossips of anyone in Rivermouth. Many times I'd heard the tales they delighted in sharing with each other, given in a flurry of bright chatter and sharp judgment. I had always ignored it before — until today. Until *I* was the subject of their whispered amusement and side glances. But the idea that I had acted rashly was unthinkable… certainly not anywhere Connor was concerned.

I grasped for some way to defend myself. "I conduct myself honorably —" I blustered.

Connor roared, "Don't I know it!"

"I've never kissed a boy in my life!" I spat out. *"No less sported with him in the forest.* You should have heard how the woman said it, as if I was — " I struggled for the words. Drew myself up with dignity. "I won't *repeat* what I think she believes of me — *and you* —"

Now Connor was undone, nearly doubled over with laughter. The entire matter appeared to give him greater amusement than any he had known before, my reactions chief among them. Even in my anger, I was keenly aware that the rumors did not trouble him in the least, though his name was tangled in them too. This disgusted me afresh. In my mind his response made him guilty of spreading them, at least planting the idea in someone's head, else he would act with dignity and care. At the very least, if he held even a scrap of decency, he would show some kindness toward my discomfort.

I stared him down. "I think you did say it," I challenged. "I think you set those lies loose all through Rivermouth. How else would our names have been so easily joined? It's called bearing false witness. You should be ashamed! My name matters to me. I'm the next High Priestess. That may weigh little with you, but it means something to me..."

Connor was not stirred in the least by my fury or by the accusations I laid upon him. His grin was rakish as his mischievous eyes caught mine. "You sure are fiery for a priestess, Eren. What would your grandfather say?"

The reminder of Malachi was like cold water dashed in my face. I truly was coming undone. All at once I rued coming out here; it was plain I had done nothing but worsened the matter. An entire field of workers were watching us from the distance. I could hear them making laughing comments, enjoying the sight of me snarking at Connor and him heedlessly laughing back. They would likely press him for the cause of my fury once I had gone; and as unbothered as he was, Connor would probably tell them the full story without any thought for me, just as something to entertain them with. I cared little what he personally thought of me, but my reputation would take another blow as the rumors traveled through all the homes of the field workers. I had foolishly managed to spread the story even farther.

I quickly composed myself and gave Connor a curt nod. "I'll thank you to keep your mouth shut about me, Connor Shannesee."

"Or else *what*?" he roared. "You're going to stop *praying* for me?"

This was just too much. I turned and stormed away from him. As I did, I could hear his irreverent laughter following me all the way out of the fields.

I went home that day headed directly for the comfort of Malachi's counsel. I knew he would make things as right as he could. He was my greatest source of comfort aside from the Whisper Himself, even when I fell short, such as moments like walking out to the fields to confront Connor directly. He had such an endless grace for my youthfulness and occasional moments of impetuosity. But of course he surprised me with what he said, he always did.

"There will always be those who take pleasure in gossip, Meeshka," he said to me. "It may be that young Connor has learned this truth sooner than you. We do what we can to walk our lives above reproach — yet the passing on of shameful tales is a common bent in the heart of man, and one we must learn to endure."

He was actually painting Connor in a good light, which was unbearable. I had hoped for at least some measure of sympathy over the young man's lack of respect, if not outright assurance that Malachi privately held Connor to be the author of the grievous rumor. And even beyond that, I had looked for some comfort over the bitter, shaming tale that was moving through the market, and doubtless now through all the Planters Tribe as well. I had likewise secretly hoped that Malachi would be as repulsed and disturbed by its salacious matter as I was.

"But my name, Malachi — what will become of it among the people?" I cried. "How will I ever be heeded if they put their faith in these tales about me?"

"You must do what you are given to do — to please the Whisper — and let that be enough," he said. "Many dark things have been spoken of the Halevi through the years, yet we prove our true nature by our steadiness and our faith. No doubt you will bear a small portion of this suffering as well, little Meeshka. There are many reasons for the unholy to resent the holy. They delight to catch us in a moment of frailty, as though it might ease their own sins to see it. You must remember — even our favor in the eyes of men is first given by the Whisper. All that we have has its beginning in Him. You must lean on Him to enlarge your life. We keep ourselves low in spirit — and He is the One who lifts us high."

He could see I was wrestling with his answer. I would have better accepted a scolding from him for outright challenging Connor. Malachi smiled kindly at me. "We try our best to urge people towards better choices, but the truth of it is this — some will always fall back upon the baser part of their nature."

And then after another moment of strain, he said into the tension, "Perhaps it would be wise for you to keep from the market for a little while — to let the gossip die away, and the attention of the women turn on to some other matter."

At last, this soothed me. I held back a small sniff as I answered, "Very well, then. That is what I will do."

Only a few sennights later, I exited the front gates of the Temple with the intent of visiting the Meadows for a late afternoon walk.

The weather was beginning to cool, the leaves were changing into beautiful hues and blends of autumn color, and Malachi had encouraged me to soak up the season for as long as it lasted. Soon enough, the rains of fall would come and along with it, heavy winds, followed shortly after by the snowy cold of winter. This was the way it always was on the edge of the sea.

"You're young yet," Malachi told me. "You need to get out as much as you can, Meeshka. The day will come when the responsibilities of the Priesthood will keep you occupied all times of day and night and you'll find free times rare. Fill your lungs with as much fresh air as you can."

As it stood, he showed no sign of aging to the point where I would need to take on more of his duties, so I took his counsel gladly. I had just come from a glorious hour of worship with all the priests in the Temple, and my spirit was near leaping with gladness. Between the life-giving time we had spent in the Presence of the Whisper and the thought of an entire evening in the Lush Meadows, my heart felt light within me and my outlook renewed.

Just as I moved beyond the compound into the street before it, I heard my name called and looked up, in time to discover Garwin and Connor walking past together. The two were dressed in plain, yet clean fare, as if they were in town looking for recreation of some kind. Though both young men were burnished bronze and muscular from a summer just spent in the fields, they were distinctly different. Garwin most often showed himself calm and steady in spirit, while lively Connor ever looked as though he were hatching some mischief or shaping a grand tale to delight his companions.

My first thought was a small disappointment that Devland wasn't with them; I always hoped to catch even a glimpse of him and the three still often spent much of their spare time in each other's company. My second thought was relief that, if I was going to run into Connor, at least Garwin was present. The sharp heat of my feelings over the marketplace gossip had dimmed by now, but I liked the incorrigible boy less than ever. The mere sight of him all but stole my joy away completely.

Garwin hurried over as I paused and waved in a friendly manner, his face pulled into a bright smile. Though we saw less of each other these days, he was always glad to catch sight of me if we did cross paths in town. Devland may have had no wish to be seen in my company, but Garwin did not share in that feeling.

"*Eren!* So good to see you."

I had observed that when we were alone he took care never to show me affection, as though he judged it improper without a chaperone, and I had always respected him for these quiet manners. Yet today, with Connor present, Garwin felt at ease enough to draw me into a warm embrace, his hands reaching out to do so. Connor was close on his heels just then, and in the next instant he looked up and did a startling thing — with lightning-swift reflexes, he caught Garwin and pulled him sharply back, stopping him short.

"Don't touch her," he cautioned. *"Look at her."*

This quick action caught me by surprise as much as it did Garwin. The warning provided Garwin enough time to pause and take me in carefully.

"She's been in the Temple," Connor announced.

I knew that at times I shone a little after worship, yet it was not an awareness I kept with me continually. So few ever saw me but the priests in the pattern of my daily life, and they made no mention of it. For a moment I stood there in some awkwardness under the shadow of the boys' quiet scrutiny.

Garwin looked suddenly uncomfortable. "Forgive me, Eren. I didn't notice — I meant no disrespect — "

I smiled at him a little hesitantly. "It's no matter — I didn't think anything about it —" But it was Connor who had surprised me.

I shifted my gaze to meet his evenly. He was the last person I would expect to take notice of such a thing… or bother to show any regard for it. After our last exchange, I was fully convinced he bore not even a shred of respect for what was sacred. Yet he had acted instantly. And he was standing here before me saying nothing, doing nothing. There was no quick smile to follow his reaction, no cutting word. Unlike Garwin, he wasn't surprised or taken aback in the least. Nor did I think I had ever seen such a look upon his usually smug face.

In his guilt, Garwin did not perceive my preoccupation. "I forget sometimes… who you are…"

This stirred me, and I turned and smiled at him. "It's no matter, Garwin. It really isn't. I was just making my way to the Meadows. And what, pray, are you both up to on so fine an evening as this?"

It was in this conversation that I learned news of Devland. He had decided to join the Governor Tribe after all, and intended to do so on his eighteenth birthday in six months.

"I suppose he's doing it for our mother," I commented softly.

Garwin considered this. "He did love her a great deal. Her death was a terrible blow."

Garwin was a good friend. I saw the softness in him as he held these thoughts, his care for others settling around him like a gentle warmth.

Connor, however, was never shy with his thoughts, and gave them voice as loudly as ever. "Dev is all for change of late. I can't say I fault him for it. Everything's been wretched in the community since the plague."

I disregarded his complaint and turned to Garwin. "She always wished for him to be one of the Governors."

Garwin nodded. "He believes he might one day take a seat with the Board of Traders and help draw buyers back into the community. He even hopes to travel to Periburn, if the chance is given to him, and speak with the merchants there to renew trade with us. We are in need of food… and of those who would buy. He is young, to be sure, but I think there is wisdom in some of his thoughts. My father thinks so as well."

But Connor overrode this also, with a knowing smirk. "Oh, Dev's had no shortage of words, to be sure. He's all stirred up."

I never quite knew what weight to give Connor's words. I could not tell whether he meant that Devland was shaping his discontent into some good for the people, or whether he was slyly letting on that Dev was far more restless than Garwin would admit. Or perhaps he was only speaking out of love for the sound of his own voice. He was a born talker, and rich in opinions. All the same, I judged him to be a harmful influence upon my brother, as I always had. No one could kindle Devland's restlessness as Connor could. Even then I wished they were not so closely knit.

As was to be expected, Devland never spoke to me — nor to Malachi — of any change in his plans. It was I who made mention of it after encountering him in the street days later, yet he acknowledged it only with a dismissive shrug. He gave no sign of the eagerness Garwin had spoken of, nor did he voice any of the fervent notions Connor claimed he carried. Whoever my brother was and was becoming, it was evident that he wished to keep these matters to himself. Painful though it was for me to accept, he had firmly shut me out of his life. Something between us had indeed been broken during that long winter of separation, when Miri died.

If Devland had ever asked me for my thoughts about his new plans, I rather liked the idea of him carrying out Miri's wishes if that was what he wanted. He would help govern and administrate the people, while I would serve as High Priestess in the Temple. Surely this was the way it was always meant to be… though my heart ached for the widening space between us, and many of my prayers in those days were long pleadings with the Whisper, that He would yet give me an occasion to restore what had been lost between us.

Early that winter, new rumors began to spread in Rivermouth, which were of such an alarming nature that Malachi brought them to me himself.

"Word has reached us that rebels are gathering not far from here, in the Silent Heights to the west," he reported. "They have begun to waylay travelers on the road into Rivermouth. We know little as yet, only that they are no loose rabble but an ordered band, and a cunning one. For the present they chiefly trouble the wealthy and the merchants — yet even so, Meeshka, this spells real danger for Rivermouth."

I had not seen Malachi so grave since the time he brought me tidings of the plague. His eyes, so often lit with quiet mystery and a thread of humor despite all troubles, now lay dark and still.

"As you well know, Meeshka, we already labor to draw the merchants back to trade. And the people here are much weakened now by fear and by loss. Winter is ever a hard season, and this will lay yet another weight upon us. We stand vulnerable in this hour — both in body and in spirit. The Priests must therefore remain without ceasing in prayer for all the people."

Rivermouth had no armed forces, no walls or gates at our entrances. We were a peace-abiding community and had been so for generations. Not even sentries walked our streets at night. If there was discord or strife between households, this was brought to the Governors, who involved the Chief Priests and sometimes the High Priest, and it was addressed fairly and quickly. No one I had ever known sought after trouble… except, perhaps, Connor.

I asked quietly, "What can be done about the Rebels, Malachi? Anything?"

He shook his head, as if he didn't think the efforts that had been made would do much good. "A messenger has been sent on to Periburn to lay our request before the King, that he would send men to see to this matter," he said. "We can only pray the poor fellow does not fall into the hands of the Rebels himself — and that the King will, in fact, give ear to us." He gave a small shrug. "At times he listens. At times he does not. We have known other troubles from beyond our borders in years past — we cannot be assured of his answer.

"In the meantime, men from each tribe have offered themselves to walk the outer bounds of the community by night, as a show of strength meant to turn the Rebels away, should they think us easy prey. And the Governors have set a law now that none of our women are to walk in Rivermouth without an escort, at least until the turn of spring. In winter there is too little life abroad in the community to risk it."

Malachi's wise, sober eye landed on me. "This holds for you as well, Meeshka," he said. "If you must go to the market, you will need to take two or three of the priests with you. I do not wish you to leave the village for any cause at all — not for the shore, not even for the outer houses. I fear another long winter is before you."

It was indeed a long winter, broken only by those few journeys to the market for what we needed. To my quiet delight, Garwin learned that I was with a priestly escort and offered himself for the task instead. His people were less occupied during the winter months, and he had leisure for it. Malachi approved this arrangement particularly, since the priests were often engaged elsewhere and Garwin possessed the strength of several of them combined. So began a little weekly tradition between us, where Garwin showed up at the Temple and walked me to the market in the cold air and often wintry weather. We hunched down in our warm clothing and chatted happily the entire way there and back, both of us glad to be out of confinement and eager for activity.

I liked this arrangement for several reasons, the first being Garwin was such wholesome company. He seemed to sense my isolation and was happy to fill my ears with casual talk of his daily activities. His life followed its own routines beyond the fixed order of the Temple, though these altered with each season, and the steady manner in which he explained it all was soothing and settling to my heart. Even as young as he was, he had a rhythm much like the consistency of the sun rising calmly and falling every day.

Now and then he would also bring tidings of Devland, and this gladdened my heart. I did not see my brother at all through that winter, yet I still felt some measure of connection to him. If I could not learn directly from Dev what lay in his heart and mind, I could at least hear it from one near to him in whom he confided.

I was privately delighted as well that Garwin served as my weekly escort, since it planted a measure of doubt in the minds of the marketplace women about their tales of my wayward behavior with Connor. I had accepted Malachi's counsel that there would always be those who resorted to their baser nature and thought to myself, *If they must gossip, then all the better that they gossip about Garwin.* It seemed to me that his very face reflected only goodness and kindness. Our calm, weekly appearance in the market communicated the message that we were not sneaking around in the forest in the shadows, but rather, were good friends in the open light.

It was Garwin who told me that some of the young men wished to take on the Rebels themselves — Connor and Devland being among them — especially as the winter wore on and the King did nothing. News began to increase of the Rebels' activity in the mountains. They had raided two or three homesteads in the Silent Heights for food and coin.

For a moment this struck fear in my heart. The notion of Devland standing in battle against rebels chilled my heart. "You don't truly believe the boys will dare to do such a thing, do you?"

But Garwin assured me it was only talk. He added with a quiet smile, "We aren't fighters, any of us. We hardly know how to handle a pitchfork without bringing harm to ourselves. And Connor himself is too intrigued by the idea of joining the Rebels to actually confront any of them."

We were making our way once more toward the marketplace, wrapped thickly against the cold. Around us the village street lay hushed beneath a veil of gray winter light, frost clinging to stone and timber as though held by a quiet spell. Heavy drifts of snow banked the road and sagged from the bare limbs of trees, yet a broad path lay open before us, already packed hard by the day's passing feet. Only a few souls moved through the dimness, and each time we spoke a pale breath of fog spilled from our lips — small proof of our warmth against the bitter air.

A new horror took hold of me then, this time for another reason altogether. *"He is thinking of joining them?"*

Garwin shook his head. "You know the sort Connor is. He makes for a good Planters tribesman, but he longs for adventure."

I wanted to reply in wry disbelief, *"Adventure, is it?"* But I chose self-control instead. Garwin believed in the goodness of everyone and I liked him for it. He would have made a good priest.

"My father thinks he will leave Rivermouth for several years," he continued, "then return and settle down after he works free of his wandering spirit. He says he's seen it before. Some of our best Planters have lived out their youth in other places just to see what there is to see. I myself don't have any need for that. I like it here in Rivermouth just fine." Garwin grinned over at me suddenly.

I grinned back. This was another thread he and I shared. For how different our purposes were, I was finding we were akin in more ways than I thought. "So do I. The thought of living anywhere else feels near unbearable to me."

Garwin shrugged. "For now, Connor is offering himself as a night sentry." He gave a small laugh. "It lets him feel dark and dangerous, as he likes it."

Soon enough, the long winter passed and spring awakened in a fervor of light and beauty. The Rebels confined their villainous activity to the Silent Heights and other places, which caused everyone to sigh in relief and a little hope to stir with the change of the season. The Governors decided, with reluctance, to ease the law, and women were allowed to return to their activities in the community without escort. Spring did not come all at once, but in whispers — thin grass at the road's edge, swelling buds along the branches, and here and there a woman stepping back into the street as cautiously as the season itself, beneath light that lingered a little longer each day. Those who had stayed away from Temple services through the winter came back; the streets slowly filled again; the Builders resumed their home building, street mending, and building constructions; and the Planters began to prepare for planting season.

Garwin arrived to escort me at his usual hour, and for a brief sennight or two I thought he might continue the habit if he could. But one day, as we followed the familiar path to the marketplace, I could tell something was weighing on his mind.

After some while, he made a timid start. "Eren — I have something to tell you —"

I looked over at him in surprise. This was the first time since our walks began that he seemed slow to speak. I quickly reasoned that he must be merely feeling guilty because he couldn't escort me anymore due to busyness. He was a tender-hearted man and showed especial gentleness toward me, which I had always appreciated. "What is it? You know you have nothing to fear in telling me anything, Garwin."

But he continued to look ill at ease. "It isn't that I fear telling you, only — " He lingered in the moment, his face drawn tight.

I stopped in our tracks and turned towards him in the street, hoping a pause in our steps might help him come out with it. Fortunately, there was no one on the little tree-shaded lane where we stood, and we had privacy for the moment.

"What is it?" I pressed again, more softly. "We are on good enough terms between us — you may speak freely to me."

My words did little to ease him, but they prompted a shrug of resignation. His eyes met mine with a near-shy look, and with it a guilt I plainly recognized. "I have always held a fondness for you, Eren — almost from the first hour I knew you. But on the day Connor and I saw you coming from the Temple after worship, something settled in me. All at once I saw how far apart we truly were. I knew then that there could be no shared future for us. You could never live the life on a farmstead beside me, bearing my children and setting my supper each night — and I could never belong to the Temple at your side. We were simply fashioned too differently. I know some of the priests have done such things — married into the community — but they were men, and I understood this could not be for us. We may be friends, of course," he added with care, "but nothing beyond that."

Several emotions pressed upon me in that moment as I listened to his words and observed the shy strain in his face. But my feelings were too much to grasp all at once. Instead, I surprised myself by asking with quiet patience, "What is it you wish to say to me, Garwin? Is that all?"

He shook his head in quiet misery. "No — not all." He drew in a breath. "I — I will not be able to walk with you anymore. Not alone, at least. I have found a girl — a girl I wish to pursue — and —"

The truth struck me suddenly. *" – and you'll be with her now."*

He looked relieved. *"Yes."* He hastened just as quickly to explain, almost stumbling over his words in his anxiety. "Not very much, of course. It's planting season now, so I'll be busy, but when I do have the time —"

I finished again, "You'll be seeing her."

Some part of me wished he had spoken all this sooner, and the realization surprised me. I had not seen until then how attached I'd grown to him. It was not love, I supposed, but a friendship in which I had placed a measure of hope. I would miss that most of all — *the friendship.* A sense of disappointment washed over me.

I tried to swallow this down without giving myself away to him and smiled with as much brightness as I could manage. "I understand, Garwin — I truly do. It would not be fitting for you to be seen on long walks with me while your heart is set on another. Of course I set you free from our friendship. Do not trouble your heart over it at all."

He looked more relieved than ever. He reached out and took my forearms in a brief, earnest hold. *"Thank you, Eren.* I am grateful for your understanding. It means a great deal to me. I did not wish to hurt your feelings in any way — or make you feel awkward about yourself —"

*He really was a sincere soul,* I thought. I smiled at him again, through the disappointment. "Of course not. You're a good man, Garwin."

Afterward, long after we had gone our separate ways that day, I realized with surprise that I disliked how he had drawn the differences between us. I felt more odd than ever, more peculiar. For the first time, the destiny which Malachi had always painted in such wondrous terms for me meant something far different than it ever had. Instead of an extraordinary life of holiness and dedication to God, rather than an exceptional opportunity for intimate experiences with the Whisper, this path separated me from everyone else, kept me from the same privileges they enjoyed.

In my now nineteen years, I had never before considered marriage much, but now I only looked at it as an unattainable dream, one I could never experience even if I desired it. I was even different than the other priests, even different than Malachi himself. No one in our community would ever want to marry a priestess. *Probably no one anywhere,* I thought. In point of fact, if I remained in the Temple, I could never give them what they would want as a wife and a mother to their children. In addition, my life as a priestess would keep me from close friendship with any man — villager or priest, either one — for the rest of my days. Malachi would not live forever, I realized. How many other women were priestesses? And how many outside the Temple would ever be able to understand with compassion the life I led? *None.* At least not in Rivermouth, and probably nowhere. I was set on a path of severe aloneness for the rest of my days.

This realization was far more difficult for me to accept than the loss of Garwin's friendship. For some days afterward, I stayed in the Temple and spent long hours in prayer and solitude, trying to find peace. It was not long before this drew Malachi's notice, as all such things did. One evening he managed to corner me before I withdrew to my bed for the night.

His hand caught mine as I rose from our little table across from him and held it. "What is wrong, Meeshka?" he asked quietly. "What has disturbed my girl? You have lost your peace."

The words spilled out then, along with a convulsive shower of tears. I couldn't help myself. Garwin's words had made me feel more alone than I had ever felt before. I was that little girl again, watching the Rivermouth Community cheer for all the runners in the Tribal Fair, striving to understand why the Halevi must be so different in so many ways… why *I* must be so different in so many ways.

As was his way, Malachi neither scolded nor preached. He did not tell me I should have grasped this by now, nor did he demand that I hold true to my commitments. There was no fear that I was threatening to abandon my calling; he neither patronized nor offered assurances as you would a child. Instead, he kept hold of my hand across the table and waited to speak until after the storm of my tears had lifted, addressing me for the first time as a grown woman. I will never forget the holy words he gave me then.

*"It is true,"* he said to me softly, "there are costs to the calling of a priest. For the King as well — but for you in particular, as the one who is to come after me. You are only now beginning to glimpse an image of it. I will not sweeten the truth for you, Eren — I have long seen that a great price will be asked of you in your life because of your own call. Your road will not always be gentle beneath your feet.

"But hold fast to this — the cost will never outweigh the reward. You will see it. In the end. You will not lose your soul… though there will be hours when it feels as though you have. *The cost will not be higher than the reward."*

Tears stung my eyes again — both from his compassion, and from the weightiness of his words. "Has it been too high for you, Malachi?"

At this, he released my hand and sat back, eying me with a hint of humor. "You are truly coming into your years now, my dear," he said softly. "Your trials — and even your questions — they are changing their shape." Then he weighed his next words with that same rare, gentle equality. "It is true, I too have paid a price. I do not often speak of it — I do not know that I have ever spoken of it to you. I lost my wife while I was still a young man, to an illness, though I later ministered to many through that very same sickness and watched them rise again. And though I loved my only son deeply, and longed for him to follow me into the Priesthood, he chose instead to leave the Temple and join the Planters Tribe — all for the love of a woman who did not love us, nor our ways. For a time, this was a wound of great sorrow to me.

"But God has given me you. I will not be alone another day of my life — for not only has He given you to me, but you yourself have chosen the Priesthood." His remarkable eyes were alight now, shining at their full brightness. "You have come to us bearing many promises, and not the least of them is this — that you run for us, for the Halevi. Through you, my line will yet go on. And the Whisper has said that you will walk among kings and princes. You are our bright road ahead. Tell me this — *how could the cost ever be greater than such a reward?* This is good. *More than good."*

Malachi always had a way of calling me back to the greatness within me. He spoke the truth, and that truth refocused, steadied, and strengthened me. There was nothing greater than the truth, and nothing more glorious than living out the true destiny to which I was called. This was my path, together with all its costs, and I must run it, or I would never be fulfilled or whole.

My grandfather finished our conversation that night with some final words, this time given with a quiet gentleness that was as close to a rebuke as I ever received from him.

"Never forget, Meeshka," he said; "Our life of prayer is not to be used as a place of escape. It will be difficult to take hold of this truth in moments of great struggle and mental unrest, yes. Yet remember this always, even when the storm rages most: the Whisper is a deep-flowing river within you, even in the fiercest storms of life. His waters are quiet and constant, a deep, slow, persistent force that moves with majestic patience. He is the Place of Stillness at the center of your being.

"In those waters you will find a Place ancient and eternal, where time passes unmeasured. Sink into yourself in your times of prayer and *take hold of Him,* for surely He desires for you to do so. And in His Presence, you will find peace, no matter the storm."

# 4.

In the weeks following Garwin's announcement, I resumed my visits to the marketplace, this time unaccompanied. I resisted lingering on the loss of his companionship, and instead focused on Malachi's words regarding it all. Though the community had relaxed its laws, Malachi still discouraged any outside activity beyond my weekly visits to the marketplace until he felt more confident that the Rebel raiders had moved on from the Silent Heights or had been rousted out by the King.

"We dare not risk it," he told me. "You wander freely everywhere and are a rare sight here among our people, Meeshka. From a distance you would easily attract attention to anyone spying on our community. Our Priestess is precious to us, and we must keep you safe."

He did not add that I was of an age now that men would lust for me. I did not consider myself beautiful — certainly not like the curvaceous, smokey-eyed women of our community. I knew I was not nearly as lovely as Garwin's new interest, when I laid eyes on her in the marketplace one day. She laughed with a sound like musical chimes and clung to him in a way that communicated she would do anything for him if he needed. This was a form of beauty I would never have or be able to offer a man. Yet I knew well enough that beauty alone was no true measure in the reckless hungers of wicked men, and therefore submitted to Malachi's wisdom.

As a result, this left me mostly in the confines of the compound, and I spent a great deal of time in the Outer Court offering prayers and singing so that I could enjoy as much of the outdoors as possible. Spring settled over the sacred grounds with blessing, softening stone and song alike as the priests lifted incense offerings, voices, and prayers into the brightening air. Occasionally we had visitors, and Malachi allowed me to greet them. This gave me a little company, which I was grateful for. On these days I wore my pale, official robes clasped by a gold pendant at the throat, with my red hair spilling in soft waves over my shoulders. Slowly, I was becoming more and more known by the community as a novice priestess, not just as the young woman who lived in the Temple with her grandfather.

On one such day, as I stood in the general courtyard receiving guests, I looked up to find Connor strolling into the compound as casually as though he came here every day — an odd, almost jarring sight. He was dressed as he always was, in the plain fare of a village man, a heavy pack slung across one shoulder, wholly out of place amid a courtyard that spring had softened with budding trees and fresh green shade drifting above our weathered benches of meditation. Near the center, the well and its stone trough glimmered in the pale light, and from the eaves of the walls wind chimes whispered with every passing breath of air. Holiness settled here like a gentle cloud. I think my mouth nearly fell open at the sight of him, but a desire not to let him see any reaction he might cause in me drew up a sudden self-control.

He was also clearly looking for me. He came straight over and stood waiting while I finished speaking to a young woman who wished to visit with one of the priests for counsel. *I was surprised he was not in the fields with the rest of his tribe.*

I directed the woman to the Outer Court — taking my time just to make Connor wait — and turned back to him with an air of calm indifference. "Greetings to you, Connor. What brings you to the Temple today?"

He let out a low snort, half a laugh. He had already been watching me with evident amusement as he waited. "I'm here to find salvation for my soul," he announced flippantly.

I ignored this. "What is it that you really want?"

"I came to find you."

I blinked at him. I couldn't imagine a single thing he might say to me that would be of any importance. *"Well?* You found me. What can I help you with?"

He looked around suddenly. The courtyard held a few robed priests who were speaking in low voices. Quiet activity could be seen through the open gates of the Outer Court as the priests performed their duties, and the air was filled with the low singing of a small unseen group, their voices lifted in worshipful song. The atmosphere here was always a reverent one.

"Why don't we walk?" he suggested. "This is no place for conversation."

I agreed with him; but I wasn't going to admit that this was an act of respect. "I cannot see myself walking anywhere with you. I am not sure it would be fitting. I am a priestess, after all."

He came near to laughing at my stiff reply. "You've been walking with Garwin all winter. How is this any different?"

In plain truth, he was right, but I did not wish to explain that the two of them as individuals were a far cry different from each other. No doubt he would only respond with light mockery and accuse me of being petty and unkind; he seemed to enjoy pointing out my humanity instead of recognizing what parts of me were divinity.

"Garwin was escorting me to the marketplace for the sake of my safety," I said instead, primly. "You and I have no reason to be seen together *anywhere*."

*"What a lordly prig you are, Priestess."* He didn't look at all bothered. Connor was always laughing at me.

When I held silent, fixing him with the stillness of stone, he sighed. "Look, I have news. Some of it has to do with Devland. Will *that* be enough to persuade you to walk with me?" He gestured to the open wooden gates leading to the street some distance behind us. "We could simply stand outside the compound if it suits you better, Eren."

He knew full well the mention of Devland's name would persuade me. I was always needy for any information about Dev that I could gather, like a parched throat in need of fresh water. I gave him a stiff little nod. "Very well. I'll walk to the Lush Meadows and back with you. The roads that way are very public."

Connor shook his head with a quiet, crooked laugh, his voice dropping to a wry mutter. *"Of course they are."*

To my relief, almost as soon as we crossed the threshold of the Temple compound he began talking. Connor was never one for holding back his thoughts.

"Your brother's been holding speeches at the community meetings. Have you heard?"

I puzzled over this even as I answered him. "No. But is that such a surprise? He has joined the Governors now, and you said yourself months ago that he had many ideas he wished to get across."

Connor shot me a sidelong glance, keeping pace next to me. "I thought probably you and Malachi hadn't heard."

I shook my head, immediately frustrated. I had no wish to speak with him without some true cause. "Is that all you've come to say, Connor? We would have found that out eventually, anyway."

"It isn't the fact that he's giving speeches at the meetings, Eren."

Connor sounded odd, even for him. *Especially* for him. His mere use of my name said something I couldn't quite lay hold of. "What is it then?"

"I think you and Malachi should hear for yourselves what he's saying."

*He was oddly sober.* That was it. Connor was plainly trying to get something across that he thought would matter deeply to us. This struck me as strange. I had always laid Devland's bitterness and restless spirit at Connor's door. Why would he think anything Devland was saying was in Malachi's best interests to hear, and choose to make us aware of it?

My heart lurched. *What in all this world was happening with Devland?* "You can tell me just as well. What is he saying?"

Connor's step never broke its rhythm, nor did the whimsy in his voice. "You should go and see for yourself. Also… just so you're made aware… I'm leaving."

The sudden shift of his words set my head to reeling. *"Leaving?"*

"Rivermouth. I'm leaving."

For a moment I tried reckoning with this. "When?"

The shoulder that held his pack shrugged. He nodded towards it. "Today. This very moment. I'm headed out."

This was as baffling as everything else he had just said in a matter of a few heartbeats. "This very moment?"

"The Temple is my last stop on my way out of the village."

I fell silent for a bit, feet still moving forward. In truth, I wished to tell him there had been no need for him to inform me of this either, but I could hear Malachi's small sermons on loving behavior knocking at the door of my conscience. I forced myself to be polite and replied with kindness, "I can't say I'm too surprised. Garwin mentioned some time back that you might need to get some adventure out of your bones."

Connor snorted. "Is that what he called it? That's not the word my father used. He used words like *ingrate* and *driveling parasite.* But yes, Priestess — *I'm off to get the call of adventure out of my bones."* These last words were laced with wry wit.

I couldn't exactly tell him outright that I'd be relieved if I didn't see his face in the community anymore. Until only moments ago when he temporarily confused me, I greatly wished he would leave my brother alone forever. I hoped he would find the adventure he was looking for… *and stay there.* In truth, my greatest impulse just then was to ask him if he was joining the Rebels. That thought was the most intriguing one… and would be very like Connor. I had always been convinced he had some wayward character at his core. He was the manner of boy who could easily grow into an evil man if he wanted to, and probably would.

Fortunately, he spared me the effort of trying to carry the conversation forward. "Aren't you going to ask me where I'm headed? Everyone else has."

"I'm not everyone else," I said, primly.

He laugh-snorted again. "No. That's true."

I stopped in my tracks and fixed an even eye on him. "It isn't like you to be mysterious, Connor. Why won't you tell me what speeches my brother is giving? Why do I need to go and witness it myself?"

He broke into an outright grin, as if I had somehow given him a compliment. "I think it will sound much grander coming from his own lips. Something gets lost when news is repeated, don't you think? All manner of trouble breaks out. Priestesses find their way into the strangest corners of the community," he added slyly, "leaping upon poor, blameless field workers without warning."

I would not be drawn by his bait. He was hinting that the passing on of gossip breeds only trouble — a lesson I had proven all too true. I was shamefaced enough as it was for having charged into Planters territory and made a public fool of myself. And of course he would probably never forget it, nor let me forget it. I chose to change the subject. "Well, I wish you well, wherever you're headed. I hope you find all the adventure you are looking for, Connor."

I found, suddenly, that I meant the words. Some foreign part of me I didn't recognize thought, also suddenly, that Connor and I might have been friends if he hadn't always been such an outspoken pest. *He was such a disagreeable person.*

A stray thought of his own crossed Connor's freckled face as he took me in, weighing my words. Unfortunately, the foot traffic I had hoped for on the road had been sparse throughout our conversation. The street lay quiet beneath pale spring light, dust and stray petals drifting in the air as a cool wind stirred the heavy-crowned branches and morning birds called from the high boughs above. We were about to part ways for the final time.

His dark eyes narrowed in scrutiny, gleaming. "Garwin is a loggerhead, just so you know."

I perked up at this with a frown. "Garwin is not stupid, he's a very good man. *And* your friend," I reminded.

"I *am* his friend," he insisted, "so that gives me leave to say it more than anyone. And I say he's thick-headed."

Connor had always been full of strong opinions, and dared to say them when no one else did.

When I said nothing in response, he added, "Aren't you going to ask why?"

"No. And why should I? It's no doubt something unkind. I've no idea why you even mentioned him."

He laugh-snorted again and shook his flaming red head, suddenly walking away. "Farewell, Your Holiness. I wish you well doing the — *your priestess thing.*"

That was it. He was simply going to walk away with these final words, half-flung over his shoulder. I thought to myself, *What a rude and baffling creature he is.*

He didn't look back. I know this because I watched him until he was out of sight. The over-sized pack, balanced sloppily on his broad shoulder and bouncing to the easy rhythm of his steps, shrank until he was consumed entirely by the darkened trees.

As I turned back towards the Temple, I seriously doubted that I would ever see him again. For me, there was no doubt Connor was going off to join the Rebels, else he would have said outright what his plans were. And unlike what Garwin and his father believed, I didn't think he was the kind who would ever return to Rivermouth. We were too ordinary, too lacking in spark. He would either die along the way, or live a life courting evil elsewhere.

I made it a point to attend the very next community meeting. This was held in a low wooden building in the center of Rivermouth, with an interior of stone walls and a criss-cross pattern of heavy wooden beams overhead, beneath which multiple tables were positioned for attendees. At the far end of the room a small narrow platform was erected with chairs against the wall for the presiding Governors, as well as a simple podium for the various speakers who stood to give their thoughts. Attendance by the community was heavily encouraged by all of the tribes, and at times the room during these weekly meetings was very full, depending on the topic of conversation circulating.

Over the years I had attended several meetings, some with Miri before I moved to the Temple, and a handful with Malachi when he was required to represent the Halevi. As a child I cared little for the issues that were discussed and debated. Miri was the greatest source of interest for me when I went with her, seeing as she came to life as I had never seen her. The woman who at home was merely fiery and strong, preaching her values to Devland and me every night, became a whirlwind of emotion and wild unrest. In due course her face would redden until she could restrain herself no longer, and she would spring to her feet in sudden bursts, arguing fiercely until her meaning was made plain. The subject at hand was of no consequence — she had something passionate to say about everything. Her voice thundered and raged and tore through the room, a lightning storm of wonder and force. All of the community had been familiar with my fire-brand mother.

On this night I asked Liev, Cohen's eldest son, to accompany me and we arrived just after the meeting began, settling ourselves in wooden seats along the back wall, which were reserved for latecomers when seating at all the tables had been filled. Already the tone of the room was serious and all the faces around me were focused towards the front where the speaking was taking place. Standing behind the podium was two figures, one of which was my brother.

My first reaction was a quiet swell of pride at the sight of Devland standing beside one of our community leaders in the Governor Tribe. I had not seen him all winter. Now, in the dim glow cast by the candlelit chandelier overhead, he looked far older than his eighteen years. His expression was set and determined, and I found myself thinking with surprise how much he had aged since I last saw him. He wore the gray robes of the Governor Tribe now, along with the woven headband at his crown — the final mark of his new station.

Just as quickly, my pride turned to another emotion altogether as I caught what the community was discussing. *The Halevi.* It was no wonder Connor thought Malachi and I would wish to be here.

Recently, Devland had put forward the notion that the Halevi contributed less to the community and were therefore not entitled to the full ten-percent tithe that had long been allotted to them. He was petitioning that the amount be reduced by more than half, so that the funds might be released for the prosperity of the community at large. To my surprise, in the few sennights since he had argued for this change, he had already gained some support from members of the other three tribes, who approved of the proposal in light of the growing strain upon purse and pantry for everyone.

"The Priests have not suffered as we have suffered," Devland contended firmly that night. "They have not tasted our loss… and still we go on paying them from our scant store."

With every measured argument he offered, coolly and sensibly, my quiet dread began to rise. Unlike Miri, he was not fiery or explosive; he was making a very wise approach. Devland was young and these men would have quickly dismissed him if he had sounded like her over such a new thought. After all, the Halevi had been provided for by the entire community as long as they had been part of Rivermouth, from its founding days onwards. We were a community who prided ourselves in our holy men, in our shared belief in the necessity to pay homage to God and His priests in return for His favor, and in our need for their counsel and spiritual oversight. Some of the priests had raised children within this very community, who had since been assimilated into the tribes and were now full members of Rivermouth. We were connected at our very core. Slowly and with careful purpose, my brother was dismantling a foundational value long held by all of Rivermouth.

I wondered a dozen things sitting there next to Liev, thoughts spinning. Last fall Garwin said that Devland had ideas for restoring our patrons and enriching our commerce; I hadn't expected *this.* This was not a solution to our problems. *Why weren't Malachi or Cohen notified that the tribe was a point of discussion? How had these discussions already reached such a point of agreement between the tribal leaders, and so quickly?*

As Malachi's novice, and having been raised in the Temple, there were certain realities I understood with clearness. Without proper funding, the priests would starve within a short time — it was as simple as that. They had no other means of supporting themselves as the rest of the community did. Many of them were elderly, long past the strength for the kind of hard labor that might make up for what would be taken from them. Liev alone, who was one of the youngest, was sixty. In addition, the Temple would fall into disrepair. We regularly employed young laborers from the Builders Tribe to tend the grounds and keep the walls in good repair. Devland knew all of these particulars; most everyone did.

I thought to myself — *How could he do this us, his own flesh and blood?* I felt ill to my stomach.

I waited until after the meeting to catch him, hoping to understand. Some part of me hoped I might be able to persuade him to withdraw his arguments and petition for other, more worthy causes. He was young, I thought; surely I could make an appeal to him and guide him back to a better path.

My brother was already headed home with a few of his companions when I was at last able to sort through the departing crowd to find him. When I called his name in the street, he caught sight of me under the shadowy light of the flickering streetlamps and paused. I was grateful for that at least. At the outset, I had no idea of what he might do.

He spoke a few words to his companions as I drew near, and they quickly fell away from him. Liev, meanwhile, lingered back and left us a small space of privacy. He had been as unsettled as I during the meeting and, without need for words, understood why I would wish to face Devland.

Dev's dark eyes passed over me as I approached — he, too, had not seen me in months. There was no concern on his face, yet the quick sweep of his gaze told me he was noting my condition all the same, as if quietly assuring himself that I was well and unharmed.

Around us there was the sound of boots on stone, murmured farewells, the creak of carts, the peal of voices rising beneath the open sky. I smiled, allowing the street noise around us to diminish a moment as the crowd filtered away. "Devland —"

*"Sister."* He took on a formal reserve at once, though his bearing stayed respectful. "How are you? I saw you were seated in the back during the meeting."

I hadn't been aware of this. "You did?"

"You have a way of standing out," he pointed out; but I wasn't able to tell from his tone whether he meant it as praise or as a slight.

For a moment I searched for the right words. Neither of us had stirred toward an embrace; no warmth or affection had passed between us. Only a wide gulf lay here in the darkness — one I longed, with all my heart, to cross. "I'm — I'm truly glad you've taken your place among the Governors, Dev, if it gives you pleasure. It suits you well."

He paused to take this in, considering my tone, weighing my expression. The yellow glow of the streetlamps caught in the gold of his headband as he shifted, scattering brief sparks of light across his brow. How dignified and austere he looked in this warm lighting and scrutinizing mood.

"Are those your only thoughts, after all that passed tonight? You sat in the back in silence, though you could have spoken. I watched for it. Surely you have more to say to me than this alone."

*"Of course* — of course I do. But I have not seen you in so long — I am first only glad to see you —"

His eyes — *Miri's eyes* — probed mine for the briefest of moments. His tone carried the slightest hint of asperity. "Perhaps the first thing you ought to give voice to is your thought on what was spoken tonight. It concerns you directly, and touches every member of your tribe."

What he said left me uneasy. He stood strangely removed and without feeling. I sensed that he would have held me with greater respect had I first confronted him, instead of greeting him as family.

"You will always be my brother," I told him gently. "Before all else. You're my flesh and blood, heart of my heart, always somewhere in my soul. That is first for me."

In the shadows, the faintest sneer came and went across Devland's face, gone so quickly I almost thought I imagined it. His eyes sharpened and hardened, catching in the light, though his tone stayed even and controlled, as if he had dismissed my words the moment I said them.

"Will you tell me what you think of tonight?" he said levelly. "Or will you yet again take refuge behind that meek stillness of yours, Eren, as you always have?"

*How could he dismiss my love for him so easily?* I thought wildly. What had changed his values so greatly that my being his own flesh and blood now held so little weight? I could only imagine that Miri's death had squeezed the love out of his heart and gave way to some hurt that still afflicted him.

"Truth be told, I was left confused," I said to him quietly. "I remember when you first came to the compound as a small boy, and the words you spoke in those early days. Do you recall it? You said the Temple was a wondrous place where God draws near. You were changed by it. It sits strangely with me now that you would plant the thought that the Halevi give nothing to the good of our people. The two stand at odds with one another."

He dismissed these thoughts at once, easily. "I was a child. Those moments meant little, if anything at all. I was merely seeking to please you and Malachi. It is you, Eren, who has made them into far more than they ever were, or ever will be."

I shook my head. I could not fathom that such words were spewing out of his mouth. They pierced me through and through. "You are not only seeking less provision for the Halevi, Dev. You are setting a division between us and the rest of the tribes with this thought. That is what will come of it. The end will be grave. It is a notion that breeds discord and separation. Is that truly what you wish for? Think of Malachi. Think of me," I urged in a low voice. "We are your family. We stand with you. Should you not, then, stand with us?"

I had told him my thoughts at last.

Devland's eyes flashed over at me instantly. Though he had said he wished to be challenged, it was plain he did not welcome the way I had chosen to do it. His composure fell away from him, as it hadn't done the night through. In an instant, he was a young, stubborn boy.

He growled out, "Remember the absurd meaning you gave to that dream I had, Eren?"

"I remember it well — the dream and its meaning both. Of course I do. I have wished to speak of it with you since the day Miri died —"

He leered at me. "Not a whipstitch of what you said was true."

"I but see in part, and prophesy the parts I see," I said at once, with sudden alarm. *This explained so much...* "Parts of it were kept from me. I told you what I knew — that portion at least proved true —"

*How angry he was,* I thought. I could see it suddenly. His very countenance was turning black with bitterness.

Devland leaned in toward me, as if he feared his words might spill into the street around us — almost as though he dared not let anyone hear his true thoughts, lest he risk the fragile respect he was only just beginning to earn. His eyes glinted with a cold, knowing light that sent a shiver from the base of my neck down the length of my spine.

He hissed through gritted teeth, "Your faith may suffice for you and the Halevi, Eren, but to the rest of us it is little more than a child's wild stories. Your people give nothing to the strength or the good advance of Rivermouth. You are a waste of both our regard and our treasury."

Even then, stunned as I was by the horror of his words, I felt his fury and bitterness had hardened into a fearsome power. He suddenly loomed over me in the darkness like a figure out of prophecy, a dark-robed stranger filling the night with his shadow — a man who had the power to move whole communities, summon armies to his will, and reshape the destinies of men.

*"Hear me out,"* he vowed darkly; "At the first chance I am given, I will cast you all out. I will scour your memory from Rivermouth... until no living soul ever remembers that the Halevi ever mattered."

Then he turned swiftly and strode away with a clipped, firm step, his robes sweeping the ground behind him in a cold surge of fury, while I was left shivering beneath the menace of his words.

Malachi and I had many talks about Devland over the next several sennights. He and Cohen himself went to the next weekly community meeting and not only spoke to those gathered on behalf of the Halevi, but also spoke to Dev afterward same as I had.

Yet he came back to me with a grave face and much the same report as mine. "He takes my words for the empty rambling of an old man, Meeshka," he said heavily.

"He said that to you?"

"He did."

I was shocked beyond speech. I could almost understand why Devland would be so bold with me, why his tirades would be so severe. I was his sister. As he grew older, some part of him had always responded with impatience to my quieter counsel and my habit of silence. Our differences had long irritated him. Where I waited for a chosen hour to speak with prayerful care rather than open challenge, Devland leapt gladly into the clash of words and heated dispute. He and Connor were kings of it, even at twelve and thirteen. If he was angry with me, I was not altogether surprised to hear him issue threats greater than he could ever fulfill.

But Malachi was different. He carried an authority which everyone in the community respected. Devland had always loved him and deferred to his wisdom in the little that they interacted throughout his young life. It seemed to me that, even if he was angry and too emboldened, he would yield to Malachi's authority.

"We can only pray for him now," Malachi said soberly. "Reason will not reach him, not in private at least. He carries a deep-seated bitterness toward authority, that much is plain. It may be that I should send Cohen to the gatherings in my stead, to speak for us there. Your face and mine seem only to quicken Devland's fire." He paused, then added with quiet resolve, "Still, it is certain that one of the Halevi must be present. The community is walking swiftly toward a choice that will weigh heavily upon the welfare — and perhaps even the future — of our tribe."

"Can they be convinced, do you think?" I asked him."If they are put in mind of our needs and what we give in return, might they yet be persuaded not to cut or cast aside the tithe, Malachi?"

He was ponderous, but sounded certain. "I still believe the leaders and the governors can be spoken to with reason. Cohen and I have known these men and women all our lives. We have brought many of their children and their children's children into the world; we have joined them in marriage and laid their dead into the earth. We have prayed over them, loved them, and given them counsel in their hours of trouble. This — this still carries weight with the human heart."

He turned a wise, knowing smile on me. *How well he knew my every shift and change in emotion.* "Do not let your heart be troubled, Meeshka.

As Cohen would say, 'There is still time to turn the wheel before it begins to move too fast.'" He winked at me. "He's a good man, our Chief Priest. *More than good.* But he has a touch of vanity."

I knew he was only trying to make me smile and I indulged him, breaking into a small laugh. Malachi made the world a better place with his light.

He was moving away from the intense subject at hand now, steering the conversation with an expert hand. Even the tone in his voice changed to one of more playfulness. "He likes to sound very wise with all of his little sayings, Cohen does. But I don't mind so much."

As the days passed and Cohen brought his weekly accounts of how the gatherings in the village were faring, our talks followed the same familiar course. Malachi and I would speak gravely on the matter; I would set forth my questions and he would answer them; and then, without fail, he would gently guide the discourse back toward hope, toward prayer, and toward an assurance that would not be shaken. This was Malachi's way — a discipline he had practiced all his life, and one he embodied with quiet faithfulness.

There came a day sometime in mid-spring when Cohen brought troubling news that sent a ripple through the priests. *The judgment had passed; the tithe would now be cut down to three percen*t. Though the Chief Priests and Malachi had made many personal visits to community leaders in all the tribes those early sennights of spring, these efforts had little or no effect.

"This marks a grave turning," Cohen said announced to the priests, as we gathered in the quiet sanctuary of the Temple. "The community has spoken. By this heavy choice they have altered their bond with us. They have made plain that they now judge us of lesser weight than the other tribes. Still — *though we cannot control the wind, we can adjust our sails,* I always say. Am I not right, Malachi?"

Malachi grew ever more silent after the announcement. That night he and the Chief Priests concluded there was little that could be done for the present, save to strictly order what funds we did receive and seek prudent ways to lessen our spending. One of the priests proposed a garden, and the idea was readily taken up by several others. No one spoke aloud of how disappointing the community's choice felt, nor of how it weighed upon their hearts. Instead, they carried on in quiet endurance, with the unspoken hope that the matter might be raised again in due time with the other tribes, once Rivermouth stood in a better situation financially.

After the first hard wave of feeling had passed, I felt easy enough to ask Malachi in private, "How did Devland manage to persuade them all so quickly, especially with you and Cohen appealing to all the leaders? I am astonished. He is scarcely even a man."

"Devland has a destiny," Malachi told me quietly, "same as you do, Meeshka. Yours might be in the Temple with the Halevi, but that does not make his any less great. He is my grandson; I am not surprised. The Whisper has blessed me richly. Like you, his destiny comes with an equipping, tools necessary to accomplish his purpose. His gift is influence. You have great favor with God, while he has great favor with man. Young as he is, Devland's smallest words carry the spark that can set off mighty conflicts.

"Whether he chooses to turn his gift toward good or toward harm — that, Meeshka, still rests with him," he said. "It is so for you as well, as it is for every soul. The Whisper assigns the destiny, but the individual faces the same decision — to use it for good or for ill. We must pray that Devland's heart will yet be turned toward the good. There is still time."

Even then Malachi did not sound disturbed. He was sobered, but steady. He added, "There are other choices here as well, little Meeshka. Rivermouth stands more exposed now than at any time I have known in my life. They have borne great losses, weathered many trials, and even now the Rebels wait beyond our borders, ready to fall upon them. Our trade withers, the cupboards grow lean, and people struggle simply to endure. You have seen it with your own eyes. Their hearts are pressed by fear and want, and so they hunger for change and reach eagerly for any new word that promises it."

He set his next words before me as a question to weigh. "Has not Devland given them a solution that feels easy to the hand, Meeshka? In their eyes, they have relied on the Whisper — and our favor with Him — and yet they have suffered. Now they ask for something better. Your brother has offered them someone to bear the blame, a way to loosen their strain for bread and coin — and he has promised them safety beneath the strength of his leadership. This, too, is the choice the tribes have made. And yet we must still keep room in our hearts for understanding. Their wounds may yet be made whole with time… and with a measure of prosperity and blessing. Their hearts will turn again. This is how we must pray for them."

"This is also why the King matters so greatly," he added, always using every circumstance to continue my lessons. "He has the power to ease these burdens for his people. He can stand as a good shepherd — a firm and steady hand of safety, of order, of swift action when trouble rises. And when wolves come dressed as sheep and seek to lead the innocent astray, the King may guard his land, confront them plainly, and drive them out if need be."

"As priests, we must even now lift Cyric before the Whisper, that he would yet act rightly for his people," he said. "Though the King has not heeded our cries, the Whisper surely does. It may take time for the fullness of His purpose to be worked and made plain, but He softens stony hearts, labors with stubborn men, and teaches what must be learned.

"So we must pray now more than ever — for Rivermouth, for Cyric, and for our small nation of Avan. We are not the only ones who suffer, that much is certain. If the King deals loosely with us, he most likely deals as loosely with the burdens of others in our land as well."

For a few sennights the Temple was occupied with making adjustments and considering new alternatives for food and provisions. A change came over the compound, but there was still a strong and steady hope that we would endure this temporary hardship.

But then the worst happened. Within only a few sennights more, Devland managed to convince the Governors and all of the tribal leaders to remove the tithe altogether. The priests were utterly stunned when the news was delivered to the compound by courier. We were, in effect, being cut off from the rest of the Tribe; they had determined that our contribution was so insignificant that we were not deserving of even the slightest income. It was a cruel, heartless action, taken out on elderly men who were not accustomed to toil or labor except in prayer and incense offerings.

This time the priests held a flurry of meetings to discuss what could be done, what solutions could be reached. It was determined, to our shock and woe, that the food supply would be gone within two sennights. The little garden plot which the priests had already begun would not harvest food by the time we needed it, and certainly not enough for the entire compound to survive on. Some of the priests could fish in local streams, but this also would not be entirely sufficient and would only last until autumn when the season would be too cold. With every idea that was suggested, all the priests knew with heavy hearts that it would not be enough. By the beginning of the summer, we would most likely already be starving.

It was Malachi who suggested the unthinkable. He gathered Joel and Cohen privately and said, with a somber spirit, "For the sake of the priests, my brothers, I think we must take a little action here."

As his novice, I was allowed to be a quiet presence during this exchange and witness the conversation. He had called them into his chambers and the four of us sat at the little stone table deep in late afternoon shadow. Only a dim light cast by the fading sun illuminated the stained glass windows, producing a hushed environment. Malachi had already given what oil we had to the priests for their use in the compound housing, and the two of us were conserving what little firewood there was left for any unexpected cold nights still remaining in the spring season. Within only days we would be forced to travel outside the village and make use of the woodcutter's huts located halfway up the forested mountain paths where timber was chopped and hauled by various members of the tribes.

"There are many risks to what I am about to suggest," he said. "It could be it doesn't even work, who knows? But I want your thoughts on the matter."

"What is it, Malachi?" Joel asked. "Tell us freely." He was an old bent man who required the use of a heavy crook, with long gray hair and a heavy beard that streamed nearly to his chest line. As the eldest of all the priests, the concern on his face made his deeply weathered features appear even more ancient.

"I have been going through the articles in the Temple," Malachi said with calm measure. "It seems to me we must part with some of the adornments. Not the sacred vessels, of course — never those — but the decorations may be taken over the mountains to Periburn and sold in their market. Some, like the silver crown, carry great worth yet serve chiefly for beauty and for the honoring of the Sacred Text; they are not themselves consecrated. And the heavy tapestries as well — those would surely bring a fair price."

Even this would have been unthinkable only days before, yet it was now soberly weighed among the three men. The alternative, quite simply, was starvation. Many of the priests were very old men and could surely not survive very long without adequate food. Joel was one of them.

"If we send two of our strongest priests across the Silent Heights," Malachi added, "they may pass unnoticed by any Rebels nearby. No one would think such men carry coin or goods of value with them. We still have enough silver to purchase a small cart and a donkey to draw it. It is a risk — yes — and a hard giving of what little we now possess. Yet it may be that they could reach Periburn and return again in time, before hunger begins to claim the weaker among us."

How still the air was after these words. How quiet the silence was that fell. For a moment the Temple itself seemed like a tomb, as though death had chosen to settle there in the aftermath of such an announcement. In the near-ten years I had lived here, I had never sensed such a thing in this atmosphere of constant holiness. Even if the items were not sacred, this was a terrible desecration to historical relics that had been part of our tribe for generations. They represented who we were and what we believed. I nearly wept simply to be present and witnessing it.

After a moment, Cohen shook his head with quiet uneasiness. "I would fear greatly for the priests we send. It will be danger enough even to send a few of them into the forest for firewood, which is fast becoming a necessity for us. *But some roads are not taken by will, but by necessity laid upon the soul,* I always say. I think we should do this, Malachi. We have no choice."

So it was decided. All of the priests were told about the plan, so they could pray, and so they could be present on the day that we sent the two priests away. With heavy hearts, the entire compound gathered to pray for the volunteers in the courtyard before departure, then stood in the early morning hours outside the gates of the Temple as the donkey and the cart pulled away.

A mix of emotion hung thick in the air. These were men of faith and self-control; they had seen the Whisper answer many of their prayers and perform many miracles in their lifetimes. Yet they also loved their brothers and were sharply aware that few of them had ever traveled outside the confines of Rivermouth. There were many unknowns before the two who were riding away, and many unknowns still lingering for us as well.

At the close of the farewell, I searched for Malachi but couldn't find him at first, only to discover him at last in the Holy Room hidden behind the sanctuary. The narrow chamber was filled with shadow and flame, its modest altar draped in sacred cloths and ringed with low-burning candles. The air pressed close with an unseen Presence and the faint breath of myrrh and cedarwood.

Malachi knelt there in stillness, a quiet and sorrowful majesty in his posture, his most regal robes pooled about him in the dim inner chamber, his silver head bowed beneath his prayer cloth. This silk prayer cloth was set apart for the High Priest alone, and for this one sacred place, and it seemed to me it lay upon him today like both honor and burden. Scarcely a sound escaped his lips, yet I could sense his prayers rising in the hush like unseen incense, laden with unspoken weight. Silently, I went and knelt at his side, and stayed with him that day until he was finished.

At one point in the days that followed, I questioned him quietly, "Why is Devland so angry? Why has he done this to us, Malachi?"

My heart had begun to feel a pain over the events that were happening, a pain I had never before experienced. Miri's death had been the closest I had ever come to feeling such brokenness, but I had had the safety of Malachi and the familiarity of the Temple. Those hard emotions had passed soon enough as I accepted her passing and moved on. This experience was more severe and was accompanied by a looming fear that was almost impossible for me to shake. For the first time in my life, I feared for the priests.

Malachi, of course, though more somber, was never fearful, nor did he lack for energy or unwavering devotion to his duties. That sparkle was still in his eyes, and a quiet joy still present in his countenance. He had an abundance of affection for me, and an encouraging word for every priest who crossed his path.

"Your brother's deep pain and hurt have turned to anger and grown hard," he said. "We see such things in the world, too, Meeshka. Sand and mud, given time, become stone. This way of hardening was shown to him by Miri. He is very much like her. She set this pattern before him, showed him how to carry his hurt and anger so — and he loved her more dearly than anyone.

"I have spent time in prayer, weighing what has come to pass with our little Devland. It is plain that he felt abandoned by us in his darkest hour. Most of all, I did not allow you to leave the Temple to be with him and Miri through the plague. In his heart, he believes he suffered alone. And when suffering comes — especially when we are certain we are alone — there is great temptation for the eye to turn crooked. Truth becomes hard to see unless we cling fast to the Whisper and to His ways. Many come out of such storms like a tree after fierce winds — twisted at the roots, and now growing towards the sun in mangled ways.

"You told me of the dream Devland had, and of how you read it to him. It is plain now that his seeing of it has been bent by a heart that feels betrayed and misled. He trusted what you said and held to the hope that all would be made right — that Miri would live — and she did not. And so he has been growing in a wounded and crooked way, with a vision that is twisted now. He has chosen to let these things harden him, and to believe that none of what the Halevi place their faith in is true or living. He is being driven by a spirit of anger and of vengeance."

Malachi paused and shook his bearded head in somber reflection. "I believe if he can, Meeshka, he will drive us out of the community altogether. And with the measure of influence he has now gathered, I would not be astonished if he succeeds in the days ahead."

This quiet announcement, given at the end of the conversation, was more startling than anything I had heard so far from any of the priests, perhaps most alarming because it came from Malachi's own mouth. Only a scant few sennights ago he had said that there was time to pray for change for Devland, but now he seemed to have accepted that this might not be immediately possible. I still remembered well Dev's chilling vow on the night I had tried to appeal to him, but hearing Malachi agree with it made the horrible words a harsh reality. This was indeed what Devland's desire was and what he was attempting to do.

For the first time, my grandfather did not conclude the conversation with his usual note of faith and optimism. He spoke the words with finality and then moved away, leaving me to shiver in the wake of his quiet declaration. He was already preparing himself for the worst...

After the two priests left for Periburn, a strange tension increased in the community. I had never experienced anything like it before. There were sharp furtive expressions cast towards me or any of the priests whenever we were in public. Any expressions of sympathy or compassion were quickly hidden away, as if the individuals feared to be seen siding with the Halevi. A feeling of jealousy and anger hung in the air in the marketplace. Fists curled, eyes narrowed; conversations ceased in the streets as we passed by. Briefly, a few of the priests considered whether we should close the gates and assign watchmen at the walls at night, though this was quickly set aside by Malachi and the Chief Priests.

Malachi gathered them all together in the Temple to make this announcement. "Brothers, Rivermouth has never been a people of violence. It is true they are restless now, and their unease seems turned toward us — yet I fear that to close our gates would speak a message we ought not to send. They may have shifted their heart toward us, yes — but we must not shift our heart toward them. We are of them, and they are of us. The Temple must remain open for prayer, for counsel, and for refuge to all who are in need. We are not afraid."

So it was that the compound gates remained open and weekly services continued, though no one dared to come to the Temple. As the weeks of spring passed achingly slow, the priests continued their offerings, daily intercessions, worship, and study of the Holy Text. A few of our strongest traveled into the forests and returned not many days later, thankfully, with a cartload of firewood, though they were exhausted and weary. This was work none of them were accustomed to and drained them greatly. At first I offered myself to go with them, but Malachi and Cohen forbade it as one voice.

"You dare not risk it," Malachi cautioned.

"'*Forewarned is forearmed,*' I always say," Cohen added.

Malachi continued, "There are reports without ceasing that the rebels have infested our forests and keep watch on all who pass through. A few priests might slip by unseen; a lone man or two cutting firewood may be left to himself, for they carry no coin and are of little notice. But a young woman as marked as you would not go unnoticed. No, Meeshka — absolutely not."

Throughout this the Halevi prayed unceasingly for a change of heart in the community; for prosperity for its people; for help with the Rebels from the King; for the safety and success of our two brave ambassadors who were traveling to Periburn on our financial behalf; and for miraculous provision. And I prayed for Devland, that he would see the truth and remember again the Whisper who once claimed his heart.

Then came the night when everything changed. It was an unforgettable night written in the history of my life. Every detail of it is even now etched on the fabric of my soul, woven as a strong colorful thread through the tapestry that tells my story.

The first of it began in the middle of the night when Malachi's bearded face appeared over my bed in the shadowy lamplight and called my name twice. As I struggled to wake, he said, "Hurry, Meeshka. There's little time."

At first I sensed nothing. He was always calm, always unmoved, and the heavy stone Temple separated his private chambers from the rest of the compound, further insulating against any sound or movement. It was simply odd that he had departed from his usual pattern and awakened me in the dead of the night. Patterns and routines were as a gentle rhythm in a priest's life, never changing, rising and falling naturally. They had been part of Malachi's life all of his days. I didn't know him apart from them.

"What is it, Malachi?" I asked, pulling myself up to a seated position.

To which he said simply, "Your brother has managed to convince them we are a sickness that needs to be purged from the body. *Come.* Gather what food remains and as many of your things that you can carry in a pack. The Halevi are leaving Rivermouth."

This shocking statement was the last Malachi spoke for the remainder of the night, even amid all of the gripping activity that took place afterward.

I was quickly obedient, heart pounding, mind uncertain. I had no face or name for what was happening. I did not know if we were escaping before trouble arose, or whether men were at our gates demanding our departure. I only knew my stomach was in my throat as I scrambled for my few clothing items and grabbed for the bread loaf set aside for the next day's meal, cheese, and anything else readily at hand. My thoughts were numb and hands trembling.

Moments later, I emerged from the rear chamber into the darkened Temple sanctuary armed with two heavy packs, wearing my heaviest woolen cloak and fur-lined boots. It was here Malachi suddenly appeared from out of the darkness and wordlessly led me through the empty sanctuary. There was an increased sense of urgency about him in the hushed silence between us. Without a word, he led us straight out through the Temple doors and down onto the wide stone steps.

It was then I was forced to stop in my tracks and draw in a sharp breath, taking in the shocking vision before me. That moment burned itself into my memory like fire on stone, unmoving and eternal.

My eyes swung wide left to right, in surprised shock. A gathering of at least a hundred stood crowded in the courtyard, staring up at us with set determined faces. *Men had indeed come to drive us out.*

They held flickering torches aloft in their hands, the flames strong enough to wash the entire courtyard in a strange orange glow and throw a sinister cast across their hardened expressions. Even in the shadowed light I recognized most of them — nearly all were men, though a few women stood among them. These were the very ones who walked our streets, frequented the marketplace, and harvested our fields. They outnumbered the priests with ease by two to one.

Though they said and did nothing as Malachi and I emerged, there was a grim air about them that was one of constrained anger, hidden power. They had come prepared to force us out if they must, as if they had forgotten how harmless the priests were, how physically incapable of retaliating even if the old men had wanted to. In truth, by comparison, only four of them could have showed up and would have been just as able to demand our departure.

My gaze was drawn quickly to the front, where several men of the Governor Tribe stood waiting in their gray robes and gold satin headbands, standing as though presiding over the proceedings. Among them stood Devland. His expression was cold and distant, his short frame held rigid, shoulders straight as a drawn rod, as though what was unfolding was a fair justice being meted out for the good of the Rivermouth community. How my heart twisted and grieved at the sight of him. What was happening here tonight bore his mark alone — shaped and set in motion by his terrible influence.

Close at his heels was goodhearted Garwin, his face troubled and drawn in the unsteady torchlight. At the first sight of me his eyes darkened, caught between relief and quiet torment. In that brief exchange of glances, I knew at once that he had not come because he fully agreed with what was underway. He lacked the strength to halt the decision itself, but he could try and soften this event — to stand as a barrier if he could between judgment and the violence that threatened to rise from it.

Gathered also were the priests, quietly waiting before the low doorway of the Outer Courts half-way down the courtyard. They were already assembled and stood with quiet patient faces, a picture of composure and servitude. It seemed all of them — everyone in the courtyard — had been waiting for Malachi. He had brought me out last.

Something about that moment struck me for reasons beyond the terrible knowledge — caught in a quick, fearful breath — that a horrendous act was being set in motion against the Halevi. All eyes turned upon me as I emerged from the shadowed portico of the Temple and paused in shock upon the broad steps, taking in the scene before me. It would be some time before I could look back on that moment and fully understand its significance.

Malachi had no doubt chosen to fetch me last in order to shield me from the harsh words flung by the villagers, from the danger such an arrival carried, from the alarm that must have rippled swiftly through the priests and their hurried steps as they gathered their things in the dark. The entire compound had likely been a scene of frightened, angry chaos only moments before. As always, he wanted to keep me safe and as removed as possible. But in doing so, my emergence became notable, poignant even, as was Malachi's presence only a few steps below while he paused for me to catch up with him. He was the High Priest, and I was his God-given novice; and the Whisper wanted this sacred image above and before them to be sealed on their minds forever from that night. It would haunt them in their dreams, and therefore the heinous thing they had done as well. I somehow knew that.

Then, as suddenly as it had come, the impression passed. I moved quickly to catch up with Malachi. He strode toward the priests without pause, ignoring the gathered crowd, unmoved by the tense hostility that pressed in around him. There was neither pride nor display in his bearing, nor any show of humility — only the still resolve of a man doing what must be done, what he had long foreseen. I hurried in his shadow, my head bowed and shoulders bent beneath the weight of the two heavy packs, crossing the courtyard as it lay eerily silent around us.

Just as we reached the priests, I heard a rustling of some kind behind me. Then a man's voice — Garwin's, I realized — was speaking in fierce quiet tones. He was making an appeal to Devland.

*"Your own sister —"* Only snatches of words reached me the short distance between us. *"…marriage… …children… …could still contribute…"*

After a quick few moments of this, Devland spoke up from his place at the front. His voice was like a stranger to me, cold and stentorian, rising over our heads. "If Eren wishes to stay, then she will stay. Room will be found for her within the community. Let her choose for herself."

How freshly amazing it was to me that at such a young age and so new to the Governor Tribe he was listened to by all of these men and women. He truly had wrought some mysterious influence over Rivermouth with his spirit, his words, and his ideas. Everyone in the courtyard heard him and nodded, murmuring agreement. Looking at me — a young and innocent girl — they thought he was a fair and equitable man.

In the stillness that fell, I glanced around the huddle of priests. Joel, Cohen, Liev and Anshel, his second son, were situated at the front next to Malachi, their ancient faces already showing signs of tiredness at having been so roughly disturbed in the middle of the night. There were over fifty of us in all. Some of the men looked weepy and their faces were filled with heavy sorrow; others stood unusually quiet, clearly in unspoken prayer. I quickly recognized the items in many of their weathered hands which were catching the light in muted tones — an odd assortment of parchment scrolls wrapped in linen and wool, leather bound volumes, golden bowls and yads, silver trumpets, jeweled ornaments, brass lamps, and hand-held lyres and harps. In the moment of being cast out, they had chosen these sacred and precious items rather than blankets, clothing, or food. These were the things that must live on, that must not be desecrated or forgotten; they represented a way of life that must be upheld even above their own physical preservation. They lived as living temples of the Whisper, to bring Him pleasure.

At Devland's command, all of them were watching me now, taking me in. Beside me, Malachi did not say a word, though his bottomless gray eyes as I caught his gaze said much. He was willing, just as my brother was, to let the decision be my own, without interference from him. All of the Halevi were pausing for my decision before they turned and left the compound behind forever.

They need not have stopped at all, I thought. There was never a choice for me, not even for a moment. If Devland had hoped in anyway that I would choose the tribes over the Halevi, he had been sore mistaken. And Garwin, though kind and desperately trying to show mercy in anyway he could, had measured me too small in the weighing if he thought I could abandon everyone and everything I had known for the hearth-tied life he dreamed for me. As much as I loved the Rivermouth community, I knew I would rather be mistreated along with the Priesthood of God than enjoy a life cradled in comfort and calm outside of my destiny. I slid my hand into Malachi's leathery one and gripped it, standing next to him. *I, too, lived to bring the Whisper pleasure.*

Lifting my chin, I turned and raised my eyes to Devland's proud gaze across the way. "I am Halevi," I declared. "And I will die as one of the Halevi."

The words rang out in a way that surprised me, echoing in the air like a resonant bell, their vibrations washing over the gathered group of hard-hearted men. This was another impressionable moment that night, as if our conversation — and my decision — was being recorded in the very courts of heaven.

I did not know right then what suffering lay ahead; I only nervously feared it. I was not yet aware of the twists and turns of the journey that lay before me, complete with all of its sorrows and sufferings. The cost to go with the Halevi — to be one of them — was only just beginning. Yet even now, looking back, knowing what I know, I would have made the same choice. I belonged with them, as they belonged with me.

Devland lost a fair bit of composure over my answer, as if he had stooped to offer me a moment to redeem myself in his eyes and I had failed even at this. For a moment he strained to keep hold of that proud show of cool command. In the orange glow of the dancing torchlight, his angry dark eyes glimmered at me; his jaw clinched and un-clinched; his lips thinned to a bitter line. He nearly snarled, face clouded and black.

*"Then so be it.* You heard her," he growled at Garwin. "She has made her choice. Let no man claim we denied her mercy." He swung on the Halevi and barked, "Away with you, the lot of you — *crawling parasites."*

His command stung the cold night air, driving us forward like cattle being driven by the sting and snap of the whip. A few of the priests recoiled slightly. The hatred that surged from the words swept over us with greater force than the words themselves. The Halevi had been here for generations, giving of their life to these people, bringing favor into the community through their own favor with God.

I felt my heart crumbling in pieces before we had even taken one step. *My own brother has done this,* I thought, ashamed and broken. My sweet, wonderful Dev has betrayed us all.

Then, in that horrible moment, I became aware suddenly that Malachi's dry hand had closed more firmly over mine. When I looked up, his eternal eyes were fixed on only me. He was not seeing our immediate future — homeless, penniless, defenseless, and hungry. Neither was he aware of Devland, his cold hate-filled words, or the set-faced horde of merciless men surrounding him. Many of these people were my grandfather's friends and life-long neighbors. Their cruel intention to condemn everything he held sacred and drive the priests out of their very own Temple was completely lost on him for a long, slow heartbeat. In Malachi's deep gaze I saw a spark of tearful joy, and a fierce pride which I will never forget. That pride was for me. In the hour of decision, I had chosen the Halevi, my part in God's holy priesthood, and I had chosen him.

I could almost hear his words echo in my head: *"You run for us now, Meeshka. It is you who runs for the Halevi."*

# 5.

In the first hours of travel through the darkness, lit only by the torches borne by a few priests in our silent caravan, the weight of what had just happened began to settle upon me. A heavy pall of gloom descended, threatening to overwhelm me entirely. We passed beyond the village and began our slow ascent through the low foothills beyond it — hills that, after dawn, would deepen swiftly into the treacherous Silent Heights. Cohen and Joel led in quiet watchfulness, and few words were spoken among the priests, yet I learned that Malachi had been warned by loyal informants that the community would move against us that very night. My grandfather was far more shrewd than he ever let on.

In advance of that momentous event, he had stocked the Halevi's single cart with as many supplies as we could afford, and kept this, along with a horse and donkey, housed with Halevi sympathizers whose home was on the edge of the village. In recent weeks he had known which friends to call on and made use of their quiet allegiance. We paused on our way to gather these much-needed items before moving on.

Thankfully, the wagon allowed for the priests who were most feeble to ride, while the donkey could haul the heaviest items that had been carried away from the Temple. This still left at least forty-three priests on foot, and our progress was slow and painstaking. They weren't accustomed to moving fast; the way was dark and unknown; and they were beginning the journey already tired. The trail lay as a narrow, well-worn ribbon of earth, so tight we moved in threes and fours, each of us drawn in close against the cold night — a long, hushed column of hooded, cloaked figures, with me carried somewhere in the midst beside Malachi.

For a little time the darkness pressed in as we began our journey. Fear and the terror of the unknown hovered just on the edges of the light cast by the torchlights. It seemed to me that the Rebels could be anywhere — behind every tree and bush, hidden in the dark shadows that lined the way, perhaps perched above in the heavy branches that stretched like black twisted snakes to the sky over the lonely trail. We were vulnerable, we were outcast, and we were wanderers.

The only sound for some time was the shuffling of tired feet; the creaking of the wagon; the clod of the horse's hooves on the dirt track. The forested foothills, normally so alive at night, were silent and still, as if nature itself had paused to quietly watch the forsaken Tribe pass through.

Then, from somewhere in the back of the little caravan, one of the priests began to sing. *How the priests loved to worship.*

Very quickly, more voices took up the song, until at last they were all joined — low-throated voices woven into a single, wondrous harmony that drifted through the dark as breath became prayer. That night they chose a ballad from our oldest history, telling of our encounter with the Whisper and of His faithfulness carried from generation to generation. This might not have been advisable for a defenseless group seeking to remain as discreet as possible in a landscape where Rebels were said to roam free, but the song rang out as a shield against the darkness, against the anguish of what had just been done to us. I took comfort in the peace and Presence that fell; and we walked on beneath the stars until the first pale sign of morning touched the sky.

By the following morning the priests were too weary to press on, and the mountains loomed ahead like a vast, unfathomable shadow, so a rest was called and we made the first of many camps beside the dirt road. Beneath the heavy forest canopy, the caravan of old men sat upon the cold, dew-slick ground and broke bread, speaking in low, weary murmurs. Some nodded off between bites, exhaustion pulling them under. I was surprised so many had lasted even this long without collapsing on their feet.

It was during this that Malachi stood and made an announcement. I had no real idea why he selected this particular moment, nor why he had chosen not to speak the night before. There were moments when he was a man of profound mystery, one whose spirit ran so deep that in the sharpest hours of his distress he could withdraw from all about him and find shelter in the Place of Stillness at his core. I'd seen this in him many times of late as times grew harder for the Halevi. Unlike myself as of yet, he knew when words were important, and when they were as dust on the wind. He truly was our High Priest.

In a quiet solemn voice, he told us that morning he had foreseen that the Exile would reach an end, the Whisper would restore the Halevi to the Temple, and we would return to Rivermouth.

"We must place our faith in that truth," he said. "The Whisper has assured me it will not be so very long."

Even then I suspected there was more, but he did not add anything to this. It was simply enough that we had these assurances after a long hard night, facing a bleak future. Many of the priests who were scattered around me broke into quiet murmurs of praise and thankful relief. Some of their eyes misted with unshed tears.

He then explained he had become aware recently that there was a handful of abandoned farmsteads to the west just over the Silent Heights. In the past short run of sennights he had hired a messenger to go by secret methods and purchase them for the Halevi, paid for with the sale of some small silver items from the Temple to certain members of the community who were willing to purchase them in private. There was little coin left after the selling, yet enough for a humble beginning — enough, he believed, to keep the tribe from hunger.

"For those among you who are willing and who desire it," he said, "we may settle there and work the land until the Whisper restores us to our rightful place. None of you is bound to remain. I know that some of you have kin in distant parts of Avan whom you may wish to seek out in these times."

A surprised rumble broke out amongst the men. This presented several new thoughts for all of them. Some of the feeling was tremendous relief, a rising hope, followed quickly by questions of how they could possibly work the land when they knew nothing of farming. The task was daunting at best, especially for men of their age. My first thought even before these was how discreetly Malachi had sat on this plan without telling anyone, not even Joel or Cohen. He had planned a temporary rescue long before any of us even knew there was a need for it. I suspected the Whisper had forewarned him ages ago.

After this, the men were simply too tired to even discuss it or ask further questions. They merely gave verbal thanks to the Whisper that there was hope; that Malachi was as cunning as a serpent and as innocent as a dove; and then they huddled down in their cloaks and slept.

For a short while I slept heavily along with them, as the warm spring sun rose above the forest and burned away the dew and early morning fog. But I was younger than all of them and my thoughts more restless; and I stirred long before the priests did and withdrew a short distance from where they had settled in little clumps and clusters under the trees. The forest was noisier and less forbidding in daylight — squirrels darted among the brush in quick flashes of motion, birds stitched song from the treetops above, and a cool wind combed softly through the tangled green below. Life had mysteriously continued on in spite of the turmoil of the night before.

None of these things seemed to settle me, however, as I turned my back to the others and sat in silence. With waking came a sudden tide of feeling that I could not seem to master. That pall of gloom from the night before returned, stronger than ever. Not only was Devland lost to me completely now, but his betrayal had led to the entire community rejecting us and the loss of our home. I already missed the compound sorely. I knew from experience now that the ground was a hard, unforgiving place to sleep on; and I felt the anguish of being cast out, as if all of life promised to be just as hard and cold. Even with Malachi's message of hope, I still felt a great pain that was difficult to set aside.

After only a few moments, I heard a stirring behind me and realized Malachi had awakened and was making his way over to my side. He was wrapped in one of many thick woolen blankets he had managed to bring in the wagon for the priests, a tall wise figure only slightly rumpled after the long relentless night we had.

"What is it, little Meeshka?" he murmured in a dry morning voice, as he seated himself beside me.

I was staring back down the path we had come from, though there was nothing to see but dark forest and an empty dirt trail. I felt reluctant to speak my true thoughts to him. "I was unable to sleep."

"I see that. But why is it you are sitting here looking back at where we've been? The future is before us."

He was somewhat teasing, and I smiled slightly at his effort to cheer me. It was a wonder that he could even attempt it after the terrible thing that the community had done to us. "I shouldn't speak of it, Malachi. You have given us a way forward. That should be enough. I should be like you and the priests in this moment and simply be grateful that we have a promise from the Whisper and hope for the future. All of you have had no trouble sleeping at all."

While I studied the road behind, he was watching me from the corner of his eye. "I am still your grandfather," he said gently. "That place binds me to you for more than the office I hold, Meeshka. If you are not well, then I am not well. What is it, child? Tell me."

So I told him, in a quiet broken voice I scarcely recognized. "They've cast us out, Malachi. We mean nothing to them. Devland has betrayed us, our own flesh and blood."

*"Ah. Yes."* Malachi drew his blanket closer about his shoulders, squinting slightly as a blade of golden sunlight slipped through the treetops and came to rest upon his face. In that fragile light he looked both wise and holy, serenely untouched by the hardship that surrounded us. Yet he never made light of our sacrifice or our suffering, and when he spoke of it, he did so with a quiet truth that gave it dignity rather than diminished it.

"It is no small thing to be misunderstood, to be set at little worth and left uncherished; nor for the labor of our love to be taken in hand and then cast aside as though it were nothing; nor to be turned away and scorned — most of all by those we have loved, and who once loved us. It is not a dream alone that has been crushed beneath careless feet, but our own hearts as well. I know how this feels, Meeshka. I know it well."

I believed him. I could hear it in his voice, as if he had traveled the long mile I was and knew its every step. Then he added, with his eyes closed and his bearded face raised to the warm sun, "The persecution is wrong, but it can produce something good if you will let it."

*"What good could this possibly produce?"* I burst out. "The pain is so intense I can scarcely bear it."

"It is already at work within you, even now. It is in such moments of persecution that our calling — to be set apart as God's own, to live as His treasured dwelling, to follow our way of life to carry that calling out — grows only more dear to us. As you feel the cost more sharply, as the ache of loss settles deep, the truth of who you are becomes all the more precious. Its worth rises in your heart. You come suddenly to know where your true treasure lies, and your hands close upon it with iron strength."

His voice grew more and more hushed, as if he had walked these very steps himself, every one of them, perhaps many times. "If you will allow this hour to do its full work in you, nothing will ever be able to divide you from who you are and why you were sent into this world. Nothing and no one will ever lessen its worth. Nothing can pry it from your grasp or steal the call of the Whisper from your soul. You will not let them."

I found myself weeping for a moment. Even then his deep sea of words were hard to take hold of. They may have been true and beautiful; I wanted greatly to be like him; but there was no immediate reward in it. I still felt the sting of rejection; the absolute betrayal. I still saw the hatred in Devland's face, and could only think of the loss of our beloved home. These truths seemed much stronger than Malachi's revelations.

He caught this. "Do not forget, Meeshka," he said tenderly; "The cost is not greater than the reward."

My emotions were so deep I could scarcely lift my head to look over at him. "What is your reward now, Malachi?" I whispered tearfully. "It might be years before we return, and who knows what condition the Temple will be in by then? Aside from the Whisper Himself, everything has been taken from you — led by your own grandson, flesh of your own flesh, part of your very heart."

To my surprise, he opened his eyes at once with a soft, mischief-touched chuckle. I suspected he wanted to laugh outright and was smothering it for the sake of the sleeping priests behind us.

"He did not take everything, did he? Not the things that truly matter. I came away with the greatest things. You see, Meeshka, I know where my true treasure rests — and none of those people were able to lay a hand on it." His gray eyes twinkled over at me with that mysterious light.

Looking at him in that moment, I felt I was beginning, at last, to glimpse the inner secret he carried within himself with such beauty. Malachi had learned these lessons long ago, long before Devland was ever born, etched into him by years of quiet trial and faithful endurance. Truly, whatever my brother believed he had won, it was our grandfather who stood as the real victor.

Later that morning his words were still settling into my soul as we once again made our way forward and entered the paths that would take us over the sharp mountainsides. The priests had eaten a sparing breakfast and drank from a creekbed near the road. Most of them were stiff from sleeping on the ground, but they made no complaint and their spirits seemed renewed knowing Malachi's plan. Their small comments were simple and heartening as they walked, the shared promise among them that once the Silent Heights were behind them, a new life would begin.

Malachi led from the front that morning alongside Joel and Cohen, while I followed just behind him, guiding the donkey. Behind us came the long file of priests, with the horse-drawn wagon rolling quietly at their center. For a time we walked in near silence, each of us absorbed in the steady labor of setting one foot before the other as the path began to climb more steeply. All around us spring was in full motion — new leaves unfurling from once-bare branches, bright wildflowers spilling across the forest floor, and the air alive with birdsong and the soft buzz of insects. A gentle breeze moved through the trees in a low whisper, trailing beside us like quiet music as we went. Almost I could imagine that everything was going to be fine, and I began to think I could possibly take Malachi's words to heart. The pain receded somewhat. *Perhaps the cost would not prove to be greater than the reward,* I thought. Perhaps there was even hope that the situation with Devland could be redeemed. Surely even now his heart could be turned...

Then, at some point during this peaceful moment, we heard hooves and looked up in time to see two riders approaching on horseback, emerging from the forest some yards ahead.

Malachi caught sight of them much quicker than I and murmured over his shoulder, with quiet evenness, *"Eren, draw your hood up."*

This was enough to cause me alarm before I ever saw their faces. When they came, Malachi did not stop, but continued pressing forward, even as they pulled their horses to a halt to examine us from the roadside.

"What's this, then?" came a rough, half-drunken voice. "You're far from where you belong, aren't you now? And where might such a gathering of gray heads be headed, I wonder? What business brings you up into the mountains and beyond?"

The other man laughed at him as baldly. The two might have been out on a joyous morning ride for all the intention that was in their actions. But these men were not like men from Rivermouth, not even those who had angrily driven us out the night before. Their voices were testy and strangely daring, and their attitudes were reckless. From beneath the lip of my hood I caught sight of surly faces and stained filthy clothing; their underfed horses stamped and sidled as we passed them in silence.

Around me, the priests were exceedingly quiet, saying nothing. Nothing could be heard but the shuffle of feet and the creak of wagon wheels on the narrow dirt track. We were plainly ignoring them.

I took note that there was no fear in the air from the tribe, though my own breath was short and my heart was hammering wildly. *Were these Rebels? Would they rob us of everything?* I could see sword hilts hanging from their saddles. They were dangerous men at best, and were clearly up to nothing good.

The first man quickly heeled his horse in front of Malachi, blocking him from advancing. *"I said, what's your business?* Speak up." He had marked us as weak, and boldness rose in him because of it.

Malachi was forced to stop, and with him the whole caravan drew to a standstill behind. His voice was quiet and careful as he raised his face to the rider. "We are the Tribe Halevi. We are bound for our new home beyond the mountains. We seek no trouble with any man."

"Poor devils," the second man burst out with a laugh. "Been cast out, have you?"

They seemed to enjoy this thought. The first man moved his horse out of Malachi's way again. "Probably religious reasons. That always does it."

This made the second man laugh.

For a moment I thought, with relief, that they would allow us to continue, but then the second man declared suddenly, "Eh? *What's this?"*

Without warning, he brought his steed up next to the donkey. For a brief moment I thought he had found some item strapped to the animal enticing, but no, his horse reined in next to me, blocking my way in one quick move. To my alarm, he pulled his sword from its scabbard with surprisingly quick skill and cleverly used the tip to draw back the hood of my cloak. A little gasp traveled through the priests as my features were exposed to the light. I slowly raised my gaze to the man's face.

His eyes widened. "What have we here? Caleb —"

Caleb released a sound of pleased amazement from his position. "Now, aren't you a sight?" he bellowed out. "*A jewel hidden among the coal.* I thought you was awfully thin to be a gray beard."

"Tall, too," Caleb agreed, with sudden interest. He called over to me, "And what are you called, sweet one?"

My breath caught. Panic rose up inside of me, but I forced myself to stand still and unmoving. The second man's sword point was dangerously near my face, waving slightly as his horse pranced just feet before me.

Swiftly, Malachi moved himself between me and the blade, pushing me none too gently behind his strong form. "We want no trouble," he insisted again, staring the man down.

His voice was not as kind this time, nor as peace-loving. To my surprise, it held a warning, which I did not think my gentle grandfather capable of giving.

At his tone, a sharp tension rose among the priests there on the roadway. It seemed to me all the peaceful sounds of spring only moments before suddenly became a disharmonious melody that only called out doom and trouble for us. The scene careened and swayed treacherously before my eyes. Surely something terrible was about to happen and we were powerless to stop it.

The man did not take kindly to Malachi's interference; his eyes narrowed and the point of his sword lifted toward my grandfather's throat. He let out a dangerous, disbelieving laugh, as though he could hardly take Malachi seriously.

"And what will you do, old man?" he barked. "All I ask is a look at the girl. Let us see her — that's all."

In that terrible heartbeat I knew Malachi loved me more than his own life. A cool rigidity I had never seen before in him was in his face and form, in the straight line of his shoulders and the positioning of his hands. He would find a way to stop them and sacrifice himself if he must for the sake of my safety.

*And then what would happen?* I thought, panicking. *What would the priests do without Malachi's leadership? What would I do?*

The tension coiled tighter with each passing breath, as though both sides waited for the other to strike first. The priests stood in a deathly hush, watching — men of prayer, not of action, and never meant to be. Malachi met the rider's gaze without flinching, while the man sneered down at him from his saddle in open contempt. Beside him, his partner Caleb laughed softly, savoring the chaos and the suspense, as if it pleased him to torment a handful of harmless old men and one unguarded girl.

But then, to the astonishment of everyone standing on the trail watching, Joel threw himself with heedless speed between Malachi and the bandit's blade, knocking at the hilt with his staff. No one would have guessed that the bent elderly man leaning so heavily on his crook nearby would even be capable of such hidden quickness. The action was so swift and startling that the bandit was nearly thrown from his horse. He let out an angry curse as he scrambled to stay balanced. The strike lacked the force to loosen his hold upon the weapon, however; his fighting reflexes went into motion at once and he vengefully drove the point of his blade through Joel's belly with a motion as swift as a bird's dive towards its prey.

Several small actions happened then. A wretched cry escaped my lips at the horrible sight; the priests gasped aloud, as one voice; Joel staggered back, mouth opened in stunned surprise as awareness settled in that he had been stabbed through. His staff fell aside; his eyes rolled back and his head lolled. Malachi's strong hands immediately reached to catch him.

*"Churl!"* Caleb seethed, swearing at his companion. "What have you done?"

But the bandit merely muttered, *"Doddering old fool."*

He pulled his horse clear even as Malachi gently lowered Joel's body to the ground at our feet. The bandits were hardly a point of concern now; all eyes were turned towards their Chief Priest, murmuring, muttering questions, voicing their worries for him. The group of priests pressed forward, crowding the scene.

Seeing this, the bandit muttered in shame, "We only wished for a bit of sport, that's all. Didn't intend to do any true harm..."

"Come on, let's away," Caleb urged him in haste. "Murder earns a rope, you witless fool." He swore again.

Quickly, the two withdrew and only moments later disappeared into the forests from where they came.

With their departure, the danger passed, and the air fell hollow with shock and grief. By the time Malachi gently laid Joel upon the dirt road, I was already weeping. We knelt on either side of him as the priests gathered close, helpless witnesses to the horrible scene. A dark, spreading stain covered his abdomen as he fought for breath, each ragged gasp weaker than the last. It was clear he was dying — the wound was far too grievous for even the Priests' healing skills to touch.

During this, Joel's eyes rolled open, focusing on Malachi's face above him. He tried speaking, gasped hoarsely, and coughed. Horribly, blood was in his spittle, staining his lips, spilling over his heavy gray beard. The sight was almost too much to take in — watching him struggle, seeing the blood, knowing these were his final moments.

"Don't speak," Malachi told him gently. "Just rest, old friend."

But Joel was persistent. "*No.*" His kind eyes settled on Malachi as he reached weakly for the words. "You could not... be sacrificed, Malachi. You must... lead us. And Eren —" His gaze shifted to me.

What love was in his weathered eyes; what beauty was visible in his spirit; what absence of pain was in his countenance. I wept even harder at the sight. He dragged in great, ragged breaths, struggling to get his next words out. His ancient voice had always been raspy — the dry crackle of paper being folded — but just now it carried an additional tremble. *"Our little... Meeshka.* You are... our light ahead. You must... be protected... at all costs."

His hand seemed to grasp feebly for something then, until Malachi realized he was reaching for his crook nearby and quickly pressed it into the old priest's hands. But Joel shook his head. "*No.*"

With the last of his strength, his blood-stained hands returned it to Malachi. "Lead us... out of the... mountains... to our new home, Malachi." His eyes rolled around the tight group of familiar faces hovering above him, catching sight of them with a faint smile. *"Remember me, brothers."*

Then his smile grew into a truly wondrous one, one I thought shouldn't have even been possible. He looked beyond us and towards the morning sky, as if he had seen a great light; and the life-breath disappeared from his body in an instant.

A quiet pause fell as the reality of it dawned upon us all. I was filled at once with a dozen sensations — shock, horror, and a cringing, fawning fear. My hands trembled and my body shook beyond all control. I had never before witnessed a single act of violence in my life, and this had been done so callously, so without cause. One moment Joel had been standing among us, alive and breathing, and the next he lay as an empty husk at our feet, left to die in the dirt. *Surely men were the authors of the deepest cruelties.* In only the passing day I had seen the depths of brutality they could stoop to — betrayal, rejection, severe ingratitude, cold-heartedness, and now careless murder.

Malachi and the others recovered much quicker than I did. As the priests fell back from the tight circle they had formed, now completely quiet, Cohen put one hand on Malachi's shoulder in comfort. "Let Liev and I handle his preparations, Malachi."

Malachi nodded his agreement, stood to his feet, and silently drifted away into the forests, leaving us all behind. I was left to stand there, still in shock, watching as Cohen, Liev and Anshel lifted Joel's lifeless body onto a blanket and carried him to a cleared area beneath the trees there on the roadside. Already the trio were chanting soft prayers in unison, which the other priests joined from a short distance.

Everyone seemed to know what must be done. Some began gathering stones, while another fetched a wood-handled shovel from the wagon and set to digging a shallow grave. One of the priests found two sturdy branches and, with a small knife, began to whittle a cross for the marker. The rest brought out their harps and lyres and lifted quiet songs of worship, heedless of the dangers that still lingered on the mountainside and which we had only just tasted. Soon the air was filled with the soft, wondrous sound of lifted voices.

I marveled at their calm. For men who had just witnessed so savage a death, there was no outward fear, no visible disquiet — nothing like the storm of feeling coursing through me.

After several long moments, Malachi returned with a quiet strength and calmly helped wrap Joel's body in his cloak and laid him in the shallow grave, along with the assistance of Cohen and his sons. He did this, I noticed, without any heaviness. There was no trembling in his hands, no weeping or tears. Together, the four of them began wordlessly laying stones over the body.

Surely the beautiful way in which Joel passed was what made his death all the crueler, I thought, watching them in anguish. He was so harmless, so pure in heart, so self-sacrificing. The world was not worthy of him. I felt my heart shriveling even as I stood there.

It was not until Malachi spoke that I realized I had not moved from the place where Joel had died. He was very aware of my presence some feet away. When he did speak, he did not look up from the burial; his hands continued their slow, steady work, lifting stones from the nearby pile. His voice, calm and measured, carried clearly over the soft rise of song.

"You have a choice right now, Meeshka. We all do. We can either stay in a place of deep hurt and sorrow, or go to the Whisper and let Him give us a grace."

In that moment I also realized I was still weeping. I hadn't stopped since Joel fell to the ground. My earlier pain had returned, and this event only added to the great pile of my suffering. I gestured towards Joel's dead body, now half-covered in stones, my voice thick with emotion and sharp with horror. *"What could He possibly say in this moment, Malachi, that would make up for what has been done to us?"*

Then he did turn and fix me with a bold, steady gaze, pausing in the burial as the others worked on. His voice came firm at once — as firm as I had ever witnessed it. Even on bent knees, his hands stained with earth and his robes soiled with dust, Malachi was every inch the High Priest of authority. "The only way to know is to go and find out for yourself. What do you think these men are doing even now, at this very moment? Eren, only the Whisper has the way of showing you that you are greatly wanted by Him; that you are cherished and set at a worth no man could ever give you; and that you have found your eternal home with Him. No being can place that knowing in your soul. He will remind you that you are wanted — always wanted — and vital to the whole of His plans and purposes. No man or single stroke of violence can ever steal that from you, Meeshka, unless you yourself surrender it. *This is who we are. Go and find out for yourself."*

Malachi's words set my feet in motion. It was the closest to a rebuke that I had ever received from him. Like he had earlier, I withdrew to the trees and left them behind — not far enough I couldn't hear their voices ringing out softly, but distance enough I would have a little privacy.

I had always spilled my troubles out to the Whisper. I knew His presence; I'd experienced his life. But this was different. The difficulties of my childhood paled in comparison to the events of the past day. The pain I was experiencing felt as though it would rend my very person in two and I would surely never be the same again. I was lost and adrift in a turbulent sea of emotions and longing; and there was no immediate change in sight. Years stretched out before us with little hope of returning to Rivermouth; Devland had still thrown aside every bit of love he had ever felt towards me. Joel was still dead, had died partially to save my own life. The injustice of our lives — the Halevi's lives — screamed out, like Joel's spilled blood must surely be screaming for justice from the ground where he was being buried.

For a long moment I sobbed my eyes out, emptying myself of emotion. I sagged against a hardened oak and slumped to the ground, burying my fists in my face. My heart could easily cry for sennights and months. Malachi was right in that it would be easy to stay in a place of sorrow and hurt forever. Yet I was too weak to choose anything else in this moment. The hopelessness was too strong; my strength was simply not enough to stand up to it. I was too small, and surely not enough as a person to be brave or hopeful.

After a long while, I thought, *I could at least own this truth.*

So I did. I found some measure of a voice and whispered it. I weakly admitted my inadequacy, my inability, my smallness.

The Whisper did not answer, not like other times, not like times in the future when He would speak in a mighty way. Instead He simply came.

At first He was just there, just beyond my reach, not quite touching. He merely established His presence. He was almost so quiet, so unassuming, I could have missed him altogether if I had still been indulging in heavy emotion. But I was slightly quieter now, and He appeared.

For a quick instant I had a decision to make. I could yield to His Presence just a little and allow Him to move in closer, or dismiss Him in favor of my pain. It was not so difficult to yield to Him — I was already in the habit and had done so many times over the course of my young lifetime — but it did require a small amount of belief that He could do something to help in one of the hardest hours I had ever known. It required an honest desire from me for Him to help at all. *He sought my permission before touching.*

"I need... *something,*" was all I could manage.

And that was all it took.

Ancient and continuous, that River still flowed within me, still moving, undisturbed by the ripples and rapids of the surface. There was no exterior noise that could change it. Time truly did pass unmeasured here.

A deep warmth swept over me from crown to sole, soaking through me entirely. I pressed my palms to my face — more gently now — as my breath slowed and found its own steady measure.

On that day He said nothing. Somehow He didn't need to. His touch was so bottomless that it was enough. I was strengthened in an instant.

*How small I was,* I realized, *and how great He was.* Only one touch from Him could set me right... could set the entire twisted, maniacal world right.

I knew when I stood up from where I was that things would not have changed. At least not with my physical eyes. I would still face the same challenges, the same emptiness, the same betrayal. I would still have to lay eyes on Joel's burial place, and turn and walk with the priests up the mountain away from our home.

And yet they *had* changed. The Whisper had strengthened me, settled me, *grown* me even. He had infused me with something of Himself. I was less myself, and more of Him. A little divinity had been exchanged for my incomplete humanity.

The Halevi took that day to linger beside Joel's shallow grave out of respect, to worship, and strengthen themselves in prayer. Then the next morning we carried on quietly and peacefully.

As we made our way from the place, with our backs warmed by the spring sunlight, Malachi caught me looking back on the pile of stones one last time. The grave was marked by a cross bound with twine, a stark lonely place in the shadow of the dark forest around it. Surely many would walk past and never know the soulful man who had died here, nor the selfless way he had sacrificed himself for Malachi and myself.

It was then Malachi murmured to me gently, "Take heart, Meeshka. There will come a day when the Whisper will have you gather all of the scattered Halevi and return them to the Temple for proper burial. Joel will be one of them."

I knew he was prophesying, but his words also spoke the solemn truth that there would be more untimely deaths ahead.

A holy joy fell on the priests after Joel's passing that carried them through the rough days that followed. We were in constant danger of attack; the unknown was a serious barrier before us; we knew little enough of how to farm or what we would find when we reached the farmsteads; yet all their fear had vanished after the older man's death and they were filled with a profound peace. I came to respect them more and love them more preciously than ever before. During travel they sang, prayed, and even at times debated the Holy Text, not allowing their rough circumstances to change who they were, nor ever forgetting what they lived for. I witnessed a true grace given to them from the Whisper which I had never seen; I had only heard Malachi describe it.

In the following days, eight more of the priests died along our journey. The mountain trails were too steep, the nights too cold, the food too sparing. Their bodies simply did not have the stamina or the strength to uphold the strain. Amazingly, as they died one by one, their prayers were never more fervent, their hearts never more open, their song never so bright. Just like Joel, the glory of God shone with radiance upon their faces even as I watched them take their last breaths in this life. I felt so deeply honored to know every one of them. I thought surely their faith had been perfected even in the suffering; they understood something I was just beginning to attain. It was just as Malachi had said — the cost of their calling had made their faith infinitely precious. Even in the moments of their slow hard deaths, the priests were truly happier than I had ever seen them.

We buried each of them beside the narrow road that wound through the Silent Heights, each grave marked with the same small cross of twigs bound with twine. Every priest was laid to rest wearing his prayer cloth and wrapped in his cloak; and with each death, I found myself vowing to return for all of them. Somewhere along that lonely path, watching them fall one by one, I came to believe Malachi's prophecy that I would be the one to carry them home and lay them properly in the Temple burial grounds. Not a single Halevi would be forgotten. I would remember them all.

Eventually came a day when we reached the farm land that would be our home for the foreseeable future. We had passed through the mountains without detection or interference from the Rebels beyond that first encounter, thankfully. Though we were a weary band, a ripple of joy swept through the priests as Malachi paused just over the crest of a treeless hill and gave the announcement, "Here it is. Our new home, brothers."

The land had been changing for some time as we came upon it, growing flatter and thinning of trees as we left the mountains behind. We even passed a few harmless travelers on the road, returning to a distant village, which we took as a quiet sign of a more peaceful, more settled region. At Malachi's words, we could see the lonely road we had followed split, and the leftward lane unspooled like a ribbon through low, rolling ground of fallowed fields and empty pasture. Bright skies opened over the farmland, spilling light across a wide, uncluttered horizon that stretched as far as the eye could reach.

I had no immediate impression of the farmsteads except relief that we had arrived, followed by natural curiosity as we explored the property that late afternoon in the early summer season. This place was not the Temple compound, and I could never call it home; but we all understood with a thankful heart that it was a far cry better than the dangerous mountain paths we had just exited.

The property consisted of two farms: one held several small log cabins where the priests would stay, and the other held two separate homes to be shared between Malachi and me, and the Chief Priest and his sons. The land had once belonged to a large family with grown, married children, but they had been driven away when they could no longer meet the heavy taxes imposed by the King. We would all work both lands together now. It was plain at a glance that everywhere we looked there was need of repair and cleaning, work far beyond our skill, yet here at least we could cease our wandering and escape the persecution we had fled. Here, at last, there would be roofs over our heads and a warm place to sleep. Malachi had saved us with his quiet foresight.

At the outset the project seemed nigh to impossible. We knew little of the true work of farming, the priests were neither strong nor filled with vigor, and our first crop would be planted late, leaving a shortened season and the constant threat of frost before the harvest could be safely gathered. Yet the land had been abandoned in workable condition, and much of the old equipment remained. Between the two farms were three wooden, wheeled mould-ploughs that could be drawn by the donkey, the horse, or any priest stout enough to pull one himself — enough, at least, to begin the heaviest labor. A clear creek wandered through both properties for bathing and irrigation, and on the priests' farmstead a deep well with wooden water channels still stood ready, granting us steady water for daily life as well as the fields.

By the end of a sennight Malachi and a handful of the priests had returned from a neighboring village with seed and other supplies. He also brought with him a man who had farming experience and could point out many things we did not know, which no doubt saved us that first winter from starving altogether. We stumbled into many errors the first year, but at least we made fewer with his help. Then the work began, slowly at first as the priests organized, and then with great dedication as we better understood the task before us.

The cabins themselves were in the greatest need of repair, and we quickly determined they would have to remain so for awhile until we could focus on them or could pay workers from a nearby village to help us. This meant suffering leaky roofs beneath the rains, and chill drafts creeping up through the wooden floors when the autumn winds rose — among many other small woes that clamored for attention. We understood the first and most important task was plowing the fields and planting the seed, as well as purchasing a handful of cattle which would be kept in the pastures where the soil was being replenished and reserved for next year's planting.

Very quickly, our days became long and exhausting, and during these first sennights there was no time for even a moment's rest and certainly none for prayer or worship. There was too much scrambling to learn all we must, struggling to catch up on all that needed to be done if we hoped to harvest a crop, and taking on a new life filled with many demands.

Malachi decided that I should prepare and serve the meals for the four men on our property, as well as tend to the cleaning of the cabins and the mending of their clothing. I was also given charge of a small garden near our shared cabin, where we grew vegetables, and of the thirty chickens that supplied both farms with eggs. Aside from the simple meals I had always prepared for Malachi and myself, I knew little of cooking, nothing of tending chickens, and even less of raising vegetables. Until now, our produce had come from the markets of Rivermouth, our washing and mending done by hired women there. I had never chopped or hauled a single piece of wood in my life, and chickens, I soon learned, were as foreign to me as all the rest of this new existence — leaving their droppings wherever they pleased, their manure sharp and potent if not carefully managed.

Still, I applied myself to every task as best as my limited knowledge allowed. My hands, blistered and bruised at first, soon hardened with calluses from hauling endless buckets of water for bathing and boiling, and my back grew strong through weeks of aching exhaustion. I swept and dusted and washed until it seemed this had always been my life, and my days at the Temple belonged to some distant past.

Most of our meals that first summer were spare, yet in time I learned to bake bread from the little grain Malachi could afford for the two farms — well enough, at least, that the men no longer had to soften it in water or broth before eating. With great difficulty, I learned to kill and pluck chickens and to prepare them in a half dozen different ways. Through much trial and error, I also learned to use the apple and pear trees beyond our cabins, baking the fruit and turning it into muffins and butters that soon became the envy of all the priests — both the four priests that ate at Malachi's table and those on the other farmstead, where one or two among them had taken up the quiet work of cooking and mending for the rest. And I learned, too, how many predators must be kept from a flock — raccoons, foxes, and snakes, of which our farmstead seemed to have no shortage.

All of the Halevi soon understood that our survival rested on the weather — whether the crops would live, whether frost would come too soon, and whether rain and wind would hinder the work we so desperately needed to do.

"Pray for good weather," was often the parting message among the priests.

Sadly, where once all our devotion had been given to the Whisper, the Sacred Text, and ministering to the needs of our community, it was now bent toward simple survival. Our days were filled with constant concern over the harvest, the weather, and, eventually, the coming winter. For those born to the Planters Tribe, this life was good enough — even satisfying — but for the Halevi, every simple challenge made the labor all the more draining. A hard day's work was only that: a hard day's work. There was no deep fulfillment in tilling or owning the land, no joy in rising with the dawn to take up the plough, no hopeful sense that this labor was a legacy to be passed on to our children.

Many of the priests were particularly vulnerable that first year after a summer of relentless physical labor and fell sick the first winter; a few more joined the brothers in death who had died along our way in the mountains and were buried in a small cleared place at the edge of the property under a giant oak. During all of this, our single greatest comfort was in the fact that we understood who we were in spite of our low circumstances and were united in our faith that the Halevi would one day return to Rivermouth where we belonged. There was an unspoken strength among us which came from that.

My days soon fell into an endless pattern, so much so that an entire year passed before I even looked up long enough to acknowledge it. My twenty-first birthday came and went, and would have been almost entirely unnoticed by me if Malachi had not made mention of it that day at our morning meal, just before he headed out to the fields.

"I spent a little time in prayer for you this morn before you woke, Meeshka," he announced.

These days even this was a tremendous sacrifice for him. Sleep was precious and greatly coveted by everyone on the farmsteads, myself included. There were few hours left for prayer or worship unless it was done in the fields or barns as the priests worked on until their bones ached and their muscles stiffened with pain. Malachi labored harder than them all, seeing as the burden of every decision concerning the farms and our future rested chiefly upon him. Over the long months I had prepared countless warm salt baths for his feet and bound his hands when blisters burst into blood or swelling left them near useless, and even then two or three men were often in the cabin, quietly consulting him on matters of the priests, the fields, or the failing equipment.

"I was given a word from the Whisper concerning you," he told me.

I paused a moment to take him in. He looked rumpled and tired this morning in a way that he had never looked when waking at the Temple, but that mysterious light was ever present in his eye. How I wished for his sake that we were back at the compound where he could dedicate himself to what truly brought him life. For nearly two years he had labored without a single complaint, without pause or hesitation, to secure our survival.

He said, "You may not know, Meeshka, but in my younger years there were priests who went out from the Temple and dwelt in other places. Some never returned, but chose to give their lives in service to the Whisper elsewhere. We have rarely heard word of them since the day they departed. And even now, Joram and Zadok journeyed to Periburn before we left Rivermouth, and from them also we have heard nothing. I have foreseen that you will be used by the Whisper to draw them all together again. You will help gather the scattered Halevi — every one of them — and return the dead for holy burial."

He smiled glowingly at this. These prophecies gave him as much pleasure as if he was the one being made the promise. I was his child of promise, his assurance of the future, just as Joel had said I was for all of the Halevi. "You are precious in the sight of the Whisper, my little Meeshka — not only in mine. Your destiny has not changed. Though this life now pressed upon you is a hard one, you will yet walk with kings and with princes. Indeed, the Whisper has said that you and your calling are of such weight that men will be given in exchange for your life. One of them will be a prince. Of this I have seen the sign."

At the time I took his words as simple encouragement and left them there; there was hardly room in my heart or my days for more. All that Malachi had ever prophesied to me felt impossibly distant, as far removed as east from west. There was clothing to mend for Malachi, and for Cohen and his sons; food to be preserved; the quiet, unending planning of daily meals…

Part of Malachi's message became very meaningful at the end our second summer when many of the priests approached him to say they feared they could not endure the physical hardship of continuing to farm and wished to seek out what family they had left in scattered parts of Avan. A few had left their elderly wives and grown families behind in the community. They felt surely they were at the end of their days and wished to see their loved ones before it was too late. They had thoughtfully waited until the completion of the harvest season, but it was needful to make haste at once so that winter did not catch them while they were journeying.

The departure was hard for more than one reason. With the priests' absence, we lost not only strength in numbers but also the unseen weight of their presence. After Malachi gave his blessing and we watched them go, the farmsteads felt hollowed out, drained of the life their voices and labor had brought. The tribe felt diminished by their leaving, as if something vital had been taken from us rather than given away. And with our numbers thinned, the work fell heavier on the shoulders of the twenty or so priests who remained — Malachi among them.

I found myself worrying for him more. I did not like how heavy he seemed in spirit, how quickly he tired, and how exhausted he was at the end of the long days… certainly more so than he had ever been since we left the Temple.

I told him one day late that fall, "You should be allowed to pray. Your spirit withers because the priests have gone and you must work so much."

But Malachi merely shrugged this off. "All of our spirits wither when we cannot pray. The Whisper is our source of life."

"You especially need it right now, Malachi."

His eye landed more strongly on me at the worried note in my tone. "We will survive. The Halevi will survive. We have a promise. You are a part of that promise, Meeshka. I am never afraid when I look at you. God has given us you to lead us to a better tomorrow."

In spite of my concerns, he carried on as before, as all the priests were. Colder weather settled in, which was not much reprieve. This was when they turned their attention from the fields to maintaining the farm equipment, preparing for the following spring, and winterizing the farmsteads. By now the cabins were in desperate need of attention and the priests that remained were forced to learn to repair leaks, rebuild faulty furniture, and seal broken windows. This left them outside in the cold a good deal of the time.

Most nights Malachi came through our cabin door with a great weariness that I did my best to combat with warm food, providing him with blankets heated by the fire for him to wrap in, and a foot bath for his aching feet. If there was any small way I could pour life into him while he could not fill up in prayer and worship, then I committed myself to it. This became my chief concern during those long winter days.

So I was surprised one night when he arrived with a spark in his eye and more vigor than usual. It was by now well after dark and he quickly closed the rough-hewn wooden door behind him to shut out the wintry snow that had begun to flurry only hours before. I noticed the change in him at once, though I made no mention of it, except to make my usual efforts at remaining cheery and welcoming. Malachi shared his secrets in his own time and never failed to give them.

Tonight the front room of the cabin glowed against the cold with a cheerful fire crackling in the hearth, a heavy pot of chicken stew I had prepared simmering over the flames. Its rich scent filled the air as I ladled the steaming meal into wooden bowls and set them on the crude table at the room's center. Outside, winter pressed hard against the walls, but within there was warmth, woodsmoke, and the promise of comfort.

True to form, just as he sat down, Malachi announced with cheerfulness, "I've been having visions, Meeshka. They are of the most unusual kind."

This encouraged me at once. I threw another log on the open fire from a low pile beside the hearth and joined him. "What is it, Malachi? It must be a good thing. You are practically glowing."

"Two times today I saw your grandmother — my wife. She was greatly excited, more than I have ever seen her, as if she had received wonderful news. It was good to see her, and especially so happy. *More than good.*"

In my twenty-one years, Malachi had scarcely ever spoken of his wife; I knew she was among his most sacred memories in this life. Throughout the rest of the evening he lifted quiet praise to the Whisper for allowing him to see her again and witness her happiness, yet his words left me uneasy in a way I could not grasp. They seemed to point to something just beyond my sight — something I was not ready to face. Not yet. Not now. *Not like this.*

In the sennights that followed, I redoubled my care for Malachi. On the coldest days I sought him out across the property with scarves warmed by the fire, with steaming teas and simple soups, urging him to take a few moments' rest between his labors while I served him. He took quiet delight in my attentions, yet was keenly aware of all that I was doing.

One day he stopped me before I could leave. We stood in the open doorway of an old, giant-sized barn on the far farmstead near the small cluster of priests' cabins, with loose hay underfoot and the sharp scent of horse and manure heavy in the air. A wind moved through the barn's long central passage, hampered by the stalls, lofts, and shadowed storage rooms around us. It was quiet here with the priests scattered across the property, leaving the space our own.

Malachi fixed me with that firm eye of his when he felt I was not in faith. "There are some parts of our destiny we must accept, Meeshka, uneasy though they may sit with us. There is a timeline, and we are all beholden to it. The Whisper is God over all — never be fooled. He holds histories and destinies and generations in His plans, even while we make decisions independent of Him... even as we try to turn the tide of time in every which way we can to avoid, slow, or hurry its markers and milestones."

Tears stung my eyes at once. This was the nearest we had ever come to speaking about the end of his life.

"I am not ready yet to lead the Halevi," I burst out, still unable to speak directly of it. "I want you to continue to lead us."

Ever patient, Malachi smiled a wise little smile down on me. He was never afraid of anything, not even this. "Ah, but I knew my time was coming to an end the first time I held you in my arms. It is not on me to complete the work, only to begin it."

The light softened in his eye and changed, as if for just a moment he could see into the future and it was the toasty fire by which he warmed himself these days... as if all was settled and content in his soul at the very sight of it. *"But you* — you are the one, Meeshka. You will take the Halevi into the future. The Halevi will return to the Temple, you will unite them, and be their High Priestess. That is enough for me."

It *was* enough for him. I had to ask myself if it was enough for me — I couldn't imagine a future without him and didn't want to — but it was certainly enough for Malachi. Only days later he did not rise with the dawn as he had done for two years. I nursed him in bed that day, and fetched Cohen to come.

For the next two days I spent my time at Malachi's bedside, knowing this was the end. He walked towards it slowly, giving me plenty of time. How gentle he was with me even in his final moments in this life; how merciful the Whisper was as I slowly accepted the inevitable.

During these hours the little cabin room was dim and hushed with winter, the rough walls bare but for a single candle whose flame trembled softly beside Malachi's small, neatly kept bed. He lay propped beneath rough quilts, his silver hair spread thin upon the pillow in curly waves, his face worn with age and gentled by nearness to heavenly rest, breathing shallow yet steady, as if already listening for a world beyond this one. Frost pressed faintly at the windowpanes, yet the air within felt stilled and set apart, held in a quiet, unspoken holiness, as though the space itself had been appointed for this final vigil.

With each quiet step Malachi took toward his end, my heart broke a little more. He said and did all the things that must be said and done. He gave me instruction concerning the Priests and the Temple for our return. He blessed me, laid his hands upon me, and prophesied — witnessed by Cohen, Liev, and Anshel.

During this moment, with the three priests present, he asked me to retrieve an item from an iron-banded chest from the corner of his room. This was an old weathered chest that had been abandoned along with the farms, which held the few of Malachi's belongings that we had brought with us from the Temple. I had never touched it out of reverence for him, but today he had me retrieve a small linen pouch from its sparing contents.

"This is for you," he said, placing it ceremoniously in my hands.

As I opened it, I recognized what was within at once — the prayer cloth of the Holy Room, meant only for the High Priest during his times in this sacred place. The material was light as breath, woven of fine, pale silk and marked with faint, careful stitching along its edges. Delicate yet enduring, folded and refolded by three generations of the faithful hands of my forefathers, it held the soft scent of incense and oil, as though decades of whispered prayers still rested in its folds. I had no idea he had managed to keep it…

"Oh, Malachi," I whispered, weeping at once.

His eyes, though rimmed with weariness, still held their familiar spark that I had seen all my life, bright with a quiet life that the shadow of death could not dim. "Keep it safe, Meeshka," he told me. "Use it in the Holy Room when you return."

This was his final and unalterable will: that I should be the next High Priestess, and that I would one day lead the tribe back to the Temple when the Whisper made the way. This was my birthright — by design, by God, and by my grandfather's wish.

"Bring them home," he told me. "Bring them all home, Meeshka."

At another point, this time with the other men absent, he asked me to sing for him, and I chose a happy melody, so that some of his last sounds on the earth would be a song of cheerfulness and joy.

After this, he said with a quiet warmth, "You're such a good girl, Meeshka. *More than good."*

He also told me during this time, "Let Cohen say the words over my burial. He'll like that. It will be a great opportunity for him to bring out his wise sayings." And then he winked, laughing softly even then.

With each passing hour the room grew heavier with stillness. The remaining hours drew inward like a slow tide, retreating toward a shore none of us could see, but which Malachi already seemed to know by heart.

There was only once he seemed to show regret of any kind. But this was not from his past.

"I wish I could have seen it," he told me, staring off into the distance. "Seen the days when you know the King of the land... when one of the Halevi walks with kings and princes. *My own flesh and blood."*

Then, suddenly, as if he knew this would be too much for me, he smiled warmly, eyes sparkling in my direction. "But take comfort. I will hear reports of how you are doing in heaven. You must run now, child. *Run for us all."*

During this, my thoughts could not help but move towards Devland. Not only was he absent from all of this, but it was his own choices that had set the whole matter in motion. Malachi could have had many more years, I thought resentfully, if he had not been forced from the Temple. At the very least, our grandfather deserved to die in his own home, in his own place, not as a stranger in a strange land. We were too impoverished to even afford the incense we would have burned for him in this holy moment. I realized then, suddenly, that a great ugly bitterness had been festering in my soul towards Devland for some time, a bitterness that I had hardly recognized during the punishing labor that had consumed me in the past recent years. He was the fault of all of our struggle and suffering. I would not be facing the task of leading the Halevi home again had he not driven us out in the first place.

Of course Malachi discerned this. He had always seen straight through me, and what his eyes missed, the Whisper whispered to him in full.

He told me, "Resist temptation, Meeshka."

"What temptation?" I asked, though I knew at once what he was referring to.

"The temptation to hate. It will destroy you as it has your brother. Choose the way of love. *Choose forgiveness."*

My eyes burned with tears for the second time, though I had vowed to myself I would not weep in front of him. I only wanted him to experience joy in his final moments. Yet Malachi's very character demanded sincere honesty; he always had. "You are his grandfather, too. This is *his* doing, Malachi. Devland is the one who has done this."

Even lying upon his bed in the humble glow of the candle, at his most weakened state, Malachi's face still carried a noble strength and a quiet joy upon his countenance. He could never be counted the least of his brothers, nor the last of his tribe. He was surely the greatest of us all. And as with the others, the nearer he drew to death, the more joy and light seemed to rest upon his features. Even then, in that moment, he held enough inward strength to guide me toward the truth.

"The Whisper may speak to our hearts in the softest ways," he assured me, "yet do not think His quiet means He does not see. He sees all things — even the deeds man has done in secret. So, my little Meeshka, remember this. Do not take vengeance into your own hands unless He Himself stirs you to speak with a clear and steady boldness. Leave room — always leave room — for the wrath of God. He is rich in forgiveness, that much is true, yet He is also mighty, and His holiness does not bend. Do not mistake this — He loves justice, and justice belongs to Him. And it will come to you in its season, just as it will come to all of the Halevi."

His words did more than merely comfort me. There was a holiness in them; even then Malachi was prophesying. The air at his bedside seemed to still and faintly shimmer, and the restless winter wind at the small window fell suddenly quiet. The Whisper did not mean only to deliver the Halevi; He meant to exact justice for what had been done to us. I shivered in the hush and released the matter, content to leave it in His hands.

Malachi took his final breath on a cold day that began in rare winter rain and ended in streaming sunshine. At the very moment of his passing, the light broke through the clouds as if in answer, drinking up the moisture and filling the world with sudden glory. We were not left behind in cold darkness; we were left behind in the wake of his warm light.

For the better part of the day afterward, a double rainbow arced over the little cabin from horizon to horizon — an impossible wonder for the heart of winter. When the priests first laid eyes on it, all of us gathered outside in a little huddle for a brief time to take it in.

"A double rainbow," Cohen murmured. "A sign of hope, of promise, and the faithfulness of the Whisper."

"Surely Malachi was our double rainbow," Liev added softly.

And then a holy silence fell and did not lift for hours, as the priests quietly sanctified and readied their High Priest's body for burial.

# 6.

Life was very quiet as spring approached. Too quiet. I felt a little lost without Malachi, as though a familiar lantern had gone dim along the road. Even four months after his passing, I still had not fully adjusted. My days were lonely and endless. A handful more of the Halevi departed shortly after his burial, headed for other places before their own inevitable ends, which only served to add to the feeling of quiet emptiness on the farmsteads.

I was grateful for the presence of Cohen, Liev, and Anshel at midday and evening meals, usually taken at their small cabin. The other priests were near as well — steady, faithful, carrying on the labor of the farm without Malachi's guiding hand, loving in their constancy. I was far younger than they, and a woman, yet they were my people, my own. In their quiet way, they shared my grief and bore it with me.

And I had the Whisper. I always had the Whisper. I spent a great deal of time talking or singing to Him as I worked, or in the evenings when I was alone in my cabin — alone now without Malachi.

As the winter weather began to recede, all of us slowly began to prepare for spring. There would be planting soon and the soil must be assessed, the seed carted from town nearby, and supplies purchased with what meager funds we had between us. As soon as the weather was more bearable and the ground at the appropriate temperature, we would begin tilling the fields. Cohen was leading now, along with Liev and Anshel, and the three felt confident that we could still survive financially off of what little crop the remaining tribe was able to produce this year. Practically speaking, with fewer mouths to feed less profit was required.

It was still upon me to cook and serve the meals for the four of us on our side of the farm, as well as maintain our cabins, which spared me a little of the tasks that were done in the harsh weather of outdoors, but there was still more work than daylight for all of us. For the countless time these past two years, I missed the many hours in prayer and freedom I had in my days in the Temple. The Whisper had had much more freedom to visit me then. As a result, particularly now without Malachi, I was not as strong as I once was and my heart often suffered at night lying in my bed in the cabin alone. I cried many tears in the final months of that winter. I missed *everything*... but especially Malachi.

One afternoon I was preparing the evening meal in my cabin when Anshel knocked on the door. I quickly motioned him in out of the chill air, unsurprised to see him. All three of the Chief Priests were often dropping by to discuss news, plans, and tasks that were before us, especially this past winter when there was less field work. Sometimes, when the weather turned severe, Cohen would send one of the other two to look in on me.

"You're like a granddaughter to me," he told me once, only days after Malachi died. "I will always carry a certain duty toward you, from my own affection for you and for the love I bore Malachi. I hope you will not be offended, Eren."

I had smiled at him as bravely as I could. There would never be a replacement for Malachi, but at least I had the comfort of being surrounded by these men whom I called fathers and uncles. "Of course not."

"And you are our High Priestess now," he said gently. "That is also so. With or without a Temple, with or without our gathered hours of prayer… even if few remain to speak it plainly… still, you are our Priestess."

Today Anshel's face told me he had news. Of Cohen's two sons, he was the more expressive, though none of the Halevi were very effusive except in worship and in their occasional debates over portions of the Sacred Text. When they had the strength, they still liked to argue scripture while they worked.

"What is it, Anshel?" I asked him. "I can see you have news. Please, come stand by the fire and warm yourself."

His dark eyes glanced at the fire hungrily, but he didn't move from his place on the doorstep. "We have a visitor, Eren. He is asking for you. That's why I've come. Can you be spared for a moment?"

Immediately my heart quickened. This was both strange and exciting. So little changed here on the farm except more departures, more deaths, and more work. "Of course I can come."

Already I was reaching for my heavy wool shawl from the peg by the door and my fingerless knit gloves, preparing myself for the walk before me in the cool wind. "Who is it? One of the brothers? Has one of them returned from somewhere?" This was the only thing I could imagine.

"It's a young man from Rivermouth. Perhaps you remember him. Connor Shannesee? He say he has news for you about Devland. It's very remarkable that he found us."

This shocking announcement stopped me. A new thought hit, one I hadn't considered before. I was particularly vulnerable after the loss of Malachi. I stared at Anshel, stricken. *"Is Devland — ?"*

Anshel answered the question I was unable to finish. One of his hands came out to grip my shoulder. "No — do not be alarmed, my child. It is not news of harm to Devland; Cohen made sure of that at once. Still, I should not hide it from you — Connor's report is a heavy one. For a handful of sennights now, he says, he has been looking for you and for Malachi."

After this somewhat alarming announcement, the two of us set out at once, while my thoughts rolled and twisted like waves off the shore of Trowich predicting an approaching storm. *When was the last time I saw Connor?* I remembered how he had come to see me at the Temple with word of Devland, which had taken me by surprise. Later, I came to think he had also used it as an excuse to say farewell before leaving Rivermouth — no small wonder to me, given how openly antagonistic we had always been toward one another. At the time I was certain he was leaving to join the Rebels. I was nineteen then and was freshly twenty-two now, well over two years ago.

So much change had happened since. I hadn't given him another thought since he left, and especially since the Exile. I supposed it stood to reason that he and Devland might have had contact somewhat, but if he wasn't delivering a message directly from my brother, then why search so hard to find us? What news could he possibly bring about Dev that mattered so greatly... and was so troubling? How strange that Connor, of all people, would be the one to show up here to deliver it.

*Just send him on his way quickly,* I prayed, as we made our steps through the cow pasture and followed the familiar trail through the trees that separated our two cabins. *You know how deeply I have always disliked him. Just let him deliver whatever terrible news he has brought and send him on his way.*

As we cleared the edge of the belt of trees and approached Cohen's cabin from a distance, I could see the three men were gathered on the front porch, with a smattering of the other priests lingering before it. Connor stood leaning on the front post at the top of the few steps, as if watching for us while they talked.

There was no mistaking who he was. Even without the sun today, his uncovered head was a dark flame that caught the wintry gray light. He was stockier than the priests, his build naturally stronger than the older men, dressed in trousers, dark boots, and a heavy coat. As a Planter, hard labor had shaped his days since boyhood. Of the three on the porch, he alone remained standing, by all appearance untouched by the cutting wind. I had somehow pictured him fresh from battle — bristling with blades, astride a wild horse, clad in black leather, his skin marked with ink and scored with scars. This tame, farm-boy image surprised me after all this time.

Anshel was the one who called out a greeting as we drew near and Cohen answered it, raising one hand from his place on the crude wooden bench by the door. "Oh, here they are," he said.

Even as I came to a stop several feet from the foot of the little cabin, Connor was studying me curiously with that dark probing gaze, saying nothing. He looked older somehow, leaner in the face, with more experience in his features; yet there was something about him still the same. He hadn't changed so much. A wicked light still danced in his eyes. I suddenly recalled the other thought I'd had of him when he took his leave two years past — that we might have been friends, had he not been so bent on being a pest. *He was such a disagreeable person.* My first instinct, even without a shred of words between us, was to be on the defensive with him.

Cohen was the one guiding the moment, as he always was now with Malachi gone. He said warmly, "Eren, do you remember Connor Shannesee from Rivermouth? He was one of the Planters Tribe and left shortly before the Exile."

I nodded stiffly, hugging my heavy shawl to my frame. "I remember. Devland's childhood friend. I see you are well," I told him.

Connor's curious, probing expression gave no change. In fact, he didn't move an inch from where he stood, casually leaned against the post above me. "Cohen explained that Malachi passed some months ago. I am sorry for your loss, Eren."

I almost didn't know how to respond. When he left, I had expected time to draw out the evil in him, not improve his manners.

"Thank you," I stammered. "Your thoughts are very kind. We have all suffered a great loss in losing our High Priest." I included the others in my glance. "It has scattered our tribe even more, sadly."

My gaze returned. "But Anshel told me you have been searching for Malachi and myself?"

"It is not good news, I fear," Cohen added at once. "Come, let us go inside where there is warmth. You look chilled, Eren."

Moments later the five of us shuffled inside, as the other priests drifted back to work with a final wave at Connor. The men gathered around the wooden table in the center of the room, while I chose the removed safety of the hearth a few feet away, sitting on a rug kept there. I had no desire to be seated across from Connor Shannasee, forced to meet his gaze the entire time — especially not knowing what news he had brought. If I were to be shocked or undone, I did not need him witnessing it in full view.

He began almost at once, in a low cool voice, with his strong hands folded on the table before him with an easy calm. He addressed us all, as I had hoped, instead of focusing on me only. "I should begin by saying that, two years past, I left Rivermouth to join the Rebels —" He checked himself at once. "The Raiders, rather. They are better known by that name. I was headstrong, and I thought it would grant me the adventure I sought. Their manner of life seemed thrilling to me, and I excused it by telling myself they did no true harm — only caused petty harassments — and that what was taken was most often what could be spared. I was foolish. And I was wrong."

Clearly, the brothers hadn't heard this portion of the tale yet. Joel had been killed by those we had always believed were members of those same Raiders, yet the three men showed sympathy at once, sensitive as they always were to the honest confessions of the sinner.

Liev broke over him, "We have all gone astray at various times and moments, Connor. It takes courage to admit it."

Anshel murmured his own agreement.

"And even greater courage to make the change to correct your course and your character," Cohen affirmed him.

Meanwhile, I was thankful for my seat by the fire for a different reason altogether. Though it confirmed my suspicions about where he had gone, I had not expected such frank honesty — and certainly not regret for his choice. He also sounded like a man, oddly enough. A sober, right-minded man. I had to remember to close my mouth from where it had dropped open.

Connor nodded at them calmly. "I thank you. Your words are kind. I knew nothing of the Exile until Devland himself came to the camp where I was lodged with the Raiders. As I have already said to you, brothers, some months past he had grown weary of his post in Rivermouth among the Governors. He had climbed as high as the order of the community would allow for, and still found himself discontented. He believed the Raiders would grant him greater command, and a truer power to shape the fate of Avan." Connor's gaze lifted from the priests and passed over me. "It grieves me to say that he is their leader now. He rose swiftly among them. They are already called Devland's Raiders, and their name is spoken in the far south — farther than here, nearer to Periburn. Even now they are beginning to make demands of the King, and among themselves it is well known that they mean, in time, to overturn his rule. They may never bring these things fully to pass, but their numbers are growing slowly, and with them dangerous hopes."

"When they started to organize," he explained, "I chose to leave. I had not been a very needful or successful member of their band anyway, and I had no desire to be part of a rebellion against the crown. That was never the cause I meant to serve."

A shocked silence fell after these words. I was truly horrified. *Devland had grown worse, worse than I could have imagined.* He had become like a disease with his ideas, infecting everywhere he went and everyone he encountered. I had not pictured this at all...

But Connor had already gone on, not glancing over to see my reaction. "He and his men have started demanding that the people make a choice."

The priests were taking the news with as much grief as I was. Anshel asked, with a great sadness in his voice, "And what happens if they don't?"

Connor looked grim. "The Raiders have threatened to kill anyone who doesn't join in their ideas. Right now they are more voice than violence, but I suspect it will only grow worse... until Cyric is forced to bring in armed forces and subdue them by might."

*This was Miri's doing,* I thought wildly. She polluted his young impressionable mind from birth with her volatile ideas and personal hatred of Cyric, and he had chosen to take after her. Devland had truly abandoned everything Malachi had tried to give him.

I almost wept right then and there. *How could he do this?* As if dismissing the Halevi from the community and casting out his own family was not betrayal enough. Not only had his actions led to Malachi's premature death, but now he had become a dangerous rebel and an insurgent. How grieved Malachi would be to hear this news, how heartbroken. I could only be glad he wasn't here to witness it.

Cohen cleared his throat soberly in the deafening silence that had fallen. "We of course are grateful for the news you have brought us, my son. This is indeed a troubling report."

Connor nodded again. "I judged that the Halevi would hear little news in exile, and I thought Malachi and Eren should be told. For now Devland is far off, and his name is just beginning to swell, but I feared that if word of your whereabouts reached him, the two of them in particular might stand in danger. He would surely seek them out — or at the least trouble any farms or villages where he found the Halevi dwelling. His aims may have shifted, but he still holds your tribe of little worth. I wished to give you warning, so you might keep watch for any word of him and his Raiders. In times like these, it is not wise to be too far removed from the local gossip."

Cohen nodded. "Yes, yes — very wise, and very good of you. When we were sent away, there were not many in Rivermouth who took much care for what became of us. And the quiet from them since then tells us something: they are still glad enough we are gone. I only hope the long searching for us, with all its expense and weariness, has not been too heavy upon you, my son."

"It was no trouble for me," Connor said. "I had already need of distance from the Raiders. I stole away weeks ago, knowing Devland would hunt my trail for a season. He will take it as an unforgivable betrayal. As I told you, I was far enough removed from Rivermouth that I did not learn of the Exile until he spoke of it himself — but I cannot call it right. Even before my leaving the community, I feared he would try to draw the other tribes after him. When he joined the Raiders, he still gloried in what he had done and showed no sorrow for it. But the Halevi, I believe, are of Rivermouth, and rightly belong there."

*He showed no sorrow for it.* These words were like hammers hitting the walls of my soul. Even years later, Devland had not softened in the least towards us. *…while Malachi lay in his grave, dead and gone to both of us…*

Cohen's voice warmed, as the others murmured their gratitude. "Thank you, my son. It strengthens our hearts that you stand with us."

Another heavy silence fell. It was then, at last, that the eyes of all seated at the table turned toward me. I had been the one who was quiet and my reaction would be the one that interested them the most.

With their eyes now on me, I found I could not endure it. Even Connor's words of goodwill slipped past; what had come before was too crushing. I needed space to reckon with it — and most certainly not with him looking on.

I shot him a watery smile, hoping that would be thanks and acknowledgment enough. "I think I need to take this in privately," I told them, scrambling to my feet.

"Of course, my dear," Cohen murmured quickly. "Take all the time you need. We will manage for our supper."

My gaze could not meet any of theirs as I skirted the table and shot for the rickety wooden door beyond. *I needed out, away…* Perhaps to the safety of Malachi's grave under the oak tree, where I often found myself retreating these days when emotions ran especially high.

They were all still watching, observing me flee, but I paid them no bother. I threw open the door and shot into the wind.

The next morning found me better recovered after the horrible news. I had had time with the Whisper and a quiet evening to settle my emotions. I would likely not feel fully at ease about Devland for some time, but I could accept the news of what he had become and the trouble he was causing. Any hurt I felt towards him could be laid aside for the moment as I considered the danger he was in.

I was worried for him, in spite of everything. Surely his future was a doomed one if he continued down the path he was choosing. My mind was crowded with grim pictures at the thought that the King's army might pursue him if he continued to cause trouble. *My sweet little Devland.* How had the hurt within him grown to such a point of anger and rebellion?

Still, I was determined that he would not steal my peace; he had done enough stealing from me already. I had the strength to at least make that choice within myself.

Around mid-morning, Liev came to look in on me at Cohen's behest and I assured him I was fine. Then once he was sufficiently convinced, he went on to other parts of the farmstead and I returned to my work. One of my daily chores included collecting eggs from the small collection of hens who made their roosts in the little shed next to my cabin. Their laying had slowed during the winter and had not yet fully picked up in these early days of spring, but it was still necessary to ensure that I found every single egg they gave or the eggs would spoil in a short time. This I had discovered the hard way in the beginning days, along with a myriad of other mistakes that all of us had made.

It was while I was in the dimly lit shed rummaging through the hay-lined nests, trying not to disturb the sleeping hens too greatly as

I made my search, when I looked up suddenly and noticed Connor at the doorway. He was leaned on the doorframe, as casually as if he had been standing there for some time. He was dressed as he had been yesterday, and bore the same curious probing expression — nearly the same expression I had always seen on his face, when he wasn't lighting up with glee because he had managed to annoy me. This unnerved me. I did feel a mild gratitude for him, knowing he held some strange concern for the safety of the Halevi, but I harbored a sharp dislike over the thought of being caught unguarded by Connor Shannesee. In my mind, he should have announced himself straight off.

As a result, my first words were not the friendliest. "You're still here," I declared. "I thought you'd be long gone by now."

He smirked, unaffected. "Where exactly did you think I would go?"

I ignored this, feet shuffling through the thick straw lining the floor, still searching the hay-covered shelves around me for eggs. "Did you have need of something? I assume you're at my cabin for a reason."

"I came to look in on you. It was obvious that the news I brought troubled you. Anshel guided me to your door."

He sounded strangely sincere, compassionate even, much as he had the night before; yet all I wished was for him to go. Malachi would have reminded me that love does not keep score of wrongdoing, and that forgiveness was especially important when the person who has caused the offense seemed truly repentant. But I still wished for him to leave. I inwardly moaned to the Whisper, *Why HIM? Why must the one person who cares for the Halevi be Connor Shannesee?*

Even now I couldn't ignore the memory — it slipped back in almost against my will — that Connor was the one who had alerted me in his final moments before leaving Rivermouth that Malachi and I should hear what Devland was petitioning for in the community meetings. *Could you not find someone else to run your errands?* I implored the Whisper. *Surely there is someone — ANYONE — with a bigger heart than his conniving, disrespectful one.*

"I thank you for your concern," I told him as politely as I could manage. "Though it was not needful. As you can see, I am well enough."

Those probing eyes sparked with frisky light. The smirk was back. "I see you haven't changed a bit, Eren," he announced.

"I disagree. I think I've changed a great deal since last you saw me."

He gave a muttered laugh. "Well, there's no sign of it."

I paused in my search through the nests, fixing him with an even expression across the space that separated us. I refused to be goaded. "You seem very certain. You've only been here — *what*? All of five whole heartbeats?"

"It doesn't take but *five whole heartbeats,"* he countered. "I'll put you to the test this very moment. Have you still never been kissed, Priestess?"

This impertinent question, given with clear laughter in his voice, annoyed me at once. He still remembered that irritating conversation even after all of this time. *Come to think of it, I still believed he was the one who set those rumors in motion...* Today I shook my head, tucked my little basket closer to my side as a show of polite indignation, and coolly swept past him out of the shed.

Connor's laughter followed me out into the gray winter light and brisk wind. "I'd say you have a true problem on your hands, Priestess."

Then, when I said nothing, he called brazenly, "I can help you with that if you like."

My annoyance ignited into real anger. *He is just the same as he ever was,* I muttered to the Whisper, headed across the hard-packed courtyard to the cabin. I could scarcely believe his audacity — and yet, knowing the source, *I could.*

*If anything, he was worse.*

"You always *were* a thorn in my flesh," I called over my shoulder.

"And you were always beautiful," he quipped back instantly.

I was truly shocked. Stopped. Turned.

From the doorway of the little shed, Connor took me in with dark mischievous eyes. I realized, suddenly, that he meant it.

"You're surprised," he stated. "I suppose I was too much of a boy to say it before. *Devland's older sister, the mysterious priestess.* You were the intimidating creature of the Temple."

Something about his daring, yet honest confession caused laughter to bubble up in spite of myself. It seemed odd to hear words like those after the grueling troubles of the past two years. Beauty mattered little on the farm, where labor left you bone-weary, with callused hands, forever-soiled aprons, and hair at the rough mercy of the winds. Then there was the idea of being intimidating or mysterious at all to the arrogant young Connor...

"*That* was you intimidated?" I asked incredulously, laughing.

I realized now, particularly after the Exile, that his idle jabs as a boy had no real power to wound me — not then, and far less now. There were much greater insults, and actual pain in the world.

He was grinning. "Am I permitted to tell you what I once thought, now that we're grown?"

"No," I answered with laughter, "I'm as much a priestess now as I was then. It's disrespectful to bring attention to my beauty."

Connor could plainly see I wasn't offended, however. His eyes glittered at me. "I thought I was being truthful. What's wrong with truth-telling, especially to a priestess? Even you can't argue with that logic."

For some reason, this made me laugh more. "I'm sure a way could be found."

He paused in surprise. His glimmering gaze scrutinized me afresh. "It may be I was wrong, Eren. You *have* changed."

He wanted me to ask him how, and I could scarcely believe I was allowing myself to stand there and be drawn into it. "And what, then, made you change your mind so suddenly?"

"I don't think I have ever heard you laugh before — least of all at yourself." His smile carried a teasing dare. "And I, for one, only ever vexed you."

He wasn't the only one recognizing change, I realized. He'd grown more charming with age, less antagonizing. *Perhaps he had always been reaching for charm*, I thought, but in his immaturity he had been unable to master the skill. Or perhaps, with his confession, I was at last able to see his relentless teasing for what it had ever been — a way to arrest my attention.

I told myself I shouldn't encourage him, but I broke into a laughing smile just the same. "You still vex me."

*"Really?"* He half-laughed, daring me. "You're still laughing. And you're still standing here."

Then he fully laughed, as if he couldn't help himself. His laughter slipped free in a low, easy ripple, bright with mischief and warmth. To my surprise, I broke down and joined.

As the sound fell away, the air between us eased and softened. I felt warm toward him for the first time in all the years I had known him.

A silence fell briefly. Connor's dark eyes dropped to the basket still in my hands. "Can I be of use? You don't have any eggs in that basket."

For a short while, we scavenged for eggs from the little shed. This simple task was carried out in companionable silence until nearly the end, after we discovered a very satisfactory four eggs which the hens had tried in desperation to hide from my searching eyes. To my private amusement, Connor scolded the chickens for causing so much trouble, though I suspected he only did so for my benefit.

As we stepped out of the little shed and made our way toward the cabin, I asked him in an easy manner, "What will you do now, then? Have you decided?"

He had taken the basket from my hands and was setting the pace slow on purpose, as though he meant to draw the moments out before his leaving. "At the moment I have nowhere to go. I visited home briefly before coming here and learned my family supports the removal of the Halevi, and I cannot stand with them because of it — to say nothing of the fact that my father and I will never see alike on many things. I'm very unlike him. Your farm looks like it could use the help of a young man, Eren," he announced suddenly. "I was shocked to find so few of you here. If I can be so bold, Cohen is getting on in years and shouldn't be working as hard as he is." He paused then, clearly waiting for me to reach the plain-faced conclusion.

I cast him a quick look in surprise. "You wish to stay here? With the priests?"

His brows raised at my tone. "Why not? I come from the Planters. I'm used to this kind of work. I can lend what I know of the fields. You could use a bit more protection," he added. "Devland and his Raiders remain at large yet."

"Devland would never harm me," I answered quickly. "He is still my brother, whatever he has done. It was my mother who sowed these dark ideas in him. He cast us out of the community, but his quarrel is with authority — with the King. Miri did not teach him to raise a hand against his own flesh and blood. He proved as much in our final moments before the Halevi left. He offered me the choice to stay, if it was my will. I cannot believe his fury is meant for me."

But Connor looked less certain. "Possibly. Possibly not. He's drunk with power and filled with anger. He's not the young boy we once knew. And even if he doesn't harm you, his men would. But that's neither here nor there. You could still use the extra protection, you and this little farm of soft priests. None of you knows the first thing about self-preservation."

Even if he was right, I couldn't help but defend the hard efforts we had made since our coming. "We've learned a great deal in these past two years. More than any of us should ever have been made to learn."

Connor grew solemn in an instant. "I believe you. And I regret that for you, Eren."

My thoughts turned towards his suggestion. There was no doubt that we needed the relief. I didn't wish this life to weigh upon Cohen as it had upon Malachi; I had lost him to it. But neither could I see Connor, with all his restless energy and quick-made plots, fitting peaceably among the Halevi. We were passive, quiet, and soft-spoken; we avoided attention. He was opinionated, loud, and witty; he clearly enjoyed making the people around him laugh. The idea itself was laughable. But a great deal had changed.

"I thought you left to find adventure," I told him. "How could a life like this one ever suit you?"

"I could ask the same thing of you," he responded. "I've never pictured you living outside the Temple — you, or any of the priests. We are doing what we have to do. Besides, this will be adventure enough for now. At least until the Halevi are allowed to return to Rivermouth where you belong. With Devland gone, there's more hope of that." His attitude shifted quickly. He smirked sidelong over at me. "Are you going to let me stay or not?"

"I never said you couldn't."

"You haven't said I could, either. How much does a man have to hint, Eren?"

"Cohen is the one in charge," I said. "You would have to ask him."

Connor's steps halted, and he turned to me with a wry look. We were eye to eye, though I always forgot, seeing as he was built so strong. "Cohen will do whatever you ask of him. That's the way of it. By right, you're still considered the High Priestess." At my surprised expression, he added with a grin, "I know more than you think I know, Priestess."

"You know I won't say no," I argued. "Clearly I won't. For all of the reasons you mentioned. You just want to hear me ask you to stay."

He laughed outright. "I'm relieved you understand me so well. We've reached a very good understanding here today."

I dryly shook my head, turning to resume my steps, half-laughing under my breath. *"I have very little understanding of you at all."*

"Oh, I'm simple enough to read," he asserted slyly. "When you wish to."

I shook my head again. We were at the front door of the cabin now; it had taken twice the time that the distance normally took to cover the small courtyard from the rickety shed. "You should go tell Cohen your plan. He's the one to ask."

Connor grinned at me. "All right. I will."

Late that afternoon, I loaded our little cart with the evening meal as I did every day close to supper time and led the donkey over the small pasture and through the trees that separated my cabin from Cohen's. Since the astonishing conversation with Connor, the day had passed in an unexpected peace, free for once of the boredom that had weighed on me for months and the sharp loneliness left by the loss of Malachi. My mind had been strangely quiet and at ease… even in spite of knowing that Devland was rampaging across the country as an angry madman. He seemed far away at the moment, part of another world entirely. Just now, instead, I was wondering what the outcome of Connor's conversation with Cohen would be. The two would have no doubt talked by now.

As I neared the cabin from a distance, I caught sight of Liev and Anshel steadying a ladder and giving direction to Connor, who was perched above on the barn roof. He held a wood-handled hammer and was repairing a leak from the top rungs of the ladder, replacing a few old wood shingles with new. The two priests had lamented that leak for sennights, which explained why they were watching the whole business with such keen interest from below. Both men called up from time to time with heartening cries and bits of counsel that no doubt did more to distract than to help. I told the Whisper wryly, *He looks at ease here already.*

From his height, Connor was able to catch sight of me as I directed the donkey to the front steps of the cabin. For a brief moment he ignored the priests and locked eyes with me across the distance, grinning with boldness. I was surprised he didn't call out whatever words were drifting through his head. He had always been a talker and clearly still was, especially fond of emptying his thoughts on me — however daring they might be. *Life on the farm will take a sharp new turn if he stays,* I reasoned.

I ignored him, hitched the donkey to the post by the steps, snatched up the large tray from the cart — careful not to jostle the covered bowls — and vanished inside. I had no need to knock on the door during the bright hours, though the priests always knocked and waited at my door for a response no matter what time of day or night it was. We considered this the central cabin and communal space between the four of us, and there was no need to be concerned about privacy.

I found Cohen seated at the table in the center of the main room just now, where the light was brightest closest to the fire. His gray head was bent over a broad leather harness which spilled over the entire length of the large table, his weathered hands hard at work with a sewing needle and heavy thread. His lips were pursed in concentration and his eyes were squinting over the tiny stitches he was making.

At first sight of him, I determined not to disturb him, but after only a few quiet stitches, he looked up, smiled at me, and said, *"Eren.* So good to see you doing well after last night's terrible news. I can see on your face you are well rested." He quickly set aside the items in his hands. "We should speak quickly, before the men come in to eat. Will that trouble you? *Opportunity is a shy guest; it does not stay long,* I always say."

Cohen's wise sayings often made me think of Malachi and smile. "Of course, Cohen."

After I seated myself across from him, he began at once. "You can already imagine it, I think, but young Connor asked my leave to stay on and help us with the farm until the Halevi return to Rivermouth."

"I figured he might," I answered, nodding.

"I told him it was a fine idea. We have need of his young strength and his knowing of the harvest, all the more now with so few of us left, and he plainly must have a place where he can stay hidden from the Raiders. But in speaking of it, he brought before me a matter that has made him look again at whether he should remain — a matter that calls for your voice."

This last part was new. I felt certain Connor would have mentioned any hesitation he had when I saw him today if there really was one. A quiet suspicion stirred that other motives were at work here. "What is it, Cohen? You know I will give what help I can."

Cohen smiled kindly. "I knew you would. You carry your duty on your shoulders with such seriousness, Eren. Malachi did a fine, fine job in shaping you for what you are meant to be."

At the sound of Malachi's name, the old priest stilled, his weathered face softening with sudden tenderness as grief and fondness flickered in his eyes. I knew he missed him as much as I did. He quickly returned to his point. "Connor let me know that when he was a boy, and close with Devland, he gave you much grief and did not leave you in peace. This I did not know before. He is very sorry for it now, of course — we all see the good man he has become — but still he fears that what once was may yet trouble you. He does not wish to make things harder for you, especially after the disrespect he showed you as a child. He even says he will not stay, if his presence would bring you further discomfort. Tell me, Eren — is this true? Does the past still weigh on you? I have never heard you speak of it."

The depth of Cohen's concern was so apparent, so compelling. He truly was devoted to my well-being. I saw no harm in answering honestly, though I was wary, wondering what boyish prank might be coming. "I bear Connor no ill will, Cohen. Like you, I can see that he has grown into a good man. He has dealt with us generously in seeking us out to bring the news he has, and I, too, believe he would be of great use in the work of the farm. If it is your judgment that he should stay, I am of one mind with you. We are in great need of allies in this hour."

"Oh, good," Cohen said with open pleasure. "I was hoping you would feel so. You know how careful I am to hold your place as High Priestess with the greatest respect — but still I asked myself whether those old wrongs he spoke of with such sorrow were not simply the work of a boy who needed a firmer hand than he had. *A disciplined boy grows into a prepared man,* I always say. I believe he has learned what he needed to learn, and now he need not carry the weight of it any longer."

"Well, you certainly know more about the raising of sons than I do, Cohen," I told him. "I will concede to your wisdom on the matter."

The older priest looked satisfied — so fully so that I believed the matter was laid to rest and our talk was at an end. I moved to stand, thinking my misgivings about Connor may have been ill-placed after all, and turned my thoughts again to setting out the evening meal.

But Cohen's voice kept me. "Eren, one small thing more, if you will."

I returned slowly to my seat, *wondering…*

His brow furrowed deeply; a look of great concern crossed his face. "I was hoping it might come from your own mouth, the invitation to Connor. As I said, he is full of regret — so full that he thinks it is better he should not stay, for your sake. If you were to offer it, I think it would give peace to his heart and show him that God has forgiven him, that the old mistakes no longer stand against him."

*There it was.*

I sat there struck dumb with wonder, unsure whether to be amused or take offense outright. Connor had played the moment to perfection.

For a fleeting instant, I could not help but admire his inner knowing of the priests and the ways we moved among ourselves. He had been watching more closely — or listening more keenly — than I ever gave him credit for in his youth. Or perhaps it was only a gift of shrewd instinct; there was no sure way to tell. Yet one thing was plain enough: he had foreseen what Cohen would do, and what request he would lay before me. His little design was clever. I stood at a crossroads — to expose him fully before Cohen, who would well heed his High Priestess, and yet in doing so I risked seeming small-hearted and unmerciful. Connor knew this as well. He had predicted my response as surely as he had the priests.

I felt color rise to my face and hoped Cohen didn't notice. I answered quietly, "Of course I will ask him, Cohen. It will not be a difficulty for me."

The Priest was instantly thrilled and relieved. "*Wonderful.* I do not think we will regret this, Eren. Surely God has brought him to us at a most needful hour."

*A needful hour indeed.*

Only moments later, I told Cohen I would summon the men for dinner and returned outside to the barn. The three were just congratulating each other on a job well done when I appeared. I quickly greeted them and announced supper was ready inside, then added, "Connor, might I have a small word before the meal, please?"

Liev and Anshel thought nothing of this, turning aside to take the ladder and tools inside the barn. Connor's eyes were already dancing with mischief even as I took him in. We both knew very well what conversation had only just passed between Cohen and myself.

When I didn't speak immediately, he asked politely, "Priestess? Did you have something you wished to say to me?"

I was wry as I turned my back on him to move for the cabin steps. "I wonder if you are too shrewd to live among us," I tossed over my shoulder. "You might become the puppeteer and we would become your puppets."

He burst into snickering laughter — low, so the men wouldn't hear from within the barn. He followed me with an easy gait. "You're not seriously angry with me, are you?"

"I should be. You deserve it."

"But you aren't."

I stopped suddenly and faced him. He was right, of course. I wasn't angry, not anymore, not after the hardships of the past two years. "No, I'm not. Even *I* can stop a moment and admire your craftsmanship," I added wryly.

He was still laughing, but he tried to explain with seriousness. "In truth, I just wanted to —"

"Oh, I know *very well* what you wanted, Connor Shannasee," I insisted.

Standing there at the foot of the steps, revelation struck me for the second time today. Somehow, I realized, the losses of the past two years had leveled us. The title of High Priestess was little more than a courtesy — for the time being at least — and along the way I had quietly let go of the notion that I must always guard a rigid decorum, or demand it of those around me. Life as an outcast and living under the oppression of hardship had taken it from me. And I had to admit to myself, beneath my general dislike of Connor, that it was good to see someone from home — a familiar face. I missed Rivermouth, and he was the only sign of the community since the Exile. The truth of the matter was, sadly, that there probably *was* no one else the Whisper could find with a bigger heart for the welfare of the Halevi. We had been cruelly thrown out and left to wander. And here he was, filled with kind words towards us, loyal to a tribe not even his own. He had sought us out for Malachi's sake and for mine, and that was far more than Devland would have done.

I sighed at last in surrender. "Connor, Cohen and I have discussed it. We would be delighted if you would stay with us as part of our community. Would you?"

I had conceded the fight.

His dark eyes were quick to dance again. His freckles, which he had never outgrown, were strongly apparent across the bridge of his nose in the wintry light, only adding to his look of boyish devilry. "It honors me that you would ask, Eren, especially given our, um, *difficult* history. I'd be delighted to stay."

I wondered if the man ever stopped playing. It was no wonder he hadn't been all that successful in a camp full of hardened Rebels and Raiders.

I shook my head. A smile was threatening to pull at my mouth, but I worked hard at reining it in. "I only have one condition."

"And what is that?"

My tone changed to a quiet seriousness now. "You must not do it again. If you find you cannot resist the urge to trouble me, so be it — I have decided it's harmless enough and I have made my peace with it — but you must leave the other priests beyond your mischief. Their great gift for mercy and forgiveness are what makes our tribe beautiful. It is not a thing to be taken advantage of."

Connor gave a quiet smile, as if he was privately admiring of my response. "There are many things that make your tribe beautiful, Priestess."

*He was also deeply charming.* I wasn't yet sure how I felt about that.

I opened my mouth, but he hastily cut short the coming rebuke with laughing agreement. "— *but yes,* I will do as you ask."

In spite of his teasing humor, strangely, I knew he meant it. "Very well then," I declared. "You can stay."

He acknowledged this with a formal nod. "The High Priestess has spoken. I am grateful."

I found it amazing how offended I once was by these little quibs only a handful of years ago. In this bleak landscape in which I had been living for some time now, they were somehow refreshing, like a fresh wind blowing through a stale shadowed place. *How different everything was...* In my immaturity, I had misjudged him badly in those yesteryears.

I couldn't help but break into a smile, which he had surely hoped for. Liev and Anshel were exiting the barn now, approaching, and the two of us headed up the cabin stairs, our conversation over.

To my surprise, just as Connor's hand closed around the latch, he spoke quietly. "By the way, I have no wish to vex you, Eren. I never have."

As a boy, he would never have felt the need to offer clarity after relentlessly tormenting me. He had indeed grown into a man — steadier in himself, less staggered by me. Yet he also didn't see the need to explain his deeper reasons. Without another word, he stepped inside.

# 7.

I was right. Life on the farmstead changed greatly when Connor joined us. Within only a short time, his young strength seemed to burn energy into every priest left on the property. They were more fruitful that spring than we were in the two planting seasons we had known here. Malachi would have been amazed, as indeed I myself was, to see how much work was accomplished, what vigor returned to all of the men with his presence in the fields and barns. Connor did twice the work as any of them and seemed to never break into a hard sweat, yet this only served to encourage them more. He alone knew more of the work than all of us had learned together in two years, which sharpened our choices and kindled the belief that this might be our richest year yet. With his help on the land, the priests at last felt steady enough to set aside one day each sennight for prayer and worship, and it renewed them all the more.

As spring quickly deepened, there was more laughter heard in the fields, barns, and cabins. The priests took to Connor almost at once, as though he were one of their own, or at least as though he reminded them keenly of their wider kin and the Rivermouth community. A life returned to the farmsteads that had seemingly drained away with Malachi's death, one that was new and filled with the hope of springtime. Though some part of me wished Malachi was here to enjoy the change and benefit from it, I was grateful. We had needed it so desperately. I was quietly glad as well that Connor kept his word and never again made sport of the priests. He took a simple joy in them, cherished their fellowship, and freely stepped into the place of young counsel and guide over all the labors of the farmstead.

At some point early on, I carried fresh muffins over to the priests during their mid-day break. This was an almost daily habit I had formed since Malachi's death in hopes that my presence might encourage them, and to see for myself that they were staying warm and in good health. That day they were in high spirits and took glad advantage of the brief respite, then drifted back to the fields and their tasks with faces full of quiet satisfaction. They were singing as they went, which brought joy to my heart. I couldn't help but smile to see them so content.

Connor was the one who lingered behind for a moment to help me reload my now-emptied baskets back into my little cart and do the heavier work of re-hitching the donkey to the wooden shafts before I set out.

"I nearly forgot to tell you, Eren," he announced as he assisted me, "I have other news from home… though you'll probably not wish to hear it."

At my sudden change in expression, he added quickly, "Nothing of *that* sort. Garwin is married. He has a child already, and another on the way."

I was puzzled. "Why would that be bad news?"

He grinned a brief wry grin. "I figured you were sweet on him. He was certainly sweet on you."

I shook my head. How long ago that seemed, as if an age has passed since those days. "I was neither sweet on him, nor does it surprise or disappoint me to hear the news. Of course Garwin was going to marry quickly. And babies are a way of life in the other tribes; I would expect that, too. You are the one who has surprised me, truthfully," I confessed.

By now Connor was connecting the harness to the driving saddle on the donkey and looked up, suddenly delighted. "I have? How so?"

"In truth, I hadn't expected to find such astonishing *goodness* in you."

He burst into a low snicker. Done now, he extended a hand to help me step up into the little cart, handing me the reins. His eyes were laughing up at me as I seated myself on the wooden bench. "I suppose I *did* have a devilish streak."

From this new position above, I considered him very wryly for a moment. He had maintained that innocent farm-boy image since his arrival, but there was still a daring light in his eye that always sparked at the sight of me. I constantly carried the sense that he was imagining all sorts of mischief towards me. *"I'm not sure you don't still."*

He looked even further delighted. "That's why I'm here, don't you know?" he quipped. "So you can keep me on the straight and narrow, Eren."

Then he laughed outright and bounded away with that endless energy of his, off to work with the priests.

For all the newfound gladness of the farmstead and the priests, during this time I still missed Malachi sorely. Nights continued to be difficult, particularly in the evenings after Cohen, Liev and Anshel had departed. This was when I was accustomed to his company, as I had been my lifelong. Even the priests had the companionship of one another in the small hours. Old conversations with Malachi drifted back, when I had realized I was set on a path of severe aloneness without him and he confirmed there would be costs to my call as a High Priestess. Surely I was paying a little of that price now.

I couldn't help but wish Devland had made different choices; if he had, even now we could know each other, visit one another. He might have even joined me in the Temple and we could have shared both lodging and companionship. He had ruined everything with his bitterness, and even lost me Malachi early — my one companion in this life. I continued to weep many quiet tears, calling on the Whisper to give me a grace and help me endure these hard moments until my reward arrived, whatever it might be.

One day after the spring planting was finished, when summer temperatures had begun to set in, Cohen and Connor led an inspection of all the cabins on the property to find what larger repairs were needed on rooftops and in the walls and fireplaces. The project created a great excitement amongst the two little farms; this was fundamental work that had been long overdue since our arrival, and finally and at last our lives could be improved in this way.

For a few days this left a handful of priests in and out of my cabin at all hours, with Connor climbing around on the rooftop overhead calling down thoughts to the others, peering up the chimney with a thoughtful eye, or moving continually through the two-room cabin scrutinizing its condition. With him came an undeniable burst of life. He was forever cracking some joke to make the priests laugh, or calling out something witty and wry about what he found in his searching. It was plain they delighted in his company, chuckling together over his humor, doting on him with affection.

There was little of my work I could do on these days, so I spent most of it standing around watching or serving the priests cool water and small refreshments. During this, Connor seldom spoke to me, yet I often caught his laughing glance when I fell within his sight, as if all his merriment were meant for my sake. His opinions proved as plentiful as his playing, I observed, and the men seemed to enjoy them no less.

"He speaks with good sense," Cohen told the others with a pleased smile, within Connor's hearing. "An honest man."

They all murmured their agreement, nodding with warmth.

To which Connor turned slightly from his place where he was knelt by one of my front room walls and raised his brows at me wickedly, with dancing sparks in his eyes. He took a secret amusement in their praise of him in my presence.

It was at the end of one of these days that he was preparing to leave when I stopped to offer him some water outside the front of the cabin. The other priests were already drifting away, eager to be off for their supper. He was still setting down a few charcoal notes on a scrap of paper, thoughts distracted by the poor condition of my exterior walls.

"Your cabin needs the most work of them all, Eren," he announced. "It's beyond me how you and Malachi withstood the cold of the last two winters. And your chimney is in bad need of a cleaning. It must pour out smoke dreadfully."

Still bent to his notes, he failed to see the small shrug I gave him. I was remembering many days that the heavy smoke drove me out of the cabin, especially in my early attempts at cooking. "In truth, I thought it was my poor cooking."

Then he did look up, eyes sparking, unable to resist a little laugh. "Well, you were never meant for the life of hearth and home. You've been doing what you must."

I acknowledged this with some surprise. It still seemed foreign to me that Connor so readily understood my role and position in the Halevi. "*A compliment.* I half-expected a tease instead."

He recognized the mug of water I was offering for the first and pocketed his notes, reaching for it. He did not think anything at all of the fact that he had just honored me in this way.

"I can offer a compliment," he defended himself, drinking his fill. "In point of fact, I'm rather good at them."

"Is that so? I wonder if you remember when you used to call me *Air?*"

The question took him unprepared. He nearly spit out the remainder of the water he was taking in, casting me a quick, laughing grin. "I regret you still have memory of that. At the time, I meant it as a compliment, in my boyish, roundabout manner. Not the best way, I grant you, yet I still meant it as a tribute to you."

"How so? You thought my head was full of air instead of good sense. I don't see the praise in that at all."

He threw back his head and laughed outright, as though my reaction after all of these years to his boyish barbs — though calm now, more direct and unflustered — was still high entertainment for him. Or else he found mirth in his own foolish bid for my attention. "I was poor at the saying of it," he amended, "but I meant that your influence was felt everywhere you went. It was as though you moved in the very air about us, ever inspiring and guiding others to better choices. You still bear the same air, Priestess."

Then I laughed disbelievingly. Even now his words held a wry note in them. As for his perceiving any holy *air* about me, I was puzzled. It was a strange thing — strange, too, that he should truly acknowledge me as High Priestess of the tribe, and not mock or make light of my place.

Wordlessly, I retrieved the mug from him, preparing to return to the cabin. Then a sudden, unbidden impulse dared me to stop. "Did you truly count me as beautiful — or was that yet another clever bait to win my notice?"

At this, Connor's brows lifted in surprise and swift interest. In that moment the sinking sun sent fire-gold light through the trees at my yard's edge, striping his face with shadow and catching the dark gleam of his eyes as he carefully studied me. A warm wind whispered through the leaves and swept the tall grasses nearby with a sound like the wind chimes we once hung in the courtyard of the Temple.

He broke into a short laugh. "I wasn't playing with you."

At my silence, he shook his head and gathered fresh resolve, as though set on persuading me. "Do you remember that day in the Temple courtyard, when I came to give my farewells —"

"Of course."

He gave a crooked grin. "*Exquisite.*"

"I was dressed priestly that day — "

At the memory, his expression shifted, quite unmoved by this appalling truth. "I know. *Wondrous.*"

He ever had a touch of the scandalous. Before I could answer, he went on lightly, as though so intimate a confession was not a hard or uneasy thing for him at all — almost as if he took pleasure in speaking of it with me as freely as a friend. "And remember that day when Garwin and I caught you just after you'd been worshiping?"

My voice was growing noticeably quieter. "*Yes.*"

"I thought I would never recover." He laughed under his breath.

Then his dark gleaming eyes darted up and caught and held my own. "Does it flatter you, Priestess?"

When I said nothing, unable to, he concluded lightly, "I'm of the opinion it does flatter you."

How smug he was. He enjoyed that fact. He was too good at reading me… even thoughts I had not yet admitted to myself. This had been the way with us since childhood, I realized.

But he wasn't done yet. "Which," he shrugged with sudden candor, accompanied by a short laugh, "flatters *me* exceedingly."

I couldn't help but utter a compulsive laugh at his logic. *He was flattered because I was flattered by his flattering.*

Suddenly, Connor's eyes gleamed afresh at me across the two feet that separated us; he shook his head in wry amazement. "*That laugh* — it's going to be the end of me, I swear."

Then he quickly moved away, leaving me behind, as if he expected nothing whatsoever from me in return, while I stood shivering unexpectedly in the warm summer wind.

A subtle change comes over a woman when she knows a man thinks she's as stunning as Connor described — when she knows she holds some quiet power over him, drawn out by no more than the sound of her own laughter. It was, for one thing, a distraction; and for another, it kept me watchful in Connor's presence. He was not as Garwin had been, whose simple affection was plain and whose hopes were easy to read. Connor did not pursue me, nor did he declare any intent that I could discern; he spoke no open claim of feeling or desire for more. He was simply there — full of an easy, likable warmth — and he took delight in entertaining all who fell within the range of his presence.

He was ever catching my eye with that rakish grin of his, hoping, if he could, to draw my laughter with his story-telling, or at the least stir my reply by expressing some strong opinion of his own. It was no less baffling for all of that. There was no courtship in it, no singling me out in any marked way; he sought the same mirth from the priests if he could glean it. I would have better known how to answer him if he had been the man I once believed him to be at seventeen — the kind who, with oily beguiling words, would entice a girl and lure her into the woods in a fever of passion, with the wholehearted intent of stealing her virtue. But this Connor — charming, a little wicked at the edges, and yet oddly indifferent — I could make neither head nor tail of him…

Yet I couldn't wholly deny the pleasure of knowing that my laughter held a power to dazzle him. Weak though it was, the knowing of it tasted strangely sweet. It stirred a part of my soul starved of Malachi's love and watchful regard — a part I had quietly folded away when I believed my life would be spent in solitude. I wondered what Malachi would have said to all of this; how he might have answered it; whether he would ever have given his approval to such girlish whimsy in his novice. And more than all else, I wondered how he would have counseled me.

In the sennights that followed, I sought the Whisper more than once over this new frailty, yet no clear word or guidance came. Not for the first time since Malachi's passing, I greatly longed to confide in him. Of all the prophecies he had ever given me, this potentiality was not in them. He had spoken to me of knowing kings and princes; of interpreting dreams and spiritually advising men of great importance; of somehow uniting the Halevi and returning us to Rivermouth; of men so dedicated to my purpose that they were willing to make great sacrifices for me. He talked about the cost to me personally, and great rewards if I remained faithful to the call. But there had been no mention of attraction or the quiet possibility of love, and especially from a man outside of our tribe. His silence from the grave left me uncertain.

As the weeks of summer turned, I fell prey to that weakness more than a few times and sought Connor's face out when I walked past the fields where the priests were working. If the men were gathered in clusters in the barnyards on the other farmstead when I was in the vicinity, I listened for his laughing voice, trying to account for his presence. I tried to tell myself I was only lonely, but it was of no use. I enjoyed it every time his eyes caught mine. He always had an impish grin to give, or a quick wave before he returned to his work.

It was Cohen who finally broke my uncertainty on the matter. We had chosen to have supper in my cabin on this night, and he lingered behind afterward, telling Liev and Anshel go on without him. This was not so unusual upon the occasion when he had something to discuss that concerned my position as High Priestess. Cohen still held my place in the tribe in high honor, as well as the promise borne by all the priests that I would one day unite us and lead us back to Rivermouth — though for the present I was little more than his cook and housekeeper.

I was already removing dishes from our small table when he paused to consider his next words. A slight frown played between his weathered brow, making him look very wise in the feeble light cast by the flickering fireplace across the small cabin. "Eren, there is a small thing I wanted to speak of with you. Nothing serious — only… it seemed right to put it before you."

I paused to take him in more fully. Just now the fire gilded the long fall of silver hair at his temples and kindled quiet embers in his deep-set eyes. His long beard, thick and time-worn, caught the glow in scattered threads of gold, while the rest of him remained wrapped in dusky cloth and silence. He was very solemn.

"What is it, Cohen?"

He announced it at once. "I have taken notice that young Connor's eyes follow you everywhere you go."

My heartbeat quickened in surprise. "Do they?"

I had been so occupied with my own lack of restraint that I had not been aware of it. *Was this true?*

"I didn't think it had come to your knowing yet," Cohen said, at my reaction. "That is exactly why I could not keep silent about it. I am often beside him, and I have seen how he looks toward you, time and again these past sennights."

His words struck me on more than one count, though relief outweighed the rest. Malachi's eye toward me had always been tender, but keen as a hawk's, while Cohen's fondness for me, combined with my place as High Priestess, had made him somewhat blind. To him I was the purest soul ever to walk the world — and perhaps I was, in part. After all, I had not noticed Connor's attention.

I set the dishes I was holding down on the table carefully, moving slowly so as not to give myself away. My heartbeat was thunderous. "Are you uneasy about it at all, Cohen?"

He shook his bearded head sagely, considering the answer with a ponderous air. "No, no — not in the least. Only that it should not trouble you. It is your comfort I have in mind. Connor is a good young man — of the best in Rivermouth, I would say. He understands our tribe and does not force himself upon our ways. I can easily see him staying with us all his life, lending his hands where there is need. I do not believe he wishes you harm."

I attempted a natural smile. "I'm of the same mind. He seems harmless."

"Then I'll not say anything to him," Cohen decided. "And if ever you want me to, you have but to ask. '*We are not put on this earth for ourselves,* after all, *but are placed here for each other,*' I always say."

I nodded. "Of course, Cohen. And I thank you. You are ever good to look out for me and I am most grateful."

He moved for the door then, the conversation over. But then, suddenly, just as he reached for the latch, he paused and turned half-way back, his heavy robes *swishing* with the swiftness of the movement. "I think he pays us all a compliment with his interest in you," he added. "You are our High Priestess, after all. And I, for my part, believe you are the sweetest, loveliest soul God ever set upon this earth. Malachi thought so too, I know it well. Young Connor would be blind in both eyes not to see a treasure like you."

This was a rare compliment from Cohen, but not a surprising one. He had always doted on me, as had Liev and Anshel. My voice softened even more. "Thank you, Cohen, thank you. You honor me."

*"You know —"* He paused again, as if considering whether he should say what he wanted to next. "Malachi wished — and he prayed — that you should marry. I do not know if he ever told you this. He wished it for your own sake, so that you would not be alone. It troubled his heart to think of you solitary after he was gone. And yes, he wished it also for the sake of his blood, that the line of priests might not fall away with you. Still, he did not know how such a thing could ever be made in any practical way. For all his faith, until the Whisper spoke on the matter and showed the will of God, or until he saw the beginning of it with his own eyes, he could not know if it would ever come to be."

This was the greatest marvel he had told me tonight — far greater than learning that Connor's private thoughts ran towards me. My thoughts wheeled in a sudden, new course.

Cohen quickly saw my reaction. "*Ah* — so he never told you. Then it is just as well that I have. He must have kept silence so as not to raise a hope for something that was likely beyond reach."

His old eyes softened and caught the light of the fire; his whiskered mouth, nearly invisible beneath his beard and heavy mustache, pulled into a small smile. Cohen had no mischief or cunning in him, not like Malachi had had, certainly not like Connor did. He was entirely guileless when he added quietly, "Perhaps the Whisper is making a way for it after all — *who knows?"*

Then he shuffled out the door into the darkness, pulling it softly behind him.

Knowing Malachi's thoughts helped bring a peace, and with that peace, suddenly I found I was not so eager for Connor's glance. Somehow the power of it had been broken. Even hearing from Cohen that Connor stood in much the same case as I did did not, to my surprise, stir any greater desire in me. I was strong again, which relieved me, much more than the tingling possibility of what could be or might be.

I spent the next three days at my cabin, more focused on tasks that I had scarcely attended to in many days, or had put aside altogether. We were nearing the autumn months now and the little vegetable plot beside the house stood in need of harvest, as did the apple and pear trees in the front yard. After this would come the long days of canning and preserving — work I never welcomed. Once again, I missed my days of prayer in the Temple, which now seemed like a leisure beside this. Still, the solitude gave me room to pray in my own way and to settle my spirit. And my heart, for all its quiet ache, could not keep from gladness when I thought on Malachi's wishes for me. He would not have liked that I spent this year so much in tears, alone and without him.

It was at the end of the third day that I found myself perched high on a ladder leaned against the pear tree, woven basket in hand, when I heard my name called from below. I hadn't heard anyone approach and was surprised. Ordinarily in the bright hours the priests called out a greeting before arrival so as not to startle me, and I had been so caught up with the task at hand and the pleasant sounds of summer winding to a close around me that I had heard no footfalls. I glanced down through the fruit-laden branches, surprised to catch sight of Connor peering up at me.

I was immediately concerned. I rarely saw him alone or not busy at work with the others, and would especially expect all of them to be heavily engrossed right now, during harvest. Even from here I could see he had come straight from the fields, dressed in dirty breeches and sweat-stained shirt sleeves.

"What is it?" I asked him sharply, moving down the rungs as quickly as I could manage.

His hands reached out to steady the ladder.

*"What's happened?"*

He called back, in nearly the same tone, "I could ask the same thing of you. *What's happened with you?"*

Now I was confused. As soon as my feet touched the ground, I turned to him with intense concern. We had faced so many deaths, so much trouble, so much sickness among the tribe in the past few years. "Are the priests well? What's happening?"

Connor's expression broke into mild amusement over our back-and-forth. "Nothing is the matter, Eren. *Rest easy.* I have not seen you these three days, and the priests said nothing of it, so I came to see that you were not ill — or worse. I suppose I have grown to feel some small charge for everyone on the farmsteads, yourself included."

I confess, his words made my heart quicken for reasons other than relief, but I chose not to give any hint of it. Instead, I lingered a moment, studying him with a faint, disbelieving smile. Dried mud caked his boots; his flame-bright hair was more disorderly than usual; smudges of dust and dirt had left grimy patterns on his face. Clearly, he had hurried here, snatching the first spare moment he had.

"You could have asked one of the priests and saved yourself the trouble of coming all the way," I concluded.

He gave a crooked smile. *"No. I could not."* He reached for the basket and lifted it from my hands. "Just the same, I see you're well enough. What was it that kept you tucked away in your cabin, might I ask?"

I blinked at him more innocently than I felt. "I had work to do, what else? It's the season for busyness. Why couldn't you ask?"

"Even priests have a romantic bent, Priestess," he quipped wryly, laughter already rising. "I suppose you've never noticed. No doubt you're far too removed from worldly thinking for that."

This caught me by surprise. I scoffed. "The *Halevi?* That's not worldly thinking, just good sense. I hardly think they could be found guilty of such romantic notions."

He shrugged and came back to his former thought. "Speaking of good sense, I've been here these many months, and never once have you vanished for so long as this. During harvest I would have thought you'd be out cheering the priests on in the fields with your deliveries of fresh water and those terrible little muffins you make — whatever you call them —"

He was expecting a better explanation than I had given, just as I didn't believe that he came himself because the priests were impossible to ask after me. Reaching out, I reclaimed the basket with a firm hand, paying no heed to his jibe at my cooking. "You should have asked Cohen. He would have thought nothing of it."

"You're still their Priestess," Connor announced wryly. "They would have questioned my intent, no doubt."

"Since when has such a thing ever troubled you? They would only have thought you kind and full of care," I said firmly. "After all, you bear some charge for us all now," I added, coyly.

*"You're still their Priestess,"* he repeated.

I did not fully grasp what we were each driving at with such persistence, save that neither of us wished to concede our point. I met his gaze squarely, my face set. *"Yes, but I'm still a woman."*

At those words, the very air between us shifted, and a spark of awareness leapt to life in Connor's eyes. I had meant only to insist that the priests would understand any concern he held for my safety, but in that instant I knew I had stirred something far more personal in him — and, unwittingly, laid bare a motive of my own.

I blushed at my careless words and at the swiftness of his answering look, but Connor broke into a low, quiet laugh, his eyes holding mine with a new, unsettling steadiness. *"Don't I know it?"* he murmured.

Then he broke from my gaze and turned away. He knew full well what lay at the heart of this argument.

I was privately surprised. *He was never shy about anything, almost to a fault, yet he wouldn't broach this.* Heart beating quickly, I scrambled for a way to bring him back.

"Connor," I called, with a deliberate hint of exasperation in my tone. "While I have you here, I could use your help with these pears."

He turned back only halfway. Even this direct meeting of his eyes unsettled me just then, but I masked it with a brief, disbelieving laugh. "You came over for no good reason. The least you might do is put your time to good use and fill my basket — it's heavy work to haul it down the ladder."

*"For no good reas —"* His dark brows snapped together, and a spark of offended laughter kindled in his eyes, pulling at the corners of his generous mouth. My words had needled him, as I knew they would.

He didn't complete the thought. He strode back toward me, gaze flaring as he seized the basket from my hands. "Very well, Priestess. Allow me to do your bidding."

Up the ladder he shot, filling the basket with quick energy, while I steadied the wooden steps from below. At one point as he did this, I prodded him, calling up. "You know, you might just admit why you came. You were worried after me — enough that you felt the need to come and see for yourself that all was well."

Connor could never back away from a good verbal challenge, particularly not with me. His voice promptly filtered down from above, strained slightly from grasping for fruit beyond his reach. "All right, then. I was concerned for you. Are you content now?"

"I don't know why you made such a stir about it," I added. "All this roundabout speaking for no clear cause. It's no different than the day you said goodbye at the Temple all those years ago. We both know well enough why you truly came, even though you dressed it in another pretense altogether —"

There were other parts about that conversation that were just now coming back to me, parts I had dismissed and forgotten in the hardship of the past few years. He had called Garwin a loggerhead for reasons I had never bothered to understand. He had also hoped I would ask him why…

It was possible Connor was remembering the same conversation. He had gone utterly still in his work, and now regarded me through the thick leaves and dappled sunlight with a look that was no longer merely listening, but quietly intent. "I didn't dare say what I actually thought, did I?"

The secret truth was there between us, stretching its warm fingers down through the leafy branches unseen. I dared it to touch me, to be bold and make itself plain…

"Why not?" I called up to him. "You've always been too daring for your own good sense. I'm still shocked by you a good amount of the time. Why not just say what you keep circling around about?"

Even at that distance, with branches set between us, I could still catch the gleam in his eyes. His fiery red hair looked even fiercer somehow, though he was shaded by the fruit-burdened tree. His jaw tightened, then eased. My words had struck their mark.

*"Very well,"* Connor declared softly. *"I will."*

Then, very slowly, he broke into his familiar roguish grin, glittering eyes locked on mine. He didn't even trouble himself to descend the ladder. "If I ever even *thought* I had the smallest chance at winning your heart, Eren…" His deep voice lowered. "…I would call myself the most fortunate man that ever lived."

A deafening silence fell. My heart stopped and restarted again. He had given me more, much more, than I was expecting.

In a single breath, so much came to light — his persistent draw toward me since childhood, despite the river-wide differences between us; his pretense on the day he came to the Temple to say goodbye; the reason he thought Garwin was foolish to choose a

Rivermouth woman over me; and his careful hesitation to speak even now.

Memory stirred, and with it the rest of that final exchange on the day he departed from Rivermouth. I had thought he would never return because the community was too ordinary, too lacking in spark. Now I saw that there may have been a reason for the way he had always circled me. I suited his taste for the exotic quite well.

Before the Exile, I would never have been able to grasp how Connor saw me. It was only after we were cast out that the differences between the Halevi and the rest of the tribes grew so stark for me — and became something I learned to treasure, something to claim with pride. Not the hard pride that demands the world bend to its will and requires that all things fall in line beneath it, as Devland's pride had… and once, my own had as well, as I had shown to Connor. But a gentler pride, like a hidden coffer deep within the heart, glowing with the secret riches of knowing your own worth. That good pride had been gathering its wealth in me since our banishment, an iron truth at my core of who I was and what I belonged to. And now I saw, with sudden clarity, why Connor might love our tribe — and why he might hold me in such esteem. He had seen a treasure in me I myself had never been able to see.

Considering this, who could blame him, then or now, for holding back his heart or the depth of his admiration? I had harshly refused him as a girl, and now I stood as High Priestess. *The untouchable Priestess of the Temple…*

And yet the irony was sharp. I had never been more ordinary, more reduced in the eyes of the world, than I was at this very moment. Today was proof enough of that: barefoot in the fruit trees, wearing a stained apron and a simple hand-sewn dress, my bright hair bound under a dull scarf as if it were nothing beautiful at all. *Yet here he was,* still taken in, still drawn to me, just as I was to a quiet room filled with prayer.

And perhaps, in some strange turning, that was why I was drawn *to him* in return — that he could still see me as High Priestess, and still believe in me and in what the Halevi were, even now, when everything had been stripped away.

"You have a chance," I told him soberly.

One of Connor's hands tightened its grip on the ladder. *"What?"*

I smiled puckishly up at him. "You heard me, Connor Shannasee. You have a chance."

*"Since when?"* he barked. He was shimmying down the ladder now, trying not to spill the contents of the basket as he came.

He moved with such intent that I darted away from the tree, pretending to consider his question from a short distance. "If I'm being as plain with you as you've been with me — truth be told, probably since the day you arrived and warned us about Devland."

As soon as his booted feet hit the ground, I turned and accused him wryly, "You must know this. You must have at least sensed it at some point in the past short run of sennights, seeing as you've always had an uncanny ability to read me. I'm certain you just wish to hear me say it."

He didn't come toward me after all, but lingered at the foot of the pear tree, grinning, his eyes lit with a slow, dangerous fire. He set the half-filled basket at his feet with deliberate ease, each movement measured, controlled — like a hunter keenly aware of how close he stood to what he wanted. Connor possessed a startling measure of self-command when he chose to use it. "I didn't know it. I didn't dare dream of it. You forget too easily, Priestess — you're the Priestess. *But I do love it when you say things I want to hear."*

I had to laugh at this. I was glad I had retreated by a few feet; he looked playfully dangerous in this moment.

He pressed, "Was that the reason for your hiding these three days? Were you keeping from me? That much, at least, I sensed."

I refused to answer him. "You had better make good use of this chance. It's not a very big one."

*Oh, how his gaze glimmered…* as if he carried his whole heart within them, bright and unguarded. He wasn't bothered in the least by my warning. "Oh, I will. I intend to right the wrongs that have been done in your life, Eren," he declared daringly.

His words sent a quick shiver down my spine, my heartbeat loud in my ears. He was the most romantic-speaking creature I had ever heard. I laughed shortly, too quickly, as if it might save me from the effect of him. *"Like what?"*

"Well, for a beginning, I mean to lay claim to that first kiss," he decreed. "Brace yourself."

I felt my face flush hot; but to my surprise, he stalked away before I could laughingly smart something back, our conversation apparently over for the day.

A busy sennight passed. After the conversation with Connor and his worry over my welfare, I made sure I took time in my days to carry fresh water and victuals out to the priests in the fields. He was always there watching me with his wicked grin, mingled with an impish wink occasionally, but he said nor did anything unusual. I was coming to think he liked playing indifferent, as if it would draw me out more. I have to say, I was content enough with waiting until he made his move. It was a fun thing, this little game we were playing...

At the end of a sennight, after another visit to the farmsteads, Anshel happened to be the last priest to leave before moving back to the fields as the others were. As I loaded my baskets into the cart yet again and hitched the donkey, he mentioned offhandedly, "Young Connor's feelings for you have deepened, Eren."

Anshel's eyes were not even on me when he made the announcement, but on the men returning to the fields, Connor being one of them. He said it as though he had made an innocent observation.

"What makes you think so?" I asked him.

"When you used to walk by the fields, he grinned at you. After some time, he winked at you. Now he quietly watches your every move."

There was no hiding anything from the priests, I thought... except perhaps my own behavior, which they seemed entirely blind to. I hadn't done any grinning or winking, but I had certainly done my fair share of watching, and more recently, feeling self-conscious, which had to show.

Quietly, I joined Anshel in watching the men for a moment, our backs to the barns and scattered string of cabins where the priests lived. The worst of the summer heat had burned away, leaving an inviting breeze that blew over the landscape before us, parting the field crops like waves, rustling the pastures beyond dotted with cattle. We had rotated the fields again this year — corn where there were beans last year, pasture where there was corn last year. With Connor's arrival even the weather had improved, and this year's yield would be the largest we had managed yet.

Save for Connor, who was dressed in his usual Planters garb and walked with the energetic strength of a much younger man, the gray-haired, bearded priests painted a docile picture as they calmly strode out to the half-shorn corn field in their shifting robes under the late afternoon skies, their husking pegs and curved knives in hand. Cohen was already there to meet them at the edge of the field, waiting with the horse-drawn wagon for the shelled ears of corn to be thrown in. They were all listening to Connor tell some story; his joy-filled voice and their low chorus of gentle laughter drifted out to us on the wind.

"You're very watchful, Anshel," I told him.

He nodded sagely, never glancing over, as if we were quietly deliberating a scripture from the Holy Text with our eyes prayerfully focused on the horizon. "Do you agree with my observation?"

I frowned ponderously. "I have noticed the same progression, yes."

"What will you do, Eren?"

I paused long enough to give it some thought. "Feelings are not harmful, I suppose. I think I'm going to let him continue. Who knows? I might even return them."

Anshel did glance sidelong at me through his long beard then, smiling slowly. "I think you are playing with me."

I laughed at him, confirming it.

His kind eyes sparkled. "It's good to hear you laugh, Eren. It's been a hard year you've had."

"It feels good to laugh."

"Then maybe it's a good thing," he said warmly, "all that grinning and winking and watching."

I laughed again.

One early morning, in an hour of the third watch, long before I would have normally awakened, I thought I heard a soft shuffling noise on the short wooden platform that served as a front porch for my little cabin. This was scarcely loud enough to be considered frightening… though I was somewhat frightened for my chickens. I thought for certain raccoons had returned and were scurrying to the coop, ready to find breakfast. I dragged myself out of the creaky, wood-framed bed where I slept on one side of the central room of the cabin — I never could claim Malachi's room and it remained empty, with his things untouched — and wrapped myself quickly in a dress robe. This was hardly needed as a covering, seeing as my night gown was as heavy and modest as the robes I used to wear in the Temple, but it did serve to provide an extra layer of warmth for events like this. Quickly, I struck a light to my oil lantern and snatched up the whisk broom from where it stood nearby, then stumbled out the door into a rush of cool air, ready to face my intruder.

To my surprise, near my feet a pair of dusty boots shuffled, a dark-clothed body moved slightly, and I realized in a confused haze of sleep that someone was seated on the porch next to the front door. Drowsiness left me instantly. The warm light of the lantern hit the man's face, and I realized this was Connor, peering up at me with a face I had never known him to wear. He had the look of one who had been awake for hours, unlike myself. *Here was my raccoon…*

He pulled his legs up at the sight of me. "Eren —"

There was nothing in his voice to indicate that he was troubled, but I knew immediately he was. That he had come without word in the black hours before dawn was odd enough of its own weight. The priests had just finished bringing in the harvest, but there was still no end of work and the men left the fields each day utterly spent, even Connor. *Especially* Connor, as hard as he labored. He should have been sleeping like a stone in his bunk in the priests' cabins. "Connor — what troubles you?"

But he merely shook his head, as if clearing it with the dismissive gesture. Save for an occasional smile in passing, or a short exchange with Cohen about the work of the land, we had scarcely spoken at all for a sennight. He broke into a smile. "Nothing. Heavy dreams."

"Some dreams are real," I said at once. *"I don't suppose there is a need for this any more."* — This, as I set the broom aside.

His smile broadened. Tonight was a black, clouded one, which brought out the shifting light of the lantern more sharply, now flickering ghoulishly across his tired features. "Not these dreams."

"Are you sure you don't wish to tell me? I can be very helpful where dreams are concerned."

To my surprise, he caught my hand gently from below. "I'm sure, Priestess. They need no interpretation."

My heart broke into a low, contrary thud at this gesture; he had never touched me before. "Then can I offer you some food? I still have a few meat scraps from today's supper meal that I intended to make into a hash tomorrow. I could fry it up for you. You look sore-worn after all the labor of late."

To my further surprise, he tugged on the hand. "The way to please me could never be through your cooking or your serving, Eren. I'd rather you didn't do any of it. Sit here with me awhile, if you will. The assurance that you were safe was all I needed."

Now my heart melted altogether. I allowed him to pull me down next to him and we sat side by side in the shadowy darkness. After extinguishing the lantern, we said nothing for a long while, lingering in the shared warmth and the hush of morning. All tiredness had vanished the instant he touched me. His callused hand rested steady in mine, sure and unmoving. In that quiet contact something new passed between us.

The late summer breeze was mostly night-cool just now, before the sun rose and reminded us again in its plain-spoken way that it wasn't yet finished with the season. The light air moved softly through the fruit trees on the edges of the dirt-packed yard and over the rooftop of the cabin, brushing against leaves so gently they whispered, smelling faintly of turned earth drifting in from the fields and the endless odor of the manure we used for fertilizer, which seemed to linger everywhere on both farms. Now and then, mercifully, the breeze carried the pleasant hint of something blooming even at this time of year — not the loud perfume of spring, but a soft floral note coming and going. This was the kind of air that caused you to feel between things, especially on a peaceful night like tonight here next to Connor — between night and morning, summer and fall, sleep and whatever came next. For a while I breathed it in, thinking that it tasted like a promise I could not quite put a name to. I felt the Whisper's Presence and felt grateful…

Eventually, a quiet question rose and I felt comfortable asking it, as if this was the right time and place. His last statement had made me think of it. "What kind of life do you picture with me, Connor?"

His heavy boots shuffled against the old dried planks of the low porch. He answered just as quietly, but there was a hint of play in his voice. "The best kind. You'll pray and I'll pay."

I couldn't help but laugh, softly. "How will you pay?"

At my laughter, his warm hand came to life, squeezing my own and threading his fingers through mine, as if the sound of it drew him. "I'll work to pay all the taxes, and pay for the food, and pay any debt collectors that might come along."

"So you'll provide for me."

His speaking voice had a texture to it tonight that daytime never gave, softened by the darkness and the last few moments of unspoken companionship — not whispering precisely, but measured, unhurried, carrying only as far as it needed to. The sound seemed to sit in the air rather than travel through it, as though the quiet itself — or the Whisper — was listening. "Until the Halevi are restored to their rightful place and the community provides for you as it ought, yes. I will see to us. And even then, if what we have isn't sufficient, I'll take on work for hire, so you have provision enough to dedicate yourself to the Temple.

"This will never happen again, I can promise you that, Eren. When there is finally a steady flow into the tribe from the community, then I'll spend my time caring for the Temple. The tribe needs someone who will show the compound the respect its due as they upkeep it. It should not be trusted to just any laborer."

If he meant to win my heart, this was surely the way. With every word he spoke, I felt myself softening toward him, until at last I rested my head against his hard shoulder in the dark, drawing nearer to his warmth. "You've given some thought to this."

"Yes. Of course."

The answer was said simply, as though his commitment was as uncomplicated as the words. We both knew this was no easy thing he was agreeing to, however.

I said, "Malachi prophesied — and all of the priests believe — I will be the one who reunites us and returns us to Rivermouth."

"I've heard them say it in the past several months, many times. They encourage themselves with it all the time. I have no doubt of it," he confirmed. "I believe it."

Connor sensed my surprise. "There's no other way, Eren," he spoke with firm resolve. "There's no other way your story can end."

This sounded more like a personal vow than it did a prophecy or a confirmation of a spoken spiritual word, as Malachi or Cohen might have said it. Connor was not a priest or a king; he was a planter, a builder, a *doer*. But he was perfect for what we needed... for what *I* needed.

"What else?" I asked him. "What else do you see for the future?"

"I will see to it that you never lack for love... or laughter... or a warm refuge when you need it."

This was becoming too much. Tears surfaced, but I worked to swallow them back, trying to keep my voice light and the conversation flowing. "And you'll do this all while I live my days out in prayer in the Temple?"

"As it should be, Eren," he said gravely.

"And what will you get in return for this generosity? Surely you've thought of something."

"Of course." A smile played in his voice. "I'll get you — the High Priestess herself."

This went far beyond anything I had expected for my life, from the hour Malachi had warned me about the cost of my calling. This was more than Garwin could ever be. More than I ever thought anyone would wish with me and for me. Aside from the dream of the Halevi returning to the Temple, I hadn't known a hope like this these many years. What a soothing balm this was to my soul after the terrible rejection from Devland and the community, after the loss of Malachi and only a faint image of the future ahead. I could hardly take it in.

Tears came anyway, slipping down, dashing my cheeks with salty warmth. I tried to keep the emotion out of my voice, thankful for the covering of darkness. "That's truly what you want?"

"Nothing else seems right. You have to be in the Temple, Eren. I've known it since I was a boy. It's a terrible thing what Devland managed. You should never have been cast out from where you belonged. I'm going to help see you back there, no matter what it takes."

He was making self-command an intense struggle. I drew a quick breath, letting the feeling slip out with it, and offered a small laugh in return, as though I were only pleased and not so shaken. I would not spoil the moment — or the beauty of his vows — with the weight of emotion rising in my chest. "What about that adventurous spirit of yours? It drove you away from Rivermouth the first time."

He stirred then, a faint frown passing over him before a soft laugh followed. "You have to ask that? You *are* the greatest adventure, Priestess. *Look at you.* There's no one like you. I would have stayed if I ever thought there was a chance. My destiny is with you."

Now it was simply impossible to speak.

After a brief hush, Connor's hand shifted restlessly against mine, betraying the reply he hoped for before his words ever did. "You fell quiet, Eren. I'm unable to see your face in the darkness. What do you think? Of the kind of life I picture with you. Can you picture it for yourself? Speak honestly."

I took my time answering him, not to torment him, but because I needed to settle myself and felt he deserved the best answer I could formulate. I didn't know if I had the deep words to tell him how much what he had said meant to me, and why. Perhaps in time I could give him context for the weightiness of what he had just given, but for now I would simply have to offer what I had.

When I thought I could manage it, I answered thoughtfully, "In truth, I never pictured any of this. The Exile. Malachi's death — especially not so soon. Not life on the farm. Not even the chance to be loved. But I can imagine the life you've described. It's practical, and real, and —" I faltered again.

I found suddenly I couldn't say it. I was too shy, too at a loss for the intimate words that seemed to come more naturally for him. I couldn't tell him just yet that the plan held him, and that made it the best of any plan. I needed to take this to the Whisper in prayer and organize my thoughts and feelings on the matter.

I think Connor knew then, however. I suspected he understood my entire heart on all of it, and even the cause for my hesitation, when he broke into low, snickering laughter. *He had always read me with surprising ease…*

"That's answer enough for now, Priestess," he announced, amused. "No need to reach for more."

The intimate moment was broken. He dropped my hand and moved away, pulling himself strongly to his feet. He stood laughing down on me in the darkness. "I'll get more out of you yet. You'll see."

He had already stepped off the porch and was planning to move away, back towards the other farmstead, when I scrambled up to stop him.

*"Connor — "*

He paused quickly, a dark outline in the darkness. There was just enough light to glance off the edges of him, just enough to draw shape from shadow. His features were lost, but his broad shoulders were squared, his head bowed slightly. There was the slightest suggestion of breath as he waited for my parting comment.

*How I loved him in that moment.* He had not brought this dark shadow I stood in, but he meant to lead me into the warmth of the sun and keep me there. In that moment, I flung wide the doors of my heart and loved him without reservation.

I found my feet and shot off the porch, reaching for him, burying my nose in his hard chest without word. His arms folded about me as easily as breath. How warm he felt, my quiet refuge after a troubling storm. I very nearly gave way to tears all over again.

He sensed my heavy emotion and knew what to do with it. "I'll not let you down, Eren," he promised me, in the stillness; "Of that you can be sure."

# 8.

That fall was destined to be a brilliant one amidst the several that followed it, like a shooting star exploding in the night sky among the dimly lit stars, whisking past them all in a flash of light and glory. It was as if the Whisper had waved His hand and the broiling clouds calmed, tumultuous seas quieted, and the fierce gales of the past few years receded to a soothing breeze, leaving an opportunity for the earth to bear the fruit of love in warm sunshine.

The priests held a feast celebrating the harvest; we all prepared for winter in a spirit of joy; and Connor and I lost our hearts to one another more and more with each passing day. All at once, everything looked near and dazzling. The Halevi's return to the community felt only days, perhaps sennights, away. The future, so inviting and beautiful, looked just beyond the next horizon.

Connor told me once with great satisfaction, "Eren, you are the song, the riddle, the reason and the rhyme."

This made me flush and laugh softly. For all the poetry in his words, and the soft humor threading through them, I knew he meant it. He was seizing hold of this revelation more and more as he declared it.

Then I considered his words a moment, frowning. "A fine way you had of showing it in the early days."

Which made him snort outrageously and laugh much like he would have when he was twelve, with an abrupt blast that sliced through the air around us. "I will try to make up for all of my boyish efforts at getting your attention, I promise."

"I'm going to hold you to that," I quipped.

He laughed again. "I will."

We were in the belt of trees near my cabin when this conversation took place, hauling water in buckets from the little creek that ran through the edge of the property. With winter nearly here, Connor's time was freer and he liked to spare me as much work as he could. Fortunately for the priests, their homestead had two wells and wooden water channels piped to them, as did Cohen's cabin across the field; mine did not. This was a weekly chore for me that often made me miss the days in the Temple where Malachi's chambers had the ability to draw water right into his kitchen area.

Just now Connor lowered the heavy yoke from his shoulders, stopping short as we headed back toward the cabin. Around us, the late afternoon sunlight was a russet glow, filtering through the canopy of narrow trees above in warm, slanted beams, catching on drifting leaves that turned slowly in the air in colors of gold and ember-orange.

"Come here, would you?" he asked.

I presumed he wished to tell me something in earnest after our last few exchanges, and I retraced the few steps back to his side. As I stood before him, he looked into my eyes soberly with his dark sparkling gaze. As if the wind had struck some unseen bargain with him, ready with its atmosphere when he most needed it, the fall breeze rose at just that moment, threading through the trees with a restless murmur, brushing over the open skin on my bare arms and uncovered throat with a fine, papery edge, rather like the turning of a page.

Connor said with a quiet smile, "I vow to balance the scale of all of my injustices towards you, Priestess."

I stood held by his words for a heartbeat, taking them in along with the soft temper of the wind… the distant aroma of smoke from my chimney… the faint sweetness of the fallen leaves around us. There was something holy in his promise, touched by the Whisper's unseen Presence, braided with the quiet sounds and scents of the world around us.

Before I could respond, however, Connor reached out a gentle hand and pulled at the knot that held my heavy stream of hair at the nape of my neck.

Impulsively, I breathed a protest, "My hair will be a tangle." There was a day only a few years ago when the sacredness of the moment would have taken preeminence above all, but the work of things was always foremost on my mind, unfortunately, even when I didn't want it to be.

But Connor merely gave a muttered laugh. "*Eren* — let me kiss you, would you?"

This quiet rebuke was enough to see at last what he meant to do. With a soft laugh at my own blindness, I let him take the lead.

At once the air between us quickened — warm, living, *alive*. Over the span of the next few moments, Connor's magnetic gaze held mine as he slowly loosed my hair with his fingers. And then the autumn wind caught the long, unruly fall of red at my back, lifting it in a sudden rush so it billowed like a banner of flame behind me. The action became almost a sign of freedom; of Connor's promise of the future; of a change happening even now.

His eyes were wide and fully black now. Between us rose a tension thrilling and steadying, as though something unseen and mysterious, yet utterly real, was drawing us forward. Then, still with that same deliberate care, he lifted a hand to cup my face, bent to me, and brushed my lips with his own.

I gave myself to it, and to him. Time seemed to loosen its hold, allowing the world to slow. Distance collapsed. We had moved from two people solemnly observing each other with shining eyes to sharing the same breath, the same heartbeat. Something tender, holy, and deeply human passed between the two of us. In Connor's kiss was a promise I would not soon forget.

After a long moment he pulled back with a husky laugh. "Careful there, Priestess. I'm going to start to think you like this."

That broke the moment. Time began again; the earth drew near; chores beckoned. I laughed at him — happy laughter that came from the depths of my soul.

In those early days of love, Connor was forever making vows, each one sealed with laughter and good cheer; and I savored them all.

That winter we announced to the priests that we wished to be wed in the spring, which caused a tremendous amount of rejoicing. I had never seen Cohen beam with such joy. To my delight, the priests were as excited as we were, declaring all kinds of blessings on the two of us, eagerly volunteering to sing songs, say special prayers, and prepare a proper place on the property for the ceremony when the time came.

"Didn't I tell you they had a romantic nature?" Connor said, at my laughing surprise.

I thought the only way the season could have been more perfect was if Malachi had been there to share in it, but I took comfort in the fact that he would have blessed the union and wanted it for me. I knew he was watching from heaven with Joel and the other priests who had gone before us, cheering me on...

In the early months of spring, our plans were disrupted when Connor returned from a visit to the local village with news. He arrived at my doorstep with Cohen and Liev in the afternoon, all three wearing sober expressions. Seeing this, I quickly ushered them inside to the warmth of the cabin, where they seated themselves at my little table before the fire. I couldn't imagine what would make them appear so grim. Connor had gone to town for seed and other supplies we needed for the spring planting, nothing that would merit this kind of importance.

In the end, he gave the report, seeing as he was the one who brought it back with him. Whatever the news was, I thought, watching him draw breath to begin, he neither liked what it meant, nor how it would impact me. I could read that well enough just by the absence of light in his features.

"The King has ordered a census," he announced without preamble, then quickly added with wry disgust, "Though why he should be distracted by the number of citizens he has in Avan is beyond me, considering there are Raiders threatening to overthrow his kingdom. It seems to me he has other concerns on his hands."

Cohen was naturally not as expressive, but he did nod his head somberly. "I agree. It is plain his heart runs first to his own interests, not to the good of his people — such a pity. As the Holy Text teaches, *a foolish ruler brings sorrow upon those beneath him.* But go on, my son ..."

There was a quiet tension between the three of them, and it was clear they had already weighed the matter and its consequences for the tribe before arriving at my door.

Connor's eyes flicked to me across the little table. "This means the eldest child of every household must present themselves at Periburn and be entered in the castle register, or else face arrest. Cyric has even set a reward for those who name any neighbor who refuses, a kind of watchfulness meant to ensure that none hold back. And if any are too old or too frail for the journey, the next in line must go in their stead."

For a moment I was taken aback as the news of this settled in. I could see why they looked so sober. This would no doubt create unrest throughout all of Avan. For us in particular, it could force some of our priests to make the long journey to Periburn and badly disrupt the spring planting.

I looked between the three of them. "How soon? How soon is he calling for it?"

"Very — unfortunately so," Liev said darkly. "In the next two months."

I considered this with some alarm. *Did Cyric understand nothing of his own people?* Autumn would have been the wiser season for such a demand, when the harvest was in, the roads safer, and winter had not yet taken hold. Never in my lifetime had a census been called. "What is the King's purpose for the census? Do we know?"

Connor looked too irritated to answer, so Cohen provided this in his reasonable way. "We are not given leave to know the King's thinking, no."

"Cyric answers to no will but his own," Connor muttered.

Cohen nodded. "Sadly, yes. He has little care, it seems, for keeping the goodwill of his people. Most often a census serves the purpose of taxes — the more souls counted, the more coin may be drawn from them. At times a king wishes also to know how many fighting men stand ready, and who has come of age to serve should the need arise. And though it is not likely with Cyric, there are kings who seek such a count to know how many skilled hands they may call upon for the building of roads or fortresses. Any of these reasons may be at the heart of it, perhaps all of them — yet none are reasons a people greet with joy. In the end, such a demand is understood for what it is: a laying of power upon the people. You see, then, how little this speaks to Cyric's care for the good of Avan. Our King," he added softly, "is still a great needer of prayer."

Upon hearing this, my thoughts turned at once back to the Halevi. "Do we know how many of the priests are the eldest? How many do you judge will be sent?"

Cohen exchanged a glance with Connor before answering. It was plain they had already worked out a plan even before bringing it to me. "If this meets with your consent, Eren, I do not believe any of the priests should go save Liev alone. It is true, they are strong workers, and the Whisper has laid His grace upon them for the keeping of the farms — but the long road to the city would be hard and dangerous. *A fool's errand*, if you ask me. In any case," he added with quiet gratitude, "by the Whisper's mercy, few of them stand as the eldest in their homes. Most were given to the Priesthood as boys, and their families will answer to the King in their stead. Liev is the eldest of my sons — and among the hardiest — and he may stand for both the tribe and my house, for I myself am too old for such a journey now. I believe this will be enough to satisfy the King's counting."

Connor added, dry as old straw, "And any neighbors, too, who might be sniffing after a bit of silver."

"It does smell like an open invitation to turn neighbor upon neighbor," Liev said, with a small, knowing shake of the head.

We all held the Exile close in our hearts and probably always would, remembering that even the most loyal of community could turn sour if given the right motivation.

I moved on quickly, however, nodding in appreciation over the wisdom in Cohen's plan. "This sits well with me, Cohen. I give my word to it — without reserve." My gaze went then to Liev. "But you'll not be traveling the road alone, surely? It is no safe thing — with so many strangers on the roads —"

A surprising silence fell, one that was loaded with meaning and intention. Connor's expression darkened and his expressive eyes came to rest on my face as the charged stillness hung in the little cabin, as if he was disturbed by what he had to say next. It was plain that the full weight of the news he carried had not yet settled on me.

"The census beckons every man, woman, and child throughout the whole of Avan, Eren." His voice held an edge I had not heard since he had discussed Devland on the day of his arrival.

Cohen added, his voice soft with a tender ache, "This means you, Eren — with Malachi gone, you are the eldest of your house."

My heart picked up rhythm at once, considering it. For safety's sake, Malachi and Cohen had rarely allowed me to accompany any of the priests to the nearby village when they went. In the beginning months of our arrival, Malachi had merely wanted to establish a relationship with the local community first and ensure that we would be well-received. He had little idea what kind of men roamed their streets or weighed their decisions. At the least, he knew the strength of curiosity, and he would not wake it with my presence — not after what had befallen in the mountains with the Raiders. He never had to explain that my physical characteristics and age still stood out starkly, even in this community, especially as a young woman living amongst a group of elderly, mystical men. Then later, after Connor's arrival, the younger man and Cohen had agreed that it was safest for me to stay away because of Devland. Unlike Connor, I never feared for my own safety where Dev was concerned, yet I knew well how easily I might be recognized — and I would lay no trouble at the door of the Halevi, nor at Connor's, should he learn where they were hidden. All of us had agreed that we should take no risks.

At the moment, seated across from them all, my gaze went first — and longest — to Connor, whose eyes were held just as fast on mine. The meaning of it all unfurled at once — I would take to the road, far from the shelter of the farmsteads; I would stand more exposed while all the country was bound for Periburn; and, most keenly of all to my heart just then, our wedding must be set aside until my return.

"At least the spring planting can continue without interruption," I said, faintly. "There's that."

My words drew an instant, protective stirring in Connor. He growled, "You'll not be leaving without me. We've all already agreed that I will escort you both to Periburn."

Cohen was still grieved. "It is for the best, yes — though my heart struggles, this risking of our High Priestess. Would that you did not have to go at all."

"Or Connor," Liev put in. "We have sore need of him for the spring planting. *Sore need.* Without him, the tribe stands in a perilous weakness, God keep us."

They all seemed to hold the same unspoken thought — that danger would surely meet us — and it hung in the air, heavy as a storm yet to break. Even the stout logs of the cabin walls pressed close, as though casting their own silent warning against our leaving the farmsteads.

I sought to lift the weight a little. "The Whisper has dealt kindly with us these past seasons," I said. "It is not the hour, I think, to lay the worry on too thick. Surely it won't cost us too much time there and back if we take the horse and cart — and we'll be the safer for it. How long a journey will it be, then?" I asked Connor. "A few sennights at most? Might we be home before the end of spring planting? The wedding would only be put off but a month, would it not?"

But Connor was less concerned with the details and was plainly not ready to share my hope. He wished for me to see the weight of what lay ahead before anything else. "Eren, the road runs straight through lands where Devland's Raiders are well known to tread," he said, grimly. "They lie squarely in the northward path to Periburn."

Then, as the cruel truth broke open for me, he went on in a darkened voice, "The King has witlessly found a way to place every soul in peril for the sake of his own grasp on power. He has offered the people no true protection at all, sending them straight through the Raiders' lands — as though he doesn't yet believe Devland's men are a serious problem."

Liev piped up, "He is inviting trouble, that is certain."

"And you and I will especially be at risk, Eren," Connor continued. "I have no doubt Devland will be watching the roads for those he has an eye out for. We'll need to travel with others as much as possible, and blend in as best we can. We may be back within a few sennights, yes, if we meet no trouble, but this will be no easy thing ahead of us."

Cohen added softly, in full agreement, "Every care, yes — every care we must take, that is certain. *A prudent person foresees danger and takes precautions,* I always say. The priests must all be told to pray."

The three of us left only two days later, waving goodbye to the priests from our perch on the small horse-drawn cart as we made our way down the lane leading away from the farmsteads. We agreed not to put the journey off, reasoning that the sooner we were back, the sooner the priests might have help for the spring planting, and Connor and I could return to our own plans. I also suspected Connor just wanted to have it done and behind us. The King's selfish census had unavoidably flushed us both out, and in his mind Devland was a sinister face lying in wait, much like a hunter watching the heavens for water fowl after his dogs have startled their quarry from the brush. Connor was never one to draw back from a challenge — least of all when it bore the look of a fight set in his way.

Fair weather was with us, thankfully, which helped in dispelling the feeling of impending doom that had seemed to linger with me ever since the discussion with the other three. Even then, I did not truly believe Devland would ever do me mortal harm, not even at his worst — though for Connor, I carried a quiet fear. There was ill blood between them now. At the same time, there was simply no one else who could escort me, and no one I would have preferred, either. I was left merely to put my trust in the Whisper to watch out for our care and bring us safely home.

Very soon on our journey south we discovered the census had indeed brought out many caravans and packs of citizens traveling across the country on horseback, in wagons, or on foot. The early spring weather had not hampered those who needed to return home quickly and the roads were often full, enabling us to join many of them and blend in in a friendly manner for long stretches of time just as we had hoped. To draw as little notice as possible, Cohen urged us to keep one shared story, so we told everyone we met that Connor and I were newly wed and that Liev was my father. This was an easy enough story to live out and indeed seemed to help distract. In the eyes of everyone around us, Liev looked like a doting elderly father rather than a mysterious priest, while the image of two young lovers seemed to deflect from any questions I might have faced for being unnaturally tall, with flaming red hair and unusually blue eyes. Connor's physical presence — his strong build, bold tongue, and keen eye — was another natural deterrent from curiosity or harassment which I was grateful for along the way.

Aside from the new circumstances in which we found ourselves, nothing much changed for Connor and me for the first several days of travel. We were still very much in love and had eyes for only each other. I scarcely took note of my surroundings, though in truth I hadn't been beyond the farmsteads in more than a year and was little used to dealing with anyone but the priests since the Exile. Connor laughed often, told stories to entertain those around us as we all traveled together, and carried on as before, always with me at his side. If anything, the journey gave us a rare and concentrated span of time together such as we never before had. We embraced often, huddled closely around our evening campfires, and whispered sweet mysteries when the moment struck us. We drew closer than ever, eager to be wed soon and ready to embrace the next season of our lives. With each step that brought us closer to Periburn, I carried every hope that the banner of blessing blowing overhead for the past year would not waver.

When at last we were two days from our destination, the landscape changed dramatically. Dark forests grew thick on all sides of the road, falling back only slightly, running as far as the eye could see until they met a string of magnificent forested mountains to the west known as the Mountains of Purpose. These mountains separated Avan from our western neighbor, Waldony. Just at the foot of them, two days' ahead, was Periburn.

It was in this last stretch that Connor and I drew up the hoods on our cloaks and kept more discreet. This was not so unusual; the other travelers with us were more wary and cautious as well. Many of the men carried knives and swords. The groups of travelers moved in close clusters, with the women and any wagons filled with personal belongings kept in the center.

"Just as a precaution," many of them said around us.

So far, they reported, no one who had come for the census had been accosted by the Raiders or any other thieves that might lie in wait on these roads. The Rebels, it seemed, held their chief interest in the homesteads and the settlers nearby. Even so, the travelers, like us, were not willing to take chances.

Even now, many years later, I'm not sure how Devland managed to find us, nor how I was so successfully taken. The chaos that followed was too great, the noise too confusing for me to ever piece together a faithful recollection of it. I can only assume he had spies among the travelers posing as regular citizens, on the watch for anyone Devland might deem of personal interest. We had no warning and no chance to defend ourselves; what happened took place so swiftly and at once that there was no accounting for it.

One moment I was contentedly perched next to Connor on the wagon seat with Liev in the back, making our way down the little road in the midst of a small cluster of men and women on foot… and in the next moment there was a great commotion of shouting. This was almost instantly followed by constant feminine screaming, though it was difficult to tell from whom it originated. The shrilling sound pierced the air with a note that would cause even the boldest heart to cringe in uncertainty. The group of citizens we were with panicked, rushing in a thousand directions, stumbling over one another, diving aside to the left and right. No one seemed to know who the enemy was, or what he was attempting. At the same moment, a thick cloud of gray smoke rose from the sides of the road — or perhaps from within the company itself — making visibility almost impossible. The air was immediately difficult to breathe; fear clutched at my soul;

my mind whirled. There came the popping sounds of several blasts, like chestnuts cast into a fire, their shells rupturing from the heat — or like river stones hurled into flame. The horse leading the wagon screamed and whinnied, pulling at the wagon, threatening to bolt, clearly as terrified as the panicked people around him. Then Connor was shouting, most likely instructions, but the words were lost in the mayhem and only added to the confused chaos of the moment.

And then, suddenly, shockingly, rough hands grabbed me from below the wagon. This happened within mere heartbeats after the first shout. I saw no faces, heard no distinguishing voice that set these hands apart from the other individuals running and screaming in panic around us. Two hands — *no, four hands* — dragged me from the wagon seat, nearly losing me in their efforts, scarcely catching me before I fell the distance to the ground. The sky reeled; my eyes refused to focus. Before I could let out a cry of warning, a cloth was pulled tight across my mouth with efficient skill; a bag was thrown over my head; my hands and feet were lashed together with a competence that was too fast to follow. I was slung over a hard broad shoulder and promptly marched away… still with the sound of Connor's hoarse voice in the distance.

I seemed to come to my senses some moments later, as we walked clear of the turmoil and into quieter places of the forest. The strong arm around my middle had a steel grip on my form and a rough manner about him; I feared him without even knowing his face. There were the sounds of several booted feet around us, marching with a quick scurrying rhythm over the soft floor of the forest that suggested hurry, intention, carefulness.

There was the hushed crush of last autumn's leaves… Breaking twigs making fragile clicks and muffled splinters… The muted thud of leather meeting the earth… They breathed in quick, uneven pulls — too fast to be steady, too shallow to be quiet. *We were escaping the scene now, the entire group together…*

I was trembling profusely, in shock. My heart thundered in my ears; the smell of dry, dusty burlap filled my nose; my mind reeled at what had just happened. My own breath was a persistent, urgent tempo as I gasped hoarsely for air between the bonds of the gag. *Where was Connor? Liev? What was happening?*

*This had to be Devland,* I told myself. There was no one else this could be. The plan had been too coordinated, their taking of me too orchestrated.

This then led to a fresh panic over Connor's whereabouts. *What would they do to him?*

*Whisper, let him be saved. Let him be safe…*

At some point, the man carrying me muttered, "She's a tall wench. Tall as a man."

Another answered, "Tall or no, she's comely. *That red tangle of hair.* I'd have her in an instant."

"I second that," a third man answered. "I care little if she's comely or not. I'm hungry for it, too."

They all chuckled in agreement. There was an especial greed in their voices, as if the thought gave them rich pleasure.

Instantly this set me trembling again, more violently than ever. Never had I been tossed about like a thing without will, nor had brutal hands ever been laid upon me. The idea would have been unthinkable. Before I could even give shape to the knowing, I understood how little my worth was to these men — as well as my great worth to the men I had always been surrounded by before now. I was at the mercy of their savagery. A fear I had never before experienced — a new understanding of my powerlessness — crept over my body from head to sole.

"We could stop here and have our fun before we take her to him," the second man suggested.

*Whisper, save me. Save me…*

But the man who carried me decided for them all. "*Later.* I have no wish to be late and get a stern talking-to for it."

Thankfully, this refocused them and they continued without word.

We seemed to walk for a small lifetime, though it was probably no more than a little while of travel through the forest. Then, finally and at last, we stopped, and I was tumbled off the strong shoulder and tossed lightly to the ground.

A pair of hands — *new hands,* I realized, just as rough as the big man who had carried me — pulled me to my feet. The bonds at my feet were deftly cut with a blade; the suffocating burlap was dragged off my head. Immediately the gray light of day caught my unadjusted eyes and caused me to wince. My long stream of hair impeded my sight and I tossed it back, gasping for air, struggling to see my surroundings.

They had brought me to a tiny clearing in the forest, just enough space between the trees to allow for a patch of steel-colored sky to show overhead, not enough so that lanterns weren't required, which hung off a few low branches strategically to provide for additional lighting. Here there were two rough linen tents staked to the rocky ground, outside of which several barrels and unmarked trunks were situated. I was clearly in a small camp of some kind.

No sooner had I taken all of this in than a dark figure stooped and stepped out of the nearest tent; black challenging eyes met mine. He had been expecting us.

*I knew who this was.* Flesh of my flesh, blood of my blood, bone of my bone. Bitterness had etched firm lines about his young mouth, had tightened it and set the sneering glitter in his eyes. He was young to look so old.

*"Sister,"* he announced smugly.

Gone was the stately image of an important member of the dignified Governor Tribe. He had allowed his black hair to grow in a rugged fashion and was wearing plain traveler's clothing — dark, unassuming, with a cloth sheath slung around his shoulders as protection against the cool spring weather. He carried a sword at his belt, and an intimidating knife strapped to one leg beneath his short tunic. Somewhere he had learned to use them.

There was an immediate presence about Devland that had not been there the last time I saw him, as if the very air around him shifted as soon as he stepped into the light. Where before he had been forced to smother it, now he was free to give way to it. Shadows seemed to gather at the edges of his form, not because the light had dimmed, but because he pulled attention the way a storm pulls wind. He was neither raging nor wild, simply aware, in the way a predator was aware of everything it could dismantle.

*How dangerous he has become,* I thought at once, shocked. Connor had been right. Devland was more changed and corrupted by power than I had ever foreseen. Malachi would have wept; *and Miri would have quite possibly been proud...*

Before either of us could respond further, there was a scuffle, and the rough characters around me parted ways to allow for more of their kind to enter the clearing from the depths of the forest. Here were four or five more men, similarly dressed to Devland. They pushed two bound characters into the center of the clearing.

Connor had not come willingly. They had been unable to carry him and merely covered his head and bound his hands. I could already see how rumpled he was; he favored one side as he blindly stumbled forward, as if he had resisted them numerous times and was willing to pay the price for it. He was muttering furiously, swearing at the men around him. I'd never heard such savagery in his tone. My heart leaped at the sight of him... and Liev as well, who stood unharmed and docile.

As soon as the group halted, Connor became aware of the change around him. He knew who his captor was, sight unseen. "Where is she?" he snarled. "Devland! *Where is she?"*

Devland didn't respond, and the men knew what he expected without a signal or command. Quickly, they removed the burlap sacks from both prisoners and stepped back. Connor was enraged even by this and tossed his hair out of his face as his angry eyes met the light, braced for a fight. His wild gaze swung around the clearing, met Devland's with an unsurprised, spitting glare, and kept moving as he assessed his surroundings like a wild lethal cat restlessly taking in the scene of his captivity. When his eyes landed on me, he was staggered with instant relief.

Unable to control myself, I shot the three feet to him, nearly bowling him over as I clung to him. My relief showed itself in my trembling hands and a near-overpowering urge to weep then and there.

His voice instantly changed; his eyes softened desperately. "You all right? Have they harmed you at all?"

My touch seemed to soothe him some, though the breathlessness in my voice couldn't have been any comfort. "I'm fine — unharmed. I'm fine —"

It was then that Devland chose to come to life. He laughed over the two of us. "An unexpected turn, this. *The two of you.* That's not something I saw coming."

This pulled the both of us back to our surroundings. Our eyes shifted to Devland. Connor tensed dangerously.

Devland hadn't moved from his position, but stood taking us in with a confident pride. There was an evil in him that was not a display but a summons, drawing all who stood near toward fear or silence without the raising of a hand. I could feel the awe and the fearful regard of the cold men behind me. It seemed that even danger itself stood still to hear him speak.

"Where is your Whisper now, Eren?" he asked. "Sleeping at His post, is He? He must be. To meet you on these roads by chance is beyond all reckoning. I watched for Connor — I have harbored plans for him for a good while now — but you…" His voice dipped. "I had them haul you here so I could behold with my own eyes the living proof of how witless you must be."

I was not afraid of him. Nor, to my surprise, did I feel hatred toward him. My forgiveness still held. The truth of the matter was, he had betrayed the Halevi and cut short Malachi's life. By his doing, Joel had been lost as well, along with the many others whose deaths I had seen with my own eyes. Every hardship of the past years could be traced, in the end, back to him. And yet, in that moment, standing before him after so long a span of time, he was still my brother. He was still the one who once ran with me through the Temple halls as a child… still the one who knelt in devotion and took the Whisper to his whole heart, with tender tears streaming down the length of his innocent face.

"There was a time you believed in Him," I reminded him calmly.

He scoffed at me with a quiet power, amused. "You rub my nose in that truth as if it will change my mind in some way. You should have taken my offer when it was given, Eren, and stayed in Rivermouth. It was the smarter choice. You would have been safer."

"I'm of the Halevi," I reminded him grimly.

He was unmoved by my quiet insistence. For as much as it once meant, my choice meant nothing to him in light of his new endeavors. Instead, his gaze slid to Connor. True hatred passed over his face and warped it for a moment. Here, at last, was the real prize.

"*So.* I have trapped the little turncoat at last," he said harshly. "You thought to steal away without a word, did you? And after I offered you the seat at my right hand… *my so-called friend…*" He shook his head, eyes flashing. "You ran straight to the Halevi, I take it. I am astonished you didn't carry it straight to King Cyric, with that reckless tongue of yours."

Connor declared, "I would have, if I had any way to tell him what you are." Unafraid, he nodded towards me next to him. "Do with me as you will, Devland. Only let Eren and Liev go. Your quarrel isn't with them."

I was immediately alarmed. "*No —* "

Liev, who stood on his other side, also turned towards him with swift concern. The men had removed his gag and bonds, as if knowing he was harmless. "No, my son — *no —* "

But Devland gave no sign that he heard our protest, as though it had never reached him at all. His bright eyes were fixed upon Connor. He took a few slow steps and came to stand before him. It was plain that he bore a twisted hatred for what he took as Connor's betrayal. To be abandoned was a great personal affront to my brother.

For a moment he and Connor stood as motionless as stone pillars. A thin, invisible wire of strain stretched between them, quickly plain. The tension made no sound, yet it was absolute — a pressure that lived in the jaw, the spine, the set of the breath. In each man's gaze was a steady, calculating force, as if they were testing the weight of each other's will.

Devland took no liking to what he saw. Swiftly, before Connor could brace for it, he pulled back one locked fist and landed it squarely in Connor's gut. Caught off guard, I cried out as Connor bent double with a sharp, gasping sound. My hands flew toward him in tearful fear.

There was no possible way for Connor to retaliate even if he hadn't been bound and I wasn't standing so near; we were surrounded on all sides by Devland's men, who were armed, evil, and braced for conflict, besides. He could only raise dangerous eyes after the initial wave of pain passed and stare unblinkingly, with great gasping breaths, into my brother's cool gaze.

Devland purred with great evil, "I will take *pleasure* in seeing your end."

At these words I stared at him in horror. The bloodthirst in him shocked me.

At my obvious reaction, Devland's gaze shifted to my face and held there. He lingered in that look, as though caught between private amusement and careful thought. In the silence, I saw the weighing in him — and then the choice. It seemed to me that he must carry some small measure of regard for me… or else a quiet fear of the Whisper, a power still greater than his own.

"But we cannot stain ourselves with murder in the presence of our little priestess," he announced mockingly. "That would be wrong indeed, would it not?" He tipped his head toward the men behind us with a dry look. "So off you all go, until I decide when I wish to deal with you." His malicious eyes flicked back. "I have higher business at hand than you, my sanctified sister and my faithless friend."

"Keep her in my tent," he added, to his men. "Lash the men to a tree somewhere. *And keep your hands to yourself, all of you,*" he barked, as if he knew their appetite for warm flesh.

A quiet tension fell after they tossed me in Devland's tent and closed the flaps with rough disregard. There was little sound or movement outside my prison, but I trembled in fear for what would surely come next. They had left me with a small lantern which I used briefly to examine my surroundings. My brother lived a transient life; there was little more here than a cot covered in sheepskins and a pack of his clothing. There were signs that a woman had visited him recently. A blue hair ribbon, so oddly out of place, was near the single pillow he possessed; a small wooden comb tooth had been discarded on an empty trunk in the corner, with a few long strands of a woman's golden-colored hair still caught in its teeth.

For a long while, I sat on the edge of the cot and prayed. That was all there was to do, I concluded. I pleaded for the Whisper to deliver us out of this situation, for surely Devland desired for Connor's death with a spiteful vengeance I had never witnessed before in any man. I shivered at the thought. And where did that leave Liev and me? Liev, I presumed, was dispensable and unimportant. If he lived or died, it was no matter to Devland or his men. I was beginning to believe Dev might be capable of needless killing if it suited him. *And me…* There was no telling what my brother would do with me. I had not been part of his plan, clearly. Yet equally clearly, he didn't wish to see me harmed, just as I thought. *Deliver us, Whisper. Whatever it takes. Deliver us from this evil.*

As if in answer to my prayers, only moments after my pleas faded, the tent flap suddenly pulled back and Connor's face appeared, his eyes wild and breath heavy. I jumped to my feet, heart thundering.

*"Come,"* he said hastily. "I've purchased us a few moments. Let's be off."

I never knew how he managed to break himself and Liev free, nor how he overcame the guards that were assigned to watch them… nor even how he managed to find a moment when Devland's little campsite was empty. It was surely a wonder provided by the Whisper Himself.

There was no time for questions. I shot out of the tent and into his arms with a quiet grateful sob, then clutched at Liev, who stood nearby with a wide-eyed smile at the sight of me. Thankfully, he looked none the worse for wear for all the anguish and physical rough-housing of the last span of time.

*"Let's be off,"* Connor repeated, whispering.

Then we were darting into the forests and away.

It seemed to me after that that we ran for hours, though it couldn't have been so very long. We tore through the trees in a hard, breath-burning rush, three shapes weaving between the undergrowth as the evening light thinned to blue. Branches whipped at our shoulders and thighs, snapping back with sharp, startled sounds. Our boots hammered the soft earth in an uneven rhythm — quick when the path opened, scattered and frantic when roots rose like traps beneath the leaf litter.

I had always been a good runner. My stride cut through the brush like a blade, while Connor darted forward with quick, light bursts, clearing fallen logs with skilled jumps, his bruises and slight injuries from Devland's earlier treatment of him shoved aside in the desperate need for escape. Liev was the one who consistently lagged half a step or two behind, pausing frequently to draw in air with ragged pulls, causing me to often cast a quick glance behind in fear for him. He surely could not keep this up for long…

For a long while, the three of us didn't speak. We didn't look back. Shadows lengthened as the forest dimmed. Even though there were no immediate signs or sounds of pursuit, it seemed Devland's men pressed close at our heels, always a black danger we had to escape. Twilight pooled under the branches, turning every trunk into a looming figure, every thicket into a possible threat. Leaves scattered beneath my feet, and the scent of crushed fern and damp bark rose behind us like a trail. The evening air was cool, but sweat still traced lines down my temple and soaked the collar of my dress. I had long since discarded my cloak in Devland's tent, thankfully.

Then there came a time when Connor slowed to a walking pace, then halted altogether, panting heavily. He motioned to the two of us and we pulled aside into the shadow of a great tree to rest. The forest was darkening with every passing moment.

"They're following us," he announced softly.

I looked at him in alarm. I had heard nothing as of yet, and heard nothing now.

He caught my expression. "You forget, I lived as a Rebel for two years. *They're following us.* Some of the men are master woodsmen. Devland will send his best — and his most brutal — to find us."

This announcement was delivered as calmly as it was terrifying. I drew in a sharp, sobbing breath. I could already see that Liev was nearly spent. Even if he had the strength to continue, I had high doubts that he could run well after dark.

"How far till we are clear of the forests?" I asked. "Can you tell?"

Connor's expression was grim. "Even if we find the road in the dark, which I doubt, they'll surely be watching it. Our only hope is to find a group camped by the road on their way to the city and hide within one of their wagons." He did not add that this, too, would be nigh impossible at this hour.

A silence fell as we considered the difficulty of the situation. A great urgency hung in the air, rife with danger, sharp with stress. My mind whirled with the need for some solution.

Liev was the one who spoke up just then with words I will never forget. "Let me lead them astray," he said, quick and fervent. "I'll take the opposite direction with a thunder of noise, and you two will run on ahead. They will surely chase after me — and that will buy you the time you need to clear the forests."

For a moment I blinked at him, trying to grasp what he was saying. The idea was unthinkable. *"No.* We can't leave you. Absolutely not. If they were to find you —" I stopped, unable to say it. "There is another way."

The old Priest paused to looked at me with a great steadiness, his dark eyes seemingly absorbing the darkness of the forest rather than fighting it. There was a depth to his gaze. Like his brothers before him who had faced death, there was no fear, no resignation, simply clarity. "I have very little strength left, Eren. Allow me to spend the last of my moments on this earth fruitfully, in God's service."

My protest came weaker now. "I won't allow it. There must be another way." I cast a quick glance at Connor, hoping for his support; but his shadowed gaze held a grave acceptance. He already knew what needed to happen if we were to survive.

Tears immediately sprang to my eyes. I released a little whimper. Surely there was another way… *Whisper, give us another way…*

*"Eren."* Liev's voice drew me back, reluctantly, to his face.

"This is not my time," he said quietly. "My hour has passed. This is your time, Eren. Your hour is just ahead. You must run. You are the one who must survive. Connor and I both know it. All of the Halevi have known it. You must run ahead. For all of us."

I fell silent then, unable to speak, unable to fully agree, dreading what came next. He had silenced me with the holy truth in his words.

It seemed to me he was already drifting away even as he said the words, though in reality Liev's feet had not taken a step. He knew what he must do. There in the fading light he looked between the two of us with a divine stillness, his wizened face filled with a final, wordless promise, a recognition, a farewell that was not spoken aloud. In the forest's hush, his bottomless eyes held something more powerful than light: the certainty of a man who believes his life is not his own to keep but to give away. He had already given it away long ago, to the Whisper Himself.

"I will see you both in heaven," he murmured; and then he was gone, a pale robed figure fleeing in the darkness in the opposite direction.

There was no time to stand in shock over what had just happened, though I could have. I could have stopped there for the space of days and wept till my eyes had no remaining tears. *How would I break the news to Cohen? And Anshel? How would the tribe fare without Liev's gentle leadership?* He had been part of my world all of my life. *What would I do without his presence?*

But Connor was tugging at my sleeve gently, clutching for my hand. "*Come.* We have to find the road... if it's possible... This way, Eren..."

That night passed with great difficulty. Connor and I ran until we couldn't run any farther; then we walked until I was staggering on my own feet; and then we had no choice but to stop because the forests had become too black. There was a measure of safety in this, knowing our trackers likely could go no farther without risking injury as well. By then we no longer knew where the road lay. Connor was certain we had been turned around in the darkness, yet he also felt confident that Liev's sacrifice had purchased us a little time.

"It's best we stop and wait for first light," he told me. "I'll find my bearings then."

Very soon he found a little hollow for us to sleep in, hardly more than a hole carved in the earth from time and a fallen tree's roots that had pulled up before rotting back into the forest floor. A thin layer of leaf litter had gathered at the bottom, creating a muted cushion for the two of us. Low branches provided by a young tree leaned close enough to the enclosure to break the shape of anyone hiding inside if someone passed us by.

The tiny shelter wasn't spacious by any means, as we half-crawled into it, but it offered just enough room to disappear from sight and spend a small watch of much-needed sleep. In truth, I was surprised I could sleep at all after the events of the past day, without water or food, and especially after losing Liev. But exhaustion claimed me instantly, Connor's arms were a warm security in the cold emptiness of the night, and I nodded off, hopeful that we would make our escape from these terrible forests come morning.

I woke to the feeling of Connor's arms tightening around me and his voice whispering my name sharply. *"Eren."*

Even as I woke, slow and heavy with sleep, struggling to grasp where I was and why, he murmured, *"They've found us. They must have tracked us through the night."*

This brought me to life quick enough. Reality seeped in like water rushing into a hole. *He was right.* Outside of our little shelter I heard the distant sounds of approaching footsteps and the scattered call of several male voices as they scanned the area. As if in defiance of this, the song of a dove rang out blissfully in the trees, calling for morning. The soft light of pre-dawn filtered into our shelter through the close web of young leaves.

I clutched at Connor's chest, panic-stricken. *"What are we to do now? Should we run?"*

Even as I spoke the question, I knew we had no hope of outrunning them. I was still worn to the bone, sorely lacking in food and water, and just now had no feeling in my legs from the cramped way we had slept all night. I would need at least a few moments to stretch stiff muscles, to rouse myself into taking action again. By then they would already be upon us for certain.

Connor seemed not to hear my question. "I misjudged how dearly Devland wants me dead," he murmured.

Then his gaze fell upon me, and in his eyes was a knowing I had never seen before — yet its meaning, gentle and terrible together, struck me with dreadful clarity. *"Eren — "*

I pulled away from him at once, as far as the little space would allow. "Don't you say it — don't you dare say it — Not after Liev — " My voice broke.

But he was unmoved by my emotion. I suspected that he had been listening to them draw near for some time, and had sat holding me through those last moments of my sleep, knowing what he must do. "Devland does not truly want you," he said quietly. "It is me he seeks. That's why they press us so hard. If his men return without you, that is one matter — they will likely let you slip away. But if they return without me, they will answer for it — they can't allow that. I am the burden here —"

*"NO!"* I was near to hysteria now, struggling to keep my voice from carrying beyond the little earth hole. "I won't allow it — *we may yet make it — "*

*"You* can make it, yes," he answered steadily. "You were always the swiftest runner. You always have been. I can draw them off from here — there is strength enough left in me for that. And when I judge you've had time enough to be clear, I will turn and meet them. It's your life that matters, Eren."

I was sobbing. These words from his lips were devastating. *"We may yet come through – you mustn't give up –"*

"I am not giving up," he corrected me. "I'm saving you." His eyes were like black polished stone, reflecting a solemn emotion I had never seen before. He had already reached a place of quiet acceptance. "They will catch us — it cannot be helped. And without Devland near, I know well what his men would do to you before they brought you back to him. They are ruthless men; that's why I fled his camp in the first place. And we have angered them now. *They'll not lay a hand on you,"* he vowed dangerously. "Not while there's a single breath left in me."

He knew I did not hear him — *would* not hear him. It was beyond belief that such a terrible choice was before us.

He changed tack suddenly, trying to get across to me. "Eren, I have long known I would not leave these forests alive."

These words stunned me. Shook me. Pierced me to my very core. I took him in afresh. "What do you mean? *What do you mean by that?"*

He looked grim. *"The dreams.* I have had them for months now — almost since the day I found you and the Halevi."

Words left me then, stripped away entirely. Only emotions remained — deep, searing emotions that rent my soul in two. *Whisper, no… NO…*

We could hear the sounds of the men drawing closer now, sweeping the area. Both of us halted to listen. There was the unnatural disturbance of leaves… a faint rustling that rose and fell in uneven patches… the low murmur of voices, rough and hushed… Branches snapped under their boots — sharp, brittle sounds that broke the stillness like small bones. They sensed they were closer to their prey and had slowed, carefully searching one step at a time.

In response, Connor reached out and enfolded me in his arms, looking down on my stricken face. He was earnest to get my attention. He murmured with quiet urgency, "You must run, Eren. As you have never run before. You are swifter than they are, my love. The swiftest of us all."

Tears streamed down my face, blinding me. I was unable to respond. Somehow, the words felt larger than the man giving them. Beautiful, sorrowful, chilling… they came from somewhere deep and left an echo behind in the deathly silence.

Even then, even while I grappled with comprehending fully what needed to happen, *what was going to happen,* Connor knew his moment of destiny. A burning light illuminated his brilliant eyes like twin fires; a certainty came over his being. He was prepared for what lay ahead and was ready to meet it with full force.

He smiled at me, into my soul. For a moment he looked at me in a way a man memorizes a face for the final time, letting his eyes linger on every detail of my features. Then he grinned a devilish rakish grin and shook his head, laughing at his life with great satisfaction. "Priestess, you are the song, the riddle, the reason and the rhyme."

He didn't kiss me; he didn't linger over the decision or my numb inability to grab hold of this moment. Those were his final words, his final say on the matter. In the next instant, he tore away, springing out of the earth hole as a man on an eternal mission. Almost as soon as he burst into the light he sprang into action, running so hard and so furiously that I could hear his boots tear up turf as he went... meanwhile leaving my aching arms empty and my life far behind.

I didn't obey Connor's wishes, though I should have. Long after I heard him draw the men away and the sounds of footsteps had died, I was unable to move. I suppose I was in too much shock, too exhausted to make my body obey, too emptied in spirit to put any more fire into my legs and move on. Some part of me was unable to believe he was gone. So I waited... *and I waited*... until hours slipped past and the sun rose high in the sky.

At one point I wearily slipped out to relieve myself. To my surprise, I found a creek bed not twenty feet from our hiding hole and drank my fill of water, grateful for this small relief. Then, strangely, instead of leaving, I crept back into the hole and remained there. My mind was numb and my thoughts slow. I was unable to say what I was waiting for; I only knew I was waiting. There was no leaving just yet...

I slept there that night, appearing only long enough to drink again. Then the next morning, as soon as dawn arrived, I stumbled out once more and quietly set out in the direction Connor had vanished. My actions were beyond all reason. I had no surety that Devland's men had moved on. Other men in the forest he had posted could have easily found me. But I didn't care. My scattered senses — and what remained of my broken, crushed heart — were all that was leading me, not my own sense of self-keeping.

By some stroke of good fortune that could only be described as the Hand of the Whisper, I stumbled around in a meandering course until I came upon Connor, as I somehow knew I would. They had left him to die in his own blood, ruthless men that they were. They would carry the satisfaction of taking back the report to Devland that they had finished him and that was good enough for them.

As soon as I came upon him, sprawled across the forest floor in a motionless heap, I stumbled to my knees at his side. It was clear from his injuries that he had fought hard, just as it was plain his enemies had been relentless. *An instant met eternity as I looked into his beautiful empty face.* Dreams died and fell away, forever gone. I would never again have them back, not even a likeness of them. Connor was the purveyor of those treasures, and without him, they could never again exist.

Somehow, I found the strength to begin collecting rocks for his burial. I couldn't leave him here for the carrion and the predators; *I would not.*

*There were some things in life,* I discovered on that terrible day, *when you were forced to do them, they changed you.* When you had to do them alone, with no one else, they sobered you in a way all their own. Others would only ever get the benefit of later hearing about it. You had to find the strength within and from the Whisper yourself, with no support or assistance, to carry out what was necessary. It forever marked you. This was one of those things.

It took me the span of an eternity to finish burying him. I was indeed blessed by the Unseen Presence of the Whisper, who kept me safe while I did so. I had no recollection of keeping especially quiet, or making myself small to avoid detection.

Afterward, as I knelt by the fresh grave, grief finally fell over me. Dim green light threaded through the canopy onto the hollowed earth, settling between the ancient roots where I had dragged his body and covered it with shaking hands. The air was thick with damp and shadow, and the forest closed in as a silent witness. Sorrow came like a weight dropped across the world, numbing sound, flattening the air, forcing every painful inhale and dragging the exhale from my chest. It was a tangled, suffocating burden that claimed me, so heavy I did not think I could ever stand up from that place. *I was destined to remain here forever, next to Connor's grave.*

But then, the Whisper stirred. His voice reached through the crushing grief and claimed my thoughts with His quiet voice. He was the Beginning and the End, the Keeper of Time, the Ancient of Days.

*This is not your ending,* He said. *I am.*

He had to say it twice for it to really take hold.

*This is not your ending, I am.*

These powerful words did not lift the weight of grief, nor break the shock. They were spoken beneath it, into the deepest press of it. But they were enough. They were enough to pull me to my feet and stumble away from the grave.

I took to walking again, back along the way of the earth hole where I had spent my last hours and moments with Connor. By now the light was sinking towards dusk. The night forest came alive around me, though I was scarcely aware of it. The wind rose; branches creaked like old bones; needles hissed softly; the woven treetops above moved in one great, slow sigh. I had no real idea if this was the course in which I should head, but some spiritual inner sense was still leading me — that, and a numb displacement that gave no care for who or what I found — and I carried on like this for some time.

Only a short while after dark, I stumbled upon the dirt road that led to Periburn. Even then I knew nothing of whether to choose right or left; I just chose, striking out on the road with little in mind. Then, suddenly, only a few moments later, a wagon approached from behind with a slow, rhythmic creak of wood under strain, a weary groan that rose and fell with each turn of the wheels. I felt no alarm; I found I hardly had the strength to care. The muted jingle of harness rings sounded in the night air as the buckboard pulled up next to me. Several lanterns hung dangling from its bed on hooks; one was held high in the hand of the driver as he caught sight of me.

*"Hullo,"* he said. "What's this, Mother?"

*Mother* was seated in the back of the wagon, nestled among a passel of children who stared at me over its edges with a mix of wide eyes and sleepy expressions. On the buckboard bench next to his father, a young boy carried a three-pronged pitch fork, making a plain-faced attempt to look daunting. Before the last few days, I had been traveling this road for over a sennight and had never once witnessed a wagon journeying alone.

*"By all that's holy,"* the woman murmured in motherly alarm, staring me down in the shadowy darkness. "Where did you come from?"

I had little idea what I mumbled in return, if I said anything at all. I could scarcely stand without swaying on my own two feet.

"Do you think we should take her up with us?" the farmer declared. His eyes passed over me, clouded with perplexity.

"Well, I think we'd better, Father," the wife answered. *"Poor thing."*

"We're headed to Periburn," she added reassuringly, to me. "You'd better climb in with us." And then to her children, *"Make room, now. Make room for the lady."*

Then I found myself moving for the back of their wagon, half-falling in as I planted one boot on the hub of the wheel and hauled myself heavily over the rim of the wagon bed. Shortly after, with few further words between the married pair, the farmer tongue-clicked a command to his team of horses, gently flicked the reins, and the wagon jolted forward peacefully into the night.

# *Part 2: Kings*

# 9.

I woke in the jostling wagon just at sunrise, surprised to find I had been able to sleep. Not just because of the constant rumble of the wooden wheels bouncing over the low ruts of the old dirt road, though that should have been enough to keep me awake. After the last few days, I had thought I wouldn't sleep a night through for months, possibly years. But here I was, waking naturally and without fear, just as the first golden light of dawn broke over the eastern horizon to the left of the southbound road, splashing me in the face with faint color. *Light had illuminated the darkness once again.*

At first I felt nothing at the sight of it. I wondered if I would be able to feel gladness over a new day for a very long time. My eyes were still swollen from crying and my mouth was filled with dust. Various aches and pains made themselves known from the running and strain, mixed with the stiffness born of long hours taking the buck and jolt of the wagon. I could muster little more than a small gratitude that we had come through the night without harm.

Sometime in the night one of the youngest of the children had curled up next to me — probably for warmth. She was a dirty child. As I peered around through weary eyes, I recognized they all were — all seven of them, huddled together in the back of the wagon with their mother. Bless them, they were a poor family. The team of horses pulling the wagon were cleaner and better fed, probably out of necessity. I had scarcely taken notice the night before.

The father and the oldest son still sat alert from the raised wooden seat at the front, though the two were hunched forward uncomfortably, as if they were finally tiring after journeying all night. The sight of the three-pronged fork held aloft in the stocky boy's hands was as strange a sight as it was when I first caught sight of it, but he wielded the farm implement like it was a holy weapon he intended to defend his family with should the need arise.

At the other end of the short bed of the wagon, the woman was already awake and caught my eye with a warm smile in the shadows. Her arms were wrapped around at least three or four short figures who were using her plump body as a cushion. She was as kind today as she had been last night.

"We're nearly there now," she said with encouragement. "You slept all the way through, poor thing. You was truly tuckered out, just as I thought."

She was right. From my position, I could see we were fast approaching the city gates. On either side of the closed portcullis the tall gray-stone walls of Periburn, heavy in shadow just now, stretched into the dark forests, making it impossible to see how large the city was or what I could expect. There was no other activity on the road.

"We'll be the first entrants to the city for the day," the woman announced cheerfully. "It'll be a busy one today, what with the census going on and all. It's drawing people from everywhere."

*The first entrants to the city.* It felt like ages since the three of us had left the farmsteads, as if I had been traveling a lifetime. Just as with the sunrise, I could neither feel glad nor disheartened by the news that I was finally here. If I stared at her words very long, I would become painfully aware of an emptiness. That empty void was so large now it was a black cavern — a cavern filled with the exiled and scattered Halevi, with Malachi, with humble Liev, and my loyal, wonderful Connor. *With murderous Devland, too.* I was too numb to look into that emptiness. It was better to be like these children, unaware of the ache of their own hunger, carried along, sleeping soundly through the discomfort.

My eyes flicked back to the budding sun before me.

*A new horizon.*

I had reached for the Whisper without knowing it, my soul stretching upward of its own accord. And He had already answered with a simple phrase.

The budding rays of early morning sun splashed across my face again, a little stronger now through the web of trees to the east. The golden light had begun to chase away the thin tendrils of clouds that had somewhat hidden it only the space of a breath or two before.

*A new horizon.*

Sitting there in the jostling wagon, my eyes fluttered shut in the growing light. I was still in shock, so weak I could scarcely receive the words, but I did, gratefully, like a starving invalid being hand-fed a spoonful of warm broth. So weak, so dependent, so unable to do anything but rest in the hands that tended me.

*A new horizon.*

Emotion rose in my parched throat and tears surfaced behind my eyes, but I squeezed my lids tight, closing it out.

*And the Light became flesh and dwelled among us.* That was Malachi's voice now in my head, quoting the Sacred Text. I could picture his beautiful eyes smiling at me as he said the holy words. How real and true they were… I needed them just now. There was great evil in the world, but there was *this...* this great Light.

There was Light, here, with me, lighting my path, feeding my feeble broken soul. I could not take hold of the words — I could scarcely grasp their meaning — yet I could receive the life that came with them, like a small piece of warm bread drawn fresh from the oven.

*A new horizon.*

For a moment I breathed the Whisper in… breathed Him out… *The Breath of Life.*

A little strength returned to me. Not much, but enough. It was enough to open my eyes again, breathe deeply of the early morning air, and find courage to face whatever today held.

*Connor was gone, but the Whisper was here.*

I glanced over and found the woman watching me in silence. She said nothing, and I had no strength to spare for wondering what she might be thinking. Thankfully, in only a few moments more, we were granted access to the city by the armed men at the gates and continued on through a maze of narrow dirt streets.

By the time the farmer pulled the wagon to a stop in a small courtyard surrounded by tall wood buildings with thatched rooftops, the children were awake and staring around them with wide curious eyes and happy chatter. They scarcely took notice of me. Periburn was awakening, and people were beginning to exit their houses and places of occupation, arms loaded with trays of food, baskets of goods, or scrambling towards their day with frisky children well in hand. Upper floor balconies and windows were being thrown open to the budding sunlight; curtains were being drawn back in glass-front stores; colorful awnings were lowering at street-side booths and shops. A thin dog emerged from an alley and chased a mottle-colored cat through the courtyard, skirting busy feet and distracted bodies. All of this created a medley of sight, color, and disharmonious sound.

I took little enough of it in; that would have to come later. For now, in this moment, I could only tumble out of the back of the wagon with the rest of the children as they spilled into the street. Their mother issued several commands for them to stay nearby, while their father hurried away into a house across the courtyard. As if he knew what was expected of him, the eldest son wordlessly laid aside his pitchfork for the first time in the past many hours and led the horse and wagon to a central drinking trough in the street.

It was then the woman turned to me with a sympathetic word. "I regret we've nowhere to invite you to stay. I can't even offer you a meal, I'm afraid. It's my brother-in-law's house we've come to for the census, you see, and he's already got five children of his own and is as threadbare as we are."

She had clearly put together that I had nowhere to go and no money. And how could she not? I was empty-handed and exhausted, without baggage or any explanation as to who I was or why I was out in the forests alone in the dead of the night.

Before I could respond, however, her expression changed. "You'll need a new shirt. I can offer that at least. My Jenny — she's the oldest girl there — she's big for as young as she is — and you've a small enough frame. Turns out she has an extra shirt you can have. We have precious little, but I can offer you that and ease my conscience a bit."

I opened my mouth to object to this, but she shook her head, already turning away to follow the wagon. "You can't wear that one anymore, lassie. It's just too terrible a sight… and you'll need to find food and shelter soon, so you can't be wearing it on these streets if you have hope of getting work of any kind. They'll mistake you for a beggar otherwise and then you'll get no pity at all. *Come, children,"* she directed her brood, "I'm headed to the wagon. Jenny, bring the little ones there —"

At her words, I glanced down and took note for the first time that my shirt was stained heavily with dark rich blood. *Connor's blood.* I had taken no notice of it since finding him, or in the black hours afterward. No wonder I'd received such a reaction from the farmer and his family the night before, stumbling down the road in pitch darkness.

Unable to take in more than this, I managed to follow the woman and the children to their wagon, avoiding the press of other distracted souls in the street, and stood in silence as she rummaged through a cloth satchel or two of their belongings before drawing out a loose-sleeved linen shirt. She held it up to me.

*"Here.* You find some quiet alley and change into it, now. As for your next move, there's a marketplace nearby — follow the smell of spices. They grow stronger the closer you get. This here is the Serfs'

District, but there's surely work or a little kindness that can be found there in the marketplace among the sellers. Periburn is prosperous, and its people are good ones for the most part. And you've a wholesome face."

Surprisingly, she stopped to look into my face at the mention of it. I was much taller than she was, and I felt I nearly towered over her squat figure. She was like a puffing little bee, zooming here, buzzing there. She fit in well amongst the noisy busyness of these streets. All around us were shouts and calls, happy chatter, lively activity. Life was probably difficult for her on an isolated farmstead with only children to speak to.

Just now, however, the woman grew sharp-eyed and still as she locked eyes with mine. "I don't know what's happened to you, lassie — something terrible, you poor soul. But you're going to be all right. I can see that. You've got something special about you. It's like a light that surrounds you. I saw it the moment you took in the morning sun. So I won't feel as bad sending you off in the state you're in.

"But do take care of yourself," she stressed. "Keep your wits about you as best you can, you hear? There's good people here, but there's bad too. Stay away from the King's men especially. Most of them would just as soon take a young woman, if you know what I mean, than help her like they're supposed to. It's that Agnar, the Crown Prince — he turns a blind eye out of amusement when many of his men do as they please, so they do it all the more without punishment." She was trying to prepare me as much as she could, like a mother giving final instructions before her child enters the world for the first time without her.

She added quickly, "If you ever come by the township of Salsworth and hear of the farmer Glenwood and his wife, that's us. We'll be safe from what you've run from, that's for sure, and you're welcome at our table anytime..." She grinned a crooked little grin. "Though lord knows we probably won't have much to offer you in the way of food... or a warm bed, unless it's filled with a half-dozen children. There's just plenty of farm work at my place, and safe company."

I was grateful to her. So grateful, in fact, that I lacked both the strength and the presence of mind to thank her as I should have. I was still too shaken, too undone by the suddenness of it all, clinging weakly to that small sliver of life the Whisper had given me only moments before. I merely nodded.

She seemed to sense my state of mind; she had from the start. "Don't worry about thanking me, lassie. Save your strength. You're going to need it for the days ahead. Take a little water from that drinking well over there before you go and refresh yourself. You're covered in his blood, mind you, whoever the poor soul was you've lost..." And then she turned away, quickly, as if these words had brought emotion to the surface for her.

I found my way to the well soon enough and waited in a short line of early morning citizens before stepping up for my turn. A bearded man in a leather apron and small cap, who had just taken his turn filling a wooden bucket he had brought with him, cast me a quick glance and offered to draw up the water for me.

I accepted his offer with gratitude, and took a moment to splash water on my face and arms. The water was a sharp cold shock, but it refreshed me, and I stirred at once from my stupor. I tried not to notice the blood that came off with the water, dripping onto the stone street at my feet.

"Take a sip or two," the man told me kindly, when I hurried to let the next person in line step up. "You look as though you need it, lassie."

This brought attention to me from the handful of people around us, but none of them protested. After a quick glance, I saw expressions of thoughtful interest and kindness on several faces. They were very like the travelers that Connor, Liev, and I had encountered on the journey here, always willing to lend a helping hand if needed. Once again a wash of gratitude came over me, but I could give little response to my surroundings and had few words to offer the man. It was enough to just have some water, a few moments of mercy, a gentleness from strangers.

The man said, quietly, "You've come into some trouble, have you? In the forests?"

Finished now, I nodded, avoiding his dark curious eyes. I murmured, "Devland's Raiders. I'm the only one who came away alive."

I sensed, more than heard, the startled gasp that went through the tiny crowd around me. Fear buzzed instantly in the air with a sharp sting.

*"What did she say?"*

*"The Raiders. She said Devland's Raiders."*

*"Someone said there was trouble on the roads a few days back —"*

This was a name they were clearly familiar with.

The man's eyes sharpened with intensity, looking at me with fresh scrutiny. "Well, you're safe now, lassie. You're safe from them here in the city, though the King will wish to hear about this —"

He opened his mouth to say more, but I knew I had no words for him. I needed to move away from their fear, and most especially the questions he was sure to ask next. *I couldn't speak of it yet… Not yet.*

I said quickly, "I thank you for your kindness."

Then I dashed away from the well with a speed I didn't know I had just now, deliberately burying myself in the increasing crowd shifting through the stone-paved courtyard, leaving behind the kindly farmer's wife with her brood of under-fed children and the little circle of curious city people.

In only a few moments more, I had followed the moving stream of people until I found a dark empty alley that suited me and paused to change my shirt. There was no saving the camisole beneath, which was just as stained with Connor's blood. I tossed it aside with the bloodied shirt, stopping my thoughts from considering anything more than the simple action of exchanging shirts and moving ahead. I had no plan, but the woman's idea of finding the marketplace was a good one and nearly the only thought I could cling to right now.

Stepping from the alley, I rejoined the stream of foot traffic. Periburn, I would soon learn, was a large city, with three separate districts which were comprised of housing and work places for the lower class called the Serfs' District; housing and places of occupation for the upper class called the District of Nobility; and the booming marketplace where both classes mixed and mingled as their needs required. Apart from this was the King's Quarter, where offices of government were located, as well as the impressive castle where King

Cyric and the Royal family were housed. The latter could be seen from nearly every corner of Periburn, perched on the side of a low, forested mountain at the city's edge, its many round towers and strong walls hewn from the same gray stone that paved the streets.

None of this meant anything to me today, not even the distant sight of the huge castle, with its brilliant blue flags snapping in the wind at every corner tower, staring down upon its city and its citizens like a proud, well-dressed monarch peering down at his people from a lofty gallery; but it would eventually. Today this was merely a crowded busy place filled with noise, a blurry paltry location that was not my home and never could be. This was the city that had forced Connor, Liev and me from safety, and in so doing, had cost them their lives and left me completely alone and adrift, fresh from witnessing first-hand that I was sister to a cruel murderer and an insurgent. I was numb, blinded, and broken.

On the wind everywhere in the city was the smell of spices — ginger, curry, turmeric, and others I had no name for — which drifted through its streets from the massive marketplace where all of these fragrances were sold in great abundance in the form of dried flowers, botanical roots, crushed and mixed spices, and in prepared food. All of my life I would remember Periburn for that warm, aromatic scent — complex and only somewhat identifiable to my ignorant senses, with savory notes that ranged from sweet and floral, to earthy and spicy. This was a sensory experience that was exotic and new to me, even in spite of my poor condition. It served to soften my image of this foreign place slightly, today on this most brutal of days.

I knew at once when I entered the section of the city where the marketplace was held. Aside from the heavy fragrance in the air, which had indeed grown stronger as I approached, there was also a growing roar of noise and activity. This was surely the hub of commerce and trade for the great city, and by default for the whole of our little country. At one point the streets suddenly opened before me, revealing rows and rows of tables shaded by brightly colored awnings, wooden booths, curbside shops and stores, and open wagons serving as trading posts. Strings of lanterns and fanning pennants were stretched across the streets, forming a thin canopy overhead.

Although the hour was early, already there was a low roar from street hawkers and vendors. Plain-dressed women haggled over the price of household goods; a mix of bustling carriages arrived and departed, from which merchants and important-looking men exited to stroll the area, talking business with the sellers. Lone horsemen passed through with clatter and noise; servants with baskets tended the marketing for their households; curious strollers lingered over booths and shops; threadbare beggars hunched in corners, bleating for alms; and enclosed, painted wagons hauled goods to and fro. It seemed the entire population of the city made its way here at some point during their daily activities for whatever needs they had.

Most prominent of all were the salesmen, nearly accosting passersby at every turn with their wares, with their cries for attention, and their wiley efforts to entice and cajole. They were most recognizable by their vibrant turbans and possessive eye for their displays and goods. As I passed through, one man took me in with an eye for knowing who was a foreigner to his city, and announced with a brilliant smile, "Welcome to the City of a Thousand Salesmen!"

He was right. In time I would come to associate Periburn with many things, but its chief mark was the sheer number of salesmen, springing up at every turn to wave some trinket in your face and shout a tangle of words meant to loosen your purse. The effect of this place would have been staggering on any other day for a girl who had only grown up in the Rivermouth Community, and who had mostly remained within the shelter of our quiet farmsteads over the past few years. But today I merely wandered through, taking in the entrancing — and often strange — sights, until I realized how weak I was from hunger. I couldn't recall the last meal I had had; time had ceased to exist before the events of the past few days.

With the extreme hunger, it seemed, the shock began to wear off. I found as inconspicuous a corner as I could amid the marketplace's mayhem, and suddenly wondered what I would do for food… for shelter… *what I would do at all now.* My thoughts were running — a deer in the forest searching in frenzy for what was not there. None of these people around me knew me or were connected to me in anyway. I was lost in a sea of human flesh, all of whom had places to go, purposes that defined them, and relationships that kept them earth-bound. I had nowhere to go and there was no one left.

*There was no one left.*

By now I had felt and weathered many things in life, but there was no feeling like that one in the whole of the world — the feeling that *there was no one left.* Save for the few humble priests still waiting for our return to the farms, everyone I knew had either exiled me; had betrayed and abandoned me; were scattered to the winds by persecution; or had died helplessly in return for my survival. I had not lost them all at once, but in a matter of a few seasons, one right after another, like water circling down a drain, emptying out the very world I had always known. *There was no one left.*

I found myself trembling beyond control, though whether from hunger and weakness or deep emotion, I could not say. My heart raced; my skin burned with fever; my face was cold and clammy. I grew weaker and weaker, whimpering with despair as a cloud of death quickly descended upon my soul. I was certain all the life would drain from my body right then and there, until there was nothing left of me but an empty husk.

*There was no one left.* That empty void stretched out before me, black and treacherous, waiting to claim my soul.

Suddenly, without warning, I felt the Whisper come over me. It was unusual that I would be able to hear or sense Him in the chaos all around me, but He spoke above the clamor and over the death occurring within, there as I huddled brokenly in a dirty corner in Periburn's marketplace.

*There are two ways you can view this, Eren,* He said. *You may call Joel's death — and Liev's — and Connor's — and Malachi's — tragedies, and bear that grief through the rest of your life. With that knowing, you may grow angry at Devland, angry at Me, and let disillusionment darken every corner of your days.*

I wasn't certain I wanted to think yet about the horrors of the past few days. Neither was I certain I wished to name the dozens of emotions swimming through me. They were easier to push aside, to ignore them as one ignores a horrible story you can't take in fully. But the Whisper had a way of illuminating the truth, whether ugly or beautiful, no matter how difficult or uncomfortable. And I desperately needed His help now, this very moment. *Death had come for my soul.*

The Whisper continued, *The second way you can view this is that I held true to My word. Men have given their lives for you so that you can live. They did it freely, because they believed in your destiny and believed I will fulfill my will through you. I did not mislead you, nor am I misleading you now. Your destiny has not slipped from you; it lies ahead even now. You are the design I have woven, the plan I have set in motion, to save the Halevi from the cruel schemes of men. You are the means I have chosen to help shape the fate and future of this nation. There is a reward held in store for you. If you choose the second way, you cannot give up now, when you are closer than ever before. You have a purpose. Malachi, Liev and Connor said you must run… and so you must.*

There were a dozen reasons to be offended by these words. Though they were spoken to my heart with gentleness and grace, they seemed unbent by my heaviness. They did not note my great physical exhaustion and hunger, nor show compassion for the desolate emptiness of my life. They did not offer me an explanation for why these terrible things had happened — and especially to the people I loved — in order for this plan to be executed. They did not address the evil in the world, or assure me of justice in the future. There was no evidence that I was closer than ever to the promise He had given me. I was a hungry beggar; and I was alone on the street.

But He was right. Malachi, Liev and Connor had told me to run. They believed. They had given of themselves without reserve, and their lives — and most of all their deaths — could not be allowed to go to waste. The Whisper had prepared me that this would happen, and it had. This was the truth I needed right now. If I allowed it, this truth could become a weapon that was able to push back the very darkness that was threatening to consume me.

He gave me the choice. The Whisper always gave me the choice.

Sitting there in the dirty chaotic street of a city foreign to me, with my arms wrapped around my drawn knees and my face buried in my shirt sleeves, I chose the second way. I was so weak in spirit and trembling so fiercely that I could scarcely form the words, but I spoke them all the same, accepting His perspective. I would not view this as a tragedy, but as a sacrifice. I would not walk through that trauma again... the terror of running... the blood... the sight of Connor's broken body... Instead, I would receive the gift the four men had given me... and *I would run.*

I would run for Malachi, for Joel, for Liev, and my beautiful Connor; I would run for the Halevi; and I would run for the Whisper. I would believe. The Whisper had held true to His Word to me, and would continue to do so. Someday, *somehow,* He would use me to reunite our tribe and reestablish a people who would worship Him. I would serve Him by doing my part in shaping the fate and future of our nation.

*What was it Malachi had said so long ago in the Silent Heights?* "As you feel the cost more sharply, as the ache of loss settles deep, the truth of who you are becomes all the more precious. Its worth rises in your heart. You come suddenly to know where your true treasure lies, and your hands close upon it with iron strength. Nothing and no one will ever lessen its worth. Nothing can pry it from your grasp or steal the call of the Whisper from your soul. *You will not let them."*

Suddenly, that dream was more beautiful than ever. Malachi, Joel, Liev, and Connor were the precious jewels that had been paid as part of the cost. I felt my fingers lock around that dream with a death grip that I could never be parted from. Not while I had breath to breathe;

not while I had life in my bones. This was my mandate, my calling, my destiny, my purpose, my identity…

*"Run like you've never run before,"* Connor had said. *"You're swifter than they are, my love. Swifter than us all."*

I would outrun the evil; I would outrun the injustices of this life; I would outrun the forces that opposed me seen and unseen. I would run like I had never run before… *and I would run all the way to the finish line.*

My choice suddenly became a weapon — a weapon held by my trembling fearful hands, but nevertheless, a fiery tool that discharged against the darkness threatening my soul. In that weakest of moments, there in the city streets, my tiny seed of faith — my choice to believe the truth — moved a black mountain standing in front of me. I felt the darkness recede; my inner person settled and grew calm; and I sat breathing quietly.

Death had passed over.

It was then an impatient voice demanded, "*Girl.* Girl — what are you doing there? You can't sit there. *Go, beg with the other beggars."*

I wasn't startled. I lifted my gaze calmly.

A dark face moved into focus. This was a seller. His turban, rising in bright folds atop his narrow head, glowed in the morning light like a sun-warmed orange as he stood above me. His expression sharpened the moment our eyes met.

"You're no beggar," he stammered. "What are you doing here? Are you faint?"

"I was," I answered simply. "I'm improved now. Is this your booth? Forgive me if I've intruded."

My gaze drifted to a low table of goods only a few feet away, where the man had set out an odd collection of bottled spices, bolts of imported cloth, and other small items that looked little more than baubles. He was hovered near it like a hen protecting her young.

He nodded hawkishly. Something about me was still taking him aback. "It's mine, yes. No one's allowed over here but me. Where are you from? Not from Avan. And not from Waldony, either, I'd wager."

His observation surprised me. My features stood out among these people, as they did anywhere in Avan, yet no other soul in Periburn had given me a second glance today, not after I had changed my stained shirt. Since entering the marketplace especially, every seller I passed seemed far more intent on boldly guessing my needs and assuring me they could meet them before any rival had the chance. Being a trading city, and the capital of Avan besides — and especially in a season of the King's census — strangers and foreigners were plainly expected here. I had to assume the man was seeing something still lingering on my countenance from the conversation I just had with the Whisper.

"I'm from Avan," I told him. For some reason, I no longer felt the need to keep my origins discreet. "From the Rivermouth Tribes along Trowich River. I've always looked a bit set apart among my own people, too. I've come to the city for the census. I won't trouble you any longer —"

I was already on my feet, signaling that he could step aside so I might leave the narrow space. I was grateful to find I had regained enough strength to slip back into the shifting crowd around us.

But the man did not move, as if the urgency to send me on my way had suddenly left him. "My wife has grown faint as of late from the smell of the herbs in the marketplace. The spices are too strong for her delicate stomach. In other days she helps me here, at the booth." A faint twinge of color entered his lean face. "She's bearing our first child."

He was plainly holding me here for a moment, trying to work something out in his thoughts. "Congratulations to you," I told him.

He stood shorter than I did, and his dark gaze had to rise notably to find mine. A small frown creased his brow. "You're not with child, are you?"

I shook my head. "No. I only grew faint from hunger… and exhaustion. It — it was a long journey, getting here. And I lost my companions unexpectedly along the way, as well as our coin. We were robbed. You caught me using your corner trying to weigh what I'm going to do for food and shelter while I'm here."

"Ah." He took this in with a thoughtful look. He gave a half-shrug. "Well, I'm short on help. We have twice the patrons right now because of the census, but I'm losing more coin than I'm gaining because I've no one to watch while I sell. There's as many thieves as there are buyers. I have no wages to offer, but I could feed you, and my wife and I could give you a place to sleep before our fire for a day or two until you register for the census and decide what you will do more permanently."

I knew the work of the Whisper when I saw it. He had seemed uncannily near, shaping each step I took, since the moment Connor offered himself at the sacrificial altar. Relief flooded me at once. *Thank you, thank you.* To have a little food, to be safely off the streets after nightfall, and to pass the night before a warm fire — these felt like great luxuries just now. My head fairly swam with the idea of food in particular.

I smiled a little at the man — my first smile in days. The action felt like opening a creaky door on rusty hinges, but I meant it. "I appreciate your trust; I would be most grateful."

"Well, you're no thief, nor a buyer — that much is clear." His tone was blunt and practical. "And I could use the help. I was about to close down my booth for the day, with thievery running so high. You showed up out of nowhere, and just in time." He turned toward the back of his selling space. "Come then — let's feed you. My wife's an excellent cook, and she sent me off with plenty today."

As I followed him, I noted the puzzled look still lingering on his face. He had decided I was a safe enough investment, yet he could not quite place me. It seemed he sensed, in some small way, that something Divine had moved beneath the guise of a timely coincidence, come in a moment of great need for us both.

The man's name was Henri. I soon learned a great deal about him, seeing as he enjoyed talking to the steady stream of patrons that visited his stall. He had lived in Periburn all his life and came from a long line of street merchants, each passing their small trade to the next, as he meant to do with one of his own children someday. He seemed to know every seller within shouting distance — and there were at least fifty alone in the crowded quarter where his booth stood. He held an outspoken opinion on them all, and on his patrons too, once they were safely out of his hearing.

As I assisted him, I determined he was not a man who bothered to make himself very likable. He was nothing like the people of Rivermouth, who were keenly aware that the prosperity of the entire community relied upon currying and keeping the favor of buyers who passed through. Henri was fiercely competitive, and burned hot at patrons and fellow vendors alike whenever someone chose nearby goods over his. His temper erupted in constant tirades. I suspected he was tolerant and patient with me only because I followed his small instructions without fuss, and he could not afford to lose my help today.

Curiously, however, when he made mention of his wife or their coming child, Henri gave himself away entirely. His hard eyes brightened and his cheeks took on slight color; his brittle voice softened and his thin, set mouth grew more yielding. Beneath that sharp-eyed street hawker was a man whose heart had been captured by a dream, and it was a lovely one. He worked hard for them. I suspected his family would always know the best side of him.

By nightfall that first day I was feeling a little better. My companion had faithfully fed me twice from the plentiful supply of food his wife had sent with him, and my work allowed me to sit on a stool behind his booth where I could regain some of the strength I had lost in the past few days. For the most part I only kept an eye out for the swift-grabbing thieves darting through the crowd; my being there also discouraged those sly buyers who waited for the moments Henri's attention strayed. This made for easy work, which was in truth all I could manage just now.

As darkness fell over the city, streetlamps were lit in the marketplace and a cooler breeze drifted through the open streets. The spices in the air grew more pungent as many of the sellers prepared warm food for selling. With the change, a new crowd of buyers shopped the marketplace, arriving on foot or spilling into the streets from fine carriages pulled by teams of equally stunning horses. These were the nobility of Periburn, whom Henri explained dined early, then took pleasure afterward in sampling the foreign sweetmeats, coffees, and baked desserts sold along the streets.

I had never seen anything like them. The men were part of a warrior-class — burly, fierce-looking, proud fighters in dark leather costumes. Few were handsome or well-spoken; all of them carried swords and gleaming knives. They laughed and swore raucously, and spent large amounts on food and drink.

"Agnar's men," Henri muttered darkly. "Idiots, every last one. Still, they're never short of coin, so there's that."

From the hidden safety behind Henri's booth, I watched them with curiosity. Most of the strength they carried as they moved through the marketplace seemed rooted in false bravado — a proud air as they escorted their women, an arrogant nature as they cast baleful eyes about them and spoke with the sellers. I suspected they lusted for power more than any true military greatness, and took confidence instead in the knowledge that they belonged in a class set above the rest of the city. Though dangerous in their own way, they were nothing like Devland's men — desperate, mangy rebels who would ruthlessly kill with a mere tree twig if it meant pleasing their leader. The very memory made me shudder with horror, and for a moment I felt my strength falter.

Along with these rough men were their women, who browsed through the bolts of cloth and other household materials in the market. Many of them possessed a working knowledge of the spices and potions for sale. Where their men were lacking in attraction of any kind, these dark-featured women were rich in beauty and refinement, exuding a sense of great delicacy. Some were truly breathtaking. All wore flowing gowns in elaborate colors that caught the wind and lamplight of the streets, like a field of diaphanous butterflies beating their wings at dusk. They were at once a dazzling sight and a strange one, set beside a crowd of crude men who showed so little respect or evident appreciation for beauty.

One lady of particular loveliness lingered at Henri's booth, haggling with him over several bolts of his finest cloth. Two armed men accompanied her, yet I quickly gathered from their distant manner that they served as her escorts. While I would have been overwhelmed by Henri's doggedness, she appeared to enjoy his persistent sales tactics, and at one point laughed at him outright.

"You'll have me buying your entire booth," she declared. "And then how would I explain myself to my husband?"

Henri gave her a sly look. "Oh, come now, Your Ladyship. Surely the man who holds your heart would wish for you to have all that you desire..."

She laughed again. She was the most charming patron we had had all day. "That reminds me of a dream I had only last night. You aren't a reader of dreams too, are you, you crafty Salesman?" Her hands roamed over the cloth before her, as if she was truly tempted to buy more than she had already. "If you were, I would risk displeasing my husband and purchase everything on your table here tonight."

Henri's thoughts were turning at once. I had watched him work all day, well enough to know he thought if he could keep her at the table he could empty her purse. "You strike an enticing bargain for a humble seller like me. I could try my hand at it. What was this dream, Your Ladyship?"

She knew what he was attempting. She laughed a third time. "It was nothing significant, only odd. I was a lioness in the wild, living in a pride of lionesses. On a mysterious night when seven full moons appeared in the sky, I discovered I was secretly carrying a beautiful male cub." Her dark eyes, dancing and exotic, glanced at Henri with teasing amusement. "Well? What is the meaning, Wise Salesman? Do you know?"

Of course he could not know what her dream meant, and I doubted that Henri was fool enough to try — but I never had the chance to see what clever scheme he might have attempted next to win more of her business. It was just at that moment when an invisible Hand softly patted me between the shoulder blades and prompted my voice into action, like a mother using a feather-light tap along her child's back to provoke a tiny breath of release. I'd never experienced anything like it in all my living days.

To my astonishment, I heard myself blurt out softly, "You are part of a tribe of beautiful women, Your Ladyship, like these here in the marketplace tonight. You are with child even as we speak and will give birth to a male in seven months time, who will grow to be as powerful as a lion."

I could scarcely believe the words had come from me, least of all here and now, in this foreign place. My gifts were far from my thoughts; I was more than content to make myself as small as possible in this exotic city. When the woman turned to gape at me, I found myself as struck dumb as she.

For a long moment no one spoke; the two of us only stared at one another. It was as if the entire marketplace had fallen silent for the first time all day. Then Henri made some scuffle with his sandaled feet;

the cool evening wind caught the trailing end of the woman's head scarf; one of the dark-faced guards some feet behind her turned to his companion in the quiet tension with a trace of unease — and then the woman blinked, the moment broken. I could tell at once from her expression I had revealed something she had not known... something that had plainly left her shaken.

With her stricken eyes still on me, transfixed, she murmured to Henri, "I will take the entire booth." She turned away, towards her men. "Pay the man and bring the goods to the coach. Hire help if you need."

It was only moments later, after her men had departed with every item Henri had on display, that he turned to me in wide-eyed astonishment.

"Do you know who that was?" he exclaimed, all but bursting with delight. "Do you know who that was? *Lady Chatney."* When I said nothing, he leaned in close, lowering his voice conspiratorially. *"Lady Chatney.* King Cyric's mistress — every seller here knows it. She fools none of us. Her husband pays for nothing; Cyric funds her every indulgence. He dotes on her. And his emblem is the lion. *Do you know what you just said to her?"*

Henri had little interest in gossip, however, or in the mystery of how I had managed what I did. His shock gave way quickly to outrageous rejoicing. "You've made me a fortune! Never in my life have I seen such a day — from near ruin to selling everything I own. Tomorrow I'll have to haul the rest of my stock from storage, just to keep selling until I can buy more. I must go home and tell Noya. Come — come at once!"

That evening passed uneventfully. Henri's wife was a meek, plain-faced woman who quietly welcomed me into their humble, three-room townhouse in the Serfs' District and served us a warm supper, while Henri continued to boast over the day's success.

Nearly the only thing she said was to her husband, once she grasped my part in it. "Henri, did you ask her for her name?"

When he looked blank, as if confused or unwilling to admit how self-absorbed he had been, I spoke quickly, "*Eren.* My name is Eren. From the Rivermouth Community. In the east."

At this, Noya smiled kindly in acknowledgment. "*Eren.* It seems we are indebted to you twice over. *Thank you.*" She sent Henri a low, gentle glance through her lashes, which scarcely passed for a reprimand. "You must excuse my husband. He works long hours for the little we have, and sees only the needs of me and our unborn child. He is a good man, only... distracted."

I slept hard that night, and with little thought, upon a pallet by the fire in their front room. I was still mostly filthy from the trials of the past several days, yet this was more luxury than I had known since Connor, Liev, and I left the farmsteads, and my exhausted body accepted the rest eagerly. Morning, however, proved more difficult. As the pre-light of dawn crept into the house, my senses woke me abruptly, suddenly aware that I lay in a place unknown to me. I took a moment to gather myself and register my surroundings — the quiet front room that served as both kitchen and commune area; the stone hearth that gave off little heat now that the flames had burned down to dying embers; the small sounds of the city streets outside just now coming to life. I was safe; that was my first thought. Even so, with this came the sharp awareness that Connor was not here.

Tears slipped down my cheeks unbidden. No matter how restorative the Whisper had been the day before, there was no escaping how deeply I would miss those whimsical eyes and that smirking grin. Once Connor had taken up residence in my heart, I had never imagined a future that did not include him. The dream of a life together had grown terribly important to me — something I could cling to like a life raft on a restless sea. Even as the Halevi and our way of life stood on the brink of extinction, I had comforted myself with the certainty that Connor was my home and my family. I carried with me the assurance that he would always respect me and my calling, whatever life might bring.

Now, in those first raw moments after, I knew he had been sent to me by the Whisper; I believed it with an unshakable certainty. He would live in my heart forever. Yet whether he was meant to remain by my side, I could not say. There was so many signs, so many things said in his conversation — words he was perhaps only vaguely aware of, yet which pointed towards an unmistakable reckoning, as though prophecy itself had threaded its way into his speech. I did not know the full truth of the matter; I knew only that I ached for him this morning — terribly.

With these thoughts, the reality of my situation settled upon me once more. I was in a foreign city with no clear sense of what to do next. After registering for the census, I was without resources of any kind, and there was no path back to the farms. Even had I possessed the coin for food, supplies, and perhaps a mule, I could not dare the forest roads alone, not with Devland's men still keeping watch over the ways in and out of Periburn. For the moment, I was hopelessly trapped.

Tragically, I did not even know how to send word back to Cohen about Liev. He and Anshel deserved at least some small measure of news. All the priests would surely be in a panic, wondering what had become of the three of us. And how was I ever to tell them about Connor? The tribe had loved him deeply, and relied upon him all the more. This place — these people — belonged to a world I had never known. They did not even know the Halevi existed.

As I lay there, hollow and desolate, the Whisper's words came back to me for the first time since He had spoken them the morning before — *a new horizon.* I found I could meet them with less weariness now. *A new horizon.* It carried the promise of His design, and of things yet unseen. This turning of my story was new… a new day.

I held to these thoughts for a moment as my tears slowed and at last came to rest. In the space of a single day, the Whisper had already shown that He was near and faithful. Twice now His hand had turned my path toward Henri, granting me favor with him and his wife. I had to believe He would show me the next step, and that it would come soon. *I was so very small, and the world felt very large in this moment.* I did indeed need a new horizon; the old day had died completely.

The next two days followed much the same pattern as the first — working with Henri in the crowded marketplace, then returning to his house well after nightfall for a quiet supper and an early bedtime. If Henri and Noya kept any other manner of life when I was not a guest in their home, I saw no sign of it. They were as steady and dutiful as I had once been in my prayers and offerings at the Temple. Henri seemed to spend all his store of energy and conversation during the day, and in the evenings the two lived together in companionable silence.

This stirred my longing for Connor once more, all the more keenly. He had filled my world with laughter, with badgering, and with constant conversation. I leaned heavily on the Whisper during those lonely nights, in the first terrible days without him.

At dusk on the third day, Lady Chatney returned to Henri's booth, again accompanied by her two armed escorts. She appeared more beautiful than ever, clad in a deep blue gown and matching cloak that rippled and shimmered as she moved through the marketplace, graceful as a swan upon dark water. I was not especially surprised by her return — but I was startled when she fixed her gaze directly upon me, as though she had come with the intention of speaking to me alone. Henri grew nervous at once.

"Milady, my assistant meant no disrespect by her unusual gift, I assure you. I cannot offer a refund of any kind, if that is the reason for your return."

Lady Chatney's lovely gaze never left mine. "That is not why I've come, no."

Henri seized on this at once, his delight returning in a rush. "Then perhaps I might interest you in these silks! Imported from overseas, from the silk makers of the great nation of Dungh Da Ga itself. The finest material you have ever seen —"

He was already waving a tail of the cloth before her nose, but she paid it no mind. Her gaze rested on me instead, sharp with fresh appraisal. "Where are you from, Lady? I'm unable to place you. You dress like a serf of Avan, but you aren't, are you?"

This struck me with a startled jolt. Gone was the exceedingly charming creature of three days past; even the frightened, unnerved woman of those final moments was buried away. In her place stood an intelligent woman who, in that instant, looked nothing short of cunning — her thoughts clearly turning, her full mouth set in a fixed line. *She needed me for something.*

I saw no reason not to speak with unvarnished truth, not anymore. Something had changed within me, deeply and irrevocably. I had tightened my hold on what was most precious to me, and I would not shrink from the reaction it stirred in the world around me. Even the common speech of Rivermouth fell away from me, as I boldly embraced this change. "I am from Avan, Your Ladyship, but I belong to an ancient tribe of holy men called the Halevi who were exiled and scattered by our community because of our way of life. At present I am the only woman and in line to be its High Priestess."

This seemed to stupefy Henri. He stepped back in confusion, while the woman's gaze sharpened. "A holy woman!" she murmured. "That is very interesting indeed. Even better than I had hoped. What is your name, if I might ask?"

"Eren. Eren of the Rivermouth Community. From the far east, along the River Trowich."

These geographical landmarks did not seem to mean anything to her. Instead, she seized upon the name with friendly promptness. "My name is Lady Chatney. I need to speak with you most urgently, Lady Eren. And to bring you with me if you'll come."

Now my heart truly began to thud. That I sat there threadbare and grimy, laboring in a loud and industrious marketplace — far from any Temple or place of holiness — did not trouble her, nor cause her to doubt me at all. She wanted me on the merit of my gifts and my place in the tribe alone. *Surely this meant something …*

Lady Chatney mistook my quiet hesitation. "I will see you well rewarded for your time, my lady. You need not fear; as you can see, I am well guarded."

Before I could answer, Henri cut in at once, his tone sharp with demand. "You cannot take her! She is my assistant. We have a busy night upon us. She cannot be spared."

At this, both Lady Chatney and I turned together and regarded him. I could not say what showed upon my own face, but I saw clearly what lay in the Lady's. The marketplace was not busy tonight.

She addressed him in an even tone. "I think you forget your place, Salesman. This woman of holiness is no assistant, and I am not just any patron."

I marveled at this temporarily. How could I not? The Halevi had been thrust out of Rivermouth in shame, and had been the scourge of society since. Connor was the last person outside of the tribe to show us the least bit of deference or respect. It had been years since I had heard the level of honor which used to be so commonplace among our community.

Henri was not a man accustomed to yielding without first mounting a stout argument — even, it seemed, before those of rank, or at the very least those who stood near power. Though he would never have confessed it, the merchant in him knew well the gain and favor I had brought him in these past three days, and how easily it had come. Inwardly, he grappled with her words. His face flushed red with anger; his lips pressed thin in vexation, and his sharp eyes flicked toward the armed guards standing only a few paces away. He had no ground to stand on, and he knew it.

Ignoring him, Lady Chatney turned back to me with a smile of unexpected equality. "Will you come, Lady Eren? I have need of your help."

Only moments later she led us through the marketplace, weaving in and out of the stalls, tables, and loitering patrons, always with one of her guardsmen before and behind. We reached her coach within a short time, where a well-dressed coachman in black livery with gold piping stood waiting. Once we were settled inside, the coachman wordlessly drove the team of four dark horses from the box seat. I was immediately aware of the great luxury around me — the barrel shaped roof covered in brightly painted leather; the grand interior which included cushioned seats, tapestries, and rugs. I had not seen such finery since our days in the Temple, where certain tapestries, rugs, and the seats of the Chief Priests were kept with reverent care. I was certain my rough garments and unclean skin would blemish anything I touched, yet Lady Chatney appeared wholly unconcerned as we set out at a slow pace through the crowded streets.

Almost at once she asked, with a slight frown, "What name are you called by? What is your rightful title? Milady Priestess? I would not wish to offend your station through ignorance."

*Milady Priestess.* Connor would have laughed at that one… and no doubt would have begun using it to make me laugh in return. Even so, I still marveled inwardly at her continued respect. The acknowledgment felt strange, as though I were caught in a dream.

"That title will serve well enough, Your Ladyship," I answered. "Or you may call me by my name. Our people do —" I checked myself with a quiet wince. "*Did.*"

There was enough lamp light from the streets entering through the long windows of the carriage on either side of us to illuminate Lady Chatney's delicate features in the fading light. She smiled in a sunny manner, as if my words were an invitation to friendship and she was pleased with the idea. Just as before, she brushed past my admission that the Halevi were considered the outcasts of our community and no longer held any position.

"*Eren*. I'm honored, especially seeing as you are a High Priestess. There are many spiritual men in the castle who serve the King, but none are women, and all of them are raised rather high in their piety, in my opinion."

She did not seem to require a response. Instead, her attention turned to the movement beyond the windows, and she waited with quiet contentment as we traveled on. The coach had now cleared the busy marketplace district and moved at a quicker pace, rocking slightly as its great wheels passed over the stone streets.

I found myself far less interested than she in the streets we traveled, and far less at ease besides. Life was too uncertain right now to leave it at that. I needed to find a way back to the farmsteads, and she had spoken of reward for my time — to say nothing of the Whisper's thoughts over these past days.

I ventured to ask, "May I know where we are going, Lady Chatney? Is it very far?"

"Oh." She turned toward me with a softened, apologetic smile. "Forgive my neglect. I was so concerned you would refuse me that I failed to say it sooner. We are bound for the castle. I have arranged an audience for you with King Cyric."

# 10.

My first meeting with Cyric was one I will never forget — for so many reasons. Even so, on my way to the encounter, I doubted that any exchange with the King, no matter how riveting, would measure against the sharp events that had shaped my life in these last years.

Just before arriving, Lady Chatney explained that in the past two days since I had interpreted her dream she had gone straight to the King and told him, in private, that the child she carried was his. She did not tell me how he received the news or what would become of her, though she seemed content enough as she spoke, as if it had not unsettled her life in the least. She also carried no shame at all in confiding this, to my surprise, as though it were natural that I would understand, being both a woman and one who held a holy office. Her greater interest was in keeping the King happy. He had a dream recently that troubled him, she said, a dream which none of his spiritual advisors seemed able to read. After she told him how the news of her pregnancy had come to her, Cyric immediately bade her bring the dream interpreter before him the moment she could discover my whereabouts.

Before Lady Chatney delivered me to the great double doors of Cyric's throne room, she turned over her own cloak so I could wear it over my dirty peasant clothing. She brushed my hair out of its simple plait, clucked sympathetically over its rough condition, and placed a jeweled comb in it which she happened to carry in a silk alms purse on her person. In only moments, I was transformed from a dirty beggar to a dignified woman of seeming consequence. The gesture was an impulsive one, nearly unconsidered; Lady Chatney plainly set little store by coin or kind generosity.

So it was that I was ushered into the throne room of Periburn to stand before King Cyric wearing a sweeping cloak far finer than any priestess robe — or any garment — I had ever known. The fabric moved like breath, yet carried a quiet weight, its muted silver shot through with the faintest blue, like twilight woven into cloth. As I walked, it caught the light in gentle waves, shaping itself to me before trailing behind in a modest train. I can only imagine the impression I made, though at the time I was in a dazed-like state and was scarcely aware of it.

As I took my first steps, the moment fixed itself in my memory for its unearthly cast, as if I were hovering on the edge of belief. There was no way in all my days that I could have shaped such a moment by my own hand. Malachi's prophecy was ringing in my ears… his only regret in life being that he had not lived to see his own flesh and blood walking among the Kings and Princes of this world. This was a true point of divine destiny, one I knew — even before I knew its outcome — would give way to all that he had ever spoken of my future. The Whisper Himself had confirmed only a few scant days before that I would be instrumental in shaping the fate and fortune of our nation. *This moment,* I thought, *was as much for Malachi as it was for me and the Halevi.*

Cyric's throne room was less a chamber of state than a great ceremonial dining hall. Long trestle tables stretched down the length of the room, their polished oak surfaces gleaming in the candlelight as I took my first steps. Each table was flanked by high-backed chairs carved with the crests of old families — some worn smooth by centuries of feasts, others newly commissioned to impress visiting dignitaries. Above, a vaulted ceiling of dark timber beams arched like the ribs of a cathedral ship I'd seen in pencilled sketches from volumes kept in the Temple. Between the beams hung banners faded at the edges, their painted beasts and heraldic devices stirring in the faint cross-drafts. Iron chandeliers, each a spoked wheel studded with dozens of candles, shed a warm amber glow that softened the stone walls and gilded everyone in firelight.

The far end of the hall rose on a shallow dais — not an austere throne but a single armchair set in the center of a grand table. This resembled the seat of a sovereign only in height; otherwise, it was upholstered like a dining chair, meant for exchanging toasts more than decrees. Behind it, a monumental tapestry stretched nearly floor to ceiling, depicting the realm personified as a robed figure holding a scepter over mountains, rivers, and villages — an allegorical image celebrating the crown's absolute authority.

Along the side walls, arched alcoves held smaller round tables for council meetings, private whispers, and the overflow of guests during festival seasons. Niches between these alcoves displayed silver ewers, jeweled goblets, and portrait busts, all catching motes of light from the hearth. And the hearth — an immense stone fireplace capable of roasting an entire boar — dominated the room midway down its length. Its mantle was carved with scenes of harvest and celebration. Richly-robed servants moved quietly over floors of checkered stone, refilling wine pitchers and laying out dishes on a long sideboard carved with vines. Musicians played from a minstrels' gallery above the entryway behind me, the soft echo of lutes and shawms drifting down to mingle with the clatter of cutlery and the hum of conversation.

I thought, *For all its glory and splendor, the music could not compare to the hearty singing of a simple group of priests in worship to the Whisper, nor could the room be any more grand than the unadorned Holy Room of the Temple.*

At first sight of the resplendent room, I suspected that Lady Chatney had only called it a throne room out of habit. From all appearances, this was a hall where diplomacy tasted like spiced heady wine, and where the kingdom's heart beat not from an impressive seat of judgment, but from a table laden with wanton feasting. Most of the chairs were occupied by the same warrior-class of men I had seen in the marketplace in the last few days; few of them looked up from plates heaped with rich meat dishes and goblets of wine, chatting amongst themselves with hearty rough laughter. Several were seated next to elegantly-dressed ladies very like Lady Chatney, who spoke around the men in soft laughing chatter. It seemed clear that the diners were accustomed to visitors to the King during meal-time; I was scarcely noticed.

Cyric had already been made aware that I coming and glanced up from his meal with a greasy chin and a mouthful of un-chewed meat to take me in as I reached his chair. In that first exchange of glances, I tried to remember every noble, balanced thing Malachi had ever told me about kings, all of the wisdom he imparted to me on dealing wisely with the men God had placed in power, yet I was unable to recall a whipstitch of it. Too many years had passed, with too many hardships in between. I had no time to prepare my heart for this unexpected meeting. Even the Whisper was quiet, as if He was observing the events unfold in watchful silence as men made their choices before Him.

In that brief, dazed instant, I could only recall with perfect clarity what I had witnessed because of the King's selfishness and neglect — the crippling fear and suffering that Rivermouth had endured as a result of the threat of the Rebels in the mountains; the blind eye Cyric had turned to the fact that Devland was growing in power; the required census that had flushed Connor and me out of hiding; and most especially, the unprotected roads on the way here that had cost me the last, most precious person in my world. By the King's uncaring eye, a chain of events had been loosed that shattered my life, and the lives of many others. I found it difficult to think well of him, most especially at first glance.

It seemed to me he lounged on his throne-chair with the heavy ease of a man who ate well, gave orders often, and had long forgotten what it meant to truly feel compassion for anyone. His small eyes looking at me — half-lidded, yet sharp beneath the weight of indulgence — held the greedy calculation of a small king over a small kingdom. Every jeweled stitch on his fanciful robes felt less like symbols of rule and more like the spoils of an indifferent sovereign who draped the prosperity of his country around himself with an air of self-importance. Still, there was something of a lion in him, just as his emblem suggested — not the majestic king of the wilds, but the lazy, overfed predator who still possessed a sudden, dangerous strike if crossed — very like the burly, arrogant warriors who served him. I found it remarkable that Miri had never seen him, that Devland knew so little of him — and yet their notions were not so far-fetched.

I found myself praying inwardly, grieved. *Whisper, what do I do? I cannot represent you properly. My poor disposition towards this man disqualifies me to be here.*

"So you're the dream teller," he announced brashly, still chewing. His eye scanned me over. "None of my dimwitted spiritualists seem able to read a dream I've had now five times. Can you do it?"

I discovered something else about myself in that moment, standing there before Cyric, taking in his power and prestige. I wasn't afraid of him. Nor any man in power. Nothing could compare to that moment of fear only days ago as I was being carted away into the forest and my captors discussed with so little regard how they would ravage my body... or the moment I stood before my own brother and he had cast a hungry murderous eye on Connor... or the moment Connor turned to me with an expression that tore the living heart out of me because I knew he was about to offer himself up for my life. This king was unable to hurt me; I had nothing left which he could take except my life, and it was already forfeit to the Whisper Himself.

"If the Whisper gives me the interpretation to the dream, yes, Your Highness," I told him quietly.

He sat back then, taking me in afresh. His thick fingers reached for a hand towel near his full plate, wiping the fingertips clean of dark meat sauce. He was still chewing, but more thoughtfully now. "It keeps returning. What does that mean?"

"That it will surely happen," I answered simply.

"Are you a diviner, a soothsayer?" he asked bluntly. "I've heard there's a witch woman who hides in the Mountains of Purpose. Did you drift in to Periburn from there?"

This caused my heart to quicken just the slightest. My thoughts focused themselves somewhat. This manner of questioning was much closer to my heart's desire. I gave him nearly the same answer I had given Lady Chatney. "No, Your Highness," I answered. "I'm from the Rivermouth Community in the east, along the Trowich River. I serve the Whisper, the One True God, the Creator of the World and all its inhabitants. I belong to an ancient tribe of holy men called the Halevi who were exiled and scattered by our community because of our way of life. At present I am the only woman and in line to be its High Priestess. I've come to register for the census, as you commanded."

*"Ah."* This information appeared to hold little interest for him. I suspected he was only trying to place me. Whatever decision he was trying to make, if any, he put behind him. "Very well. I'll tell you. In the dream I always walk alone through a great hall. At the far end stands a golden cradle, but when I draw near, it splits into many smaller cradles, each rocking without wind. Then lion cubs spill out, yowling and clawing at one another, each fighting to reach the high seat where my crown hangs above them. And when I try to lift the crown away, the hall fills with the sound of women laughing — soft

at first, almost mocking, then rising until it drowns out the cubs' cries. *What do you make of that, priestess woman?"* he blared.

Somehow, I understood at once why his dream troubled him. It was as if the Whisper gave me an instant glimpse into the man's soul. He lived in constant fear of losing his kingdom to another power. He already knew somewhat its meaning... and that was what disturbed him most of all.

I inclined my head the slightest, acknowledging his request. "Your Highness, the dream speaks of danger to your line. The golden cradle shows the throne you intend for your true heir, yet its splitting into many cradles means your seed is being scattered, weakened, and spread even now. The cubs fighting beneath your crown are sons not born to the rightful queen — grandchildren who will war among themselves for what none of them has a lawful claim to."

This second part was more difficult to give voice to. Around us the hum of chatter and laughter continued; the music drifted overhead. We were surrounded by servants. A young fair-haired woman in lavish, fanciful gowns sat at his right, paying us no heed whatsoever. All of them appeared well accustomed to the King's private dealings being carried out in their presence; yet I lowered my voice all the same. "The laughter is the peril. It warns that the Prince's passions may leave your lineage without a single undisputed heir. If Your Highness does not secure the line, the throne will fall into the hands of illegitimate heirs who will fight over it for generations."

As I said the words, I had to wonder if Cyric even had a married son. I knew little enough about the King and his household beyond the fact that he was grossly careless. But his reaction alone served as proof enough. His jaw fell for a brief instant in astonishment, and his beady eyes bulged. Then his meaty face grew red with emotion, his hands clinched into fists on the table before him, and he bellowed, *"AGNAR!"*

The sound jolted me just the slightest. He had shouted it straight at me, though it was clearly meant for someone else.

Suddenly the entire room was brought to a stilled silence. Servants scattered; the musicians put down their instruments. The fair-haired woman looked up with bored annoyance and cast him an irritated glance, as if his outbursts were no stranger to her than his custom of conducting counsel over supper.

"AGNAR!" he shouted again, voice thundering. *"Bring me Agnar!"*

Agnar came quickly, hurrying into the waiting hall as if he had tumbled here out of bed at a headlong run, dark hair tousled, warrior-garb mussed and certain of his garments missing. The roomful of warriors broke into scattered laughter and cheered for him as he made his entrance through the double doors and shot past them all, as if he was their hero, but the King roared, "Silence!"

In spite of his sloppy appearance, the Prince appeared every bit a brash cutthroat as he came to halt before his father with a bewildered glare. He scanned me over, then dismissed me just as swiftly. I placed him at thirty or thirty-five, with arrogance in his bearing and a cold, calculating stillness in his eyes. Selfish, cold, sharpened by ambition. I remembered what the farmer's wife had told me — that he turned a blind, amused eye to the terrible misdeeds of his men.

He swore outright. *"What is it? I was sleeping —"*

The King growled loudly, "During dinner? *Warming beds* is closer to the truth! How are you doing at securing an heir for the household?"

This was clearly a familiar quarrel between them. The blonde woman snickered, watching now. Agnar's face grew sullen with anger. "I've said before — Draveena doesn't seem able —"

Cyric pounded a huge fist on the table, rattling dishes. It seemed the Royal family had no qualms about speaking of intimate matters before the whole household. "Unacceptable! You have spurned that woman since the very day I brought her home to you. If you persist in this way, you will fill the realm with a dozen sons by other women. Onyx has already managed to bear a royal whelp —" He nodded toward the fair-haired woman, who showed no offense at the remark, but instead looked pleased and self-satisfied as every eye in the room turned upon her.

"Now, Father," she purred. "There's no need to rub his nose in it."

She was a beautiful young woman, close to my own age. I thought she lacked the elegant manner with which Lady Chatney presented herself, whose very nature seemed to carry a mysterious scent which left questions in the air all around her. Instead, the Princess Onyx had mastered a stone cold beauty of physical perfection that was both smug and self-assured in her position. It was difficult to imagine her with a child.

The King ignored her cajoling reprimand. "I will not have your little reprobates tearing at one another's throats over my kingdom when I am dead and gone, Agnar, do you hear me? I'll make sure of it." His head lowered; his angry eyes glared at his son. "You know the throne will fall to Axel's heirs if you fail to produce a royal son. Your brother will think little of you if I am forced to arrange a marriage for him because you are unable to do your duty as the eldest — and I will do it, have no doubt."

"Axel will take great pleasure in hearing such news," Onyx interjected, with snide irony.

Agnar's livid gaze snapped towards her, finally roused. *"Shut it, Onyx!* You have no part in this."

"Your sister has more right to speak up in this moment than you do, Agnar," the King barked. *"Now, it matters little to me which of you gives me an heir,"* he added warningly, "you *or* your brother. But the burden of shame will be on your head for all your days if you do not produce one, as the direct heir to the crown. *So get on with it!* You can indulge your pleasures after you have provided the household with a royal heir!"

This scathing rebuke appeared to be the final word. Onyx leaned back in her chair with smug satisfaction, while Agnar begrudgingly withdrew from the hall in open resentment. Before long, the music resumed, the diners returned to their meals, and servants moved easily through the room with pitchers and platters again, seemingly untroubled. Most startling of all, the King himself grew calm and returned to his food, as though the matter had been settled as simply as that.

Standing there in the aftermath of the disturbing argument, I had to think — *these men, this household, were so very different than anyone in Rivermouth, or indeed anyone I had ever known.* Unfaithful, promiscuous, bawdy, brunt. The Princess was clearly arrogant and vain. They aired their private grievances in full view of everyone, and with a coldness that was unsettling to witness. They were as foreign to me as this city, as godless as a people who had forgotten their own names. I could only ask the Whisper, *What am I doing here?*

With the dream interpreted and the matter settled, I found myself uncertain of what should follow, or what protocol required. No further opportunity presented itself. That moment of destiny I had been waiting for had not seemingly come.

Just as I was about to withdraw in silence, the King looked up, his mouth still full, and seemed to recall my presence. His gaze swept over me once more with a probing eye. "I know of the Halevi. One of your people tutored my son when he was a boy. I was not aware there were any women."

His blunt words astonished me for more than one reason. It was difficult to imagine the rough-mannered Agnar tutored by any of the gentle, soft-spoken Halevi; the Prince must have been a dreadful student. I also could not picture a single one of our kind among these people, or in this place. "I was the High Priest's granddaughter. I inherited his position in the tribe, Your Highness. I — I was not aware any of our priests had been in your service."

He gave a brief shrug, reaching for a bread roll close at hand and tearing a chunk from it with thick, ringed fingers before stuffing the food in his mouth. "That was nigh on twenty years ago. Your grandfather was no doubt the one who sent him. Do you remember that, Onyx?"

As she glanced over, attention pulled, he added, "Likely not. You were too young."

"I have some memory of it," she objected. Her blue eyes scanned me over slowly as if noticing me for the first time, though with a different intent than her father had. She did not know how to place me… and was uncertain whether she should dislike what she saw or dismiss me altogether. "He loved that little priest until you took him away."

Once again, Cyric appeared unmoved by her subtle rebuke. "The man was not a spiritualist, though, not like you." His beady eye fixed on me with fresh interest, still chewing. "You should stay on as one of my spiritual advisors."

My mouth threatened to fall open. *There it was, the very moment Malachi had prophesied ages ago.*

However, the Princess forestalled any response I might have made by remarking with wryness, "You already have at least fifteen of them, Father."

He grunted at this. "They are nearly useless. One more will do no harm. At least you can interpret my dreams," he said to me. "They trouble me constantly — not unlike my children," he added pointedly.

To my surprise, Onyx laughed softly, as though she took his insult for little more than teasing.

"You said the tribe has been scattered?" Cyric asked me.

My heart was thundering in my ears over this sudden direction in the conversation. "Yes, Your Highness."

"We should speak of it further at another time," he said. "For now —" He scanned the room at once, searching until his gaze settled on someone out of my sight behind me. An unmistakable, covetous glitter entered his eyes; a subtle smile twisted his full wet lips. "Lady Chatney and her husband, General Chatney, can take you in as a guest in their residence here in the castle. I only have housing for male priests. She can see to it that you report to my chief counselor, Rogath. He will tell you everything you need to know." He gave a slight signal with a sparkling hand.

In another instant Lady Chatney appeared next to me, visibly breathless. I realized then she must have found a seat at one of the tables during my exchange with the King and had witnessed the entire meeting. She curtsied with beautiful elegance, raising glowing eyes to Cyric. "Milord?"

Watching her, I found it difficult to believe that the charming and goodhearted Lady Chatney had forsaken her marriage vows and laid with this man, and was even now carrying his baby without any sign of remorse. She was delighted to claim even a moment of his attention. I thought there were surely weaknesses and temptations in life beyond my experience… as well as my comprehension.

"The Priestess will remain with you and the General," Cyric commanded. "See that she reports to Rogath. He will set out her duties and her recompense. I intend to take her into my service for a time. You will see her properly clothed and provided for, at my expense. I thank you for bringing her to me, Lady Chatney. You have rendered me a great service." His eyes still held that glitter as he addressed her, his tone softening almost to a purr. "When does the General return? I have forgotten."

I had a strong sense that he knew, and was choosing his words for her alone. The air felt charged with what went unspoken between them. I would soon learn this was an art well practiced within the royal household.

Lady Chatney inclined her head in the most gracious manner, nearly bubbling with unexpressed joy. "He is with the Prince in Waldony on a diplomatic mission for you, Your Highness. I do not expect him back for at least a fortnight."

"Ah, yes," he said. "Ever faithful, the General." He waved us off with a dismissive hand. "Until the morrow, then ..."

"Very good, milord," Lady Chatney murmured, curtsying again.

In that moment, I did not follow her example, but inclined my head instead — acknowledging the King, yet withholding a full bow. I could not bring myself to bow to a man who did not bow his heart to the Whisper. I doubted he noticed at all. Princess Onyx, however, who had long since returned to her meal and her conversation at the other side of the table once Lady Chatney was called by the King, caught my eye as I turned to leave. Unlike her father, I was certain she was sharply aware of my every move.

Life took a strange new turn after that. For a time, my heart and mind were slow to catch up to the sudden change. Yet the Whisper was always with me, as was the memory of Malachi. As I moved through my foreign surroundings — and most especially my dealings with King Cyric — his words returned to me, steadying me like a fixed point by which I could set my course.

"As a High Priestess, you hold office as a mediator for the realm, Meeshka," he once told me. "The Priests stand between God and man, yes — this is true. But by your office, you are charged to intercede with the Whisper in matters of governance: in affairs that reach beyond private lives and bear upon the course of the world — in matters of public consequence, you see — in decisions and in events that govern the lives of others. All people, and all priests, should offer prayer for their leaders, yes, this is right. But it falls to you and to me to intercede for the men and women whose decisions shape the fate of many —

where power is exercised and history is set in motion. This is the charge we carry. This is the authority and favor entrusted to us."

Standing among Cyric's alien household and their heathen ways, I did not always find it easy to believe that I held any influence or weight at all — with the Whisper, or with Cyric, either one. I knew that I was precious to the Whisper in a personal sense; I felt this whenever He drew near or spoke within my heart. Yet the knowledge that my foreordained place in the courts of heaven carried authority — weight enough to bring about profound change — was harder for me to grasp.

It was true that Cyric's court showed a certain measure of reverence for those of a spiritual nature; even to associate too freely with a priestess was forbidden and quietly condemned. Even so, I was small here, unknown — as strange to them as they were to me. My prayers did not seem any more effective than had I been a humble seller in the marketplace pleading for the Whisper to change the heart of the King. More often than not, I was little more than Cyric's private curiosity, summoned at his pleasure to read a dream or deliver a prophecy — for himself, or for the guests he wished to impress.

Even so, I knew that I must try. I must at least attempt to intercede with the Whisper — and where I could, with Cyric — to bring about change from within. I told myself I should pray faithfully for him for the sake of the kingdom of Avan; for the Whisper; because it was surely my destiny and there had to be reason that I was here beyond that of merely reuniting the Halevi. God had brought me to this place… had told me that it would happen since I was a child… had commissioned Malachi to prepare me for this consequential moment… and so I would carry out my ordained purpose as faithfully as I was able.

Aside from the occasional audience with Cyric and his guests, I was also considered part of his team of spiritual advisors, led by his lead counselor. Rogath was a long-faced, middle-aged man of a pious air who floated in and out of the court in simple robes with a groveling demeanor, as if that proved his humility to the King and the many gods he served. He knew — as I would learn in time — that Cyric clung to an immovable belief that every person in the kingdom was born into a set place, ordained by circumstance, and meant to remain there, no matter how fiercely they challenged it. Their bloodlines determined their position and their status. He had little tolerance for those who stepped beyond their station.

Because of this, Rogath did not impose many sanctions upon me. If the King declared me a spiritual advisor — and I had proved myself as such — then that was what I was. He troubled himself with little beyond that. Whether I was a woman, a Halevi, from Avan or another country altogether, or even what it was I believed, weighed hardly at all with him. My lineage as High Priestess, and my continued obedience to the King, were the only true qualifications required of me among Cyric's advisors.

For the first time in years, I was free to pray and worship for as long as I desired, nearly every moment of every day if I liked, which was a great freedom I should have been humbly grateful for beyond words. Yet I worshipped in a decorated shrine filled with the stone and brass statues of other gods. I did not wish to pray in a temple where God was not. I wished to pray where God *is*.

There were no priests here lifting humble praises with thankful hearts; no shared Presence to settle the soul, steady the heart, and give life to one's steps — save for what little I could gather from within myself. There were no sacred objects to bear witness to a way of life, no orderly symbols to remind me daily of who I was, and of the great Priesthood to which I belonged. How I longed each day to be at the Temple where I was meant to be — or at the very least, to find some quiet place apart from this unholy one, where I might be alone with the Whisper.

I thought of Connor often. *How could I not?* Moving ahead was the most difficult part; embracing a future without him was the greatest challenge of all. I often found myself asking whether it was mercy that I came upon him already gone, or whether a few final moments — a handful of last words — might have given me a small eternity of comfort before he left this world forever.

These fruitless thoughts often surfaced as Devland's name began to circulate more freely through the conversations of Cyric's court. The Raiders were becoming an ever greater harassment. They were said to have increased in number, prowling the long forest roads in and out Periburn, burning settlements nearby demanding for change from the King, successfully turning every mile of open country in southern Avan into a gamble with danger. My brother was relentless in his violent efforts to make Cyric listen to his voice. Cyric and Agnar, who was the head of his military forces, sent out investigators to find men who could be bribed for information about Devland's organization, his points of vulnerability, his plans before they were executed. The royal pair were not yet prepared to act, but the matter was much discussed in the court.

I worried for Dev. I still loved him, in spite of his cold murderous heart. *And yet…* I knew with a sorrowful acceptance that his course was set towards destruction. There was a point in which his future was irredeemable, if he had not crossed that threshold of no return already.

I also understood the importance of keeping my connection to him concealed. I began to see quickly how Cyric would view the relatives of a man like Devland, as if a man's bloodline was as guilty as he and capable of the same rebellion. There was a strong likelihood that I would be imprisoned, and would almost certainly lose my place in the castle, to be turned out into the streets. I chose to remain discreet about the terrible events that had brought me to Periburn — even with Lady Chatney, who often inquired after me and sought my friendship. No one need know the specifics, I decided privately.

Throughout my days, I was left alone and unbothered. There was at least that to be grateful for. Agnar's men and many men of the household ogled me often enough, but they kept their thoughts and their desires to themselves. I roamed freely through the castle without fear. Lady Chatney saw to it with great delight that I was outfitted with robes and gowns finer than anything I had ever worn or would probably ever wear again — garments cut in the stately fashion of a priestess, their draped folds and solemn, sweeping lines whispering as I walked.

The women of the nobility, like Lady Chatney, were colorful and brilliant, but she said to me once, "See how the fabric of your clothing catches the light? When you enter, you make even the dimmest rooms feel touched by something sacred." She was practically beaming with warm pleasure. "There's no need to dress you so colorfully as the other women of the court, Eren. You *are* color."

I did not tell her that the clothing deepened my sense of being a foreigner in a foreign place. Beauty meant nothing to me here. Instead,

I let her dote on me with her happy radiance. She was exceedingly pleased that it had been she who first discovered me and brought me here.

After I had been in the service of Cyric for three months, Agnar stood during the evening meal and proclaimed with pride that his bride, Draveena, was finally with child. The entire hall rejoiced with him; wine was called for; and the King declared a celebration as soon as invitations could be sent out for dignitaries and friends in the nobility to gather for a grand feast.

When the feast was held two sennights later, the entire castle was in an uproar of activity. I, along with Rogath and a handful of other spiritual advisors, were required to be in attendance and given discreet seating along the side walls at small tables in two of the arched alcoves.

On that night the great dining hall was transformed into a living furnace of sound and color. I had never seen anything like it, nor hoped to see anything like it again. What was ordinarily a moderately active chamber now roared with festivity. The long trestle tables groaned beneath pyramids of roasted meats, trencher breads torn open like treasure chests, bowls of sugared fruits, and jugs of wine pulled so often their rims shone wet. Servants hurried between the benches in quick, darting lines, striving — mostly in vain — to keep pace with the growing chaos. At the King's table, raised on its shallow dais, Cyric sat broad and pleased, his fingers heavy with rings, with the deep-set lines of his face eased by drink. Agnar sat beside him, reclined with the triumphant satisfaction of a man who had managed at last to do his royal duty. His smirk flashed bright with wine and pride as he accepted congratulations from his armed men — men who slammed their goblets to the table as if each toast was a battle they had just won.

Across the room, visiting dignitaries draped in silks and brocades laughed too loudly at jokes not meant for them, eager to be seen raising their cups toward the Prince. Fine-dressed ladies drifted through the hall like jeweled birds, their gowns sweeping the floors in currents of silk while they whispered, giggled, and fanned themselves beside men far too drunk to speak clearly. Some perched on warriors' laps; others leaned over the Prince's shoulder, their bracelets chiming softly as they pressed close to offer outrageous, slurred blessings for the unborn child. Onyx was in attendance next to Cyric, as was Lady Chatney next to the General. There was no sign of the princess in question, who was carrying the child. It would seem Draveena had chosen to stay far away from the frenzy her pregnancy had stirred.

As the night deepened, so did the madness. Toasts turned scandalous, then absurd — one warrior swearing he would name his next horse after the Royal heir, another vowing he'd tattoo the Prince's sigil across his chest if the child was born on his birthday. Cups were raised to the baby's future conquests, to imaginary wars it would one day win, to the women who would swoon at its greatness, to the gods themselves who must surely be drunk tonight in sympathy. Everyone naturally assumed the child would be a boy; no other outcome was possible for a man as virile as Agnar.

The hall was no longer a place of courtly ceremony but a storm of revelry — loud, glittering, unrestrained. And at its center sat the King and his triumphant son, basking in the feverish adoration of the intoxicated room. Not for the first time I wondered how the Whisper could ever capture the heart of these men. They held the greatest power in our land and enjoyed it for that alone, *power,* rather than the dream of what good that power could do. Revulsion crawled through me as their laughter curdled into drunken howls, their feasting a grotesque spectacle of open mouths, spilled wine, and hands wandering where decency should have set boundaries.

At one point Agnar stood and declared drunkenly, "Here before you stands the future of Avan... and soon you will see the next generation of leaders over all the land!"

The warriors, armored even in celebration, clattered and bellowed with loud, unrestrained mirth.

Cyric took up the charge next, raising his goblet with a loud voice to brag on the great affluence of his house. This was also met with loud cheers and well wishes. And then, quite suddenly, he seized upon the notion that he also possessed the finest seers and spiritual advisers in the known world. At this, I and the other advisers were required to stand, while the room erupted in cheers and raised their mugs.

Before long, Cyric commanded me to move through the hall and offer prophetic words to his heady guests and companions, while his other advisers gave their divinations. At first I found this almost unbearable, a sacrilege of a sacred gift in the middle of their obscene debauchery, but surprisingly, the Whisper had many small things to say to several men and women as I moved among them. For one I said, *"Your season of grief is closing; a gentler road is being charted for you;"* for another, *"There is reconciliation coming to your household — do not harden yourself when it arrives."* Some were sobered and surprised; a few were taken aback at the accuracy of the words.

As I moved towards one table, I heard a man next to Agnar tell him with a drunken snicker, "One of the most desirable priestesses I've ever seen."

"The *only* priestess you've ever seen," someone else said.

The men around the Crown Prince laughed raucously.

"I'll bet she's never been touched," a third man suggested with hunger.

The first man resumed, "I'd like her to give *me* a private personal prophecy —" The conversation was clearly not intended for my ears, but the men were too intoxicated to recognize the volume of their own words.

I looked over quickly, disturbed, but Cyric had not heard this exchange; he was distracted by other activity. The men laughed a second time.

Agnar was too drunk to notice my eyes on him. He was peering lazily into his half-empty goblet. "You'll not be given the chance. Father has forbidden any contact with her. He does not wish to risk offending her God."

"It may be she'll come willingly, in private. There's no law against that."

The men roared again, delighted.

But Agnar was merely sarcastic. "He keeps his pets, and she is one of them. I say, steer clear of her. "

Hearing this, knowing it was true of King Cyric, still gave me no comfort. Not after hearing their words of open lust. I made my exit that night as quickly as I could and returned to my chambers in Lady Chatney's private residence within the castle in tearful exhaustion.

Afterward, I could only hope that Malachi's words were true: that the Whisper would use the small words I had offered to stir belief in some of them, leaving behind an imprint that might awaken their hearts to greater truth. But how I wished this entire season of my life was over and I was back with my people where I belonged. I missed the priests terribly; how happy I would be to exchange the comforts and privileges of life in a foreign castle among a foreign people for a rugged life on a forgotten farm with my own kind.

That dreadful night did cause me to seek out a messenger service in the city with the help of Lady Chatney only a day or two later. Cyric paid his advisors five pieces of silver a month and I thought the coin I had earned in this short time might be enough to hire an armed man to get word back to Cohen. Not a day had gone by that I did not think about him and the others, and how concerned they would be by the silence from the direction of Periburn.

Lady Chatney was deeply sympathetic to my cause, though she had little knowledge of the particulars. In her eyes, I had been granted a position both esteemed and coveted, and this was glad news to carry back to them, along with the assurance of my whereabouts. After the message was sent, I felt relief, and a peace returned that had left me since the night of the feast. *It would be a difficult message for them,* I thought, *but a necessary one, and at least I would have the satisfaction of making contact.* Along with the report about Liev and Connor, I had sent a promise that I would return as soon as it was safe for me to travel and as my new duties permitted.

Only shortly after this, King Cyric sent word that Onyx was requesting for her son to be tutored by me. This news surprised me.

I did not think Onyx held a very favorable opinion of anyone but herself, and she kept a close eye on all who stood in her father's good graces, as though they posed a threat to her own influence with him, myself included. Very soon, my days included morning sessions with the young Prince, where I instructed him in basic language and the Holy Text.

I soon learned Soren was currently third in line to the throne of Avan after Cyric, which made him moderately important until Agnar or Axel, the second born son, produced heirs. At such point Soren would hardly be useful at all to the household except in name; his best hope was to become a warrior in Agnar's service, or an ambassador for the kingdom like his uncle. In those occupations he would have a chance at least of catching the attention and praise of whichever sovereign was on the throne.

These things were insignificant to me except to feel compassion for the unknowing boy. He was just a small boy of five, and was a surprisingly unspoiled child, eager to learn. His father had died in a hunting accident only two years before and his future was a set one, his place in the world determined by forces outside of his choosing. Even his future wife would have to be approved by the King. Here with Soren, I found a little innocence and humanity in this great castle and I was grateful for these quiet hours away from the bustle, as well as the away from the shrine of men making their loud prayers and supplications to dead gods. He quickly grew to love the Whisper, and I quickly grew to love him for it.

After a few months more, I was also summoned by the King to visit with Draveena, Agnar's bride and the future queen of Avan. Lady Chatney was the one who brought me the news. She herself was nearing the end of her term and had confined herself to her tower house in the castle for some time now until the baby arrived. Even so, she kept her ear turned toward all matters of consequence within the Royal family.

"The King and Agnar have not yet spoken of it openly, but Draveena has lost the child," she said. "When word spreads, the household will be thrown into turmoil. She is a fragile creature — a foreign bride from Coromos, across the ocean on the Western Continent. I cannot imagine why her father thought her a suitable match for Agnar. She is not a strong young woman — not as you are, Eren. The voyage here, and the settling into life at court, have been too much for her. The loss has undone her. Cyric hopes you may be able to bring her some comfort. She must recover as swiftly as possible, so that an heir may yet be secured."

This remained somewhat of a mystery to me — the household's obsession with producing as many royal babies as possible. Even Lady Chatney took great pride in bearing Cyric's unborn child, though the General believed the baby to be his. I hoped one day to have it explained to me in terms I could understand. Meanwhile, I could hear Miri's angry tirades in my mind; she believed the entire *shoddy* bloodline should be cut off. I wondered how she would have reacted had she known how many heirs already existed — how nearly every family in the royal court either harbored an heir in secret or hoped to soon. I shuddered to imagine how she — or Devland — might have thought to improve such a system.

Lady Chatney was right. Poor Draveena was inconsolable. I arrived at her rooms the very day I was summoned, only to find a hollowed, desolate space. Heavy velvet curtains — embroidered with gold thread and once meant to keep out the winter wind — now trapped the room in a suffocating half-dark, muting the daylight into a gray that felt like mourning itself. A great canopy bed stood at the center, its carved posts wrapped in pale silks. A low fire crackled in the hearth, but even its glow could not soften the air, which carried the bitter scent of cooling herbs and the sharp tang of tinctures left half-used on a nearby table. Dried lavender hung from the rafters, intended for comfort. A silver basin sat forgotten beside the bed, its water long cooled, reflecting the trembling shadows cast by the candles burned nearly to their stubs.

Draveena's ladies-in-waiting hovered quietly at the edges of the chamber, moving like spirits so as not to disturb her, exchanging helpless looks as she lay turned toward the wall, face buried in her pillow, shoulders shaking with grief. The linens beneath her were rumpled and twisted from restless sleep. Every elegant furnishing — the tapestries of blooming gardens, the harp in the corner, the gold-leafed mirror — were reminders of a world that still expected her to rise, to smile, to produce more babies as she should. I had already been told that Cyric and Agnar would arrive soon and would look for me outside the bedchamber to give an account, as if they hoped I might conjure a miracle to restore her at once.

I moved directly to the side of the princess's bed and introduced myself in a soft voice. I doubted she heard me at first. For a long while I remained there in silence, giving her space to adjust to my presence. Then I felt the Whisper nudge me to speak of Miri, of her challenge in having children, and how her prayers to the Whisper resulted in my birth. It was then I sensed Draveena's crying stopped and she lay listening, with her face still pressed in the pillow. I told her of how

Miri dedicated me to the Temple, and then, amazingly, Devland was born.

"How she loved him," I told her softly. "Never was there such a beautiful love as she had than my brother. I was always touched by it. My brother had Miri, and I had Malachi and the Temple."

At some point I heard the chamber of the room open, but I paid little heed to it. By now the Princess had turned her head and was gazing at me with soft luminous eyes through a curtain of dark hair, listening with hopeful interest. I thought she was a lovely girl, willow-slender, with a fragile beauty I had never before witnessed. In spite of the sleepless shadows in her face and the wretched sorrow in her countenance, she carried some unbroken sliver of grace that was immediately apparent to me. She no more belonged here in Cyric's rough court than I did.

For a few moments more, I went on, explaining how Miri honored the Whisper, and how I had gone to live at the Temple full-time at the age of ten. "She never regretted," I told her. "She never grieved her decision. She was content. And I never felt sorrow over it. I knew when a child lives within its mother, love is born forever. Malachi had taught me that. Her love for me was forever."

She was weeping now, but with different tears than when I entered the room. She understood what I was saying without my needing to say it plainly. The love she carried would never perish; it had been born for eternity, and there was no natural end to it.

Suddenly, in that moment, I became aware that others were present in the room, beyond the ladies-in-waiting who lingered at its edges. I looked over and realized three men stood near the closed doorway. Two of them were Cyric and Agnar. No one had alerted me that they had entered, though I would have expected it. Cyric and Agnar in particular liked to make grand entrances. *The death of the heir to the throne had plainly drawn their undivided attention.*

I would have altered the conversation had I known they were standing there, I thought. I could only be grateful that I had not spoken Devland's name in the story, out of an abundance of caution. The less they knew of my origins, the better.

Cyric's expression bore one that said he wanted to speak to me; I knew it well. I quickly drew myself up. I'd been leaned over the bed, talking more intimately to the princess. At this, Draveena's hand shot out and clutched my own with a desperate grip.

"Thank you," she murmured, with a pitiful softness. "Please come again, Eren. *Please.*"

I spared her a warm smile, heartened by her reaction. "Of course. Very soon, I promise."

Before I had even approached the men, Agnar was already shuffling on his feet with impatience. *"Well?"* he barked. "When will she be ready to bed again? It might be possible not to announce to the household that she's lost the one if she's already due to have another."

His logic wandered so far from compassion that it might as well have been another language. Yet his cold arithmetic was exactly what I had come to expect of Agnar.

Before I could respond, the third man answered quietly. "Perhaps we should take this conversation to the other room, so Draveena can rest undisturbed. There is no need to trouble her with household concerns at present, is there?"

His soft tone, compassionate yet firm, was what caused me to take the man in more fully. The suggestion was not one I would have expected from anyone in Cyric's household, and certainly not one directed toward Agnar and Cyric. He was a man who held authority and sway and they permitted it. Almost at once the other two moved out of the room — the father with his lazy, calculating gait, majestic robes sweeping behind him, the son with his sharper, swaggering stride that spoke loudly of his impatient mood just now.

*This was Axel.* At first sight, he surprised me greatly. In my many months here, I had never seen him… or at least didn't know him to identify him if he was present in the dining hall where Cyric often called for me. From the conversations around me, I had gathered that he was gone for long stretches, or else appeared only briefly before setting out again on diplomatic business. Yet I knew it was him; there was no one else it could be.

He neither looked like his household, nor carried their bawdy air about him. He was every bit a statesman, dressed with class and precision — the finely woven doublet in dark green, decorated with silver brocade; the dark hair well-coiffed and thin beard well-groomed; the leather knee-boots and dark leggings; the noticeable lack of weapons on his person. Yet he was undoubtedly a prince — the very sort of prince I had always imagined a man of royalty to be. Clean, upright, keenly intelligent. Strong, straight shoulders gave him a decided edge over other men. He had a sharp blue-gray gaze that held mine evenly, almost curiously, as he waited for me to pass through the door before him, like a nobleman yielding to a lady. He was, if anything, deeply awe-inspiring.

By the time I joined the other two men in the adjacent receiving room, Agnar had changed his question, this time said with a grumbling insistence. "Why is she confined to the bed? It's been days. The Healers say there is nothing wrong with her."

It was difficult many times for me to have patience with Agnar. I could almost hear Malachi tell me, "Compassion cannot be taught, Meeshka. It must be born in the heart. And that birth often begins in small ways — with understanding, with patient teaching — the sort a person of forbearance may offer even to a king. The Whisper is patient with us, always patient. So we, too, must offer patience to those He has placed in our care as priests."

Cyric was on the verge of responding to his son, but I gave no sign of having noticed. "It's not the death that's so difficult, Your Highness," I said quietly. "It's the living without them here. It's the broken dream. That's the hard part."

Surprisingly, my words caused a weighty silence to fall. For once, the King looked thoughtful. I knew he had lost his wife to illness when Onyx was an infant, but I had never discerned how this impacted him or any of the Royal family. From his expression now, I had to wonder whether he had always been the promiscuous man he was. At the very least, whether as a result of the loss of his wife or no, death had struck his life at some point and caused him to pause over my words now.

I decided to take my leave then. I had no counsel to give except the wisdom I had already offered. With a deep inclination of my head, I acknowledged the three men, turned, and soundlessly left them.

Their words drifted after me as I exited the door to the receiving room and slipped down an adjoining passageway that would lead to central parts of the castle. Agnar's arrogance and warrior-like manner rarely felt the need for a discreet volume.

"There's something about her that's irritating."

Cyric quickly dismissed this. "She's powerless."

"Does *she* know that? We did not excuse her. And she never bows like Rogath does. He knows his place. What do you say, Axel?"

Axel's soft, steady voice was harder to distinguish, but I slowed my steps considerably to catch his words. I thought there was a curious note in his tone. "I hardly have a say on the matter, if you're truly asking. I have been home but a few odd days in months. This is the first time I have even heard her speak."

But Cyric quickly put an end to the entire conversation with a brusque rebuke. "Don't waste your thoughts on her, Agnar. We have greater problems — problems that need your attention far more than a priest who goes around in a skirt. You have no true-born heir to the throne. *Stay focused.*"

I began visiting the Princess daily. Though she gradually improved, I always felt a measure of conflict. Every day that Draveena grew a little stronger and more heartened was also a day closer to when Agnar would reclaim her body and this same cycle might begin again. Her spirit had nearly been crushed to be torn from her homeland, and was even more devastated by Agnar's rough, indifferent treatment of her. She understood she was here, not because she was liked or even physically admired by her husband, but because her important marriage had offered Cyric's household prestige, while giving her father a strong ally across the Great Expanse. She was reduced to a tool of production, that was all. It was difficult to know how to pray for her, and what change I could rightly hope for, except that Cyric's entire house might be transformed into new men and women altogether.

Malleable was the best way to describe Draveena, even at her strongest. *And who could blame her?* She was safest from Agnar and Cyric's harsh criticism and possible abuse if she remained this way.

She told me one day, thoughtfully, "I think I would like to pray to the Whisper as Miri did. If He were to grant me two children — a son for Agnar, and a daughter — I would give the girl to the Priesthood."

My heart broke for her, for many reasons. She and little Soren were the first fruits of my labor here in Periburn, and yet both were so utterly trapped. "And what will you ask for yourself for all this self-sacrifice?" I asked her. "Surely something."

She merely shrugged with a wan smile. "Whatever He sees best. He satisfied Miri's heart — and yours. I am sure He can satisfy mine."

I did not tell her that my heart was not satisfied — that it could never be satisfied outside my life in the Temple, and certainly not apart from my people. Without the Whisper's daily infusions of life and the promise set before me, I would have been as broken — and perhaps as malleable — as she was.

# 11.

My sessions with Soren continued through this time. Every day he was a private joy to my soul. He eagerly grasped at new things to learn, new ways to express himself. His mind was bright, and his childish enthusiasm a delight. For all her public coldness, Onyx privately poured love into her child and he was happy and affectionate for it. He often thanked me with embraces and small gifts of charcoal sketches — tokens of affection I had not known since Connor. The Whisper truly lived in the little boy's heart; Soren often spoke of child-like conversations they had held as he lay in bed at night.

There was always a pleasant warmth that rested over the small tutoring chamber where we held our daily sessions, a gentle contrast to the grand, drafty halls beyond its door. I was grateful for this place, brief though my time here was each day. Sunlight poured through arched windows, falling in soft gold across shelves of neatly kept scrolls and the worn spines of storybooks, their edges touched by eager hands from previous generations of young royal scholars. A round oak table stood at the center, polished smooth and scattered with ink pots, quills, and little carved figurines the young Prince liked to play with during moments of recess. Cushioned benches lined the walls, draped in embroidered throws that brought unexpected color—deep greens, soft blues, the hues of a peaceful garden tucked inside the stone fortress.

A small hearth faithfully crackled in the corner, its fire mild and welcoming, filling the room with the scent of cedar and warmed parchment. Upon the mantel, a vase of fresh flowers — placed there each morning by servants of the house — breathed a hint of sweetness into the air. I always sat beside Soren rather than across from him, which allowed me to guide his hands over parchment, helping him shape careful letters. He often drew quiet laughter from me when he looked up with bright, mischievous eyes — eyes that could soften even the sternest guards posted outside the doors.

It was upon this scene one day that Prince Axel suddenly made an unexpected appearance. At first Soren and I were so absorbed — and the Prince so soft-footed — that we did not notice him. Then some creak or rustle caught the young boy's attention, his face exploded with delight at the sight of his uncle, and he tumbled out of his chair and barreled across the room.

"Unkie Axel!"

I suspected few in this household, if any, addressed the impressive Prince with such easy familiarity. I had also never once observed any true sense of family or closeness during my stay at the castle — not even within Lady Chatney's household, warm as she herself was.

Axel caught Soren up in his arms, laughing softly.

"You're home!" the little boy declared.

"I am," Axel affirmed. "I've brought you something… all the way from the great land of Dungh Ga Da. I thought you might like to see it."

Today the both of them were wearing the same strong gold and midnight hues, though Axel carried his clothing like a man of stature and Soren like a costume he was still growing into. While the boy was flaxen-haired and Axel dark, there was a notable similarity between them as I watched them interact. In a strange way, Soren might have almost been a smaller echo of the grown man — softer, unguarded, less affected by the world yet.

Soren was already begging to see his gift.

Axel's mist-blue eyes looked up, back-lit by that sharp intelligence which seemed to rest upon him so differently than the other members of his household. "I'm afraid I've interrupted your lessons."

Quickly, I stood and shuffled together Soren's writing utensils on the table before me, sensing that the lesson was over for the day. "It's no matter, milord. He's clearly very pleased to see you."

"Thank you for your work with him. It's meaningful."

It was these words of humble gratitude that left me speechless. I was utterly astonished. I looked up and tried very hard not to stare. "Thank you, Your Highness."

He still held Soren in his arms, who had settled his cheek contently against his uncle's shoulder, as if he took just as much pleasure in the warmth of the arms around him as he did in the knowledge that his gift would soon be revealed. The boy responded very deeply to love.

"Onyx and I both hoped for him to be tutored by a Halevi," Axel said.

My thoughts were spinning, calculating. "I was not aware —"

"We considered it an answer to prayer that you arrived when you did."

Now I was stripped speechless entirely, for several reasons. Here undoubtedly was the Prince who had been tutored by a Halevi. I had not even considered Axel.

"She says you are doing a wonderful job," he continued.

*Was it even possible that Onyx was capable of the things he was describing?* I told myself I should speak. "Thank you, milord."

He asked me, "Do you mind if I claim his time this morning? It's not often my schedule allows me to see him."

It had been so long since I had been shown any manner of humility — and expected it the least from a man of power, who had no need to ask for my consent — that I was undone. This was surely a man among men, a prince among princes. Whichever of the priests had been entrusted with his care at a tender age had wrought a marvelous masterpiece... and what a task the holy man had had, to cultivate the young Prince in a pitiless environment like this one. He had done the Halevi proud. *"Of course."*

Then the two were out the door of the small chamber and gone, the little boy already chattering with delight over the possibilities to come, the man answering with warm, quiet confidence.

Afterward, I recognized that my encounter with Axel had given me a small measure of hope for my own work. I could not yet claim any broad influence within Cyric's household, but I could at least make a difference in the lives of Soren and Princess Draveena — and perhaps even in Lady Chatney's. With this in mind, I resolved to renew my efforts.

During this time, Lady Chatney gave birth and was soon taken up with her newborn; Draveena was pregnant once more, and held a quiet hope that the Whisper had heard her prayer. And I received a return message from Cohen. To my relief, his report was a positive one. The priests were well and the farmsteads had managed to turn a modest crop even without Connor. He made no mention of his sorrow over Liev, only his gratitude upon hearing that I was safe and unharmed. He felt surely my work at the castle was orchestrated by the Whisper Himself.

Even so, the message only served to make me miss the priests all the more. The mere sight of Cohen's sprawling handwriting on the parchment that was delivered made my heart awaken with a great feverish longing. I quickly found myself restless, which prayer in the abhorrent, godless shrine could not temper.

Lady Chatney emerged from her confinement just long enough to notice my distraction, and to offer a thoughtful suggestion I had not anticipated.

"I think you need a quiet place, Eren. This castle is often loud and full of motion, and it becomes difficult to think clearly within its walls. I would know — I have spent most of my adult years here. *I know of this place —"*

She spoke of a small lake beyond the castle, hidden deep within the ring of forested mountains, reachable by an old and abandoned passage beneath its foundations. She told me it was no longer used, and safe enough for the rare times one needed to escape for an afternoon. The manner in which she described it told me she had once gone there for suggestive purposes of her own, yet I determined to find it without delay. It sounded ideal — an answer to many fretting prayers offered to the Whisper over the last few sennights.

Shortly after, I found the passage as she described it — narrow and damp, sloping away from the castle's deepest foundations like a buried vein. Iron torch brackets lined the corridor at first in careful intervals, and then eventually stopped as the path moved beyond the perimeter where anyone ever ventured, at which point I took one of the torches and carried it with me until I found the low, concealed arch Lady Chatney had prepared me for. This opened beneath a curtain of tangled brush and ferns, spilling me suddenly into the hush of trees beyond. This was indeed an escape seam stitched secretly between the castle and the surrounding wilderness.

Just past the hidden opening, the ground leveled onto a quiet plateau, revealing a small lake only a short distance further, cupped like a mirror at its heart. This motionless body of water was cloaked heavily by the dark forests around it, and on the first day I visited, a diaphanous, lilac mist hovered over the quiet depths, creating a mysterious atmosphere that made my heart jump with joy. The mountain air was crisp here but gentle, carrying the clean scent of water and distant pine; the afternoon sun rested low enough to turn the lake's edge to molten light. Tall grasses whispered along the shore, their seed heads silvered by the early autumn season, while the dark forest rose around the clearing like a hushed audience. It was a place that felt momentarily untouched by the tumultuous world I had been living in.

For a long while I visited the place every day I had the opportunity, which was often. I soon adopted a regular spot nested between the roots of an alder tree on the water's edge, though most of the lake was ringed with silver-barked birches and whispering willows. These quickly gave way to dark pine, fir, and flame-colored maple climbing the surrounding slopes around me, providing a natural amphitheater of gold, green and shadow often reflecting in the still waters I settled myself by. It was here, at last, I could thoroughly empty the contents of my soul to the Whisper. Not since I had arrived in Periburn had I had a chance to so completely plumb the depths of my heart, to take full stock of all that I felt and all that I had experienced in the past many months. I was finally able to begin to recover my strength and drink from that fountain of life within me.

On one afternoon not long after this, I was leaned against the alder tree with my eyes closed, taking in the small sounds of the forest and lake around me. Autumn leaves were loosening their hold on the trees one by one, tapping the water with slight, papery kisses; dried grasses brushed together in the breeze along the shore; insects skimmed the lake's surface, causing a delicate ripple of the water. Beneath this all was the subtle murmur of the water lapping at the shore only a few scant feet away, steady and quiet. In the stillness, I forgot myself entirely, grateful to put the clamorous castle and its occupants far behind me.

But then there was some disturbance — a sharp sudden crunch of boots on wet leaves, and a soft splash as a frog on the shore leaped for the safety of the water. The sound of a step cut abruptly into my small, protected quiet.

I was startled beyond words. Gasping, I jumped to my feet, nerves jittering instantly, taking in my intruder in shock.

*"Forgive me,"* Prince Axel scrambled quickly. "Please — forgive me."

He was as surprised as I was, his eyes wide and breath short at the sight of me. He was dressed plainly for once, in soft leather boots scuffed from use, dark trousers made for movement, and a simple, fitted tunic belted at the waist. A light cloak hung at his shoulders instead of royal finery, its fabric practical rather than ornamental, and his sleeves were rolled as though he expected to climb, balance, and brush against the wild. For all that, he was still more finely dressed and carried himself with more dignity than any warrior in Agnar's service.

He sensed I was poised to take flight. *"Don't be alarmed.* I only came out here to walk. I saw this alder across the lake and thought it might be a good place to settle for a breather. You were so still — I had no idea these forests held anyone. I am ordinarily a better woodsman than that —"

I knew he was speaking quickly and about nothing important as a way to settle me. He had frozen in place, as if he wanted some sign that I was unafraid before he moved any.

I moved instead, quickly stooping for my little leather slippers. This discovery instantly meant I was unable to come here anymore; disappointment washed over me. *I had lost my sanctuary…* "It's no matter, milord. Feel free to take this place. I'll return to the castle."

"No — no, don't go." This sounded more like a request than an actual command. "Please don't let me uproot you from your place."

I looked up, hesitating at the kind servility in his tone. I had heard so little of it since my arrival that it almost sounded foreign to my numb ears, and was still shocking to hear on the lips of a person of nobility. Every friend and dignitary in Cyric's circle was as puffed with self-importance as he was.

*"Please,"* Axel said again, this time with a small smile. "You were clearly resting here, milady. *I'm* the intruder."

When he saw I was slowly relenting, he suggested, "We might talk for a bit. I have wished for a small conversation with you, if you are willing. Would you mind?"

Sheer curiosity was what made me take him up on the offer; and Axel was particularly guileless, which made him intriguing. Cyric's second son was a great mystery in this duplicitous place. I gave no verbal reply. Instead, I sat down again, slowly, settling against the alder tree, my bare feet tucked beneath the long fall of my skirts.

The Prince chose a position a few feet away, settled where he could watch the water. Today, as he took it in for a moment, the afternoon sun lay in a warm spill across the hidden lake, sifting through the surrounding trees in trembling ribbons of gold that turned the quiet water to glass and fire at once. This was a setting where the Whisper could easily settle, lingering in the air like an unseen Presence of peace and power.

"This is a beautiful place," Axel said quietly. "I haven't been here in some time."

At the question hanging in the air between us, he shot me a small friendly glance. "You happened to find my thinking ground, milady. When I was a much younger man, of course, and had need of a few moments away from the castle."

Another knowing fell between us. He had already realized why I was really here, away from my duties in the castle. And I had realized he had most likely not been walking, but searching for this little spot.

"In truth, I used to come out here to pray," he admitted. "It feels almost like the center of a great sanctuary, doesn't it? This little bowl in the forest?"

I still said nothing, though I agreed with him. How refreshing it was to hear someone say they sought prayer in seclusion; I knew immediately he was speaking of the Whisper.

With Axel's storm-lit eyes on the water and his knees tucked under his chin, I thought I could more starkly see Soren in him. There was a quiet vulnerability in him that surfaced here, among the forests and woods. He was a man of deep inwardness.

He proved this in the next instant when he announced, idly, "You've lost someone, I think."

I was taken aback. No one had asked me anything so personal since my arrival, not even Lady Chatney.

The Prince did not look over. "I don't mean to pry. I gathered it from what you said to Agnar about Draveena's difficulty in moving past the death of the baby. You were speaking from experience, were you not, not just from wisdom, milady?"

When I remained silent, he did turn his head now and took me in. "I've made you uncomfortable, forgive me." He quickly moved on, returning his gaze to the water. "Your words were beautiful and insightful. *The broken dream,* you called it."

I began to suspect his words weeks ago to his father and Agnar were untrue. There was little about me that had escaped his notice since the moment he first laid eyes on me, whenever that had been. Yet I sensed I had nothing to fear in his conclusions of me. I assumed the fact that I was Halevi held a great curiosity for him.

I found I could answer this at least. I stirred a little. "*Yes.*"

"But I am correct, aren't I?" he pressed again. "You lost someone?"

When his even gaze met mine, I smiled a tight smile, with great difficulty. *"More than one."*

"I would like to hear your story if you're willing, milady Eren," he announced then. His questions spilled out quietly, as if he had been pondering them for some time. "What is it that brought you to Periburn, aside from the prayers of Onyx and myself? What finds you here, away from your tribe? I heard you tell Draveena you had been raised in the Temple; I assume you were speaking of the Temple in Rivermouth. The Halevi rarely leave their own."

What ache it caused just to hear someone else familiar with Rivermouth and the Temple. I had not realized how difficult it would be to speak of these things. He was not merely asking what had become of the Halevi; he was asking after my own journey — and that was far more difficult to give voice to. There was a knot in my throat at the mere idea.

He added, "You've probably heard from my father that I was tutored by one of your priests for several years when I was a boy before he was dismissed —"

"I had heard, yes."

*Still,* I pondered, *he was a better candidate for telling the tale than Cyric.*

Even then, I quietly determined to alter Devland's name and omit any mention of his ties to the Raiders. That was a part of my story I would not tell anyone here, not even a prince who seemed so trustworthy and as warmly curious as he.

"He was a great and humble man," Axel continued. "He helped make me the man I am today. My mother died when I was just a little older than Soren, which was a great loss to me, so my father searched for a gentle man who could tutor and care for me. He had heard the Halevi might be a better choice for this type of work than the spiritual advisors who are ordinarily in his service."

Here were the answers I had been looking for. I stirred at once. "What happened to this man when King Cyric dismissed him?"

For the first, the Prince's face grew cloudy with the memory. "I don't know. He was released because my father thought I had outgrown the need for a caretaker and tutor. I was too young at the time to make use of any influence I had with Cyric to seek his whereabouts, and by the time I was able, I found nothing. There were rumors that Ezra disappeared into the Mountains of Purpose and was never seen again. So I assume he immigrated to Waldony. I've always kept my ears out over the years as I travel, but I've yet to discover anything." He abruptly changed the subject, looking over at me. "Won't you tell me your story, milady? You can see how it might be important to me. Your people — and the Whisper — mean a great deal to me."

There were some people and some words, phrased so excellently, that could reduce you from a High Priestess of authority to a gentle song-bird singing softly in the trees. Axel would often have this affect on me during the time I knew him.

"I will tell you," I agreed.

He looked suddenly pleased, like a quiet boy who had been handed a rare gift. "Start when you first moved to the Temple. Start there, if you would. I desire to hear it all…"

So that first day I told him — from the time I joined Malachi, to the moment I arrived in Periburn covered in Connor's blood. I spared almost nothing — not my encounters with the Whisper, Malachi's premature death, nor my love for Connor as a new dream with him was birthed. And once I began, it seemed a relief to say it all at last. The words came loose like beads from a snapped thread, at last released from their prison of silence after months, even years.

Through the telling of the long tale I often felt like I was speaking more to an avid, hungry listener than an important prince. I forgot completely who he was. Axel's love of the Priests and his interest in their way of life was apparent. In some moments he seemed deeply moved; others, greatly troubled. His eyes, washed in the hues of rain and twilight, dilated fully as he became angry. Some parts of the story quietly stirred his wrath.

At the end, as I fell silent at last, he was still watching me, though more carefully now. A somber air had fallen over the lake waters. I was leaned against the tree, letting it bear the weight of my head, my cloak gathered close against the cool air. I felt emptied now, purged of the emotion of it all, as if in the telling of it my heart could settle back into its place and rest quietly. Dusk was nearly here, the light thinning to cool amber and violet as the surrounding trees began to darken. I knew I must return to the castle soon.

"You have truly suffered," Axel said with quiet gravity.

He spoke to me as an equal, as if we were old companions who had caught up on the missing years between us; and strangely, I found myself able to do the same. "So have many," I told him. "But I have suffered with the Whisper. I clung to Him. That's the difference. I was not alone. So I'm better, and I walk away better."

"It is truly remarkable that you've kept your heart open in spite of all the wounds, Eren," he pointed out.

When I said nothing to this, reflecting on the surprising understanding in his words, he added with compassion, "I believe someone else's experience can never be yours. I can never fully comprehend what you have been through, from the inside out. But I hope you will still allow me to say I feel great sorrow for you and the Halevi, for what you have been through. My heart is grieved by it, Eren."

I knew, from all I had learned in recent months, that the second son of Cyric's household held no true power. Axel could influence his father and brother in as much as they would listen, but only Cyric and Agnar carried the authority to make true change. This was simply who Axel was — deeply intimate, personal, a kind soul to all those with whom he connected.

I managed a weak smile. *"Thank you.* In truth, it feels like a great relief to finally have it said after all these months."

He nodded, as if he understood. At some point during the long story he had stretched out his legs before him in a relaxed manner and leaned back on his turned wrists, but now sat upright, crossing his legs. For a moment he considered his hands, his expression ponderous. I observed for the first that on his last finger he wore a thin band of crown-gold bearing a tiny lion sigil on its head, unmistakable in meaning. He seemed to take it in for a moment.

"I'm afraid I must apologize on behalf of my father," he added quietly. "He did not take the threat of the Raiders seriously enough, and he called for the census, leaving many people unprotected. As a result, you suffered a great loss. I can assure you I will begin to petition for Devland's Raiders to be addressed with a stronger hand. I can at least give you that assurance, Eren."

I could say nothing to this. What utter conflict his words raised inside of me. His acknowledgement of the King's neglect was thoughtful and unexpected, a rarity here in the castle. His promise was compassionate and noble. But this action also meant a terrible end for Devland if his father did as he asked. Even though I knew it was a necessary and needful task for the protection of everyone in southern Avan — and would certainly allow me to return to the farmsteads — my brother was surely doomed.

My hands began trembling. I quickly tucked them in the folds of my gowns, away from sight.

Axel looked over at me suddenly, solemnly. "You will get your reward, Eren."

Somewhere in this conversation he had become familiar enough with me to call me by name.

When I said nothing in response, he added, "*Someday.* You will get your reward. Not just the Halevi. *You.*"

He was neither prophesying, nor uttering a personal promise. I knew he was trying to encourage me. Yet his words were directed by the Whisper, whether knowingly or unknowingly. He could not have known that they echoed Malachi's own so many years ago. And they reminded me that I not only ran for the Halevi, but there was a reward at the end of this journey for myself as well. I took heart in his words, in his thoughtful kindness.

"Thank you," I told him, and meant it.

I cannot recall ever speaking of it with Axel. There were no words exchanged between us. But somehow every afternoon he was always there at the foot of the alder tree, either waiting before I arrived or appearing not long after. Although ordinarily his life consisted of being off settling some dispute or another, or handling a diplomatic issue his father preferred to avoid, throughout that fall and early winter he remained at home — also for reasons never explained or spoken of between us. He never greeted me with a bright smile or an easy greeting. He simply settled in, resuming our conversation as if it had never ended and there was still much left to say. Sometimes he could only stay a short time, while in others he stayed for long watches until dusk.

Somehow the little place at the foot of the alder tree became a removed place from everything else — all that was, all that had been — a safe quiet refuge where anything could be discussed and all thoughts were welcome. It was in those unhurried discussions in the forest, as my friendship with the steady, observant, strong Axel grew, that I slowly found my way back to healing, to strength, and to a small measure of peace. Our conversation worked to restore the part of me that had been deeply broken by Connor's death.

Axel told me about his life, his duties, his precarious position in Cyric's court. He was very aware his life was changeable in an instant if his father — and eventually, Agnar — desired it. His responsibilities, his career, even his title and influence in the household, could all change in a heartbeat. Furthermore, until his brother produced an heir or two, the throne was left insecure and it became his duty to step in if Agnar should perish or was unable to bear a son.

These truths did not trouble Axel greatly. Just as I had accepted from a young age that the role of High Priestess meant dedicating my life to the Temple and my duties there, he had also accepted his destiny, volatile as it was. He felt equally confident that his father would live many decades to come; Agnar was healthy and robust; and Draveena would eventually bear a son or two. He carried no delusions about ever holding the throne, and very much doubted that there would be a need for him to step in and produce a royal heir in his brother's proxy.

"Father only uses the threat to goad Agnar into action," he said. "There is still plenty of time."

He explained what it meant to be a member of his father's house.

"In our household, kingship — *royalty* — is a family venture. Every member, even the distant ones, knows we will either stand or fall. I suppose that is partially why I am not too concerned about my father's whims, or Agnar's. There is a careful balance of power here. They carry an understanding that they need me. All of us hold the knowledge at all times that our power as a household is so easily lost… and swiftly, too. If we lose that power, we have lost everything. When threatened, it is our responsibility to fight to the end to maintain it.

"We also understand that power moves forward. It *must,* or — once again — it faces the risk of being lost. Therefore our mission as kings, as members of royalty, is to move that power forward as a joint effort. Agnar," he explained, "represents a level of power so high, he is not required to contribute as much as I am on a practical level. I have accepted that. It falls to me — and more extended members of the family, like Soren eventually — to help maintain our level of power in whatever way we can. I do so by being a diplomat on behalf of the household… and occasionally by being very stubborn with my father so he will listen," he added with a smile.

I was silent, hearing all of this.

Yet Axel was intuitive enough to sense I had thoughts on the matter. He added with a humble acknowledgement, "I don't expect all people to understand the life of a king and his household, or the requirements for this position."

He desired to be understood, though. I sensed that. At least by me.

For a moment I took in the tremendous things he had just said. They explained many practices I had observed since coming to the castle, not the least of which was why the household women reacted so eagerly to bearing a royal child. This gave them and their child status, recognition, and a coveted position. Aside from the sensual pleasure such clandestine activities provided, it also was their way of contributing to the household mission. They felt it was a noble deed to increase the Royal family.

But hearing the words from Axel also surprised me. This was not the Halevi way. I wondered if Ezra had kept quiet on these subjects out of carefulness as he raised him. Malachi's teachings came back to me now, more clearly than ever.

It was then I told him, quietly, "I believe the King has a calling just as we the Priests do. But I believe differently than you do, Axel. We do not think alike."

I would never have dared to say such words to Agnar or Onyx, and possibly anyone else in the castle, but Axel was unthreatened by anything I had to say — a remarkable quality that set him apart from the very household he was speaking of. His brow knit together in quiet concentration, curiosity sharpening his eyes. "What is it you believe? Ezra never spoke about a difference in thought on these matters… or if he did, I didn't pay close attention."

"The King's kingdom has been entrusted to him by the Whisper to rule and reign over the people," I told him. "We believe only God raises up kings and takes them down. Promotion and demotion comes from Him alone. He uses the will of man for His purposes very artfully. Power is not given or taken from you by your bloodline, or by dissensions and rebellions. It is given by the Whisper. A king is established by God."

Axel grew still, surprise flickering across his face before giving way to a thoughtful, almost eager attention, as if a door he had not known existed had just been quietly opened. "I suppose I have always believed that in a figurative way — much as one praises God for giving us all things. Never literally, though. If this is true, how do you believe a king holds onto his power?"

"If he places his trust in the Whisper," I explained, "God will help him hold his place. He need not be afraid if he has submitted himself to the authority and guidance of the Whisper. There is no need to cling so tightly to his power. If, however, he does not entrust himself to the Whisper, he is in constant danger of losing his kingdom when his people are not satisfied with his authority and leadership, nor is he safe against other powers that would try and seize it from him."

A slow smile tugged at his mouth as understanding dawned. This was unsettling his old assumptions and he appreciated it, like tasting a new bold flavor for the first time. "I have always believed that if you allow it, control can be taken swiftly for a king, so resistance must be dealt with swiftly. Is there ever a time the Whisper might guide a king to fight and defend what he has been given?"

"Of course. A king is not passive," I said. "A king is not a priest. We are not protectors and defenders. The King and his household are the gatekeepers for all the nation." I thought suddenly of that moment with Malachi and Joel in the mountains and winced a little. "It is difficult, though, when the Priest is cast out of the Temple where he belongs. We are left to the winds and storms of life."

Alex knew at once we had come upon a sensitive moment from my history. His eyes immediately darkened. "I am sorry for your pain, Eren."

But I merely shook my head. "It is no matter. In the end, the Halevi will have their justice. Tell me more about the way things are done here in Cyric's household. I've had many questions from the start —"

In another visit between the two of us, Axel admitted, "I don't always agree with my father's methods, but I agree with his thinking. I believe in trying honey first to negotiate, before threat or force. I suppose this is what has allowed us to advance in the known world and gain recognition over the past ten years. Cyric and Agnar know this and have made room for it." He paused then. "Of course, you are presenting a way of thinking I have not considered before. It bears serious deliberation..."

As my conversations with Axel began to take place nearly daily, I questioned whether I should devote so much time to him, when Cyric, Agnar, and the rest of the household stood in far greater need than simply polite improvement. Axel was already a believer in the Whisper, could hear His voice, and often did. He held an open heart, one God could quietly teach and grow. Yet he had little power, and was as bound in circumstance as Draveena and Soren.

I continued to wonder why the Whisper had placed me here — and in many ways, was *holding* me here. I often wished Malachi was with me to explain the ways of God, which felt a deep mystery to me in this moment. I knew my presence in the castle reached beyond the simple task of reuniting the Halevi. That Malachi had prepared me from such a young age about kings spoke to something greater ahead. Even the cost of reaching this place hinted at the scale of the Whisper's design. He had said my influence might shape the fate and future of the nation.

Even so, I found a deep enjoyment in my conversations with Axel. There was so much to explore, to consider, and to discuss. We seemed to make each other's thoughts come to life. I admitted to myself that I wasn't trying to grow fruit in his life; I simply enjoyed the pleasure of his companionship. He was a lamp in the darkness of this castle, a quiet burning fire of thought and strength. With him came a soft, luminous calm I greatly cherished. I came to consider him my friend — a small, temporal gift from the Whisper during my time here.

Once, Axel said thoughtfully, "Image is excessively important to the King. It helps him maintain his power. Always keeping the image of status is of vast importance to our household."

I could see this dedication in him same as the rest of his household, yet without the pride and selfishness that so often fueled it in them. His heart would not allow what theirs did.

I suggested just as thoughtfully, "Surely the heirs to the Kingdom — and the King himself — should dedicate themselves to the needs of their people instead of concerning themselves so much with their image of status and power."

Axel surprised me by bursting into a low, brief laugh. He didn't always use it, but he did that day. "You're bold, Eren. I suppose that's what Agnar has seen in you that irritates him so. He senses your disapproval," he teased.

His laughter was infectious. I smiled freely at him. "I do not mean to be defiant, nor to appear pious, either one. Yet it seems to me that a selfless life spent in serving others would be far more effective in keeping the love of your people than a life devoted to preserving an unwavering image of rank and unquestioned authority. Surely we are called to better the world from whatever station in life we are born into, by serving those placed in our care. An entire nation has been placed in the king's keeping, and he has greater power than any man to do so."

At this, Axel admitted, with a smile and a shake of the head, "You constantly put me out of my depth, Eren."

I smiled back at him. "You do the same for me, Your Highness," I returned, and meant it.

This — and the ironic use of his title — made him laugh softly.

There were occasions I did see Axel in the castle outside of our meetings by the lake, especially now that he was home, but for the most part I was never required to interact with him. My dealings were chiefly with Cyric, his many guests and visitors, with Onyx concerning Soren, or with Agnar regarding Draveena. If Axel happened to be present, he was the perfect nobleman, as he always was, and gave no sign that he knew me beyond courtesy. When Cyric summoned me to speak prophetically or interpret dreams at yet another state dinner or court banquet, Axel did no more than offer a polite smile as I passed, as he would to any lady of the court. Once or twice, I noticed him suppress a smile when I answered Agnar or Cyric in a particular way, but he never mentioned it afterward. We lived two quiet, separate lives — holding to our duties and obligations within the castle, and beyond it, a growing friendship shaped by weighty conversation.

As freely as he and I spoke with one another, there were certain matters we never touched upon. One such subject was whether he had ever followed the example of the other men in his household in pursuing secret liaisons, or leaving behind an illegitimate heir or two in the kingdoms he so often visited. I did not doubt that Axel had received many offers. A man as distinguished and handsome as he would have been sought after often; and the simple fact that he was Cyric's second son, and still unmarried, made him the most tempting prize in the castle.

Still, I knew — without knowing how — that he had never given himself to such indulgence. I could only ascribe it to the quiet way he had chosen a life set apart for the Whisper. I never asked him of it, and he never offered it voluntarily. Nor did we discuss his thoughts on marriage, or of any love he might have known in his twenty-eight years. Though he knew of my love for Connor, and the grief of losing him, we both instinctively left his own history untouched.

There was also a quiet understanding that romance had no place between us. For all his openness, Axel guarded both his words and his manner. He held me as a priestess, and I held him as a prince. Each position was hemmed in by strict castle protocol, forbidding open intimacy or alliance — rules often broken behind closed doors in the Royal household, but never by us. Both of us honored the weight of our callings and did not treat them lightly. Between duty and conviction stood a boundary neither of us ever crossed, however familiar we became with one another.

Once, he confessed, "Part of the image the Royal household presents is the appearance of being unaffected. So in growing up, I learned the discipline of concealing my feelings to preserve that image. I have done it for my father, and for our throne."

Axel made many quiet confessions, and I was always slow to answer each one, taking them in carefully beforehand. But this one struck me in particular. I was uncertain whether he meant that some things remained beyond what he could tell me, even now, familiar as we had become, or whether he was only admitting to a habit long ingrained by the discipline of royal training.

As I considered it, I could see clearly the training he spoke of. For all the intimacy with which he shared his thoughts, that royal discipline revealed itself again and again — both in our conversations and, more plainly still, in his conduct within the castle walls. There was a stillness he practiced before reacting, as though weighing his expression before allowing it to surface; the brief tightening of his jaw or his mouth that appeared, then vanished, when strong feeling threatened to show; his habit of deflecting with courtesy, guiding difficult subjects aside rather than refusing them outright; and his quiet withdrawal from moments that invited overt vulnerability — never abruptly, but with quiet grace. Most of all, there was his ability to bear insult or discomfort from Cyric and Agnar, as though endurance itself were a form of loyalty. In public settings, he was impeccably composed, nearly unreadable, no matter the provocation.

I said to him, "Showing weakness is showing strength when we have the Whisper, do you not think?"

Though this could have been perceived as a challenge, Axel was unaffected. He looked over at me and smiled with a quiet light in his eye, amused. *"When do you ever show weakness, Eren?"*

This baffled me. "How do you mean?"

"You are the most self-composed woman I have ever met," he insisted, "and I have met plenty by now. I've traveled the known world many years over."

"I — I feel I show weakness constantly," I stammered. "Tears, frustration, agitation, hopelessness. I admit to all of it."

"You may admit to it all," he pointed out, entertained, "but you never show it. At least not outside this little haven in the forest. You carry a great air of mystery about you… which, I suppose, is very helpful in being a priestess in a castle so very different than your beloved Temple. Everyone in my household is in a little awe of you."

I had the distinct sense that he included himself in that number. For my part, I was careful not to tell him that I was not the only one in the castle who stirred a sense of awe.

In the course of our quiet talks, Axel would sometimes ask what I would do when I returned to the office of High Priestess and took up the labor of restoring the Temple.

The first time he asked me, a bleakness settled over me like a shroud. Even if I were free to return to the farmsteads, we had no means to reunite the tribe or rebuild. And even if we somehow had the means, the community had already cast us out. We were not welcome there, nor had we any way to sustain ourselves.

He sensed my unspoken despair at once. "You should dream, Eren. Dreaming keeps hope alive. You should speak your faith. *When you are High Priestess,"* he insisted, *"what will you do?"*

He was right, of course. Until then, it had been too hard to give voice to these hopes, but his strength and quiet confidence drew me back to them and allowed me to see them again in my future. Over several afternoons, I began to unfold the dream to him. I would find the priests who still lived, scattered though they were, and return them one by one to the Temple grounds. We would restore the building if it stood in disrepair, and fill it at once with prayers and offerings. Then, once this was firmly established, I would return to the mountains — and to the farmsteads — and hire men to bring the remains of the priests home to Rivermouth. Malachi would rest at last in his honored place among the High Priests.

Afterward, as the silence settled and the magnitude of my plans lingered between us, Axel said thoughtfully, "It's a good plan, Eren. A truly worthy endeavor. I know the Whisper wants it, and wants it for your people. I only regret that I am little more than my name. I wish I could do more to bring it about."

On some days, we spent many long conversations comparing the role of the King and his household to the role of a priest. We discussed the weaknesses of a king, the vulnerabilities of a priest.

At one time, he declared, "The King needs the Priest, just as the Priest needs the King."

This was a new thought I had never before considered. "What does the King give the Priest that he needs?"

He added idly, "I would look out for you."

I looked up quickly.

But Axel cleared his expression, as if suddenly conscious this was too intimate, too personal for the two of us. "If I were king, I mean," he added. "I would ensure there was a place for the Priests and see to it that they were honored as they should be."

This was the only time I ever heard him admit what he would do if he were king. He was too loyal to his father — and too mature in his acceptance of his station — to give it much thought.

He shifted the subject suddenly. "What does the Priest give the King?"

I answered with ease. "You know the answer well enough to that one. The Priest shows the way forward from God." Then I added wryly, "If the King will listen."

Axel knew I was referring to his father. He smiled in laughing amusement. "Agreed."

Winter came late that year, for which I was grateful. This allowed my almost daily meetings with Axel to continue uninterrupted. The air carried the sharp, clean bite of winter's edge — cold enough to sting the lungs, yet gentle enough to linger without pain, as if the season were holding its breath before the final plunge into true cold.

Then the true cold descended at last — sudden, unanticipated, and carrying sharp change in its wake. One day, late in the afternoon, Axel froze suddenly mid-sentence.

"I think we are about to be discovered, Eren," he announced tersely.

At first I was unable to hear what he had detected... *and then there it was.* Heavy steps, branches snapping, wet leaves tearing under stamping boots. This was a careless force moving through the trees.

Even if they did not know of the little place beneath the alder tree itself, their unmindful disregard would lead them to us all the same.

"They're coming from the direction of the castle," Axel said.

I realized just that quickly how fortunate we had been not to be discovered these many sennights. Axel had known the place in his youth, and Lady Chatney had hinted at her own familiarity with the lake, for purposes better left unnamed. It stood to reason that others, too, knew of it — and would make use of this quiet way out of the castle in search of some secluded place by the water's edge.

"You could steal away," I murmured.

But Axel refused. "I'd prefer to face possible dishonor than leave you unprotected." Then he confessed something he never had. "I have no trust in Agnar's men beyond the castle walls." His gaze was as sharp as I'd ever seen it as his eyes raked over mine. *"And never with you."*

So we waited as the footsteps drew nearer. The surrounding trees stood mostly bare, allowing us to see the two who approached well before they broke into our clearing. My breath caught — then stilled — as I recognized the man in the lead. It was Agnar, unfortunately, his breathing heavy and his features flushed with arousal as he dragged a young woman by the hand through the brush. She was giggling freely, enough so that they did not notice us at once.

With calm resignation, Axel rose and turned to face him — a movement among the trees that made Agnar halt in abrupt surprise. *"Wha — ?"* His bawdy eye slid past his brother and found me. At once his expression shifted. *"What's this? What's this, brother?"*

As he made his final steps towards us, crashing through the forest, his voice was, as usual, overly loud, overly brash. *"You and the Priestess?"*

He laughed with open glee, his coarse laughter rolling through the trees and profaning the holy hush that hovered over the little lake. "I would never have pictured this, I tell you —"

Axel sighed heavily. "Don't exaggerate, Agnar. You've clearly stumbled into a perfectly innocent situation."

The young woman with the Crown Prince was a lady of the court I had seen now and again at the dinner banquets. She stared openmouthed with undisguised interest at the sight of Axel and me, while continuing to be dragged along by the hand, her steps clumsy beneath Agnar's thoughtless direction.

Heedless of Axel's words, Agnar amused himself with whatever salacious picture he had fashioned in his mind. He had never liked me, and the moment was too ripe not to make sport of. He laughed again, casting a leering, triumphant glance at his brother as he drew near. "I never thought you had the stomach for it, Axel."

He seemed to forget entirely that he had come out here for a purpose of his own — and not a blameless one. *"Just wait until I tell Father.* He will choke on his own spit — all that castle protocol shattered by the son with no faults. And with the forbidden Priestess, no less. He'll be counting the days, wondering when the next royal brat is coming. *Good on you, brother, for bedding the Priestess."*

It was these words that caused me to take flight. I could bear it no longer. The heat of humiliation was already burning up my neck and into my face. Gathering my skirts, I quickly fled the area and back to the castle, knowing in that wretched instant my conversations with Axel had come to a final and unalterable end.

# 12.

Even if I had not fled from the scene in disgrace, I knew Axel would never meet with me again. There were many things I understood about him and this was one of them. It was sacrifice enough that he stood his ground and faced Agnar out of protection of me.

Even so, I had not expected him to vanish altogether. He took the first diplomatic assignment he could claim and departed the castle at once, gone for the foreseeable future. Seen plainly, his behavior served as a stark reminder of how little power he truly had, save to return to his duty and bury this indiscretion behind him. I told myself this was for the best — that he had acted in both of our best interests — yet the decision was still a hard one for my heart. I had lost the only friend I had found here without word or warning, and with him a great pillar of strength was taken from me.

Left with no choice, I went on, little knowing how much was about to change, the loss of Axel's company being only one thread among many. All of the household, including Agnar, were very soon caught up in a report that came in only a few days after Axel's sudden departure.

Lady Chatney was the one who brought me the news, looking flustered and alarmed. "Three days ago Devland's Raiders attacked two royal messengers just outside the city and seized messages meant for the King."

This was not the first time this had happened. Devland had slowly been finding more ways to get Cyric's attention. Most of the messages he had intercepted were filled with harmless information, however — a missive that the King's vineyard in the north had had a generous harvest; a dispatch that the fall trade caravans had been delayed by bad weather but would soon arrive. I could tell from the tremor in Lady Chatney's voice that the news was far worse.

She continued, "The Raiders then used what they learned to strike a convoy of visiting dignitaries making their way to the city through the mountains northwest of Periburn. His men have never ranged so far, nor moved so swiftly — their reach has spread across much of the country. Two of Cyric's friends were killed — nobles traveling here from across the sea, from Krouba. Cyric is beside himself. *And those poor souls* — I knew Lords Rurik and Thorin. This is a grievous thing."

Any bragging and gossiping that Agnar might have spread about Axel or myself was cut short and immediately forgotten. Finally, Devland's actions had pressed close enough to Cyric's house that he was roused to fury. This strike in particular made a mockery of his strength before his allies and the crowned heads across the Great

Expanse. It gained him tremendous attention, but not in the way he would hope.

In the wake of the grave incident, Cyric and Agnar organized several armed companies and sent them into key regions of Avan where Devland's men were said to be gathering in small numbers, intent on open war. Additional forces were stationed along the roads leading into the city, both for protection and to make plain to the Raiders that Cyric was fully prepared to defend his people. It was said the King also tracked Axel down, already bound overseas by ship, and sent him on to Krouba and other countries on the Western Continent, to reckon with the damage left in the wake of the terrible affair, leaving the Prince wholly taken up for the remainder of winter.

Yet for all of Cyric's efforts, Devland struck again and again throughout the winter — attacking here, stealing there. He had indeed amassed enough power and resources to purposefully target the King in a way that most infuriated him. Armed royal messengers were harassed and waylaid, their messages destroyed or stolen and used for nefarious purposes. Convoys of visiting dignitaries to the city were robbed, very occasionally murdered, until Cyric was bleeding friends and noblemen who once so gladly accepted his invitations to visit. Supply caravans loaded with goods that were specifically intended for the castle were plundered and burned. A shipment of iron and weapons was taken; a large consignment of bread and reserves was stolen and some of it trampled, rendering it useless even to others who might find it.

Through his actions, it was plain Devland was deliberately trying to rouse the citizens of Avan against Cyric, inciting a rebellion. He desired to make the King look weak and vulnerable. He sent several messages taunting Cyric, accusing him of neglecting his people and ruling by tyranny, demanding his abdication. These were all pinned to the massive wooden gates of Periburn in the night, left there with a knife driven through its center, a blood-stained scarf knotted to the hilt. Once, a nobleman's gold chain and signet were attached. The underlying message was horrifically clear — Devland was nearby, bloodthirsty, and well-able to deliver on his threats.

For all that it unsettled Cyric and left him in a foul temper through much of the winter, Devland's efforts scarcely touched life within the castle. The Raiders were little more than a serious nuisance, and an embarrassing one at that, but few gave heed to them or their leader. No riots followed; the people's anger lay dormant. Only a small number of common citizens lent any ear to the Rebel leader, most being occupied with weathering the harsh winter or quietly tending their families. Avan was a prosperous country, and Cyric had ample resources to draw upon in order to continue without any real threat to his lavish way of life. On a more personal front, Draveena was well into her pregnancy, which satisfied his unceasing desire for an heir. For all his anger, he remained confident that Axel and his ambassadorial company could soothe any unease among the crowned heads across the Great Expanse and restore Avan's standing. He placed great faith in Axel's ability to ease tensions and manage appearances.

After all of these developments, I was more than glad I had kept my connection to Devland hidden. Of all the things I knew, this was certain now more than ever, shaped by my many conversations with Axel and the principles that governed his household: Cyric would never look past the fact that I was in any way related to the Raider leader who so thoroughly damaged his public image. Devland was a traitor and an insurgent, and I would be regarded with suspicion, if not outright contempt, for the remainder of my days.

In the first days of spring, I resolved to return to the little lake in the forest. I had not gone back since my last mortifying meeting with Axel, but the long winter indoors at last drew me out. My encounter with Agnar, and Axel's final words to me on that afternoon, had sharpened my awareness of the dangers that lay beyond the castle walls, yet I chose to take the risk all the same. The madness of Cyric's court had been a demanding drain, though I tried ever diligently to remain faithful to intercession for Cyric and to do my spiritual duties when he requested them. Throughout the empty winter, I had watched and waited for that ultimate purpose for which the Whisper had me here, but could not see it as yet. My greatest hope was that I could return to the farmsteads within the year, seeing as the forest roads outside Periburn and the northeast were better protected now. *Devland's increase in activity had won me that much at least.* With the coin I was slowly collecting, I hoped to be able to hire a security envoy to accompany me home to the priests.

I found the little lake lay newly awakened beneath pale spring light on that day, its dark water feathered with drifting petals and the tender reflections of budding branches just beginning to green the quiet forest. The Presence of the Whisper — ordinarily so greatly hindered within the walls of the castle — came quickly and with nurturing calm. As a result, I began visiting again — always with an abundance of caution so as not to be caught unawares.

But then one spring day, just as the weather warmed pleasantly and activity in Cyric's court reached a bustling height of feasting and celebrations brought on by the season, another change happened. I was returning to the hidden opening, prepared to pull back the curtain of foliage that separated the passageway to the outdoors, when I heard the telling snap of a twig breaking behind me. Aside from this small, traitorous noise, I would have had no indication that intruders had entered my space at all. Just as I tensed and turned, a dark bag was soundly dropped over my head, I was grabbed and held by strong, warning arms from behind, then bound effortlessly at the hands with strong cords. This instantly reminded me of that terrible moment on the road to Periburn when Devland's men cleverly took me into custody. Even at my most cautious, they would have caught me. They were exceedingly skilled in secrecy and surprise.

This time I felt no less fear, and my every sense strained with the effort to take in everything around me behind the dark blind. They had not gagged me this time; but there had been no need. They seemed to know I was harmless, the castle walls too thick for anyone to hear if I did cry out. I knew at once who my captors were… and I knew, for whatever reason, Devland had ordered them to bring me to him.

The walk took at least the bright half of the day. I assessed before very long into the journey that I was accompanied by three men, all of whom were light of foot and nearly soundless as they carefully navigated through the steep forests beyond the castle. The one who had the care of me guided me with a strong, firm hand that relaxed somewhat after realizing that I was willing to come without resistance. He was careful with me — more careful than the rough men who took me a year ago. They stopped only once briefly to pass a waterskin between them.

I was able to remain calm until memories began returning of that terrible incident in the forests. I had never forgotten the lustful conversation between them when they marched me to Devland last time. *Were these the same trackers who had relentlessly pursued Connor and me? Were they the same men who had killed him?* Connor had given his life because he did not trust them to deliver me safely to Devland. *Would they grow weary of the long journey through the forest and turn their thirst toward me?* These uncertainties left me trembling and freshly afraid, gasping for air the longer we journeyed. I was soon staggering and stumbling fearfully, wondering how long this would take, what they intended to do with me, where we were going.

My fear proved needless, however. We arrived in due course, and they had neither spoken among themselves nor addressed a single word to me. They delivered me straight to Devland.

When the dark hood was at last removed, the afternoon light swam and the forest trees were a blur around me temporarily as my eyes struggled to adjust to the change. I stumbled to my knees, realizing how tired the journey had left me. The climb had mostly been uphill, and they had not offered me water.

A voice I recognized commanded, "Give her water."

There was a shuffling of feet around me, behind me. Then someone slashed at my bonds with a knife, and a waterskin was placed in my hands. My fear subsided when I heard Devland's voice, but my grip was still weak from emotion. The cool liquid refreshed me some as it made its way down my parched throat. After only a moment, my eyesight sharpened into focus and I took in my surroundings.

This was a much different campsite than the last one they had brought me to — more temporary, as if they had merely stopped here for a day or two. Bedrolls surrounded a small campfire in the center of a tiny clearing; horses were tethered to a low-hanging branch a short space back; saddle bags and piles of tack were settled in a bulky pile nearby. As my gaze swept the little area, I counted four dark-faced men. They had already peacefully dispersed to various tasks throughout the campsite, as if they counted me harmless and calmly left me to Devland now that their task was done. They spoke in low murmurs amongst themselves. One of them was preparing food in an iron pan over the fire.

To my surprise, Devland was not standing proudly over me as I would have expected. He was seated at the foot of a large maple tree, half-leaned against it with his knees drawn up. I had been led not far from his feet. He met my gaze evenly.

I knew without any sign or evidence that he was wounded. Later, looking back, I wonder if the Whisper told me; but I knew it instantly. There was a formidable darkness about him which had not changed since the last I had seen him. Even seated so informally and without weapons, dressed in the dark travel clothing of an outlaw, he carried a presence that could rival Cyric's. Devland was a king in his own right. But his wounds, whatever they were, had left him without color in his face, and the evil light in his eye had cooled.

"I swear, sister," he said, without any weakness or struggle; "You grow more beautiful every time I see you."

Strangely, the rest of my fear drained away. I was not — could never be — afraid of him. Just as last time, I was convinced he would not harm me. For as evil and powerful as he had become, for as much separated us, he held some protective love for me. We were connected somehow, by blood, by our shared moments, by our love for our mother. It flowed there between us like an underground spring — hidden, unrelenting, and still alive.

"Why have your men brought me here, Devland?" I asked him. "What is it you wish with me?"

"My men have kept watch on that egress behind the castle for days." His tone changed abruptly; an impatient light sparked in his eye. "What are you wandering out for? Men could have laid hands on you and torn you to shreds."

*He was chastising me.* A heat rose in my veins at once. "Your men among them," I reminded him archly. "They chased us down only this side of a year ago —"

He gave a dismissive shrug. He knew the *us* I was speaking of. "You had Connor at your side. I knew he would keep you unharmed."

That heat rose now in full force. It was more than I could bear. Even the sound of Connor's name upon his lips was an affront. Mindless of the men all about us, I broke out in quiet shock, *"They murdered him!* He gave himself up for me —"

But Devland's bright eyes only gleamed in answer. For all the greatness he believed he had gained in the past year, the thought of Connor's death gave him a dark and personal satisfaction. "And a fine, noble ending it was," he snarked.

I swallowed down the sick feeling that rose. It was plain that he was cut from the rock of bullying and violence. His heart stood cold and untouched. He would not listen to any sisterly rebuke, nor would my distress have an affect on him. *Whisper, help me... Give me strength...*

I took a calm steadying breath, looked him in the eye, and said quietly, "All of that aside, I have forgiven you, Dev. For the exile of the Halevi, for Malachi's early death, for Connor's death. For all of it."

This, at last, roused him. He flinched as though I had struck him. "Why should I care?"

"You seem to forget — every act is born of a cause, and God reserves the final judgment of that cause to Himself. Even in your case. It is my calling as a priestess to plead that cause before Him, not your deeds alone. You *need* my forgiveness, Devland."

This both unsettled him and stirred his wrath. He shifted restlessly at the base of the tree. One of his hands moved for his side, and he winced as if it pained him suddenly. "You fancy yourself sitting in a place of power," he threw out. "But you hold none, Eren. *None.*"

I didn't believe he meant it; he was only reacting. I was indeed the one in a position of power in this moment. The power I held as a priest frightened and disturbed him. He hated it. He resented it. He despised the fact that he believed in the Whisper; that belief was a constant conflict within his soul. He was warring with God as much, if not more, than he was warring with Cyric himself.

"What is it you wish with me, Dev?" I pressed. "Did you bring me here for nothing but a warning? Take me back at once."

He nodded towards his men, who were still paying no heed to us as they went about their activities. "We need supplies, enough for the five of us for a fortnight. Travel food, more blankets, some fresh clothing. We've no time to live off the land — we must keep moving for the sake of safety. We were cut off from my other forces in a recent clash with Agnar's men and have lingered here awhile before rejoining them. Our most basic stores are nearly spent."

He had no need to tell me that he had been wounded and that they were unable to travel. This was what had held them back.

"And what claim have you upon me that I would help you in anyway?" I demanded.

He looked sure of himself, as though he held no doubt at all as to the answer. "Because I am still your own flesh and blood, am I not?" His jeweled eyes sparked with quiet smugness. "And because I hold a spy within the castle. I would be only too pleased to have him spread word that you are my sister, far and wide. Then we shall see how well the King favors his little pet priestess."

This news surprised me, though it shouldn't have. I had been in Cyric's court long enough — and had conversations enough with Axel — to know that these games of subterfuge and treachery were played by all men in power. I drew my cloak around me in a sudden wind that sprang up in the trees, using the excuse to hide my fear. I had fooled myself into thinking my identity was safe. *Even Devland would use it against me if it worked to his advantage…*

Dev marked my reaction at once. "You are surprised," he said. "My power is no trifling matter, sister. It would not be wise to make too little of it. Yet I must tell you — I found it rather a remarkable thing when the report was brought to me where you were and in whose company. You once said you would walk among kings and princes." His voice wavered, caught between scorn and a grudging, unwilling respect. "Your labor will come to nothing all the same. There is no altering what dwells in the hearts of such men." His tone turned to iron in a cold heartbeat. *"And no so-called power from the Whisper can work that change.* The crown itself must be torn out by the root and smashed to dust. The power must be flung back into the hands of the people — through me. Only then can they rise and rule by their own will."

I shook my head at him quietly, unmoved by his passion. "We will never come to agreement on this, Devland. You know this. It is not the Whisper's way, this path of destruction and violence that you have chosen. He has another plan for the future of Avan."

An angry light flared in his eyes, instantly deaf to all that I had said. *"When can we expect the supplies?"*

I told him, "So you will obligate me by blood, and extort me as well..."

"I will do what must be done to save myself and my men."

*"Name your spy."*

Devland scoffed. "He's the same man who knows every secret in the King's household. Do you truly think I would be foolish enough to name him to you? *When can we expect the supplies?"*

I weighed what he was asking — the impossible charge he was laying upon me. There was no question that Cyric would have me killed or kept in chains for the remainder of my days should he ever so much as catch a whisper of it. "If your spy truly knows all, then you already know I have no true power in the King's household and no resources. And even if I did, discovery would mean my death or a lifetime in chains. You have declared open war on Cyric. You know I am not able to do this."

Yet Devland pressed his demand with smug insistence, heedless. "You will find a way. From what I'm told, you have great favor with several figures of consequence in the King's court. I have great faith in you, Eren."

At the look on my face, he just as quickly grew agitated. *"Do it, Eren,"* he spat out. "We need no more than enough to feed and supply the five of us for a fortnight. I am not asking you to betray that *canker of a king* squatting on his bloated throne."

I continued to hold his gaze. I could easily have argued that to give him such supplies would be taken by Cyric as open treason against the crown of Avan. Of that I had no doubt. Axel would see it no differently. Nor even Lady Chatney. This was much more serious than being of relation to him.

"Show me the wound," I declared.

The request took him off his guard. He had not known that I was aware, nor did he welcome the thought of seeming weak before me. Devland hesitated.

"You're still my flesh and blood, are you not?" I asked wryly, quoting him. "You know the Halevi are taught basic healing skills. Malachi trained me. *Let me see it."*

Slowly, he opened his cloak as I pulled myself to my feet and moved over to him. His men looked up, alert at once, but he gave them a resigned nod, assuring them of my continued harmlessness.

As I knelt beside him, I could sense his physical pain and weakness. He had not fared well since he had been injured, however long they had stopped here. He had hidden this skillfully in the past several moments. As I watched, he pulled back his linen shirt with fumbling fingers, revealing old blood-crusted bandages. The bleeding had been contained, but the small blade wound in the fleshy part of his side was still dangerously open.

"This must be cleansed with wine or vinegar," I announced. "Have you either on hand?"

I could see from his strained expression that he did not. For a moment, he looked like the small vulnerable boy I had once cared for when he visited the Temple, his eyes dark with pain, features marked by quiet uncertainty. The injury had frightened him.

"The bleeding is stopped, and this wound will not kill you if you keep it from corruption," I said at once. "You will need yarrow to hold the blood fast, and honey with garlic for the dressing. You will also need clean linen in good supply to bind it as it closes, and comfrey for the healing afterward. I can instruct your men." My voice grew firm. "And you will need rest. You should not move for several days — not even for gentle walking."

He accepted this. His mood turned as quickly as that, and he fell quiet and subdued.

A silence fell.

I stood to my feet over him then, looking down on his short sprawling figure and dark bent head. An unspoken question lingered in the air between us. I knew there was no way I could turn from him or deny him help, not in this condition.

"It will take me a full day at least to gather what is needed," I told him. "How am I to signal your men when the time comes?"

With a faint, restless motion he sought a more bearable posture, trying to ease his pain. I sensed that my kindness had softened his temper. "Come to the edges of the lake. They'll be keeping watch for you."

Before I left him, I held Devland's dark gaze for a moment. He sat there half-hunched over in pain, with that familiar, vulnerable stillness I had known in him since boyhood, dark curls falling into eyes that once laughed with mine and now measured the world like a blade's edge. Wickedness had carved itself into him — in the hard, unyielding line of his mouth, in the guarded, powerful set of his shoulders — but in that moment, softened by my small kindness, I thought I saw a flicker of the man he once was. Something fragile and human softened his sharp gaze. For all the harm he had done, for all the shadow he now walked in, we were still brother and sister.

"I dare not risk coming back here, not even for you, Devland," I told him. "Take care of yourself."

He nodded. We both knew this was our goodbye, perhaps for a long time, perhaps forever. His tone was quieter now. "Once you've brought the supplies, don't stir from the safety of the castle, Eren — not for any cause. These woods are thick with men who would seize you and think little of it." He could not help but add, dry as dust, "You should have stayed in Rivermouth when the chance was given to you."

He had said this a year ago, I well remembered, but just as then, I could see he meant it because he wished for me to be safe instead of exposed to the dangerous wilds of life outside the safety of the community. For all of his embittered, violent ways, I was a point of vulnerability for him, strangely. After this meeting, I did not truly believe he would tell his spy about my connection to him. It would place my life in peril. Devland was a living paradox, breath and bone at war within the same flesh.

I could do nothing but shake my head, my gaze still fixed upon his unwaveringly. "I am one of the Halevi, Devland. The same Halevi who believe in the mercy I've shown you today."

He sighed instantly. *"And stubborn to the bone."* He nodded to his men then, who were standing by now. "Take her back."

As I took the first few steps away, he called my name. "*Eren.*"

I turned back partially.

"These are my best men," he assured me quietly. "You will come to no harm by their hands."

I nodded at this before continuing on, aware his black eyes were following me as his men wordlessly led the long trek back to the castle.

Only after the fact did the visit with Devland fully settle upon me, like breath leaving the lungs once you realize how near you have come to drowning. By the next morning, I was fraught with mental unrest. I'd spent the night in prayer, seeking the Whisper for solace and wisdom, but my thoughts had gotten the better of me, unfortunately.

I had no idea how I would obtain the supplies Devland needed. I was certain I could not — *would not* — take from the castle's stores. That would be too risky, absolute foolishness. I would have to make my way into Periburn to the marketplace and gather them there. This alone would be risky enough, I determined. I took a terrible chance at being recognized by any of Agnar's men, or any women of the court who visited there. They could easily report back to the King that they had seen me, which could just as easily spark his curiosity as to what business I had there and why. I knew he and Agnar had an eagle eye out and a close ear to their networks for anyone giving aid to the Raiders. Additionally, I had no coin except the little I had gathered for my return to the farmsteads; there was no one I could turn to for help.

Then there was the rest of it. The treason of it. This carried a weight I could not easily dismiss. For certain it was not merely fear of discovery that troubled me. I would surely not be judged for charity of motive if my actions were found out. And now not even Axel was here to offer that steady strength he had.

Thoughts of the Prince only made the situation more agonizing. On the way back to the castle, after leaving Devland's side, I had suddenly remembered a part of one of Malachi's last prophecies that had never occurred to me in all the sennights I had become acquainted with Cyric's second son — that a prince's life would be given for mine. I could have argued that this idea was extremely unlikely, that Devland and Axel could hardly ever be expected to cross paths; but the unexpected encounter with Dev had proven, for a second time, how swiftly my circumstances could change. Fear churned within me. There was surely more trouble ahead, no matter what solution I was able to find in purchasing the supplies. *Everything else Malachi had said had proven true... and I had lost Connor tragically and horrifically.*

Around mid-morning, I found myself trying fruitlessly to concentrate on Soren's lessons, watching as the sun shifted through the arched windows in our little tutoring chamber. Every changing angle of the shadows on the grand carpets meant time was passing me by, and I still had no solution. But then, as the Whisper so often provided, a strange peace came upon me. I knew at once that some way had been made, some solution had manifested that was on its way to me even now.

I could hear Malachi's voice in my memory, saying, "There are hours when the only choice left to you is to let a thing be as it is. In such hours you must not move — not until a new door is given to you. Even the choosing to let it be is still a choice. And that choice, whether it feels so or not, carries freedom within it."

I had just calmly accepted this when the door opened and Princess Onyx walked in unannounced. In my many encounters now with Axel's younger sister over the past year, I had learned well that she maintained a certain image in the public eye. She, just as with the Prince, had adopted the importance of protecting their family image in order to maintain their power, and this manifested upon her like armor — chin always held high, eyes cool with practiced arrogance and vanity. I made it a point to never approach her, and avoided addressing her if I could. In private, however, and especially in the presence of Soren, I found her sharpness fell away into something softer and more human. The weight of her performance was set down, her posture eased, and her expression became unguarded. Surprisingly, she gave compliments and ready praise. She was, in short, a thorny rose in this castle of pretense and power.

Today, as soon as she entered the room, her countenance was soft as she laid eyes on the two of us seated at the table. Even as Soren cheerfully greeted her, she said to me, "Lady Eren, two guests have arrived at the castle to see you. I brought them to my personal receiving room and thought you might like greet them there."

My heart leapt at once. This was odd. Never once in the past year had I had a visitor, and it was even odder still that Onyx had conducted them to her private rooms. She told me nothing more than this, and quickly led the way; but I knew somehow this was the answer I had been praying for, whomever it was that was waiting.

Just as I crossed the threshold of the Princesses's receiving room after her and Soren, I froze in my steps. The room itself was hushed, as if holding its breath for me to arrive. Pale silk draped the walls in soft folds, catching lamplight that glowed like melted gold across polished marble floors. Small tables stood precisely spaced, each bearing a vase of fresh flowers or a tray of untouched crystal. But my eyes had brushed past the finery to the center of the chamber at once — lighting on two ancient priests in simple, time-worn robes, standing side by side with their hands folded before them, their bowed, patient stillness starkly out of place against the room's lavish grandeur.

A cry escaped my lips before I could contain myself. I recognized both of them immediately — this was Joram and Zadok, who had left the Temple just before the Exile to sell some of our items in Periburn five years ago. Malachi had mentioned them often in the months before his death, hoping they would find their way back to us, eventually contenting himself with the fact that I would be the one the Whisper used to find and unite all of those scattered and missing.

I rushed over to them, heedless of Onyx or Soren. Their weathered faces lit up at once at the sight and sound of me, softening into sudden, unmistakable joy. Soon I was enveloped in their warm embrace; patted gently on the back; kissed soundly on the cheek. Happy tears filled our eyes and streamed down all of our cheeks. How precious every single priest was after the terrible loss of so many of them to death, in addition to this long, desolate time of separation from any of their beloved faces. What a miraculous wonder that they were here after all of these years. I could feel my being filling with strength just at the sight and feel of them, here, *alive,* and in my presence.

*"How did you find me?"* I cried, laughing with joy. "I'm so glad to see you alive and well. Tell me everything!"

They soon explained that they had return to the compound years before, but could find none of the Halevi and no one in the community knew where we had gone. The reception they had received had been cool at best, and they had hurried on their way with heavy hearts, eventually making their way back to Periburn.

"We have held out hope for three years of finding any members of the tribe," Joram said. "We have kept the money safe, Eren, living off as meager a portion of it as we could. Only recently did we meet a salesman in the city by the name of Henri who knew you and said you had been taken to the castle. Through the great goodness of the Whisper, the Princess Onyx's lady-in-waiting was nearby when we were explaining our wish to see you to the household steward. The lady told the Princess, and the Princess came personally to usher us here."

At this, I looked up and realized Onyx had disappeared with Soren, graciously emptying her rooms for us. I was still half-laughing, half-crying. What ache filled my heart, knowing they had been here all along. "This is surely a gift from God," I declared. "You have come at a most needful moment. Let us sit and I will tell you everything."

My plans quickly formed that very morning. It was indeed a great miracle that Joram and Zadok were so acquainted with the city, and even knew Henri. I swiftly sent them to the crafty salesman and the marketplace, using a small portion of the tribe's coin to purchase the supplies and medicinal items I needed. They soon returned, with the goods cleverly stored in multiple heavy packs that looked excessively unassuming in the hands of two elderly priests. By the day's end, Devland's supplies had been delivered without incident, and my heart was filled with utter joy that my way back to the farmsteads was well in hand. I would put this time in Periburn behind me, put my encounter with Devland aside, and the three of us would return to the tribe at once.

Even then I knew this was the moment I had been waiting for. A moment for change had come, and had come all at once.

"We will go together," I told the two men, sharing my plan with great satisfaction. "I wish to return home as soon as possible. Give me a few days to find an opportunity to ask King Cyric to relieve me of my position here and we will hire an armed escort to take us to the farmsteads using the tribe's money and what coin I have collected. This is the perfect season for travel."

Joram and Zadok were as thrilled and pleased as I was, and we cheerfully parted ways that evening, with them headed back to their lodging in the Serfs' District of the city, and all of us promising to see one another soon.

My hopes for a swift departure were soon delayed, however, and quickly turned into a stressful series of events that left me reeling with exhaustion.

The first began with a midnight summons to Draveena's bedside only a day following the return of the priests. When I arrived, it seemed half the population of the castle had been called in. A team of castle healers were already there, giving quiet orders, making requests to her ladies-in-waiting, who were darting in and out of the chamber with anxious obedience. Also hovering near her bed were Rogath and two other spiritual advisors, chanting prayers in monotone and waving burning incense sticks that left a foul odor. Agnar was present, mostly in the way, swearing impatiently at everyone in sight, along with Onyx, who stood aside from a distance and watched with a sympathetic expression.

Draveena herself was in terrible distress. The princess was rigid against the sheets as the violent waves of pain tore through her, her breath breaking into sharp, helpless gasps. Sweat had darkened her hair at the temples; her hands clutched at the bedding with desperate strength as her contractions came faster and harder than they should have, stealing her voice and leaving only strangled cries in its wake. There was terror in her eyes beneath the agony — an unmistakable knowledge that this was wrong, that her body had turned on her before it was ready — while the room was filled with the blood-sharp scent of fear. The baby was coming far too soon…

I stood back until she saw me. Then she gasped my name and beckoned for me. "Eren — *please* – *please come* – pray with me… *Please…"*

So I stayed with her. I held her hand through the long, merciless hours, my own hands slick with sweat and blood by the end of it, whispering prayers and words of encouragement even as her cries tore through the room like a living thing. The labor dragged on far beyond endurance, pain stacked upon pain until I lost all sense of time. Hours passed, possibly a day or two. The Healers applied every bit of knowledge they knew to ease her suffering and hurry the delivery; but there was nothing much to do but let nature take its course. When the child was finally born, too small and too still, the room fell into a stunned, awful quiet that no prayer could mend in that moment. Onyx respectfully drifted away, tears streaking her face; Rogath and the other advisors slipped into other parts of the castle with a solemn air, leaving the Healers to do the final work.

Agnar watched in speechless stupor as one of the Healers washed the infant and placed the baby briefly against Draveena before the stillborn child was taken away from this world as quickly as it had come. It had been a boy-child — most terrible of all for the entire household to bear. Draveena's scream then was not one of pain but of something deeper and more final, a sound that broke open all the walls of the chamber and left only ruin behind. At the sound, the Crown Prince fled the room as if he was haunted by evil spirits, devastated beyond words.

I could not leave her, not like this. Draveena had depended on me so greatly and still did. In the days that followed, she drifted far from herself, quiet and hollow, her eyes fixed on places only she could see. Even as everyone else in the household chose to remain away, I stayed near her constantly — spoon-feeding her herbal broth that her ladies brought, smoothing her hair when she wouldn't move, speaking when she couldn't answer, sitting when even words were too heavy. Agnar never returned to her chambers; and part of the grief she carried was the knowledge that she had failed him. She had hoped so terribly to at last please him. How desperately she had longed to be loved by him even in the smallest way.

I prayed over her in the dark hours and coaxed her through the mornings, hoping to guide her back into her body, back into breath, back into the faintest will to remain among the living. Grief did not leave her, not truly, but slowly it loosened its grip enough that eventually she could stand, could weep without breaking, could look at me again and know she was not alone. And that, at first, had to be enough.

Meanwhile, in what little moment I could claim, I seized the chance to send word by castle courier to alert Joram and Zadok that our plans would have to be set aside until I could find a way clear of my duties. This alone was draining and discouraging. I had hoped to be gone within days, and already those days were turning into sennights.

When I finally emerged from the blurry fog of those long days and nights, both exhausted and weary, I found Devland's Raiders were being mentioned in every hall and corner of the castle. News of his evil activities had intensified by at least ten-fold through the early summer months. During my absence, Devland had escalated his onslaught of terror across the entire countryside, wreaking more havoc than ever. After seizing what he needed, he was burning granaries and fields, leaving famine in his wake as both punishment and leverage. Wells were being poisoned and supply depots contaminated that were used by Cyric's men. Royal patrols and isolated garrisons were ambushed and robbed of their weapons and supplies to equip his forces. Along his path deliberate symbols of rebellion were carved into gates, churches, or keeps — marks meant to spread panic faster than armies.

My thoughts grew restless with fear. The longer I stayed, the more certain it seemed that my connection to him would be uncovered. There was still a spy in the castle working for Devland. Though I no longer feared that Dev would reveal our familial tie, I had no idea who the informant was, or what he might be capable of. It left me deeply uneasy to carry such treasonous knowledge with no way to remove myself from it. And there was always the chance that Cyric might learn of my aid to the Rebels, a danger that only increased with every passing day. He and Agnar had promised rich rewards to any who could bring word of the Raiders, their networks, or those who aided them.

The only small reprieve I had was that Axel was still gone, safely away from Devland's reach. Malachi's unfulfilled prophecy hovered like a dark shadow over my mind. Somehow it seemed to me if Axel was not present and I could escape the castle before he returned, then I could keep him safe. I knew the thought was irrational and ridiculous, yet I found myself wishing for it all the same. For many days I kept long vigil in prayer for our safety, and for the nightmare to be ended. I longed more fiercely than ever to be loosed from the bonds that held me in Periburn and returned to my own people. Freedom felt painfully near — near enough to ache for — and still it lay just beyond my grasp.

One day in mid-summer, I was summoned through courier to Cyric's ceremonial hall at dinner time. I had not been called by the King at all this summer, seeing as the household was aware that I was with Draveena. They still had hopes that she would eventually recover and could bear children successfully, though after the terrible death of the baby no one had said as much yet. For once, everyone was silent on the matter.

Even before I swept through the double doors of the throne room, I could hear Cyric's foul-tempered bellows rolling unchecked. He was already drunk, and clearly in a sour mood. Voices were cautiously low as I stepped in; there was a noticeably soft clink of cups and an uneasy stillness in his court. The very idea of being called here after many sennights made my stomach clinch. The message came without explanation, and though I tried to believe it concerned some spiritual matter, my mind went instead to the many secrets I was striving to protect.

As I reached Cyric's seat at the Royal table on the far end of the room, my eyes were immediately drawn to the right of him. Agnar was there, lounging with his usual air of entitlement — and next to him was Axel, whose storm-washed gaze was locked on me. I had never seen him seated at his father's table before, as if Cyric had insisted after his long absence.

*Oh, what conflict the very sight of him caused me.* This was utterly the wrong place to discover the worst had happened — *he had come home.*

It had been nine months since I had last seen him. He looked well. While time had seemed to drain the color and vitality from those in the King's household — bleaching some, bloating others, dulling most — it had worked the reverse on him. He glowed with color and vitality.

Agnar elbowed him with a muttered snicker, but this only diverted his brother's attention for a heartbeat. Axel's gaze flickered briefly to the Crown Prince, aware of the jab — then his eyes were back, fixed on me with a light like the blue of distant mountains fading into mist, so intensely directed my way I had to look away.

My breath was a little short as I inclined my head to Cyric. "You called for me, Your Highness."

The question caught him while biting into a turkey leg. He tore the flesh loose and snapped at me mid-chew, grease dribbling from his heavy beard. *"You took your time. Why are YOU late?"*

Cyric did not allow anyone to dispute him, and I was too shaken by the sight of Axel to find something diplomatic to say that would turn the King's attention away from this untruth. Instead, I stood quietly, waiting to see if he was demanding an actual explanation or this was merely an impatient grumble.

But Cyric was in a particularly foul mood today. No doubt the death of the baby, coupled with Devland's continued attacks, had made him intolerable to be around all summer. I did not grovel like his other advisors and he seemed to have less forbearance for it today.

His lazy eyes raged at me. He slapped his turkey leg down on his plate, food forgotten. "Tell me, Priestess," he growled, "Do you think of yourself more highly than everyone here? Higher than the Royal Family? *Higher than my sons here?"*

This line of questions made the room go silent as I became the center of attention. Cyric had never confronted me before. All that Agnar had said over the past many months in muttering asides had been true; I was easily Cyric's favorite, his spiritual trinket, his symbolic talisman used to maintain favor with the Whisper no matter how poor his behavior.

Agnar snickered; Axel's eyes continued burning into me. Just now I felt the pressure of that moment more than understood it. Of everyone here, even Draveena, I was lower in life than any of them. I had lost more than they could ever know or understand. I was exhausted, spent, and lightheaded with containing these terrible secrets. *How I wished I was away from this terrible place and back with my people where I belonged…*

I paused a quiet spell to draw strength from the Whisper, pulled in a steady breath, and said softly, "I was in intercession for your family, King Cyric."

To my private satisfaction, this had an immediate effect. His bluster fell away; his mood tempered. He bumbled, "Is this true?"

"Yes."

He was wretchedly unhappy, that much was plain. He glanced down at his food, unable to look at me. "And what does God say about us at this time?"

I had, in point of truth, been praying for his household since the night I had been called to Draveena's chambers. They could surely not hold on to their power for much longer, no matter their efforts, if they did not begin to put their trust in the Whisper. The signs were clear. But these things I did not tell him that day. Instead, I told him what God had told me, and was perhaps the word that would comfort Cyric and his household the most in this moment. They would have to make their own choices about the Whisper. With the arrival of Joram and Zadok, I had come to a decision — I was no longer here in hopes of saving this household. I had done my part.

"He has said your heir, the King, will have many sons, milord. You should take heart."

This seemed to settle on the King like cool water on a burning wound. He nearly heaved forward over his plate, taking in the words. He was not accustomed to being brought to a place of such vulnerability in front of his court.

"I will continue to pray for your household, milord," I told him then, in the silence.

He said nothing further — I was not sure he was capable of it — so I inclined my head once more, turned, and strode from the dining hall in full view of the room.

Axel found me only moments after the confrontation with Cyric, intercepting me in a narrow passage that led toward Lady Chatney's tower house in a distant corner of the castle. He called *Priestess* after me; and when I did not stop, his voice grew more urgent. "*Eren.*"

I came to a halt with slow reluctance. Somehow I did not want to look into his face, *not just now*, not when I was so weary, not so soon after the clash with Cyric. He would surely get every secret out of me that I held so closely to my chest.

Slowly, I turned, finding a look of intense concern on his face. He quickly came to a stop just before me.

*"Eren,"* he repeated, as an exhale.

*How reverently he said the word, as if it were a prayer rather than a name.*

The passageway where he had caught me was a whispered corridor between grander rooms on its either side, short and narrow. The pale stone walls were worn smooth by age and the warm light of shaded sconces, which cast a honeyed glow across human faces. Graceful arches and a runner of dark velvet gave the small space an air of quiet elegance. We were alone for the moment, though I was aware members of the household could pass through at any time.

"Milord," I answered stiffly, forcing myself to meet his gaze.

The light here flickered gently with the flame, giving Axel's pleasing features a quiet, shifting softness — neither fully revealed nor fully hidden. In that instant, as I faced him evenly, all of my memories and moments with him came rushing back, like a wave sweeping over ground I thought had long since dried.

At my expression, his look of concern changed to one so tender and intent that it stole my breath away. *"Eren —"*

His look undid me. It felt like being seen again after a long empty season of invisibility. In that moment something gave way — as though a second wave, even heavier still, had surged over the sea wall I had always so stoutly held between us, leaving me unsteady.

"I never said goodbye," he said quietly. "I owe you an apology. You deserved better —"

I nearly took a safe step back, surprised by his deep affect on me. "It's no matter, milord. You did not — *do not* – owe me an explanation or an apology. Your actions were for the best, considering the situation —"

But Axel was not deterred. His tone changed slightly, pressing. *"How are you?* Forgive me, but you're very pale, Eren. I expected to find you —" He searched for the words. "— in better spirits. Onyx told me two of the Halevi priests found you in the spring."

This quickly gave me something to grab hold of. I nodded, glad to follow the conversation into calmer water I could hold against. "I was deeply glad they did, yes. They have been missing for five years. We hoped to return to the farmsteads together at once, but the death of Draveena's child delayed our plans. I've been with her since. Now with Devland's Raiders so fully occupying the conversation in the household, I haven't had the opportunity to ask Cyric to release me from my position here, but I intend to at the first opportunity."

*"Is that what you want?"* Axel asked with quick concern, as though he scarcely believed it. "To return to the farms?"

We were keeping our voices low by instinct, careful that our words would not escape the corridor, yet with each passing moment I ached to be free of this conversation. Fear was already snaking its way up my spine, and with it came the urge to shrink away from him. I did not wish to trouble him by damaging his standing within the household. Worse still, I was a traitor to this house, a traitor even to the cause Axel fought for. And Malachi's prophecy came back to me then, with its own weight — I did not want him to pay any cost for the destiny bound to my life.

*No more, Whisper,* I thought, in my weariness. No more should die for this. *For me.* No more. My heart could not endure it, not again.

"You know what I want, milord," I said, straining. "But it's simply not possible yet. At least this way, by returning to the farms, we will be united and can help each other survive."

To my chagrin, Axel searched my face with acute discernment. "Something has happened. More than just the delay. What are you keeping from me, Eren? *Why are you so disturbed?* Are you sure my absence hasn't been the cause?"

"Yes. *No.*" I quickly corrected myself, mind whirling. *Where was my self-control in this moment?* "No, of course not. I knew our acquaintance would one day run its course, milord. It was always meant to be temporary."

He frowned. "How very formal you sound. What am I seeing on your countenance? Why did you blanche at the mere sight of me in the dining hall just now?"

"It's nothing," I assured him. "I apologize for that. I'm merely weary from nursing Draveena these many sennights. I need rest."

"I find you difficult to believe," Axel insisted. "In any of this. *You forget how well you let me know you —"*

How trying it was for me to hear these words, almost as challenging as witnessing the expression that had crossed his face only moments before. I had indeed let him know me very well — something I both regretted, and yet cherished in a way that troubled me to admit even now.

*This will never do,* I told myself. *Whisper, give me strength...*

Quickly, I drew myself up. *Surely someone would walk through this passageway at any moment — and then where would that leave the two of us?*

"I assure you, it's nothing, milord."

His stormlit gaze intensified, holding mine. He muttered, *"Another lie."*

At this, I felt a sharp stab of emotion surface. Utter weariness seemed to grab at my soul with suffocating fingers, throttling me. I had always valued Axel's respect so deeply; this small reproof, though true, was simply too much to hear on his lips just then.

To my horror, I burst into tears. *"Axel, please —"* I implored desperately. *"You must stay away from me —"*

It was then the weariness and strain of the last several sennights caught up to me unexpectedly. Suddenly, my head grew light; my thoughts left me. My stomach turned with nausea. The room grew dim in a strange way, and I found myself swaying on my own two feet.

There was no time to reach for something to steady myself. Axel moved with the swiftness of lightning, catching me with strong hands, his eyes aflame with shock and concern. In another moment, he gathered me up as lightly as a feather and bore me from the corridor without a word.

Later, I scarcely remembered the length of time that it took him to carry me to Lady Chatney's residence, but I did recall the utter weakness that I felt. I buried my face in the comforting warmth of his chest and cried helplessly the entire distance, exhausted beyond measure. Axel said nothing, intent on reaching his destination, until he had safely arrived at the front door. He said something low to Lady Chatney that I did not hear; then her sympathetic murmurs and soft whispers of concern followed us all the way to a quiet bedchamber on the ground floor closest to the door.

She quickly took command of the situation in a soft flurry of sound and motion — calling for servants to light a fire and bring something warm to drink, hurriedly following Axel to the bed where he gently delivered me. I had frightened her; I recognized that much through the hazy blur that had settled over my thoughts. But I found I was unable to answer any of her quiet questions or gentle probing in the moments that followed. No sooner had she tucked a sea of soft blankets around me and I drifted wordlessly into sleep, no longer strong enough to stay awake and face my circumstances.

When I woke hours later, I knew where I was instantly and why. The windowless bedchamber where they had brought me lay in a hush of shadow and firelight, the hearth across the room casting slow, amber flickers that warmed the round stone walls and low-hung tapestries. Elsewhere, the magnificent tower house was still and silent, leaving the space sealed away in a private, breathing quiet.

I became aware, slowly, that I was not alone. As I turned my head, I was surprised to find Axel in a low chair nearby. I had thought he would quickly flee the indelicate scene and leave me to Lady Chatney's care. He certainly would not be here, in a private room unchaperoned.

He sat in still attentiveness, forearms resting on the arms of the chair, fingers loosely steepled before him as if he was being exceedingly careful not to disturb the quiet. He had changed his clothing since the last I saw him, though the richness of his garments was forgotten, softened by the fire's low light and the gravity in his eyes. His expression held neither impatience nor command, only a steady, guarded watchfulness. He had been waiting for me to awaken.

*What a sight I must look*, I thought. I had fallen apart completely, and he had witnessed every part of it. I was aware of the faint, aching heaviness in my chest, the residue of heavy tears clinging to me like a damp fog. My body felt spent and misaligned, my clothing creased and uncomfortable. Emotion still lay thick and weary within my soul, as though a slight pall of grief had settled there while I slept.

Axel knew the instant my eyes found him — and knew I would try to gather myself at once. "Don't move," he said quietly. "Just lie there, Eren. We can talk just as well while you rest."

I did not try to protest. With the exit of my strength, a meek obedience seemed to have taken its place. He had a calm, assuring command that I mutely surrendered to.

"I've sent for the priests in the city," he added then. "I think their company will do you some good for a short while. Lady Chatney has agreed to host them here in her home at my expense. Of anyone in this castle, I think they should have the care of you. You've exhausted yourself."

This last was said without reprimand; he was simply explaining the situation. It was the thoughtful understanding in his message that brought tears. They slipped free from the corners of my eyes and slowly made their way over my temples. *How weak I felt. How vulnerable I was to the gentleness in his every word.* I desperately needed time with the Whisper to regain my strength.

Even in the heavy shadows of the small room, Axel caught this. "I think you'd better tell me everything," he continued. "I know this is more than simply helping Draveena, Eren. You are a woman of great composure. You would not be so shaken without cause. Something serious has happened."

I knew he would accept nothing but the truth — not after the unguarded display I had made of myself. My eyes drifted upwards, unable to look at him. The carved canopy above swam dimly into view as firelight flickered softly along its shadowed beams and velvet coverings.

Somehow I found my voice, crusty and broken as it was. "The only safe secret is the one that is never told."

He could be quick, Axel could. This confirmed for him that his suspicions were true. "And what is never spoken does not always keep you safe," he returned in a voice deep with gravity. *"Sometimes it only buries you alive.* Tell me why you begged me to stay away from you, Eren."

"In part, I am trying to spare your reputation. You should not even be here."

But Axel had already formed his answer to this, long before I awakened. "That is not so difficult to cover. I found you in a faint in a passageway near here, and you are now in Lady Chatney's care. Now I've returned to see that you are well and safe, as any honorable man would do, especially to a valued member of my father's court. No one would expect differently of me. Lady Chatney and the few members of her household will remain discreet while I visit with you in private. They know the consequences of not doing so."

"It's risky, Axel," I said, tears breaking into my voice. I had never desired to be as the others in this household were — given to clandestine trysts, talking in coded speech, giggling over their forbidden secrets.

"I will take the risk," he insisted. "Tell me what has happened. Why do I find you in such a weakened state?"

I did not know where to begin. Of all those here, I cared most deeply about what Axel thought of me. I was not certain his view of me would remain unchanged once he knew Devland was my brother. There was a small chance he would not believe Dev had captured me outside the castle, but would instead think I had been the spy all along, feeding him information from within. After all, Axel was his father's son. He had admitted himself that though he did not always agree with Cyric's methods, he shared his thinking. The King would surely believe I was a spy. At the very least, my bloodline — and my act of loyalty to Devland — would mark me as untrustworthy from that moment on.

At my continued silence, he spoke again. "You cannot carry this by yourself anymore, whatever it is, Eren — not alongside the heavy burden of being cut off from the Halevi. Not after all you have endured. Let me help you, if I am able."

How well his heart ruled him, I thought. His great love of the Halevi was what taught me to trust him in the first place. Even now my plight was so very plain to him, and he understood my needs with uncommon clarity.

So I told him, haltingly at first, then with more swiftness as he sat silently listening without interruption. My voice never rose higher than a low, steady murmur, sometimes competing in volume with the soft crackle of fire and setting stone in the hearth across the room. I told him the hidden story of my brother — of Miri's death and Devland's anger; of all he had done in driving the Halevi from the community; and all that had followed since, from claiming leadership of the Raiders to the deaths of Connor and Liev. I told him how Devland had found me outside the castle and taken me by force into the mountains, where I learned he had a spy within the King's household — knowledge I had longed to share with someone, yet feared would betray me if I did.

In broken words, I confessed that I had supplied him with medicine for his wounds, and that after this, his terror had only grown stronger through the summer. *His strength might not even have been possible without my aid,* I admitted. I also knew how such an act of mercy would be judged here — as treason, beyond forgiveness. It would seal the belief that, as Devland's sister, I could never be trusted.

And finally, I told him how all of this, together with the strain of longing to return home with Joram and Zadok, had worn me down completely. I wished only to return to the farmsteads, to be free of this place at last, back where I belonged. *I could not endure life here another moment.*

A weighted silence fell after the long story and full confession. Weak tears were slipping down my temples again as I wondered what Axel's reaction would be. The only sound in the room aside from the gentle hiss and pop of burning logs was the faint, uneven rhythm of my breath, rising and falling as I wept. My eyes had never moved from the velvet canopy overhead and I found I was unable to look over.

At last his hushed voice reached me. *"Eren —"*

This slowly drew my attention. He was leaned forward, elbows on his knees now, hands entangled loosely, as if the story had drawn him in and absorbed his attention until its ending. His magnificent gaze was greatly sobered.

His voice was quiet, measured. "I am only sorry your life has been what it is. My heart is truly grieved for you. You are in the center of so much terror and conflict. Yet you remain guileless. I could never believe differently of you. You are too holy and pure to be otherwise."

Relieved emotion broke over me in a sudden rush, and I fought to contain it. If there was anyone I had wanted to hear the whole truth and believe in my innocence, it was Axel.

My fresh spate of tears was little more than a faint hitch of breath, so slight it barely disturbed the silence, but Axel's voice softened at the sight. "I must ask you to trust me with this information. It can't stay only between us. For the safety of my household, as well as your own life. Can you do that?"

Immediate questions arose. *How could they not?* I knew the limitations of his power and influence. I knew the traitorous acts I had committed. I knew Cyric's unyielding distrust for any man or woman who stepped out of their place in life.

"Of course, Axel," I said softly. "I trust you more than anyone. *Only —*"

He understood my hesitation. His face grew still and solemn, taking on the look of a man on the brink of a vow. "I give you my word — I will ensure that you remain safe. No harm will come to you or the Halevi for confessing this. I *do* have some leverage in this household." Then, with a more thoughtful air, "And I will see to it myself that you get home to the farmsteads. I can see now, when all is said and done, that is where you belong, Eren. You should not be here any longer. You should go home. I will go now and begin to address all of this."

How deeply grateful I was to the Whisper for him in that moment. If our friendship served no other purpose in my time here, this alone was enough. Axel was my advocate and my friend.

With these weighty words, he stood to his feet. He looked down on me soberly for a moment. "I still hold onto faith that you will be rewarded for your faithfulness to the Whisper, for being who you are in a sea of people who do not choose the holy reactions you always have. You will have your day of reward, Eren."

Without further word, he crossed the room to leave. He had been here for hours, waiting for me to wake and tell him my story.

But then, he paused before the hearth, as if one last thought held him there before he took his leave. The firelight flared behind him at the foot of the great bed, outlining his broad shoulders and casting his features into a quiet play of shadow and gold. As he turned, steady and contemplative, the flames caught in his eyes, the heat at his back seeming only to sharpen the stillness of his gaze. There was an intimacy to the small chamber that neither of us had failed to notice during the conversation, and it lingered now in the silence.

Axel said quietly, "There has never been anyone I have admired more, esteemed more highly, or measured myself against so often as you, Eren."

The words were said in a voice lowered with feeling; the light in his gaze was brilliant moonlight filtered through storm clouds. This was the closest he had ever come to breaking the unspoken barrier we had always held up between us.

I said nothing in return, unable to. He was still a prince, and I was still a priestess, each held fast by destinies already set.

Then the moment was over and he was gone, disappearing to other parts of the castle to handle the many things I had revealed to him.

# 13.

A peaceful sennight passed, perhaps the most restful since my arrival in Periburn. Joram and Zadok were a great comfort to me. Now that Axel had been told the truth and had made the promises he had, all I needed was a quiet space with the beloved priests, where prayer and worship could fully restore my strength. Lady Chatney offered a private receiving room where we could meet daily while the other two stayed in her home.

During this time, news from the castle was quiet. Even Lady Chatney, who was frequently a bearer of all the household gossip, did not presume upon our privacy. I was grateful for the silence, while also wondering what developments were taking place as a result of my confession. I expected that any day Axel would arrive, or would send word of what came next in our return home.

On the eighth day, Lady Chatney appeared in my rooms that afternoon with the message that Cyric wished to see me. This caught me by surprise. There was no explanation for the summons. She herself did not know what he needed me for. I dressed quickly for a royal appearance, told Joram and Zadok where I would be, and left Lady Chatney's residence for the first time since I had collapsed.

I felt stronger as I entered the dining hall, ready to face whatever lay before me. Axel's support had given me a strength and confidence I needed, for which I was grateful, and the priests' loving company had done the rest. The Whisper had sent me help in a time of great need. For once, the room stood emptied — only Cyric sat imperiously in his chair, Axel beside him, with the usual guards posted rigid at the doors. Even the massive hearth mid-way along the room had been allowed to burn low, as if the servants had been forbidden to enter the room for some time while confidential matters were discussed. Seeing Axel, I had to wonder if this would be the official dismissal of my duties as a spiritual advisor.

As I approached and bowed my head in respect to them both, I took in the temper of the room. Axel was focused yet at ease, and he nodded to me as though satisfied with how matters stood. Cyric, by contrast, bore a cunning glint in his eyes unlike any I had seen before.

*Axel had told him.* I knew it as sure as the stone beneath my feet.

There was also something else here, something that was not part of my conversation with Axel a sennight past. Something new. I could feel it hanging in the air, and read it plainly in the Prince's face. Mostly, I knew it by the quiet insistence of my spiritual instincts.

"You sent for me, milord?" I asked.

*"Yes, I did."* Cyric was behaving deliberately shrewd, his tone coy. He drew his royal robes around him, allowing his impressive rings to glitter and dance in the low light of the dining hall. "I trust you are

feeling better after this time of rest, Priestess. Axel informed me you were ill."

I was exceedingly wary, but I made an effort to appear at ease. "Thank you, milord. I'm very well now. It seems I simply overtaxed myself nursing Lady Draveena back to health. How very good of you to inquire."

But Cyric had little real interest in my well-being or my thanks, and we both knew it. He waved a bored, dismissive hand and moved ahead quickly, plying me with a sudden, sly smile. "Devland's Raiders have seen fit to leave a message on the city gates today, calling for a meeting. This is the first of its kind."

*There it was.* I could feel my skin crawl for a moment.

He continued, "He has called for parley, with the hopes of striking a deal for peace." He rolled his eyes with exaggerated contempt. "We are unlikely to grant any of his demands, but I will send Axel, with an escort for his protection, to assess the situation and hear Devland's conditions."

My eyes quickly swung to Axel, heart fluttering nervously. His expression made it evident he had already known of this and agreed to it. Probably he had volunteered himself for it.

But Cyric was in no way interested in any response from me — not yet, at least. He continued on, coyly, "I imagine this would interest you especially, Priestess Eren, seeing as your *brother* has long been at the heart of the troubles that have plagued us for *years* now."

He seemed very proud of himself for holding this knowledge, and announced it to me with the quiet triumph of a predator springing a trap. He was practically gleaming. There was also an underlying fury in his words, carefully hidden by his silken-tongue and fluttering smile. In that moment, I think that if he could have, he would have torn me apart with his bare hands. There was no way to know whether this would pass once someone else drew Cyric's ire away from me, but today he plainly wished to feel my throat in his hands.

I told myself this was to be expected. Axel had told me the truth could not remain between us, and that he must take action to protect everyone involved, his household included. He had also said he held leverage with his father, which I could see was true, given that I had not already been tossed into a dungeon or found Agnar's men at Lady Chatney's door in the past sennight, ready to march me to the nearest gallows.

Recognizing this, I raised my chin slightly and murmured, "I fail to see how this concerns me, milord. Perhaps I am blind to what it is you require of me. Is there something you need of me at this time?"

*How he hated me in this moment.* Cyric's eyes gleamed darker, richer, with more poison. He seemed to hit upon an idea suddenly. *"Why, yes…* Now that I have seen you… and see what good health you are in… I believe I will revise my plans somewhat."

I sensed, more than saw, Axel tense in the seat next to him. Whatever was coming, he had not been privy to it.

"I think you should go with him," Cyric said, a note of gloating satisfaction in his voice.

A small whimper escaped me. *No… No, Whisper, not again. Not Axel…* I almost staggered on my own feet.

A protective flare lit Axel's eyes. He turned sharply and warned, *"Father — "*

"You've had your way, Axel," Cyric snarked, his gaze never leaving me, enjoying the tension he had created. "I've given you everything you asked for. This is where I draw a line in the matter. I want her to go. I think she could be very useful in negotiating terms with the man."

They could not possibly know why I was stunned speechless, unable to move and scarcely able to think. This had nothing to do with fear for my own safety. *Hadn't I said after my last encounter with Devland that I was learning just how swiftly my circumstances could change?*

Axel objected roughly, "You made no mention of using her as a bargaining pawn —"

Cyric was smug, his snake eyes glittering at me with satisfaction. Just now he held a plain, unmistakable pleasure in being feared, obeyed, and absolute. "Oh, she won't be. I merely want to assure Devland and his Raiders that our intentions are good and we mean no deceit. The sight of his sister should soften him considerably."

"He may also interpret it as a veiled threat," Axel insisted. "An indirect message that her safety depends on his compliance. Her presence could jeopardize the negotiations and sharpen his hostility rather than lessen it."

Cyric ignored him. "No more arguing. All of your plans can resume when you both return." Then to me he added, "You'll be relieved of your duties to this household as soon as you complete this final task."

It was then, finally, I found my voice again, dragging it from the panicked place it had fled. "I'll be happy to take the journey and be useful to your household in this way, milord. I only humbly ask that you leave Prince Axel behind. Send someone else in his place. Or — if you consider me worthy enough — allow me to do the negotiations for you. I would gladly speak to Devland on your behalf."

This surprised the both of them. The conversation stuttered, stopped.

For a moment Cyric looked bewildered, and then recovered quickly with a snark. *"I'd not trust you to handle the negotiations for all the kingdoms under the sun.* What a fool idea. Your actions in this matter have been suspect at best. Axel can handle himself." His voice rose suddenly. *"Now get out of my sight* — before I begin to ask myself why you are suddenly so concerned about my son."

I knew the situation was hopeless. There was no changing this. He would never believe me if I told him I carried a prophecy that his son would give his life for mine. At least for today, while his fury was still hot, I had lost all standing with the man. But I'd had to try something at least. For Axel's sake. Even at the risk of causing his father to suspect an untruth about the two of us. No doubt I had disgruntled Cyric on the merit of my indiscretion alone. He despised those whose sins lacked subtlety.

Left with no choice, I turned with swift steps and fled their presence, sobbing out my fears in the hallways beyond.

There is a small valley known as Borderfall on the eastern side of the Mountains of Purpose in the center of Avan, cupped between green, rising walls of forested mountains, a broad, living bowl where mist lingers and the light filters soft and pale through layered ridges. The valley floor rolls gently there in a long, velvet sweep of grass, broken only by scattered old trees that lean as if listening to the slow passage of wind through their leaves. Shadows drift steadily across the slopes as clouds move overhead, and thin ribbons of fog curl out of the higher woods at dawn and dusk, giving the place an air of quiet watchfulness. It feels both sheltered and exposed at once — a natural threshold where paths converge, a part of Avan not meant to be passed through, but remembered. I have revisited there in my dreams many times, *remembering.*

It was this location that Devland set as the meeting place on that eventful day, a full day's journey on horseback to the north of Periburn. This required at least the better part of the day of light riding, accompanied by ten of the Royal Guard and sixty of a heavily armed company sent for additional protection. The air over the troop was tight and expectant, charged with purpose as we rode toward the meeting. Warmth lay heavy along the open, little-used paths we traveled, dust lifting in slow veils beneath a late-summer sun that poured down in broad, unbroken light.

Axel and I rode in the center of the Royal Guard at the head of the line, mostly silent, sobered by one another's presence. Today he had set aside his finery and doublets for dark, finely tooled leather traced with gold, yet he still bore the composed elegance of a statesman. A jeweled sword was rested at his saddle, and another, slimmer blade hung at his belt, a sight I had never seen before. He often liked to claim he was not a warrior… not like Agnar, who prided himself on his many weapons.

At one point he turned towards me compulsively, as if the question had been burning at him. "What is that you fear? What haven't you told me?"

Since we first greeted one another early that morning, he had not asked why I had begged his father not to bring him — though I knew the question still lingered with him. I could read Axel well. He had realized, in that moment two days ago, that it was not for myself that I was afraid, but for him.

This was the final fear I had kept to myself, in the hope that I might not be forced to speak of it. I had clung to a thin hope that he would not ask, and that I would not have to place another burden upon his already taxed shoulders. It was plain enough that my presence troubled him as it was. We both knew my involvement greatly increased the volatility of the meeting, for all the reasons he had already given Cyric. Yet he would never oppose his father; he had no choice but to bring me with him.

Even so, I made a swift decision in that moment. It was better that we enter this with our eyes wide open, facing the future head-on, whatever it might hold. Better to put our trust in the Hand of the Whisper to guide us, protect us, and steer the outcome, rather than sit in cowering fear of the future, or worse, try to fight it and only get in the way of His plans. His plans took all things and all people into consideration and were written for our good. I reminded myself that Liev and Connor had given their lives willingly for a greater cause, and that I could not allow my fear for Axel to eclipse that truth.

So I told him, surrendering, using a low voice for the sake of the men around us.

Afterward, Axel pondered Malachi's prophecy in still silence, his steady gaze darkening with the grave weight of a man measuring the cost of his own possible death. He had never doubted any word or prophecy I had given or repeated, and I had the clear proof of many of them by now, besides. For a moment the soft clink of tack, the faint scuff of hooves, and the low creak of leather were the only sounds beneath the wide skies as the quiet troop moved in subdued rhythm.

Then, finally he said with measured thoughtfulness, "You *are* precious in the sight of the Whisper, Eren. There is no doubt of that. But there is more than one way to give your life for the sake of another."

This statement caught me as much by surprise as my plea to Cyric on Axel's behalf had for him. I had never considered this before. Sometimes Axel spoke with a wisdom that truly only kings were blessed with.

Just now he was grim, but not without hope. "We will see what today holds," he assured me. "Try not to be afraid."

We arrived at our destination in late afternoon. Borderfall broke open in a sweep of bright grass and rising slopes before us, the heat lifting off its broad floor as the troop rode down into it, small and exposed against the vast, waiting land. The men did not dismount and we held in silence under Axel's command, examining our surroundings, waiting with sharp anticipation for our hosts to be alerted to our presence.

Axel had already explained the role of the Royal Guard. These were men assigned to protect the Royal family beyond the castle walls. Since he was the one who most often journeyed outside Periburn, and Agnar held command of the kingdom's army, this small band traveled with him everywhere. He trusted them with his life.

"I have already given them orders to treat you as they would me on this mission," he told me. "Stay close to them when we meet with the Raiders. You'll be safest."

Just now, surrounded tightly by the Royal Guard on all sides, I watched their dark faces scan the perimeter with a stern eye and deadly expressions from atop their tall black steeds. They carried twice the weapons that the company of men behind us did — pairs of crossed swords for every man; arbalests, steel shields and full quivers at their saddles; sheathed knives at their belts; silver daggers at their boot tops. In contrast, Agnar's men were great hulking brutes in brown leather armor and steel helmets who handled their horses with a heavy hand and rough commands, but these men were sleek, lean, taut with readiness. Their horses moved with them as smoothly as though they were one in thought.

A tension built while we waited, tightening like a drawn wire, unspoken but palpable. In the strained stillness of the valley, only the soft click of leather, the slow breath of horses, and the faint whisper of grass in the heat broke the silence. My stomach clenched and unclenched; my grip on the reins of my horse was sweaty. I had not thought to see Devland's face again, and certainly not on these terms. I wondered again, as I had been wondering all day, what his reaction would be when he saw me here among these men; what he would say today; how the events would play out; most importantly, how they would end.

Then, finally, a pair of horsemen appeared from the trees on the western edge of the valley, then three more, followed by another six. They came in a loose formation, riding with unmistakable intent. Devland was at their head. He rode his horse with a calm, dangerous ease, his dark gaze fixed forward, the blade at his side catching the open sunlight like a quiet promise of violence.

Even as I saw his face come into plain view, my breath tightened and my hands went numb on the reins. How I wished I did not have to be here to witness this. Our paths kept being pulled back together again and again, two vessels representing warring forces, inescapably entangled in a struggle older than either of us.

Looking at Devland now, it was difficult to imagine that he had once come from the humble Rivermouth community. The darkness that clung to him felt too deep, too deliberate to belong to a boy who had known simplicity and shared labor in the Planters fields only a handful of years ago. This grim personage bore little resemblance to the life he had left behind. Somehow I knew he had come charged with high emotion and half-hoping for trouble… or already intending to make it. Not merely because he was a man who lived in expectation of threat, but because I could read him… because the Whisper was always whispering, even when I did not wish to hear the things He said. This was no meeting of peace.

He and his men drew up some few yards before the Royal Guard, his eyes instantly lighting on Axel, who had moved his mount to the front at the sight of the approaching horsemen. Those were Miri's eyes at their coldest and most calculated. Then, as if by instinct, Devland's hard gaze slid to me, buried just beyond amongst the Guards. I was still the tallest person here aside from Axel, and my hair, all fire and sheen, betrayed me at a glance. There was no hiding from him.

His face went black. His jaw clamped shut with iron fury. "That's the game you wish to play, is it?" he snapped in a dark, guttural tone.

His words held a double-edged meaning, one I knew was meant for Axel as well as for me. He viewed my presence exactly as the Prince had predicted, and perhaps precisely as Cyric had wanted it to — as an unspoken threat. His actions to spare my life twice now had shown Cyric that I was the frailty in his defenses, the chink in his impenetrable armor. Devland immediately perceived my life was being dangled before him like bait before wild prey, in mortal danger from these men.

At the same time, he cursed the very sight of me at a time like this. I was the unwavering voice of his conscience; the relentless ache of his better self; the blinding light of truth and conviction he could not seem to escape. He had chosen his methods of making change, and I had chosen mine. His involved brutality and violence; mine involved faith and surrender.

I have no recollection of who made the first move towards violence. There was too much madness and I was too much in the center of it — madness that seemed to last for ages and refused to stop. Every scene of horror grew worse than the last.

Suddenly, the entire valley was flooded with a score of men rushing from the trees, all of them in dark leathers, metal accents, and plain traveling clothes, armed with swords and knives. They came with a deafening roar and a spirit of violence that swept the entire valley before they'd even met a single weapon.

At the same time, my head snapped around as I heard a blood-thirsty shout from Agnar's men, raised in one lusty voice, embracing the challenge with upraised weapons. Axel gave a roaring command for them to back down, trying to restore order to Agnar's overeager warriors; but by this time it was too late. They had already jumped from their horses with brutal intent, running forward on foot to meet the fighting steel to steel.

Like a beast roused from blood-hunger, one of them savagely threw off the helmet which had covered his face. His features caught the glaring afternoon light, revealing Agnar himself. It seemed Cyric had had no intention for peace, either, anymore than Devland had. He had sent the Crown Prince, cleverly buried in the troop, to finish the Uprising and destroy its leader in one swift blow.

Around me, the Royal Guard pressed their mounts in closer, reaching swiftly for their arsenal of weapons. There was the ring of steel as swords were drawn; the swift, dull click of metal teeth catching as arbalests were loaded and drawn; the brief scrape as hand shields were pulled free from their saddles.

From the front of the column, Axel's horse was turning restlessly, made uneasy by the sounds of mayhem. I had no idea where Devland was, nor the ten that had come with him.

I heard the Prince shout hoarsely, *"Get her to safety! The rest of you — come with me!"*

And then he charged into the fight on horseback to places unknown.

This is when the fighting quickly grew to complete chaos. While Agnar and his men had the element of trained strength and brute force, Devland's men were crafty and had had time to build their resources in the past two years. A great deal of them carried leather pouches of powdered quicklime, which they threw into faces and aimed at fighters, causing chaos and screaming as it caught eyes and skin. Others were armed with overpacked powder horns used as noise weapons, causing confusion, startling the horses, allowing themselves to escape and evade during the fighting. A few carried cloths soaked in pitch and resin, which were ignited and thrown, creating a thick white smoke in patches throughout the valley. Men ran, darted, dashed, some coughing, blinded, and struggling, others pushing forward with grim determination to exact their vengeance.

For all of the Raiders' cleverness, however, sword points still met flesh on both sides, and men fell right and left with sharp cries and piercing screams. Blood ran, burst, and exploded from torn bodies; heavy boots trampled the velvet grass of the valley, staining it with blood and churned earth. Horses ran from the scene, scattered and adrift in terror, only adding to the confusion.

For a very brief time, the tight circle of men around me were able to shield me from direct contact with any of it. They worked to lead us towards the trees, remaining in tight formation, but soon came under too much attack. A few were forced to dismount and take on the enemy; others engaged their arrows, firing into oncoming forces.

By now I was in a near panic. Even the brutal harm Connor's body had suffered paled beside the slaughter unfolding around me. Steel rang and shrieked in frantic clashes… fists thudded into flesh… arrows tore through the air with hissing snaps… horses screamed in blind terror as men shouted in rage… fighters cried out in agonizing pain… powder charges cracked and boomed through the chaos like breaking thunder. A few moments stretched into a small eternity. I irrationally wanted to scream for it all to stop, for the chaos to end. I wanted the Whisper to lift me from this terror and set me down in a time where violence did not exist in my world.

At the same time, I could not help but wonder where Devland was… where Axel was… who was winning… who was losing… *Could anyone be a winner after this madness?*

After a time, one of the Royal Guardsmen suddenly dragged me from my horse, catching me with rough, clumsy hands before I struck the ground. He pointed to the trees not six yards away.

*"Run!"* he shouted. "I'll guard you."

Reeling, I paused long enough to grasp what he had said, then found my feet and surged forward in a mad frenzy. For all that I had always been a good runner, in this moment my feet felt like lead, the long skirts I wore like chains pulling me toward the earth. My heart thundered in my temples; sweat ran in my eyes, blinding me. In another five steps a wild-faced man from Devland's company crossed my path with a raised sword, but the guard cut in, raised his own blade, and dropped the man where he stood.

I pulled up short with sharp swiftness at the sight, horrified, but another guardsman pushed me firmly from behind. *There were two of them,* I realized, both driving toward the cover of the trees with me as their charge. Quickly, I lunged forward again.

I dared not look down at my feet too closely as I skipped over objects and obstacles in my path. Some were dead or dying men, their limbs out-flung and eyes bulging. Others were discarded weapons — a torn cloak here, an abandoned helmet there. Dragged blood trails, churned mud and grass, trampled flowers, scattered pack cloths — I tried not to consider any of it.

Where was Axel? I thought, my thoughts in a breathless, slightly tumbling panic. And Devland? *Where was the Whisper?* How I needed His reassurance right now. *I needed this madness to end.*

As my escort brought me to the edge of the trees, a frenzied shout I recognized rang out, and I instinctively pivoted on one heel, daring a sharp glance back at the bedlam behind me. This revealed a blur of clashing steel, screaming horses, and flaring violence. But what drew my attention was a horseman tumbling off his horse — *Axel,* I realized, in shock — and thrown to the ground. An opponent was quickly upon him, but he was already on his feet, heavy sword in hand, swinging with expert skill. He was fearless. Sweat darkened his collar and hair clung to his brow, but he fought with blazing ferocity, every strike measured and deadly. Then he was lost again, swallowed by smoke and motion.

The battle did eventually come to an end. As the men guided me deeper into the trees safely away from the chaos, the clash of steel thinned to scattered rings and dull thuds behind us, shouts faded into groans and ragged cries, and one by one the terrible noise fell away.

It was then I paused, steadied my crashing heartbeat, and turned back. Even had the men with me refused, I was determined. *I needed to see the outcome of the battle…* while every part of me recoiled from what I might find.

Only moments later we emerged from the trees slowly, the weapons of my companions still drawn, not yet willing to risk our safety. I was thankful they were allowing me to lead the charge. My security was their only concern, not my obedience. With a quivering breath and unsteady hands, I paused and slowly took in my surroundings.

This was a scene I would never forget. Borderfall lay broken and eerily still, the grass crushed and darkened with blood, bodies scattered where they had fallen among dropped shields, scattered weapons, and torn cloth. Smoke drifted low over the ruin, horses moved restlessly among the dead and wounded, and the air itself seemed heavy with the cost of what had just passed. There was only the faint sound of labored breathing, the whimper of wounded horses, and the soft, stunned quiet of what remained. Very few men walked among the shattered fragments of battle, but all of them were Agnar's men — more subdued now, either limping towards their other living companions, or assisting their wounded fellows away from the site. *Cyric had won.*

*I needed to find Devland.* I had to know if he was alive… injured… had escaped… or worse.

This thought jolted me into action. I began to pick my way over the broken and blood-splattered ground, searching faces, avoiding Agnar's men. At any other time, I would likely have been sick at the sight of such butchery, but I had already seen too much. The time was past for such a delicate reaction. My escorts stayed with me faithfully, scanning the smoke-covered area, also looking for any of their comrades in the carnage.

Then there he was, sprawled on his side in a close press of two other fallen men under him. I would have recognized his short, stocky figure and mop of wavy curls anywhere. A cry tore from me — emotion I did not know I still had to give — and I lurched forward, grasping at his sleeve without thought until his body gave way and turned onto his back.

Like Connor, he was already gone by the time I found him. Death had claimed him quickly, unlike many of his companions strewn out across this desolate battlefield who were still suffering in their final moments. His dark eyes were empty and the life gone from his features, void now of all the anger, pain and hatred that had consumed him since Miri's death. With one swift plunge, a blade had found his heart, the force of it ending his life in a single, final instant.

Somehow I was unable to shed tears for him, though I wanted to. Instead I felt a quiet relief. There could be no sorrow over Devland, no grief. I had already cried my tears over the loss of him; I had already mourned the little boy I once knew. He had been gone to me for some time now.

The Whisper was there instantly, bringing His decisive perspective. *The account is settled.*

*He was right.* Justice was done. Right was restored. The balance was made. The battle was over.

*Malachi had foreseen this moment.*

After a time, I stood to my feet and looked down solemnly, taking in my brother one last time. The late summer wind lifted the damp strands of hair clinging to my face and neck, brushing over me with a faint, cooling touch that felt strangely gentle after the recent violence. I could hear Malachi's words floating through my mind in his calm, unhurried voice, worn smooth by a lifetime of gentleness and quiet authority: "Some choose to worship their pain, Meeshka. Some worship love. Some worship power. They pay homage to what they worship. They nurture and nurse it. They find their identity in it. *But all things were created to worship."*

No one I knew was outside the design, I thought then. Not Devland, who had chosen pain, and not Cyric, who had chosen power. *No one.* All living beings were created to worship. And what we worshipped led us to life... or to death.

Thoughts of Cyric caused me to return to my senses again. The two Royal Guards had stopped with me and were scanning the area, wordlessly allowing me to have my moment. I had to presume they were much more accustomed to battle than I was; they seemed alert, watchful, entirely unmoved by the terrible sights and sounds around us. I would have asked them if they had caught sight of Axel yet, but just then, as if the Whisper was supplying the answer to this unspoken question, the wind shifted, the smoke cleared somewhat, and my eyes lifted in a new direction. *There he was.*

He was sweat-stained and looked battle-weary, but he was uninjured, thankfully. The circle of Royal Guards who accompanied him were standing back a respectful distance, turned away. Just now Axel stood with his head down and gaze lowered in still silence, his strong shoulders set and unmoving as the summer wind stirred faintly through his dark hair. There was something in his stillness that spoke more clearly than any outward emotion — a gravity that made the moment feel sealed and irrevocable. I could see from here that a man lay crumpled at his feet, already dead and gone.

*Agnar was dead.*

My thoughts scattered into nothing.

*Agnar was dead.*

All the gold, power and status in this world could not purchase one more instant of his life.

That moment was the one when Axel chose to look up. His vision focused as he caught sight of me, and his memory returned.

A slight wind swept between us, rifling loose artifacts of battle, tugging at cloaks, whispering through blood-stiffened grass.

*The unthinkable had happened.*

*Agnar was dead, and Axel was alive.*

In only moments the rest of our senses would return to us. We would emerge from our shock, our grief, the terror of the last few moments. We would gather ourselves and face the truth of it — *Agnar was dead.*

*Nothing would ever be the same again.*

For now, the one thing I did recognize was that Axel was standing there, *alive*, with a look so agonizing, so sharply aware that we were the two who had survived this, that it drew me intensely.

*Agnar was dead. And everything was changed.*

We would never know each other again after today. In the final breaths that both Devland and Agnar had exhaled, a new destiny for both of us had been instantly forever sealed. Axel would be direct heir to the throne, and I would be sister to a murderous dissenter who had killed the King's favorite son.

Suddenly, my feet dragged me forward, stumbling, staggering, picking up speed across the broken trampled terrain that separated us. I found myself desperate to reach him. Where the ground was not covered in the bodies of slain or fallen men, it was churned into a dark paste of mud and blood, trampled grass flattened into the earth.

Axel's eyes intensified as I came upon him, burning with an impenetrable heat. Then I was throwing myself heedlessly in his arms, even as he caught me up with a strong embrace and crushed me to him.

I'd never felt a moment of passion like that one, an uncorked rush of emotion forcing its way out into the open, refusing to remain bottled any longer. Desperation, agony, grief, blinding relief: these were the impulses that fueled it and set it free. An awareness that this moment would pass, would forever be gone, would be stripped from us the moment harsh reality returned — this drove us to reach for each other more deeply. Axel's hungry mouth found mine, taking claim, exploding with life, filled with desire. One of his hands twisted in my hair at the base of my neck, sign that he'd wanted to touch it long before this. His iron strength bent me back somewhat with the force of his fire, but my own rose to meet it, giving back. In spite of the sweat of battle and the stench of blood, he was velvet-skinned fruit bursting on the pallet, nectar-rich flesh flooding the senses.

I felt certain I would never feel this way again — *could never* allow myself to feel this way again. We were forever doomed to a life apart. We stood in a blood-stained field of death oblivious to all else — one figure, one whole of two halves, each drawing life from the same endless fount. For just that moment, we made our destiny what we wanted it to be.

Later, much later, after a mass grave had been dug for Devland and his men, and Agnar's slain body was carefully wrapped in a wool cloak and led away on horseback, the survivors slowly made our way home.

As we traveled through the night in quiet silence, my thoughts were strangely clear. I understood the plans of God now. Some plans could only be grasped in the moment they unfolded, undeniable once seen. *"A king is established by God,"* Malachi would say. *"He uses the will of man for His purposes very artfully. Promotion and demotion comes from Him alone."* The Whisper had given Cyric's household many chances, many times. He had let them choose their ways. Then He brought down one with their own foolishness, and rose up another. He executed judgment swiftly, with great finality, for the good of all, even for the Halevi. He honored those who loved His people, and became a stumbling block for those who did not.

I could hear even Malachi marveling at the cleverness in the Whisper's plan. My path had taken many turns, had held many obstacles, yet God had overcome them all. Every investment Ezra and

I had made in Axel would flourish. All those weeks of conversation with him had indeed been the Whisper's design all along. Many years would likely pass before Cyric died, but the new heir would steer the direction of his father's hand in many ways until then. And when the old King eventually died, the country would be utterly transformed under the leadership of one solid, good man — whose name was Axel.

Everyone would taste of the goodness of this great plan. With such a virtuous gatekeeper at the doors of Avan, communities like Rivermouth would be safe from outside threats and would never again be brought so low. Roads would be protected from raiders and outlaws; men like Devland would never rise again, able to devastate the countryside as he had. Axel would have many sons, just as I had prophesied, and he would raise them to love and honor the Whisper. He would honor the Priests. For that reason, his reign would last, he would hold onto his power, and Avan would know peace and prosperity.

*Yes, the Whisper's plans — and the ways of the Priests — were so much better than the ways of man.*

Only two days after our return Cyric executed his final judgment on what had happened. He was fresh from the ceremonial burning of Agnar's body, heavy with grief, numb with the pain. He wanted me removed from his household, but could never destroy me. Not with Axel looking on. Not as long as he still somewhat feared the Whisper. I was both an enemy, and a friend. So he called me into the throne room with little pomp, without ceremony, and declared that the Halevi could return to the Rivermouth Community, by will and right of the King. The tithe would resume, as it has always been. As the tribe's High Priestess, I would be given resources to find the priests who were scattered, to rebuild the Temple, and we would honor the Whisper with our lives as it should be. *A safe distance from him.*

I knew I would never return to Periburn. Cyric would never summon me. The knowledge that I was Devland's sister would sit with him for the rest of his days. He wanted nothing to do with me or any reminder of his son's death.

Within a single sennight, all the necessary resources were gathered, the caravan assembled, and the armed men appointed to escort Joram, Zadok, and me back to the farmsteads. We would gather the priests and return to Rivermouth.

In the hours and days leading up to my departure, a few members of the household said their goodbyes — Princess Draveena, whose future remained unclear now with Agnar's death; Princess Onyx, who brought little Soren. He presented me with a small bouquet of flowers and happy thanks for tutoring him. I knew, with a thankful heart, that under Axel's rule all of them would be treated fairly and would live out their lives for a greater cause than power and prestige. I was glad for them all. Lady Chatney said her goodbyes through tears, graceful as ever, and pressed me for a promise to visit her if I ever returned to Periburn — a promise we both knew would go unkept.

As for Axel, he waited until my final moments before making his appearance. I had not seen him since the day of our return, and even now was not certain he would give his goodbyes until he presented himself at Lady Chatney's door. She came and escorted me to her most formal receiving room when he arrived, where she bowed and took her leave of the two of us very graciously. I could only assume everyone in the castle was behaving towards him with the highest regard now. He was their next king. To have his favor was for their good.

Axel, however, was unchanged. I found him dressed as he always was, in a richly woven doublet and fine attire, his fastidious devotion to careful grooming as evident as ever. He had always had the air of a prince, of the best kind. His steady gaze as he took me in at a safe distance across the room was especially pronounced today, like the frost-blue shadow at daybreak.

"I came to say goodbye," he said needlessly.

For a moment I allowed myself to simply stand and look at him. Pale daylight poured in through the broad, beautiful windows of Lady Chatney's receiving room, tracing the high walls and polished floor with quiet elegance. As the light caught him in its embrace, softness gilded the well-drawn lines of his face and the calm of his posture, as if the Whisper was offering me a final, wordless image to seal into my memory forever.

*Whisper, thank you...* I would always be grateful to have known him, to have had him as my friend for the years that I did, to have been a part in the making of him as king. These would be among the best memories of my life thus far that I would tuck away.

I responded just as needlessly. "You caught me leaving just now. The caravan is waiting in the city."

Of course he knew this. The entire castle was buzzing over the flurry of activity surrounding our departure. He nodded.

There was a great deal unspoken between us that was beyond friendship, so much we both acknowledged quietly but would never be free to name, an entire richness we had shared that we could not dwell on or touch. With this farewell, all of it would slip silently into a moment — a person — we would forever leave behind.

Axel's royal training was in clear evidence today. That stillness he practiced before reacting — the habit of weighing his expression before allowing it to surface — settled over him very briefly. His jaw tightened as strong feeling threatened to show, then eased again.

At last, he broke the silence with quiet words. "I will miss you sorely. I gave my soul to you."

His natural ease with intimate words was devastating. I broke down weeping. *Everything made me weep these days.*

He softened at once. Took a step in my direction. *"Eren —"*

But I drew myself up quickly, shaking my head, stopping him from approaching. "No. *Don't.* This is the only way. The *best* way. Any more interaction would only be unbearable. Goodbye, Your Highness." I smiled at him through the tears. *"May you know peace and greatness all the days of your life."*

Then I fled the room before I lost what little composure I had left.

# 14.

The first moment that the little group of Halevi and I crested a sharp hill and caught sight of the Temple rising from the forests was an unforgettable one. We had traveled over the Silent Heights for days, moving slowly and with great care for the aged among us, retracing those terrible steps from years ago. The entire caravan of wagons was forced to a halt as every priest paused in their tracks together, almost as one, and took the Temple in. The sight stilled us. Wind brushed the mountainside in a low, reverent whisper, and for a long moment no one spoke.

At the foot of the mountains, far below where we stood, the holy structure rose from the unseen community around it like a quiet declaration of stone and light. Its great A-frame roof lifted in pale strength against the early-fall sky, the cross at its pinnacle catching a faint, steady gleam as if answering the heavens. The Temple did not merely stand — it waited, solemn and enduring, a fixed point of meaning set against the slow turning of eternity.

For a moment I felt the Whisper's Presence move in strongly. He whispered, *"I AM."*

There were some moments where you were so rested in His Presence you simply existed. There were some instances where His faithfulness was so plain that you were left speechless in awe. This was one of them.

I did not need to look to know many of the priests were weeping. We, the living temples of the Whisper, created to bring Him pleasure... *had come home at last.*

Two years passed. Two years of putting feet to prophecy, and hands to a destiny. Cohen, Anshel and I labored hard to restore our broken relationship with the community. We oversaw the repairs needed for the Temple, and worked to rebuild all that had been lost. I traveled to find the priests who had been scattered, and sent out messengers to look for them high and low until they were discovered. Slowly, they began returning one by one, filling our courtyards once again with their prayers and their worship, just as it was always meant to be.

On the third year, I began the slow arduous process of moving the remains of the priests from the mountains and the farmsteads to the Temple burial grounds. It was hard, grueling work for the paid laborers I traveled with, but by year's end all had been recovered and were laid to rest in holy ground. Only Liev and Connor were left where they were — Liev, in whatever holy place deep in the Periburn forests where he had breathed his final breaths as a sacrifice to the Whisper, and Connor, in his resting place beneath the great tree where I hand-buried him. Inscribed stone memorials were placed for both of them in a quiet sacred place in the Temple compound, always remembered, never forgotten by the tribe as men who gave themselves sacrificially for the Whisper and for our return home.

It was also on the third year that the tribe began to grow. The priests had influenced and affected many places where we were scattered and this had a great draw for several young men and boys who were eager to join our numbers and dedicate their lives to the Whisper through worship, prayer, ministry to the community, and study of the Holy Text. Ishtob was among them. They came from all parts of Avan, causing a great joy and encouragement among the older priests. These were our light ahead for the Halevi. They would be the ones, we knew, who would carry our calling and mission forward. The Whisper had truly wrought a wondrous miracle out of great disaster.

On the fourth year, I began to wish I could do something more for Malachi than had been done. Though we held a beautiful ceremony when his remains were returned, a lingering dissatisfaction remained within me.

I told myself that I was only missing him. His quarters were strange and hollow without his presence; for as honored as I was to be High Priestess now and the one who worshipped in the Holy Place, the small sacred chamber was different without him there, leading the way as he had always done. I told myself I simply wished he were here to witness all the good that had been done, and I sought comfort in the knowledge that he would hear of news of it in heaven — but the feeling would not lift.

Towards the end of spring that year, Cohen found me in the Temple sanctuary instructing the new young priests in our proper rhythms and routines and summoned me outside to the courtyard. The interruption was unusual for him and I followed without question, wondering what dilemma was upon us now that would need my oversight. It seemed there were new challenges for us almost daily — from water management and pest control, to noise levels and keeping order while rebuilding was done on certain parts of the walls.

"A woman has come," he told me, as soon as we cleared the front steps of the Temple. "She has fallen upon our mercy."

At first I assumed someone in desperate circumstances in the community had need of our medical or financial assistance. In the days before the Exile, this was not so unusual once or twice a year. Malachi had always given them what he could, drawing on his ties in Rivermouth to find them a way forward. Even so, since our return the people here had been slow to ask for help. Devland had worked with great skill to erode a cornerstone of our community's beliefs regarding the Halevi and during a time of great vulnerability; then Cyric had commanded them to accept our return and resume the tithe. Their pride was still healing, and admitting need did not come easily to them.

Cohen signaled across our central courtyard to the front gates, where I saw a mule-drawn cart. At its bench seat sat an old threadbare man, waiting with reins in hand. His clothing suggested he was from other parts of Avan, which caused me to reconsider whether this was anyone from the tribes. As we approached the wagon, Cohen waved in a friendly manner toward the man and steered me to the bed.

What I saw there struck me instantly. A fair-haired woman lay curled in the wagon floor under ragged blankets, worn thin by obvious hardship, her unwashed face pale and slack with exhausted sleep. A crease of pain pulled her brows together intensely, sign that she was wracked with discomfort even in slumber. What I could see of her rumpled, impoverished clothing hung loosely on her slight frame, suggesting both serious illness and long neglect.

This was not what left me speechless, however. My eyes quickly passed her over for the small, solemn child of four or five who was crouched in a fearful huddle next to her, clinging to his mother with wide, dark, watchful eyes. *Miri's eyes.* A smudge of worry sadly etched his soft features as he glanced up at Cohen and myself, his face pale in the bright sunlight of spring weather. A worn cloth cap and scarf framed his tousled dark hair. This was Devland's child. I would have known him anywhere.

I almost wept at the mere sight of him. *"What's happened?"* I asked Cohen. "Who is she?"

Cohen's ancient face read that he had already recognized the child as well and understood my reaction. He quickly pulled me aside out of hearing distance of the little boy, his expression grim. "Her name is Fiona. She has traveled a great distance to come here, the driver says. She used all of her coin to pay him to bring her. She is in her final moments now, I'm afraid. She is — " he corrected himself. "She *was* Devland's woman. She has wandered since his death, not knowing where to go. I'm uncertain if they were ever married. *The road that brings one here is not always lit by hope, but it is never without purpose,* I always say —"

I did not need to know anymore after that. These words were enough. I quickly moved back to the wagon in a breathless rush.

The little boy's sad eyes flickered to me again with uncertainty. His slight figure, buried in scuffed rags, looked both guarded and vulnerable, as if he was far too young to carry the weight of whatever he had already seen. He knew his mother was dying…

"What is your name?" I asked him softly. "What do we call you?"

*"Aaren."* His voice was treble-like, airy.

My heart crumbled into a thousand pieces. I loved him instantly.

Very quickly, we housed Fiona in Malachi's own chambers, now mine, while the priests cared for her in her final hours with great tenderness. She understood where she was and spoke to me briefly.

It seemed that I had not been Devland's only point of vulnerability. He had loved her and the baby, though he had not lived to see it born. At some point he had told her about his childhood, and about me.

"If you ever need to find her," he had told her, "search for the nearest Temple. She'll be there. There's no doubt of that."

I assured her that I would care for Devland's son with the same devotion as she had. "He will be raised here, among his father's people," I promised her; and I did not mean the Rivermouth people.

After her death, Aaren was quickly drawn towards me. He was a good boy. *More than good.* I dressed him in fine linen robes, fed him on good cheese and the Holy Text, and allowed him to trail after me everywhere I went in the compound. I knew he was God's reward to Malachi, as it should be. *A kiss from heaven.*

The Whisper had seen the cry of my heart and had already made plans for honoring my grandfather, our beloved High Priest. Aaren would be the fifth generation of priests in our family. Malachi would live on, and Devland's sins would be redeemed through the son as I saw to it that he was brought up as a member of the Halevi. I determined I wouldn't raise him as Miri had my brother, fueled by anger and full of aggression. I would give him everything Malachi had given me.

One day, as I stood with him in my arms, looking around the courtyard in the shadow of the Temple, I whispered to him, "You run for us now, little Meeshka. *It is you who runs for the Halevi.*"

Another year passed. The fifth year since my return.

Aside from the many joys that Aaren brought me, the work of the Temple was difficult and wearing. A slight shadow fell over me that spring, threatening to upend my happiness. I was often weary and longed for time alone with the Whisper, which was difficult to find with all the responsibilities that constantly pressed on my shoulders. Malachi would have hated seeing it, just as much as I hated seeing him toil away on the farmsteads so long ago. A Priest's primary role, especially the High Priest's, was prayer and worship. Even so, I reminded myself this was still a thousand times preferable to laboring on a farmstead, or enduring life in a pretentious castle.

From time to time I did consider, weakly, how high the cost had been for fulfilling the prophecy that I would reunite the tribe and do my part for Avan — the Exile; the great number of deaths I had witnessed and relationships I had lost, including Devland; the violence I had endured at Borderfall; the loss of knowing Axel. This especially came over me as I passed Connor's memorial in the central courtyard, or visited Malachi's grave in the burial grounds.

In these moments, I found strength in the Whisper, and attempted to find contentment in the fact that I had been obedient to His call. I told myself that what reward I had was enough — but I did wonder privately. The cost for me personally felt very high after five years of grueling work and little left for myself at the end of long days.

It was during this time that Ishtob came running into the Lush Meadows where I was attempting to find a moment of peace and declared Axel had come. *Axel had come…*

I had no idea why, only that whatever lay behind it filled me with unease. I both wished to see him, and wished desperately for him to leave. *Did Cyric want me? If so, why? Was there some decree or command for the Halevi that would affect our future? If this was true, why had he sent Axel?* The answer could be a dozen things.

And now he was being deliberately evasive, wanting a tour of the community from no one but myself.

Axel took his time coming to it. After a viewing of Rivermouth, he then requested an expansive viewing of the Temple compound, asking dozens of interested questions regarding all the work that had been done in the past five years. There were many instances I wondered if his questions were deliberate, as if he was asking for a specific reason that went beyond polite curiosity. In considering it, however, I chose to believe he was guileless. If Axel was here on behalf on Cyric, or had some motive of his own, I was convinced that it was in our best interests and he would come forward with it. We had nothing to fear from him.

If he had hoped that time together over a handful of days would soften my reserve, he was correct. How could it not? He was unchanged after five years, save perhaps for the better. He had come into greater stature now that he was Crown Prince. I found myself glad of his presence, taking quiet pleasure in his company. He showed such careful interest in the Halevi — in our lives, our customs, and especially our well-being.

On the first day of his viewing of the community, he was in the courtyard of the Temple when Aaren came running out to see me as we stood talking. The little boy reached for my hand as soon as he joined us, glancing up at the newcomer with large intelligent eyes. He was proving to be a sober boy, but he laughed and smiled for me often enough.

Today he knew what to do. I had taught him how to greet leaders of the community when we were in public together, and at first sight of Axel he had quickly surmised I was in the presence of someone of importance. Dressed in his little linen robe and leather sandals, he bowed his dark tousled head with dignified respect. "Greetings to you, sir."

Axel was clearly charmed and smiled down at him with warmth.

For a moment the Prince stood watchful while I stooped to address Aaren. After I had answered the question that had sent the little boy running out, he darted back to the Temple to find Cohen.

Axel's eye followed him keenly as he dashed away. "He is Devland's son."

It was a shrewd guess. There was no hiding the truth from him.

I had not intended to tell him, but now that he knew I made no attempt to deny it. "*Yes.* His mother died of illness just after they arrived last year. He never knew his father. I plan for him to be High Priest, like his grandfather." I paused significantly. "That will be his heritage."

Axel knew what I meant by this. The underlying message was clear.

He reflected on this for a moment, eyes still on the place where Aaren had disappeared into the Temple. I knew too well how Cyric ruled, what he believed. Devland had torn through Rivermouth and Avan alike, and Agnar's death lay squarely at his feet. Bloodlines mattered greatly to Cyric, and Aaren would be judged a direct danger to his power.

Finally, Axel added simply, "As it should be."

"I know your father would see it differently —" I began.

"I am not my father."

The flat statement stopped me. I took him in closely. He would never have made such a bold declaration five years ago.

His sharp gaze flicked to mine with a faint smile. "Just as Aaren is not his father."

It was these pleasing words that drew a warm smile from me. They were as sweet as honey on the palate. Axel's surety on the matter was itself the fruit of my labor. Here was living proof of some of my very efforts…

"I do ask, if you would, to remain discreet about his existence," I asked him then. "Perhaps King Cyric could not be told —"

Axel broke into a slow, wise smile of his own. "Consider it done, Eren."

Then we moved onto other things.

After three days, Axel appeared at the compound just before dusk with his company of guards and asked me to join him in the Lush Meadows for a walk. He had shrewdly discerned that this was nearly the only quiet hour afforded to me, when interruptions were least likely. It was the time when the priests were given over to evening prayers, their duties for the day complete; when most of the day's troubles had been tended to, at least for the moment; and when even Aaren was safely settled in his bed for a pre-dinner rest.

As we set out, with his company of guardsmen safely scanning the area before and behind us, I had to wonder if this was when he would tell me the purpose for his visit. I did not think he could be spared from the castle for much longer — not for what appeared to be so frivolous a visit — and now seemed the likeliest time.

Axel was silent until we reached our destination, then gave a quick command to his men to remain on its outskirts in the trees, providing him privacy. Then we resumed our walk into the Meadows, as a cool blue light slowly settled over the tall wheat grass. The distant trees and the low granite rise of the Silent Heights kept the sounds of the world at bay, leaving the glade hushed as the last strains of pale gold drained from the sky on the western horizon. A soft wind passed through, brushing my face before slipping back into the dark. The deeper shadows of twilight would be upon us soon.

I waited for Axel to speak, wondering; for surely he was coming to some thought that he had arrived with. I felt the hush sharpen in that unmistakable way that meant words were gathering.

"Do you ever think about Borderfall, Eren?"

This was not a question I had been expecting as a starting point. I shuddered. "I try not to."

But his voice was quiet, ponderous as he took long slow steps in the tall grass from a distance of a few feet away. "Not all of it was bad."

This stuttered my thoughts at once. This was very bold of Axel to admit even in coded speech, I thought. Nothing had changed for either of us, not even after a few days in each other's company. Not even after five years. He was still the Crown Prince, and I was still the High Priestess whose bad blood was privately despised by his father.

I was at a loss, grappling for what to say. I had vowed to myself never to think of those moments in particular during my waking hours. They had visited me in my dreams as much as the rest of it, to my chagrin. "I've tried to forget all of it in order to move on with any happiness," I said, faintly.

"Well, I have never moved on from it," he admitted.

*Was that why he had come? Had he sneaked away from the castle and his father after five years because he could no longer stay away?* Surely not. Axel wasn't capable of being that starry-eyed. He was a deliberate man of self-control.

"This is a very cryptic conversation, milord," I told him, puzzled. "I'm afraid I don't understand what you are trying to say."

I had used the title intentionally, trying to restore a little formality to my running thoughts.

But Axel merely glanced over at me with luminous eyes and quipped, "Ours has always been a very cryptic relationship, wouldn't you say, Eren?"

My steps faltered altogether in the deep grass. Suddenly I didn't know the unspoken rules to this conversation, though I had always known them with him. "Axel, you were always a prince of Avan, and now you are the Crown Prince —" I stammered, as if that somehow explained everything.

"Then possibly that is the very reason I should talk more plainly. Perhaps it's time."

His decided tone took me aback. His logic made no sense.

He stopped and faced me, his stormlit eyes catching what little light remained, restless and reflective as a gathering sky. In the cool blue hush of dusk, the barest wind slid through his dark hair and over the clean planes of his face.

"I have a dream, Eren. A dream I have never been able to escape since the moment it was born by that lake behind the castle where we met. A fortnight ago, I pulled it out of the hiding place where I've kept it and decided to make my way here to tell you of it."

For all the restlessness in his gaze, his voice was firm and unhurried, carrying a quiet certainty that left no room for doubt. "Since our conversations, I have wanted to build a Temple in Periburn and fill it with priests who worship the Whisper. I want to give Him a holy place — a place where the people can come and make offerings, seek peace, and receive spiritual counsel when they need it. This is a great dream in my heart. Surely God deserves this Place, Eren. Not just here in Rivermouth, but in the city where the King lives. How much *more* should it exist in Periburn, as a sign that even the King submits to the authority of the Whisper. There the Priests can be honored for their service to Him. And the people will have a refuge. *I want to do this…*"

My heart leapt at these low, impassioned words. I could see he really meant it. His eyes were practically blazing now.

"Axel, you might have just said this," I stumbled. "You know you have my full blessing and support — the Halevi would be deeply honored. When you are King —"

But he cut me off calmly. "That's not all. I want you to lead it as High Priestess."

Once again he had shocked me. *"What?"*

"Leave Rivermouth's Temple in the care of Anshel," he said then. "He will make an excellent High Priest here and has plenty of years left before you'll have need of another one. You know Cohen will be thrilled and honored. You have done what you set out to do — you reunited the tribe and restored order to the Temple. The two of them can handle the work you have shown me you've been doing. It's not work that is appropriate for you, anyway. You should be in the Temple praying and worshiping, which I will ensure happens in the Temple in Periburn. I will give you men that will handle administrative matters — holy men that you approve of — so you and the priests can dedicate yourselves purely to leading, ministry, and prayer."

I had been right. He had clearly been assembling private thoughts — an entire plan — while I led him around for the past three days. My thoughts were left whirling over the idea. I had never had any intention of leaving Rivermouth for the remainder of my days, and certainly never in exchange for a life in Periburn.

"I intend to raise Aaren here —" I began, stuttering. "There is no possible way —"

"Bring him with you. Raise him in the Temple."

My mind quickly grappled with all that he was saying, considering it. I reached for every reason I could find to weaken his certainty. "You know I will offer you every support I can for the building and establishing of it, Axel. I will send priests — those who will go. But I could not possibly leave here. I belong here. I don't belong in Periburn. I *never* belonged there —"

"Not in the castle, perhaps," he said, "but you belong in the Temple."

"Possibly we should revisit this when you are King," I objected. "You know your father will never approve of me in Periburn. Never. And you'll need his agreement if I were to return, you know you will. Not even your status as Crown Prince will move him."

His voice flattened then, losing its fire suddenly, admitting the truth he had been keeping from me. "He's dead."

There was no recovering from this. I stared over at him in shock, openmouthed.

The light had sunk into a dim blue hush now. Axel's face was nearly unreadable, while his eyes remained ablaze. "I haven't announced it yet. No one knows. He had been ailing somewhat since Agnar's death, but a few months ago he never rose from his bed. During this time, the household was told only that he was in and out of recovery — it was what Father wanted. He never believed in appearing weak, as you know, so the true seriousness of his condition was kept closely guarded. He passed a fortnight ago. I swore the Healers and Onyx to silence until I was ready to speak. It is not unusual for royal deaths to be withheld for a time, in order to prepare a measured public response. I wished first to come here — to speak with you —"

"Axel —" I was still floundering for words. *Axel was king. Odious Cyric was dead, and Axel was king.* "I leave it to your wisdom on why you felt telling me about your dream for a Temple in Periburn was more important than the announcement — but we can surely discuss it after you've settled into your new role. I will clearly be here when the time is best for you to discuss it —"

"I want you to come back with me," he declared. "Since the moment of Agnar's death, I knew I wanted you to be my High Priestess when I took the crown."

I was amazed by his persistence. I half-laughed at him. "I can hardly imagine that my agreement to this plan is your highest priority right now —"

*"The King needs the Priest,"* he pressed passionately.

I think I gasped.

Once Axel said the spirited words aloud, he stopped, changed course, and admitted in a quieter, slower tone, "I need you, Eren. I don't want to rule a single day without you by my side."

A silence between us fell so quiet and deep that I could hear my heartbeat thundering in the stillness. The shadows of deepening twilight stretched long and cool across the glade around us, quiet and insistent as the last light finally thinned away. By now Axel's face was nearly gone to me, but I could see by the blaze in his eyes that I hadn't mistaken him. He did not mean that he needed a priestess alone to be at his side while he ruled.

*Malachi had never prepared me for this.*

Axel's voice carried a restrained intensity, a feeling kept carefully leashed now after his small outburst. "I have held onto faith that there would be a time for us someday, Eren. *You and I.* I always have. From the moment you fled the little lake when Agnar found us and I disappeared out of shame-faced misery for losing you —"

I could hardly believe my ears. My hands were trembling. "This is — this is impossible. *I'm a priestess.* Even if you were to overcome every obstacle in your path, the practical truth is that I will be busy. I will not be around."

His tone gentled at once, smiling at me in the darkness. "You forget — I know your life, Eren. Even priestesses have an evening meal. You don't pray *all* the time."

I shook my head in shocked protest. "You need a queen who will produce proper heirs for you, do you not? A production tool. That's the way of it. I saw it for myself."

"So your argument is compatibility."

I refused to answer him. "It will also be scandalous. I know the household of Periburn, how things are done there. I'm a priestess, and Devland's sister."

Axel's voice changed to one of quiet command. "I'm also King. It's a new day. Things will be done differently, whether you agree to be my love or not."

Even the words on his lips — *my love* — were stunning. They produced in me a terrible ache I couldn't deny, and yet I couldn't see how this was even possible. This was something I had never pictured for myself. Every room in the castle was extravagant, needlessly lavish, save for little Soren's tutoring chamber. There was not a single memory of the place that did not unsettle me. I belonged in the Temple.

"I belong in the Temple," I bleated.

"And possibly you belong with me," he responded.

This Axel was entirely new to me. This one had boldly destroyed the boundaries between us in one direct conversation and was as resolute in winning my heart as he once had been to broker peace on his father's behalf. I was shocked and overwhelmed.

When I said nothing, at a loss, he added, "You know I have always disciplined myself to hide my feelings. It became especially necessary where you were concerned, Eren. I've done so for five long years. For longer than that — almost since I met you. But I need not do it anymore. *I won't even require you to ever make an appearance in the dining hall,"* he added, a smile in his voice. "I know you secretly hated it. Your official duties will be to serve as High Priestess to the King, and wife to me. If you want children, we will have them and I will make a way for your life as Priestess. If you don't desire them or they are outside of the Whisper's plan for you, so be it. I will place the call on your life first, as I always have."

"Axel —" I began miserably.

But his words cut over me, soft and quiet. "In truth, I didn't know if you could ever feel the way I did, knowing the way you loved Connor. But you more than admitted the depth of your desire for me at Borderfall. I've never forgotten it. My faith was determined from that moment on. I was willing to wait decades for you, no matter what tradition demanded. I've just waited until I could speak... until the way was clear for building a Temple and I could present a future that was worthy of you. As soon as Father passed and the essentials were handled, I came. And even in coming here, I've been slow to speak. I wanted to ensure that I understood the totality of your life first, and to reassure myself that my offer was the right one for you before I asked. *But I won't force you, Eren,"* he stressed. "You are right in that Periburn is not your home. I guess I had hoped the Temple would be."

I could see his faith. There was no denying it. Just as I had believed the Whisper through the years for many unseen possibilities, so had he. *Even so…*

"I am unable to give you what you're asking for," I said then, heavily. "Even now, even with all these concessions you are willing to make. Life there — with you —" I shook my head. "It's just not possible."

He paused, considering in the darkness. "I can see this decision causes you conflict. You have had a specific image in your mind for your future. I knew it would be no easy thing I was asking of you." I could already feel him drawing away in disappointment.

Even the thought of it troubled me. The truth of the matter was, he had the authority to command me in anyway he liked, or punish me for not acting as he wanted just as well. *What a man of humility he was.* Even as King, he considered the Priest his equal.

*"Axel — "* My voice reached out for him.

"I leave tomorrow morning," he broke over me, quietly ignoring my plea. "I shouldn't delay any longer." Then he added softly, as direct as he liked, without any coded words at all, "I'd enjoy the sight of you one more time before I go, Eren. I hope you'll come see me off."

That night was a terrible, restless one. I woke just after dawn and slipped into the Temple. There, in the early hush of morning, I looked around the stone sanctuary, taking it in as I prayerfully considered my conversation with Axel the night before. How hard the priests and I had worked to restore everything here that had been neglected and defiled during our absence, following every instruction Malachi had given before his death with great care. For weeks after our arrival we had reestablished daily rites with scarce materials until things were brought to order again. This morning its broad pillars were still caught in shadow while pale gold light filtered through the stained glass along the eastern wall. Color spilled quietly across the worn floor in muted reds and blues, touching the edges of pews and the cold curve of the altar stone. The air held the faint scent of smoke and warm incense. *This place would always be home for me.*

For the next space of time, I received nothing from the Whisper in prayer except His reassurance that He was present, and then quietly made my way back to the rear chamber and to Aaren.

A short time later, the two of us stood with Cohen at the front gates of the compound as Axel and his men departed. The group of Royal Guards looked especially formidable this morning as they waited silently on their black steeds, fully armed and sharp-eyed. A few villagers moved along the road toward the deeper parts of the community, some skirting by with quick, nervous steps, all of them staring in open curiosity.

Axel looked particularly arresting as he respectfully said his goodbyes to Cohen first… though this might have only been in my own eyes. Somehow the news that he was king had added a measure of immensity to his stature — the cut of his shoulders in his familiar green doublet, the tight line of his jaw as he spoke, the glint in his eye as he turned his head and his pleasing features were caught in a beam of morning light severed by the thin line of trees across the little road. He would be a good king. *More than good.*

To Aaren he had a few simple warm words, which the little boy received with quiet soberness. But for me, he came and stood before me with eyes that were steady with recognition, carrying all that he had confessed the night before. For once, he let his love show plainly on his face.

He shook his head at me, smiling. "You constantly put me out of my depth, Eren."

His choice of words made me smile back. He had said this before, long ago. "As do you, milord."

"I gave our conversation some thought and prayer last night," he announced. "I think I will only ask one final question for you to think on in my absence."

It was then I almost laughed at him. He didn't intend to quit so easily. He meant to return.

Then he reached for one of my hands with a quiet soberness, holding it between each of his own as he looked into my eyes with great kindness. "This is a good life for you, Eren. There's no doubt of that. But at this point the Whisper simply returned everything to the way it was... with the addition now of a lasting ache in your heart because you carry the knowledge of having lost so much. It's written all over your countenance. I saw it from the moment I laid eyes on you. You have not moved ahead, not truly. What He did was nothing short of miraculous, and beautiful, but I have to ask — is this reward enough for you, this life you have here? Is it enough for the terrible price you paid? Because if it is, I won't trouble you again."

He didn't wait for a response, though I was too disarmed to give him one anyway. With these astonishing words, he turned, caught the reins of his horse, and swung easily into the saddle. He looked down on me for a moment with a lingering expression. "I'll be back for the answer after my business in Periburn is handled."

Then he gave some signal, and the troop moved forward without a second glance.

I watched them go for a moment in stunned silence. The narrow road curved out from the hush of the trees around the compound and descended toward the louder heart of the village beyond, where smoke and movement could already be seen this morning in the distance, hinting at busier life. The few people on the road stepped quickly aside as the small company of impressive riders passed, their horses settling into a gentle, measured trot.

Cohen had just witnessed the entire interaction between the two of us. Since leaving the farmsteads, he had taken to using Joel's crook and leaned on it now thoughtfully — a quiet image of the wisdom of our beautiful people. "*What truth he holds.* Those thoughts were surely given, not gathered," he said quietly.

My eyes returned to the departing horsemen. The soft drum of hooves followed the line of the road as it carried them toward the press of the community.

*Some things dawned on you slowly,* I thought, *and some things — some things came by lightning flashes.*

My love for Connor had dawned slowly. But standing there, watching Axel ride away, I had a lightning flash.

*Axel was my reward.* Not the Temple in Periburn, not a life of splendor. Not an entire kingdom at my disposal. *Axel.*

*The Priest needed the King.*

There was that urge again, suddenly. That impulse that had always been with me and would never go away. *Run.*

I heard the Whisper say it again, and with it came a great burst of energy. *Run.*

I could never stop running towards my destiny. I would run ahead for the rest of my days. This was who I was. Running ahead *was* my destiny. I could almost hear Malachi whisper with warmth, *"As it should be."*

Cohen sensed my inner urge. *"Go, Eren,"* he said suddenly. *"Go."*

This was the final prodding I needed to stir me into action. I bent, murmured reassurance to Aaren that I would return shortly, and then burst forward, away from the compound.

I ran until I caught up with the last horseman in the group and shouted Axel's name, no longer caring that I had lost all dignity or faced the possibility of causing a public stir. Let everyone make of it what they would. *I was running for my reward…*

Axel's neck whipped around at the sound; he pulled up short, so quickly that the horse beneath him danced on his heels briefly. The Royal Guard parted way for me. Then, suddenly, I was alongside him. Through the broken web of sunlight overhead, I saw a flash of his face… his rain-washed eyes… his hands steady on the reins…

Without thought, he leaned from the saddle to meet me with outstretched hands. As his grip closed around my wrists, he drew me inward in one swift pull, using the forward momentum to swing my weight up and across the front of the saddle. My hip struck leather first before the rest of me followed; then in the same fluid motion he shifted me lengthwise before him, one arm cradling my shoulders, the other steady at the reins across my waist, until I was pressed securely against the strength of his chest.

I could hear his heartbeat thundering a wild rhythm. Heedless of the world around us, I rested my cheek against his collar bone in surrender, as if I had always belonged there. "Forgive me, Axel," I murmured.

His arms tightened around me. His lips brushed mine before his voice broke into a low rumble meant only for the two of us. "There's no need," he said simply. "I knew I was your reward the moment I heard you tell Draveena part of your story, the first time I ever heard you speak. Even before I loved you. The Whisper told me so. And I wanted to be, as impossible as it seemed — more with every passing day. I have held onto faith that somehow He would see it through."

And with these profound words, he steered the company of horsemen back to the Temple... and towards our future beyond.

## FROM THE DESK OF THE AUTHOR:

Stories are not written only to be read — they are meant to be carried on.

If this story of calling, cost, and reward stirred something within you, a short review — even a line or two — helps other readers find this world, and helps this story continue its work beyond these pages. I would be grateful to hear your thoughts.

If you would like to journey further, I invite you to subscribe to Evie's World The Journal, where I share personal reflections on my music, my stories, and the spiritual work that shapes them. subscribe.evelynmexley.com

You can also connect with me at evelynmexley.com

Thank you for reading.

## ABOUT THE AUTHOR:

Evelyn Exley (Evie to those who know her world) fell in love with mythic fantasy as early as age five, when her minister father had her tested and discovered she was reading over two hundred words per minute. Seeing the need to feed her thirsty young mind, he placed epic fantasy books (most of them beyond her comprehension) in her hands. She likes to say she has lived most of her life seeing the world through a coke-bottle-thick lens of metaphor and imagination.

Her fascination with stories that impact the soul comes from her own need for it. That need has shaped both her life and her writing far more than any list of qualifications — which include being a licensed minister, a professional pianist and cinematic composer, and now a published author. In of all her creative work, Evie seeks to use imagery with intention, believing that art can teach the heart without preaching and heal the soul without patronizing — ultimately changing culture through the divine work that takes place within.

She resides with her husband in the Southeastern United States in a musical and somewhat magical house, where conversation is often full of talk about real-life legends, fantasy stories, and other timeless tales.

## MORE SELECTIONS FROM EVELYN M. EXLEY:

### *Cavalcade, Book 1: The Nepa Republic*

Juliet of the House of Apelles moves easily through every layer of the Nepa Republic, quietly observing how even the noblest pursuits leave the soul restless and unfulfilled. But when a buried secret upends her life, she's drawn toward a mystical people whose defiant beliefs stir something deeper. A mythic fantasy about the limits of human love, the futility of human pursuits, and the soul's quiet hunger for something more.

★★★★★ *"Imagine if Tolstoy had written fantasy..."* **~Erika Stone, *The Aureate Review***

★★★★★ *"Mind captivating, hard to put down, well-written..."* **~Daisy M., book reviewer**

### *King Justice, the Legend Begins*

When shame drives Deut-wah into hiding, he is unaware that the known world is about to forever change. Just before giants and dragons awaken and dark sorcerers arise, an assassin's secret sends him on a journey that will demand a choice — a choice that will unknowingly shape his future. Will he become the legendary King Justice, the hero who leads an army of legends... or the coward history never forgets?

★★★★★ *"...a compelling journey through a fantasy universe, grounded in profound spiritual insight..."* **~A. Jenkins, book reviewer**

★★★★★ *"A true work of art."* **~Blythedale Booklist**

### *Red, A Novel of Alameth*

When Red's life collides with the royal family of Alameth, she is drawn into the haunting mystery of the wolves and the sinister Wood that preys on her and her people. A dark, allegorical tale of spiritual battle and a love strong enough to overcome the powers that seek to break us.

★★★★★ *"Hit very close to home..."* **~Danny Agassi, book reviewer**

★★★★★ *"...emotionally rich and moving, couldn't put it down..."* **~Elizabeth S., book reviewer**

EXLEY BOOKS
EXLEYBOOKS.COM

Made in the USA
Monee, IL
19 October 2026

66036543R00262